Elizabeth Buchan spent her childhood moving home every three years, including living for brief periods in Egypt and Nigeria, before moving to Guildford, York and Edinburgh. As a writer she has continued to travel across the world. Her short stories have been broadcast on BBC Radio 4 and published in a range of magazines. She reviews for the *Sunday Times* and *Daily Mail*, has chaired the Betty Trask and Desmond Elliott literary prizes, and has been a judge for the Costa novel award. Elizabeth is a patron of the Guildford Book Festival, a past chair of the Romantic Novelists' Association, and sits on the authors' committee for the Reading Agency. She lives in London.

You can discover more about the author at elizabethbuchan.com

THE NEW MRS CLIFTON

As the Second World War draws to a close, Intelligence Officer Gus Clifton surprises his sisters at their London home. But an even greater shock is the woman he brings with him — Krista, the German wife whom he has married secretly in Berlin. Krista is clearly devastated by her experiences at the hands of the British and their allies — all but broken by horrors she cannot share. But Gus's sisters can only see the enemy their brother has brought under their roof. And their friend Nella, Gus's beautiful, loyal fiancée, cannot understand what made Gus change his mind about her. What hold does Krista have over their honourable Gus? And how can the three women get her out of their home, their future, their England?

Books by Elizabeth Buchan
Published by Ulverscroft:

SECRETS OF THE HEART
REVENGE OF THE
MIDDLE-AGED WOMAN
THE GOOD WIFE

ELIZABETH BUCHAN

THE NEW MRS CLIFTON

Complete and Unabridged

CHARNWOOD
Leicester

First published in Great Britain in 2016 by
Michael Joseph
an imprint of Penguin Books
London

First Charnwood Edition
published 2017
by arrangement with
Penguin Random House UK
London

*A catalogue record for this book is available
from the British Library.*

ISBN 978–1–4448–3279–2

Published by
F. A. Thorpe (Publishing)
Anstey, Leicestershire

Set by Words & Graphics Ltd.
Anstey, Leicestershire
Printed and bound in Great Britain by
T. J. International Ltd., Padstow, Cornwall

For the ship's company,
with thanks for golden holidays,
and in memory of
Paul Sidey (1943–2014)

The Germans call the months after the war *Stunde Null* ('Zero Hour') — the implication being that this was a time when the slate was wiped clean, and history allowed to start again. But it does not take much imagination to see that this is a decidedly rosy view of post-war history.

Keith Lowe, *Savage Continent*

1

1974

They had alighted on Clapham Common by chance. A friend recommended it as an area that was still affordable in London for young couples. Then he had read an article in an evening newspaper extolling its virtues — its greenness and the inexpensive period-housing stock — which sold it to both of them.

Once installed, they relished the Common's space and freedom, the pleasant streets and the late-Victorian and Edwardian architecture. Cheered by the brightness of the rooms, their contentment blossomed. It was an area where they felt they could put down roots and, all being well, have a family. If the house required refurbishment and ongoing repairs, at least it had the benefit of being roomy and filled with light.

Inch by inch, they were kicking it into shape. There were priorities, of course, and the basic upkeep, such as replacing windows and gutters, had first claim on their meagre budget. It was not until they had been living there for a couple of years that they turned their attention to the garden.

It was a long garden, sixty feet or so, with a south-west aspect which meant it should have been sunnier than it was. A mature sycamore tree had been allowed to grow unchecked thanks

1

to a preservation order put on it by the council, and, because she craved the sun, the plan was to create a seating area beyond its perpetual shadow.

The digging began. Except for the smack of the shovels, and the hiss of earth, there was silence in the garden. Both of them enjoyed it, although she tired more quickly and had to break more frequently for coffee. On the first day, they made good progress. On the second, less so. The soil was tough and smelled rank. The roots from the sycamore writhed in misshapen snarls and fought back. He was mocking her lack of grit when his shovel struck an unyielding object and he bent down to take a look. When he straightened up, every iota of colour had drained from his face.

'I think we have to call the police,' he said.

Many months and an official investigation later, the forensic pathologist's report detailed that the skeleton wrapped in the roots of the sycamore was that of a female between twenty-five and thirty years of age, and five foot four to five foot six inches tall. She had had a child.

The position of the skeleton indicated that she had been buried lying on her back and had been wearing, or wrapped in, a garment made of blue wool of which several traces were exhumed.

The pathologist also gave a detailed description of the bones; they indicated that the victim had suffered from osteomalacia — bone fragility — as a result of a Vitamin D deficiency. The trauma to the back of the skull was considerable and she had probably been killed by a blunt object.

The date of death was placed between 1945 and 1947 and the police were in the process of identifying the body and tracing the next of kin.

2

1945

Krista had heard about the battle of Waterloo, of course, but not of the London railway station. Gus, her husband, had put her right.

As she stepped down from the boat train at Waterloo, on to a platform littered with cigarette ends, a light spilled over the hard ground. Dazzled, she lifted up her face and felt its promise.

It was the first September after the war ended in Europe and she possessed nothing but the clothes she was wearing, the one photograph she had of the parents she had never known and the notebook she had kept in the Berlin convent as Germany fell.

From the taxi, she watched an orange-gold leaf-fall sifting down on to a cityscape substantially different from the one she had left a couple of days earlier. Once so confident and solid, her Berlin was flattened, smoking and stinking, whereas this city appeared to have kept most of its profile. But it was not unscathed — her country had seen to that. Rolling out before her was a bombed-out landscape of potholed roads and ruined buildings rearing against the autumn sky. Here also were gap-toothed terraces of houses which, like clapped-out cancan dancers kicking up grubby skirts, revealed intimacies of a previous life. As they passed, Krista spotted a paraffin heater, a doll's cot, a torn and grimy towel.

The cityscape was familiar, and yet it wasn't. The route from the station to Gus's house in Clapham Common wound through streets where people appeared to be living like human beings, not the animals they had turned into in Berlin. Houses which looked as though they were functioning more or less normally were a rare sight over there and the damage was wholesale. Once so efficient, the railway had been reduced to a jumble of shattered rails. Potsdamer Strasse played host to the blackened skeletons of offices. Kleist Park was a wasteland, seething with tormenting flies, piled with faeces, picked over by a Third Reich of beggars. Everywhere was coated in white dust and plagued by germs and a smell of death.

Gus took hold of one of Krista's gloved hands. She forced herself to allow him to do so; it was his right. He was her husband.

Turning it over, Gus inspected her wrist. 'How frail it still is.'

He looked up at her. Their gazes met, fell away.

The gloves had been bought — at vast expense — on the black market in Brussels. Gus knew all about black markets. (She was discovering he knew about a lot of things.) Trains from Berlin to London were unreliable and they had ended up stranded overnight in Belgium. There was no need for the gloves, she had told Gus: 'I'm used to the cold.' 'Precisely,' was the reply. Everything

5

Gus now did was to ensure his new wife's comfort, her warmth, her survival. 'I'm going to make sure that life is the opposite of what it has been. My aim is to make you fat and rosy.'

Her hand moved in his — *Don't touch me* — and she pulled it away.

They spoke in German and she never failed to marvel at how expert Gus's was. Her English was almost as good, but not quite. Krista did not have Gus's grasp of idiom, which came from living in a country, as Gus had done before the war. His German needed to be more than good. After the Allies reached Berlin, Gus had been seconded to the unit interrogating suspected war criminals and he was there to pick up on every hint, every evasion, every lie, every innocuous fact, and piece together a truth — even though she had learned in the rubble of her country that absolute truths were as precious and as fragile as life itself.

'You are very thoughtful, Gus, and I am grateful. Please don't think that I'm not. I know how lucky I am.' Krista used, as she always did, the formal *sie* not *du*.

Gus was usually matter-of-fact, a practical man, but he surprised her. 'If I knew you better, and I wish I did, I would know what you're thinking.'

Why should he? No one knew anything about anyone else and would it be a good idea if they did? Much of what was hidden in people's minds was shocking.

'Does it matter?'

'You can argue both ways. But if we are to

have a marriage . . . '

They contemplated in silence the implications of what had been done and what lay in the future.

Once or twice, she and her friend, Lotte — beloved Lotte — had talked about marriage and what they would like from it. Unsurprisingly perhaps, as they were orphans and as neither had experienced much of it, kindness was the top of both their lists. As she was dying, Lotte reminded Krista: 'Find a kind man, my friend.' She paused for a difficult breath. 'My darling friend.'

That was that.

Every so often, the blackness prompted something to shut down in Krista's head. Like now. It was as if she could not process as many moments as there were to be processed — as if her mind needed a second's rest. Then it lifted.

Krista probed the crack in her bottom lip with a tooth. It stung and she could never work out why she continually provoked such discomfort. Not that she was much interested in explanations. All she knew was that, in relation to the hunger and savagery she had weathered, this small pain offered a diversion from the big picture.

The tiny drop of blood on her lip tasted salty. 'Gus, you should have told your sisters about us.'

Both sisters were living in Gus's house. The elder, Julia, had been widowed nineteen months previously and Tilly was unmarried. 'I hope they learn to love you,' said Gus when he told Krista about them.

'I think people more often want to kill each other than to love,' Krista replied.

Reaching for his cigarettes lying on the seat, Gus lit up. 'Perhaps.'

What was she doing with this man?

'What's the time, Gus?'

Gus frowned at the question. He didn't like to be reminded; but Krista didn't mind one way or the other. In Berlin, no one possessed a watch because the Soviets had stolen them wholesale. The more watches a Soviet soldier possessed, the higher his status.

One of them — a sergeant, as he boasted to Krista, who understood a smattering of his language — cornered her in the ruins of the convent. He had raised his arm and there they were, a dozen or so of them stacked up over his wrist. 'I make sure I have the fancier ones,' he explained in broken German, 'and I can trade them.' He had taken care to point out the one where a jewel winked at the centre of its face. Fascinated by this reminder of luxury, she had stared at it, finally reaching over to touch it with a fingertip. 'What a beautiful thing,' she said.

A couple of minutes later, he raped her. But she had been expecting that. Her main feeling was of anguish that her one remaining pair of knickers had been ripped.

'Are you ever sorry?' she asked the Russian sergeant.

He shook his head. 'It's war,' he replied. 'That's what happens. We expect to do it.' He pulled down his cuff over the watches. 'You women expect it.'

'I'm going to buy you a watch.' Gus looked out of the taxi window. 'That's a promise.'

Gus was telling Krista that she had a new life. No longer would she creep through the ashes of the city, no longer would she fight for bread: loaf, slice, crust, any bit of bread. No longer would the soldiers come and go, doing what they wanted, when they wanted. If she now found herself in England, about which she knew nothing, it would be worth it for that release.

What would she remember of her old life? Certainly the nights, which had belonged to the British bombers. Or had it been the days? Often Krista became confused but, actually, it didn't matter which. Night or day, the sky turned violent red, pierced by flashes. Those still alive burrowed like rats into the rubble, the only difference being that the rats did a better job of surviving.

Occasionally, in the aftermath of their fire and destruction, she thought about the British airmen who flew the planes. What did they imagine they were doing when they sent down the bombs? She had prayed that they, too, were rotten with fear, because, down below, they breathed, ate, slept and excreted terror. Or, if those bombers were the fearless types, Krista prayed they were rotten with conscience.

'Not long now,' said Gus. 'Another five minutes.'

The taxi had slowed right down and Krista found herself peering into the front garden of a terraced house bordering the road. It had a workable gate, a front door with a brass door knocker, windows streaked with dirt and a rose bush growing unevenly in the front garden.

How grey, almost apologetic, it looked, and yet how reassuringly respectable. She imagined submerging herself with relief into its dreariness, its lack of imagination.

She struggled to assemble a mental geography of the city. 'Do you live in a smart area?'

Gus was amused. 'Anything but. But those who live there come to love it. The houses are beautiful and there are plenty of trees and grass and it's quiet. Which makes up for not being smart.'

Quiet.

When the Soviets did reach Berlin, Krista understood the saying that hell had many rooms. The mother nation could no longer protect her children and they were for it. Crouching in the convent's cellar, she and Lotte, plus the one surviving nun, Sister Eva, listened to the boom and bang of the *Stalinorgel* — the dreaded Soviet land torpedo. Smoke from the fires enveloped the streets and buildings rocked. Venturing out to forage, Krista ran up against the body of a German boy hanging from a lamppost. The notice tied around his leg with string by the retreating SS read: 'Deserter'.

Still tuned to the daily rule of the convent, Sister Eva knelt stony-faced in that cellar even while her faith fell visibly away from her, like the hair that was falling daily from Krista's head.

Mein Gott, mein Gott, you have abandoned us.

Inside that drab English house with the rose

bush, routines would not shift and its inhabitants would assure each other: *Things will go back to normal.* There would be set times for meals, for housework, for listening to the radio, for shopping.

Paradise.

Krista gave an audible intake of breath.

'All right?' asked Gus.

Nothing, but nothing, was more desirable in heaven or on earth than a grey house with routines.

The taxi moved on along Clapham High Street, where many of the shop fronts were either smashed or boarded up. Yet there were signs of life. Some of the shops displayed goods in the windows and queues had formed outside.

'Nearly there, Krista.'

'That's good.'

Dusk was mustering and ineffectual lights struggled to illuminate rooms into which Krista was peering. As they approached the end of the High Street, Krista's apprehension deepened, for the next step was crucial.

'Gus?'

He turned his head to look at her.

'I shall try to be your wife and make the arrangement work. I hope we can manage.' She spoke in German.

'Arrangement?' His eyes questioned the notion. 'Yes, of course.'

The High Street opened up on to a large space criss-crossed with earthworks and vegetable patches and fringed by trees. Yellowing leaves dripped from the branches.

11

Glancing round, the taxi driver said, 'Road's a bit of a problem here, sir, so hold on. They haven't got round to mending the bomb damage.'

He wasn't joking. The road was so potholed that Krista was forced to cling to the strap. The taxi drew up in front of a house and the driver hauled on the brake.

They stood on the pavement outside the gate.

'Hello, Clifton!' A figure in a brown demob suit had materialized from over the road. 'Back again?'

Gus turned round. 'Hello, Mr O'Connor. I hope you are well.' He turned to Krista. 'Mr O'Connor is our neighbour at Number 18. Let me introduce you. Mr O'Connor, my wife, Krista.'

Krista held out her gloved hand. 'How do you do?'

Mr O'Connor did a double take at her accent and she could see the thoughts sledging through his mind. Accent. Foreign. German? For God's sake. 'How very nice.' He dripped hostility. 'But I must be going.'

How we all hate each other, she thought. Germans. English. Soviets. French. Italians. And she was as good a hater as any.

'We'll be seeing each other,' said Gus to Mr O'Connor's departing back.

The driver searched in a leather wallet for the correct change and jerked his head in Krista's direction. 'Was the missus talking German?'

'Yes,' said Gus.

'Right,' he said. 'Right. If you want my advice,

12

sir, best not to round here, you know.' The hand with which he handed over a sixpence had black fingernails. 'You're in luck, sir. Sixpences these days are like hens' teeth.'

Krista remained rooted to the spot.

3

A figure stood at one of the windows on the first floor observing their arrival.

The presence was rendered shadowy by a lace curtain sagging from a pole. The silhouette revealed a woman about the same height as Krista and there was a glimmer of fair hair rolled back from her face. Her pose suggested extreme tension. One hand rested on the window frame, the other was clasped tightly across her body.

The house?

It was nice, Krista thought. No, it was more than nice.

In the middle of a terrace of handsome semi-detached houses that faced on to the Common, it had an innate elegance. To its right, further down the block, several of the houses were badly damaged; to the left only a couple of them had shattered windows and cracks in the masonry. Somehow, because it was central in the terrace perhaps, Gus's house appeared to have survived intact.

With sound and lovely bones, complemented by large sash windows, and steps leading up to a portico at the front door, its quality was obvious. Gus had said it was the kind of house built by early developers for the city workers who wanted to ape aristocratic tastes. And why not? A few plaster cornices here and there were harmless enough in the imitation game.

Krista wriggled her fingers inside the expensive gloves. Was it a place of safety? Please, God, it was.

'After the bomb,' he had said, during the course of one of their curious, getting-to-know-you conversations that had leavened the interminable train journey from Berlin, 'the ruin recorder sent to check it over passed it as safe.' Apparently, the ruin recorder, who wore a boiler suit with his ribbons from the last war pinned above his council badge, had spent considerable time knocking at walls and peering out of windows.

'Do they inspect all the houses?' She had been curious. 'I don't think there are any houses left in Berlin to do so.'

She could not but applaud British thoroughness.

'But,' Gus dropped into the silence which had fallen in the railway carriage, one of many silences full of unspoken tensions, 'a tight rein is kept on anyone wanting to improve their home. You're only allowed to spend £100 on paint or distemper and it's a struggle to get anything looking reasonable. Anyone caught using too much paint is reported.'

Would people report each other for using too much paint? Yes . . . oh, yes . . . Krista understood that better than anyone. By the time Hitler's National Socialism collapsed in flames, every German, apart from babes in arms, knew all about people reporting each other.

Herr Miller leaves by his back door . . . Fräulein Best is wearing a surprisingly expensive perfume...

15

Gus picked up his suitcase. 'Come.'

She placed a hand on the railing leading up to the front door.

'I ought to carry you,' said Gus behind her.

'No,' flew from Krista. 'No.'

The front door was painted iron grey and had a big brass knocker in the shape of a hand. Gus was searching for his key when the door opened.

A woman was framed in the entrance to Number 22 — possibly the one who had been watching them from upstairs. She was wearing a blue wool skirt and cardigan and lace-up shoes. '*Gus!* Where have you come from? I was expecting Mr Forrest, the ruin recorder, for tea.'

Gus dropped the suitcase and kissed her on the cheek, and she clung to him. 'It was impossible to get a message to you.'

'Never heard of the telephone?' She sounded very dry.

'You've no idea, old girl, how difficult things are out there.'

'Never mind,' she said with a glimmer of a smile. Turning to Krista, she asked, 'Who?'

Gus tried to take hold of Krista's hand but she avoided him. 'Julia, this will come as a shock, but one I hope you will welcome. This is Krista, my wife.'

A pair of bruised-looking eyes widened in the pale face.

'Krista and I got married while I was in Berlin.'

Married.

The word ricocheted between them, catching all three in its passage.

16

'Good gracious.' Julia's hands flew up to her cheeks. '*Married.*' She stepped back and her shoe clicked against the door. 'I don't believe it. You can't . . . There's . . . Does Nella know?' She checked herself. 'Look, this is a shock.' She flashed a strained smile at her brother. 'You always loved surprises.' She called over her shoulder. 'Tilly! Tilly, *come.*'

Gus shrugged. 'Whether you believe me or not, I refuse to stand on the doorstep of my own house to debate it.' Picking up the case, he ushered Krista through the front door.

'Your own house,' Julia echoed. 'Yes, of course.'

Stepping into the hallway, Krista felt as if she was walking out of a cold and dark place into sunlight. There were not many sensations to match it — perhaps the assurance of a blanket on a freezing night, or hot soup settling on a screaming stomach.

As she took in the curved banister, the sash window and the room flooded with light opening off the hall, her depleted imagination soared and leapfrogged over the black holes of the past. Yes, the paintwork was knocked about and the banister looked rickety but, in two seconds flat, she had mended it and polished it into gleaming beauty.

Unsure what to do, she fiddled with her gloves, eventually stripping them off and stuffing them into her coat pocket.

Julia banged shut the door behind them and leaned back against it. 'Well . . . ' She brushed down her skirt and began again. 'Well . . . '

17

She was a beautiful woman, elegant and long of limb, but her beauty was marred by the tight set of her mouth, which suggested that, in the struggle to control strong emotions, she took refuge in permanent disapproval. 'You could have told Tilly and me, Gus. About something so important.' She glanced down at the brass ring on Krista's finger. 'I'm sorry, but you will realize that we need a little time.'

'I know,' said Krista.

She pronounced it: *I now*.

She was aware how odd it sounded, and how marked her accent. In normal circumstances, Krista had no need to worry about her English; it had improved many times over from working on Gus's interrogation team. But it was not her language, nor the language of her heart, and, in this unfamiliar situation, it might fail her altogether.

Julia flinched. 'You're German?' Her voice rose in scandalized question. 'German?'

'Yes.'

It was said and everything was set in stone.

Julia looked absolutely dumbfounded. She turned to her brother. 'And you brought her here, to us?' She stopped herself, wrestling visibly between her shock and the need for good manners. 'I'm sorry. I didn't mean to say that.'

Gus used the quiet, but deadly, tone she had heard him employ in interrogations. 'Krista is very tired.'

That was true. Her bones were tired. Her spirit was tired.

'Yes, of course,' said Julia quickly. 'Let me

18

think. You're home for a while?'

'Yes, we are,' Gus replied. 'As far as I know.' He spread his hands in a gesture which took in the house. 'Here, the job, normal life.' He looked at Krista. 'Doesn't sound much, does it? But it is.'

Julia checked the front door was properly closed and hooked up the front-door chain.

Krista watched her. The outside world was locked out.

Julia was still casting around for something else to say. 'I hope you will think that I have kept the house in order, Gus?' she said. 'It hasn't been easy.'

Gus took hold of one of Julia's hands. 'I'm very grateful, Julia. I could have trusted no one else.'

Julia looked everywhere but at her brother. 'I didn't mean to be snippy. Sorry, sorry, Gus. Please don't think me horrible. It is a shock . . . I mean . . . ' She glanced up at Krista and pulled her hand away. 'It's harder than ever to get things now. Would you believe it? Rationing's still awful. And we all long for pretty clothes and nice food.' She was almost gabbling. 'But you must have been all right wherever you were. I know you can't talk about your work, hush-hush and all that, but it was Berlin, wasn't it? The wireless says that supplies are going in.'

'I believe they are.' Gus did not elaborate.

'I suppose it is the right thing to do.' She sounded unconvinced and more than a little antagonistic to the idea.

Yet, sour or not, Julia was pulling herself

together: straightening her shoulders, adjusting the cuff of her cardigan. Once upon a time, in another world, Krista had read an article about Englishwomen in a magazine that a visitor had brought into the convent. How she and the other girls had enjoyed reading about the English *memsahib* (as the article referred to her) who took for granted that the atlas was coloured a reassuring red more or less across the globe. The article had not been particularly kind or reflective and it had struck Krista then that its writer was recycling received wisdom about the British woman's stiff upper lip without examining it. Stealing a look at Julia, she felt more in sympathy with the writer now.

Her knees were threatening to buckle. 'Gus, could I sit down somewhere, please?'

Gus touched Krista's elbow lightly — *she could bear that. Just.* 'We can discuss all that later, Julia, but at this precise moment.' He steered Krista towards a staircase leading down into the basement. 'Could we have a hot drink? We've been travelling non-stop.'

'Of course. Where's Tilly?' Julia stood at the bottom of the staircase which curved up two storeys and called, 'Tilly! Come at once. There's news.'

Situated in the basement, the kitchen did not have much natural light and the single, unshaded light bulb hanging down from the centre of the ceiling did little to lighten its gloom.

There was an elderly stove and a wire rack for vegetables but, otherwise, it appeared to be practically empty. There was no food; no shiny

20

pots and pans to be seen either. No jars of spices. No onions. No dried herbs. No loaf of bread waiting to be sliced. No flitches of bacon. No sausage. Nothing familiar: no meat or herb scents, no aromas of vanilla and cinnamon.

To be fair, she was comparing this dingy, damp-smelling and sparsely stocked kitchen with the well-appointed convent one which had existed before the war but which, of course, didn't survive it.

'Pride is a sin,' said Sister Hannelore, who had been in charge, repeating it frequently (oh, so frequently) before she died of starvation. 'But when it comes to my kitchen, well, my Sisters, you must excuse me the sin.'

Julia seemed at a loss. Gesturing vaguely at the kettle, she said, 'I'll make some tea.'

Krista looked at the surface of the wooden table that had been scrubbed so hard it had turned chalk-white. The what-had-been was just that. Gone.

After boiling the kettle and filling the teapot, Julia sat down. 'The tea isn't up to much.'

No, it wasn't; and the cups into which she poured the brew were of such an intense blue that the tea sheltering in them appeared even weaker and more beige.

'It will do,' said Gus. 'Is there sugar, by any miraculous chance?'

'You *are* joking?' said Julia tartly. All the same, she got to her feet and searched in a cupboard by the window. 'There might be a few grains. Nobody can get anything . . . Aha.' Triumphantly, she pulled out a blue paper bag.

21

'There's a tiny bit.' She placed a teaspoon and the bag in front of Gus. 'Our last.'

Gus dug into the bag with the spoon. 'Krista, you should have it.'

Krista longed for hot, sweet tea but reckoned it would be prudent not to accept it and shook her head.

'Nonsense.' Gus tipped the sugar into her cup, leaving a tiny portion for himself.

Julia observed the interplay. 'Sugar is almost too precious to cook with. Do you remember, Gus, when we used to make toffee? There was tons of it and we never gave it a second thought.'

'Toffee is a sweet,' Gus explained. 'I was good at making it.'

'Good at eating it, you mean,' said Julia. 'Since you've been gone, Gus, we've had no help in the house. Everyone's vanished. I say they can't all be dead or working in factories but they seem to be. Whatever the reason, I'm left with the chores and don't say there's Tilly because you can't count on Tilly. She's useless.' The hot, resentful words spilled out. 'Sometimes, I think I'm going to murder her.'

Gus wasn't that interested. 'I agree; you can't be expected to run this house by yourself.' His tone acted on Krista like a prod. Gus was, apparently, including *her* in these calculations because she was his wife.

'If Martin hadn't been killed it would have all been so different.' Julia was taking great care to fold up the empty sugar bag. 'Those bloody . . .'

'Don't,' said Gus.

'Martin deserved to live.' Julia got up and

inserted the bag into a drawer. 'Not to end up smashed into a French field by . . .'

'*Julia*.'

Krista concentrated on the tea. Its sweetness. Its warmth. Its comfort.

'So it *is* Gus,' said a voice from the doorway. 'I knew it had to be something to make Julia shout like a fishwife.'

Julia raised her eyes to the ceiling.

'Tilly . . .' Gus rose to his feet.

Tilly advanced into the kitchen and it flashed across Krista's mind that she had waited to make this entrance; it was a successful ploy as three pairs of eyes were now trained on to her.

She wasn't as conventionally beautiful as Julia, but her face was the more interesting of the two. They shared the same colouring but Tilly's rumpled hair flowed unchecked over her shoulders. She was in black from top to toe, a whiff of the Gothic which was complemented by bright-red lipstick and dark mascara. The overall effect was young, louche and suggestively fatigued.

Grasping Gus by the shoulders with a pair of neat, almost childish-looking hands, she kissed him, European fashion, twice on his cheeks. '*Ciao*. Why didn't you let us know the prodigal was returning?'

Julia looked up from her tea. 'Gus has some news.'

It was only then that Tilly let on she knew there was someone else in the room. A pair of intense blue eyes fixed on Krista.

Gus explained.

Krista got to her feet. 'How do you do?'

23

'How perfect!' Tilly exclaimed. 'German.' She shot a look at her brother. 'How wicked of you, Gus. How brilliantly perverse. That will set the cat among the pigeons.' The blue eyes were alight with interest — and mischief? 'We'll have to make sure that you get the welcome you deserve. But it's lovely news. Of course it is. Congratulations.' She reached for the teapot. 'Obviously, it's a whirlwind marriage.' Her gaze rested for a second on Krista's stomach. 'Or have you known each other for some time? Either way . . . ' Tilly thought better of what she was going to say and flashed a genuine smile at Krista. 'Either way, it is delightful.'

'Yes, isn't it?' said a cold, stiff Julia.

Krista drained her teacup to the last drop, and used a teaspoon to scoop up the dregs. Observing this, Julia remarked, 'You can have a second cup, you know.'

Krista flushed. She was forgetting. She held out the cup with both hands and Julia refilled it.

Tilly asked, 'Where on earth did Gus find you?'

She and Gus hadn't finally agreed on their stories. If truth be told, they didn't *know* each other's stories.

'In a convent in the Charlottenburg district. Quite near the centre of Berlin.' she began. 'I had been brought up there by the Sisters after my parents died. I did not like it much but, at the end, it was a sanctuary.'

She hated to think about that terrible end, but it never took much — the scream from an aircraft engine, a car exhaust, even — and she

24

would be struggling not to relive the moments when the distant thuds of the Soviet guns rolled closer and turned into a roar. Then Berliners knew they were for it.

Her face must have reflected her terror and Tilly jumped in, 'There's no need to talk about it now, if you don't wish to. There will be time for us to find out about each other.' She glanced at her sister. 'Won't there, Julia?'

Julia picked up a teaspoon and put it down again.

'When we realized the Soviets were coming, I took my friend and some others back there to hide. I knew the convent well, you see. The women had to get out of sight. We had all read of the violence that was happening on the eastern approaches to the city. We knew what they would do to us.'

Tilly seemed fascinated. 'But what on earth was Gus doing in a convent?'

Krista did not look at Gus, refusing to give him that lifeline.

'When a city's flattened you don't take much notice of what buildings are,' said Gus. 'My unit needed an office and someone suggested the convent, which still had a wing standing. I found Krista trying her best to get the library cleaned up.'

Part of that was true. The rest was not.

'Terrible times,' said Gus. 'I will never forget Krista's heroic efforts to save the books.'

There was almost a touch of envy in the way he pronounced 'heroic'. 'But stupid,' said Krista. 'And impossible.'

25

'Heroic, all the same,' he repeated, this time with a decided bitterness.

Tilly looked from one to the other. 'It makes for a good story.'

Krista went to Gus's aid. 'The Sisters were proud of their library. I was proud of the library. In a small way, its collection was famous and the most famous book was the Magdeburg Book of Hours. Scholars came to see it. Sometimes, when I lived there as a child, I was allowed to unlock the cabinet in which it was kept.'

She, Lotte and the others living in the convent had been starving, for God's sake, and their bodies were falling to pieces. A Book of Hours could not feed them or keep them warm. Yet she had clung to the irrational belief that, if it was destroyed, nothing would be left for any of them. So she had heaved up a marble slab behind the altar in the chapel and hid it. It was probably still there. After Gus began bringing in food to the convent and her mind and body began to function more normally, she had set about salvaging what she could of the remainder of the collection. As a child, she had hated the Sisters. Now they were dead, she felt impelled to honour them.

Or, perhaps, she had just been bloody-minded? The Tommies or the Ruskies were not going to get their hands on German things.

'Gosh,' said Tilly. 'I know we were bombed but one forgets that we didn't have foreign boots trampling all over us. That I can't imagine. It must have been terrible.'

Julia frowned.

26

Julia probably had no idea that, if you are deprived of fat for weeks, odd things happen. How would she? A persistent mist in front of the eyes was one; the sensation of floating while walking was another. Lotte's back teeth fell out and none of the women had menstruated for months. Their physical predicament left no energy to deal with the Sisters' god, not even to ridicule him. *Ach so*, ran Krista's reasoning. *How glad I am that my faith went. In that way, I cannot be disappointed in how all this has been allowed to happen.* The body and mind were no more, or less, than a mix of chemical compounds which reacted to certain circumstances.

'Gus gave me a tin of spam,' she said. 'It was the best thing I had ever tasted.'

Could she ever describe the joy of encountering the small fat deposits encasing the meat? Its damp, meaty smell? Running a finger around the inside of the tin, she had licked it until it was almost raw.

'Be careful,' she'd warned Gus. 'If anyone sees me with this, they'll kill me.' And she had wondered if Gus would prefer her dead.

'We knew nothing of what was happening to us, Gus,' said Tilly, thoughtfully. 'We had no idea that we had a sister-in-law, and a German one at that.' Her voice inflected the word 'German' but not in a hostile way. 'Congratulations, again. No, really. This is very exciting. Have you been travelling day and night? Those trains are a nightmare.' She sprang to her feet. 'Jules, they must be dog-tired and will want an early night. We should make up a bed.'

Aware that her accent was becoming more marked through fatigue, Krista said, 'Please let me do it. I do not want to be any trouble.' Using the table for leverage, she stood upright.

'It's no trouble,' said Julia insincerely. She got up and reached for the apron hanging on a peg by the door.

The three women faced each other. They were of the same height, more or less, with Julia just a fraction taller, which made it easier for her to look down at the other two.

'On second thoughts, I'll leave you to Julia,' Tilly said, suddenly losing interest. 'She's much better at the boring things. I'll see you later.'

Julia's brown leather lace-up shoes sounded hollowly on the carpet-less stairs as she led the way, ushering Krista into a room off the first-floor landing. 'This is Gus's room. It used to be our parents' room. The bed isn't made up.' She shrugged. 'We weren't expecting you. Normally, with guests, I would have made sure. A well-run house . . . ' Her voice trailed away. 'I'll fetch sheets and towels.'

Krista hovered in the doorway. With relief, she saw that it was a large, airy room with a smaller one opening off it. Yes, the paintwork was blistered, the window and bed sagged and there was only a modest-sized, faded, green rag-rug to cover the expanse of floorboards. But it looked solid, sheltering, ordinary — oh, so wonderfully ordinary.

At the window, she was able to look over the Common, dotted with those golden-tipped trees and scarred by the trenches. Across it, a row of

28

fine period houses flanked a road running parallel to the one outside Number 22, and a church spire poked up through the trees clustered at its middle. Traffic moved sedately on the encircling roads. Three or four cars. Two buses. A couple of carts.

Normal?

Yes, yes, what she was seeing was normal.

Perched on the edge of the bed, she imagined the conversation which would later take place between Gus and his sisters. She pictured their fair English complexions, faintly flushed with indignation, and heard the intonation peculiar to a certain type of English person.

She's a German, Gus.

We'll be a laughing stock.

Her life will be a misery.

Who is she?

She was frightened that she was no longer capable of feeling. Yet she was a past master at practising deception on herself and on others, so that no one could know about the fear which traced a spider's web through her mind. *I am fine. My body is fine.* Those were her counter-deceptions which lapped and overlapped each other, until her life was covered in liar's dust.

Julia returned with a pile of linen. Stripping back the bedspread, she thrust a sheet at Krista. 'Let's get on with it.'

Getting ready for bed later that evening, Gus undressed in the small room off the main bedroom, which he explained was his dressing room. Seizing the chance, Krista fled down the

29

passage to the bathroom and undressed there. The hot water had run out so she splashed her face with cold and made herself clean her teeth. Cold water on her bleeding gums was still something from which she shrank.

The toothbrush bristles searched out the sore places in her mouth.

Someone clattered down the corridor and banged on the bathroom door. 'Sorry,' Tilly called out. 'Didn't know it was occupied.'

On that long train ride from Berlin, Krista had asked Gus about Tilly and he told her that, before the war broke out, she had disappeared off to Italy for six months. 'Umbria. She's got this idea she's Italian in spirit. It took me many telegrams and the threat of coming to fetch her before she came back.' His description was tender and indulgent and, from it, Krista deduced that Tilly held her brother's heart in those childlike hands. 'During the war, she analysed photographs taken by the RAF reconnaissance planes. Apparently,' Gus rolled his eyes, 'working out what lay behind, or below, an image helped her poetry. Tilly *is* clever. She's also . . . Our parents died when she was only seventeen. It's had an effect. She's full of energy one moment, and immovable the next and you never know quite where you are with her. My parents worried about her. To them, she seemed so extreme.'

Tilly definitely had her brother's heart in her keeping.

Slipping back along the uncarpeted corridor, Krista sneaked a look at the back garden but the

30

dark prevented her from getting much of an impression of it except for the outlines of some trees. Still, she sensed its presence, a place where it was possible for life to stir and to grow and which was as far away as possible from the wasteland of Berlin.

In the convent garden, she — the child — had watched the ivy mobbed by hoverflies, and bumblebees driving their tongues into the lavender flowers to take their last feed for the year. She had gazed on autumnal spiders' webs and picked up the ripened quinces lying in the grass beneath the tree. She — the adult — had dug with a spade in that same garden to bury the Sisters.

Returning to the bedroom, she was confronted by Gus in his dressing gown. 'Would you like me to sleep in the dressing room? There's a camp bed.'

Oh, yes, she would. Very much. She yearned to capture the smooth empty kingdom of the bed for herself. 'Would that seem odd?'

'It doesn't matter if it does.'

She swallowed. 'Stay.'

'Thank you.' Gus folded his dressing gown, draped it over the chair and got into bed. Krista did likewise.

A space stretched between them, over which neither would travel.

Much later, she was aware of the noises in the house: a brief exchange between the sisters on the stairs, a chair scraping across an uncarpeted floor, the outraged shriek of a bedspring, the rattle of a window.

31

She tried to pinch the flesh over her hip bones between finger and thumb, but there was none to spare. She was well aware that her extreme thinness was off-putting to some. Despite the rationing, the two sisters looked reasonably well fed. Beside them, she was a figure from a medieval painting depicting creatures in hell. Shrunken, wild-eyed, with knees that were far too big.

The house was settling around them. She knew nothing about its history. Who had lived here, who had cared for it? Who wanted to live here, now the war was over, especially since she, Krista, had arrived?

'Are you comfortable, Krista?'

His voice sounded companionable.

'The sheets,' she said. 'They are so clean. So civilized.'

'I want to make sure that you have a chance to heal. Find time for the soul again.'

'There's been no room for the soul.' The words were dry and bitter on her tongue. *The soul.* 'It wasn't the soul that foraged for food, or a light, or fought to keep warm and dry. The soul was useless.'

'Look at me.'

Obediently, she shifted over to face her husband, searching to make out his shape in the dark.

'That's the point,' he said sadly. 'There is a roof here.'

'Ah.'

Having gathered like the high tide waiting to strike the shore, fatigue hit her, drawing her down under the waters.

4

The following morning, Julia woke early, as usual.

Another dull, if not shading on unbearable, day to be got through.

Between this point of sleep and wakefulness, she often tantalized herself by fantasizing about food. What would she choose if there was no rationing: curried prawns, roast veal with a wine sauce, asparagus and chocolate mousse? Or perhaps a fresh pea soup with a dash of cream before the veal?

Mr Forrest, the ruin recorder, had sent a message apologizing for his failure to turn up the previous day and adding that he hoped to make it today. He came so often that he was in danger of becoming an irritant, but he said it was necessary to keep a close eye on the bomb damage in the street and Julia couldn't quarrel with that. She would have to give him tea but, before that, there was the ironing to tackle. No doubt Tilly would make sure she got out of it, as only her sister could.

During her married life with Martin she had looked on this first moment of consciousness as the gateway into a larger dimension — a threshold which admitted her to the delight of feeling and hearing the rhythms of the new day. It was the moment when she turned her head to look at her husband sleeping beside her and experienced happiness and anticipation.

Husbands. Wives. Gus. Krista.

With a start, Julia remembered the previous day's bombshell and struggled to sit upright.

What strange, mad, foreign entente had Gus entered into? How cruel of him not to give his sisters any warning, let alone the rest of the family and their friends. What had he been thinking?

She threw back the sheets, her feet hitting the bare floorboards with a resigned slap. Padding down the corridor to the bathroom, she turned on the tap, and as she splashed water over her face she summoned Martin's shade. *Calm down, darling,* he most probably would have said. *Gus is entitled to marry whom he pleases, even if she were sky-blue pink.* Possibly he might have dropped a kiss on Julia's cheek, or nuzzled her neck, which he once said was so beautiful that it would drive any man mad.

Having towelled away her angry, aching tears, Julia returned to her room, pulled on her girdle and stepped into her knickers. These had been bought for her trousseau and were made of fine, white lawn. Increasingly worn thin, there was no chance of replacing them.

Rolling a stocking up over a leg, she tried not to brood over — among other things — the unfairness of Gus inheriting the house while the sisters got only a small pot of money between them from their parents. Sons inherited and that was that. Somehow, Number 22 had survived, and now it was going to be occupied by a woman from the country which had tried to flatten it.

No wonder she had forgotten every shred of her mother's training: 'Julia, remember politeness and calm under stress. *Especially* under stress.'

The girl had looked thoroughly cowed, which was understandable, and had glanced at Gus as if to say: *I told you so.* Her copper-coloured hair was cropped. She was appallingly thin and pale, had a sore on her bottom lip and a rash on her hands and neck. God knew what that was. Yet, as Julia had fought for her composure and good manners, the girl had raised her eyes and sent Julia a fierce, hard look and Julia knew at once that she was no innocent.

Oh, my God, she thought. In bringing Krista home, Gus had whipped the lid off Julia's carefully damped-down hatreds and she did not know how she was going to deal with them.

She buttoned up her blouse, a thick wool one with ugly buttons, which was both warm and sensible — how she disliked it — and put on her tweed skirt.

There. All done, dusted and assembled: the unremarkable widow who gave no trouble.

On her way downstairs, she paused (as had become her habit) to stand by the window which overlooked the Common, hoping to draw calm and steadiness from its familiar aspect. All her childhood, it had been a green, slightly unkempt domain which was almost, but not quite, rural in feel. For a city child, though, it had been full of magic and mystery and the memory of its subversive delights had never left Julia. The entrenchments now slashed across it, the digging of secret underground rooms, the gun emplacements, the bare, depressing allotments had put paid to all that. Its wildness had been replaced by layers of coal and bomb dust, upturned earth and fallen trees.

Stomach knotted, Julia went downstairs to face the day.

★　★　★

'Gus.'

It was after lunch and, once Krista had been ordered upstairs to rest by Gus, Julia tracked her brother down in his study just off the hall.

Originally, it had been their father's; he always maintained it was the only place in a house filled with women where he could think straight. After his death, Gus took it over, hanging a painting by Christopher Wood — anemones on a windowsill overlooking a Cornish seascape — above the fireplace and rearranging the desk. The study wasn't that different, Julia thought, but it had obliterated the traces of the parent for whom she felt mixed feelings.

The peace their father craved had been compromised with the installation of the house's telephone — the sisters had seen to that. Between them, they had cooked up a scheme to get their friends to ring constantly, which they knew would drive him mad.

Gus was dialling a number. During the morning, he had been to the barber and looked freshly spruced. He took one look at her and replaced the receiver in its cradle. 'No need to explain your feelings, Jules.'

36

She leaned against the lintel. 'What have you done, Gus?'

'I'm sure you'll get to like Krista in time. If you allow yourself.' Gus sounded like his good-humoured self but his expression was watchful and guarded.

'And Nella?'

Gus regarded the blotter on the desk. 'Julia, you must wish us well.'

She stared at his profile, which told her nothing. 'What happened? Your fiancée has been waiting for you all this time. Are you going to tell her that you stumbled across this girl in Berlin and married her on the off chance she would make a better wife?' She couldn't help adding, 'Teddy will hit the roof.'

'Julia, shut up, please.' Gus didn't sound so good-humoured now. 'I wrote to Nella in Egypt and, as soon as she's back, I'll go and see her. Apparently, her ship docks at the end of the month.'

A hidden, unexplained element hung over her brother. Even she could sense it. 'I don't understand. *Make* me understand. Nella loves you and you gave every indication that you felt the same.'

'Things change. Feelings change. People change. Don't tell me that Martin's death hasn't made you look at things in a different way.'

Earth turned to dust. Life to ashes. Yes, it had. 'I still don't understand.'

He fingered a corner of the blotter and she noted automatically that the blotting paper needed renewing. 'The secrets and the shadows of war.' He spoke lightly, as if he was making a joke about it. 'I can't pretend it will be easy for you and Tilly. All I ask is that you make Krista welcome and you don't blame her for what's happened between me and Nella. It is not her fault.'

Julia placed both hands on the desk and leaned towards her brother. 'Martin would never have behaved in this dishonourable way.'

For a second, Gus's features registered unspoken anguish, which alarmed Julia. 'I don't expect to make you understand.'

'Nor do I.' She could almost taste her anger — sour and unpalatable. Gus had been away a lot, doing the work he wouldn't talk about, but she and Tilly had managed somehow and kept the house for him. They had got used to making do and Julia had learned to cope with each day by refusing to think about the next one.

Gus pushed back the chair and got to his feet. 'You know, Jules, when it all kicked off we were persuaded to think about fighting in simple terms. Good versus evil. Us versus a stupid man with a moustache.' Julia met his gaze and couldn't read it. 'But it's never simple.'

Gus could be fluent and persuasive and his dark eyes could burn with feeling. But he didn't fool her. 'Gus, what did you do?'

He seemed to be deciding on what he could, and couldn't, say. 'It doesn't end overnight, either. Just read the papers. They're full of violence. There's a story of a man who kills young women with a tin opener but can't explain why. And it's all kicking off in Palestine.'

Julia helped herself to a cigarette from Gus's case. 'Good lecture, Gus.' All the same, he had a point. Being normal again was going to be difficult, and it was complicated. And frightening. She tapped ash into the ashtray. 'The last thing you said to me before you left for Berlin was: 'Look out for Nella if she gets back before I do.''

She had brought him back to the point and, with obvious emotion, he said, 'You must look after Nella for me, Julia. Please. Will you?'

'What makes you think she'll want to see any of us any more?'

Gus's eyelids closed briefly. 'Because we are . . . were . . . so close once. Because you and Tilly still are. I'm sure of it.'

From where brother and sister were standing at the study window, it was not possible to see the house next door, only its garden, which was covered in debris and scattered masonry, with the sycamore tree at its furthest end. Strangely — creepily, even — within days of the V1 dropping directly on to Number 26, pulverizing the house and inflicting major damage on the adjacent ones, ivy had begun to slither over the heavily damaged wall separating the Johnsons at Number 24 from the Cliftons at Number 22.

'The poor Johnsons,' said Gus, almost reading her thoughts. 'I'm sorry about their house.'

'Gus, it's precisely people like the Johnsons, and anyone else with holes in their houses, who are going to find a German living here very difficult. We are not going to be top of their guest lists.'

39

'So it's the social life you're worried about,' murmured Gus. 'Good thing you're not in Germany. There are no starched tablecloths there.'

'Stop it.' She grabbed his arm, gripping his flesh tight and hard. 'How can you not see? My husband *died*, Gus. How can you not understand?' There was a silence. 'Nobody will actually *say* anything to our faces. But we will feel it. What you've done will affect us, all of us.'

The stubborn tone that she knew so well was back. 'It's nobody's business whom I marry.'

'Tell that to the marines.' She couldn't control her bitterness. 'And your betrayed ex-fiancée.'

He turned away and, again, she glimpsed deep trouble in the dark eyes. There was something buried under the rubble. Something harmful and poisonous.

Gus went back to the desk and dropped a hand on to the phone. 'You and Tilly must both stay here, of course.'

'I'm not sure that's possible.' Julia had spoken off the cuff but, underneath, she was thinking: *But where would Tilly and I go?*

'You must have thought it possible when I was going to marry Nella,' he countered impatiently.

'Nella's part of the family.'

The phone rang, as Gus — clearly — was expecting.

He picked it up and said: 'Clifton.' Covering the receiver with a hand, he said to Julia, 'I have to take this.'

Baffled, she left the room, shutting the door behind her with a click which she hoped

40

registered her feelings.

★ ★ ★

Supper for the four of them that evening was a less-than-exciting meal of oxtail and pearl barley which Julia had eked out as there had been no time to obtain coupons for Gus and Krista. Tilly had decided to dress up for it in a full black skirt made from the remnants of blackout material and a threadbare jumper which she wore only in the house. Infuriatingly, she managed, as ever, to look interestingly chic.

They ate in the kitchen. The dining room had not been used since Martha had departed to work in the local factory and Julia said she was not carrying the dishes upstairs. At the table, Gus explained that Krista would require a special diet and he would talk to Dr Lawson about getting vitamin supplements. He asked Julia to help him get hold of a good winter coat for Krista, and a pair of shoes that were properly soled.

A tinge of pink stained Krista's cheeks. 'Gus, there is no need to bother your sister.'

'While you're at it, get some vitamins for us too,' said Tilly. 'We could do with them. The British probably have first dibs.' She sounded rueful. 'Don't take offence, Krista; it's bound to be like that for a while.'

The unlikely bride looked up from the struggle with the oxtail on her plate. 'In Germany we would not give to the British.' She gave a tiny shrug. 'It is to be expected. We see

41

things from our different sides.'

Julia stared at her. 'Yes, we do,' she said pointedly.

Gus shot Julia a look. *My lovely sister*, he used to say in the days before the war. *Talk to me.* All that had been replaced by wariness.

The meal ground on. Julia found herself riveted by Krista: by her German accent, by the enormous eyes which appeared to float in the pale face and by her fingers which were so white they were almost ghostly. She had to concede that Krista possessed a kind of starved, pared-down beauty which many a heartier English girl did not. The meal was finished off with a cup of acorn coffee, then Gus and Krista pleaded exhaustion and went upstairs to bed.

In the hallway, Julia watched them slowly mount the stairs and disappear into their bedroom. Envy and her ever-present grief burned as savagely in her breast as they had ever done, forcing her mouth into the thin line which had become habitual and which she hated seeing.

She missed Martin's companionship. Apart from anything else, they had been great friends, enjoying doing the same things and laughing at the same jokes. She missed those mess nights with him when, as the commanding officer's wife, she had to make sure the evening went with a swing. Most especially she loved those nights when, positioned at the bar with a glass in hand, she felt herself to be glowing and radiant and young and invincible.

All gone. Vanished with the Mosquitoes that

had flown into that dark February sky.

It was too bloody early to go to bed and she went into the drawing room. The fire had died down but there was no question of putting on another log as the day's quota had been used up. When they were alive, her parents almost invariably took up residence here mid-morning. In those days, the room had been cluttered with newspapers, spectacles, their mother's sewing boxes, of which she had several, the drinks tray on which were arranged a half bottle of sherry and five small glasses.

Nobody sat here much now, and the room was icy — almost as freezing as that terrible day in February 1944. Then, the arctic conditions had been relentless. The evening before Martin's big op, the wind had dropped a little but the cold tightened over the landscape. The married quarters she and Martin had been allocated in RAF Hunsdon were pretty dismal and she had rushed to light the fire before he came home.

Despite the stringent temperature, against which the fire made only feeble inroads, despite knowing that Martin was due to fly on a dangerous sortie the next day (naturally, he couldn't tell her where), she moved around the room buoyed by the perpetual airiness that was her love for him. The baby kicked away inside her. On her knees in front of the fireplace, where she was twisting newspaper into firelighters, she lifted her eyes to the mirror above the mantelpiece in which was reflected a slanting winter sun. It seemed fitting that, in this pose, she prayed for the radiant, precarious bubble in

43

which she was conducting her life never to burst.

'Julia,' said Tilly now, coming into the room, 'what are you staring at?'

Julia turned her head and looked up at Tilly. 'I don't know.'

'You're thinking of Martin.' Tilly leaned over the back of the sofa and dropped a hand on to Julia's shoulder. 'I hope it was good thoughts, not negative ones.' Her fingers tightened a fraction on Julia's collarbone. 'Negative thoughts damage the spirit.'

Tilly was doing her best to help but she didn't — couldn't — know. 'If only we hadn't had the disagreement.'

Tilly slid an arm around her. 'Don't.' She nuzzled the top of Julia's head.

Julia stiffened. 'It's so easy to say, Tilly. So hard not to.'

That last night, Martin had been tired and almost speechless — often the case — and they ate dinner at the table without saying much. Just: *Pass the salt, old thing.* Or: *Darling, do you want a second helping?* They had made a rule: never touch on serious matters while eating. It was only in the intimacies of a shared pillow that they allowed themselves to voice what was on their minds, however haltingly, however imperfectly.

There they were: two people enjoying the awful pie that she had produced. She remembered him laughing and, after the meal, racing to get the chair nearest the fire. They had listened to the BBC News.

They went to bed, a place where she felt at her

44

most elemental and daring — a shared arena of discovery where her good, but dull, upbringing fell away.

'Martin?'

His fingers gripped hers.

The blood rushed into her cheeks and she was thankful they were in the dark. 'Martin, do you have to fly this one?'

Martin released her hand. 'I do.'

She remembered giving a little shiver. 'Martin, please, could you not go? You need to survive for our baby. You've done your bit. Your flying record can't be matched. Time to let others do their bit.'

'Shush, darling.'

'*I beg you.*'

What did she think at that moment? Having a baby was the one way she and Martin could create order out of chaos. To give birth during a war was to make a statement of faith and trust, but a child needed both parents.

'Julia, we agreed. Please don't.' He turned his back on her. 'Please don't.'

They slept as far apart as possible and the empty stretch in the bed between them grew cooler as the night progressed.

Martin had been a man who rarely complained. He saw life as a balance. It went one way, then the other, and for him there was no stopping this momentum or wasting energy on the bad times. That serene, all-seeing vision of his was one of the many reasons she had loved him. Even so, towards the end, the gruelling sorties, the bickering of men pushed to their limits, the bone-deep fatigue, had affected even him.

Why, oh why, then, had she allowed him to leave their lodgings with their disagreement still rankling? She couldn't bear . . . she couldn't bear that he might have briefed his men and taken off with the taste of it still in his mouth.

How could she have sent him out to that operation with an unquiet mind?

It was a question which she asked herself over and over again, obsessively and hopelessly.

As Tilly released her, Julia reached for a cushion and clutched at it — trying to hold down her wilder feelings. Her anguish. Her anger. 'Do you think Nella knows yet?'

'Gus will tell Nella as soon as he can,' said Tilly reasonably. 'It's his business and we mustn't interfere.'

Julia considered. 'Do you think she's Jewish or something and Gus rescued her? It would be very like Gus to do something like that.'

'Who cares what she is? What's much more interesting is what she has over Gus to make him marry her.'

Like Gus, Tilly had never discussed her war work with her sister — 'Too boring, Julia' — but apart from six months stationed in a remote part of Scotland, she had been tucked up in a station somewhere to the north of London from which she had emerged with a taste for conspiracy theories.

Tilly was giving it full rein. 'It might well be to do with Gus's hush-hush work.'

Martin had always impressed on Julia the need

for discretion. 'Perhaps we shouldn't talk about any of that,' she said.

'Oh, for goodness' sake. The war's over. No one is going to report us.'

The exchange was threatening to become bad-tempered, which happened from time to time. God knew, the sisters viewed the world differently but, normally, their spats meant nothing. This time Julia was aware that neither was of a mind to row back because they were both deeply disquieted by Krista's arrival.

'Tilly, Gus *loved* Nella.'

Tilly's angelic blue eyes signalled agreement. 'Do you suppose she might be pregnant?' This was followed by a curious little heartbeat of silence. 'Are we going to have a baby in the house?'

'Look at her.' Julia was aghast at her mean spirit but couldn't stop the words. 'I mean, she's skin and bone. Gus wouldn't . . .'

Tilly cut across her. 'Things happen in war. Appetites arrive. Cravings. In strange places with strange people.'

Julia lit a cigarette and made no comment. Tilly pulled a strand of blonde hair over her shoulder and twisted it between her fingers. 'You've got to get over Martin,' she said. 'Otherwise your life will be poisoned.'

Again, there was an odd little silence.

Julia smoked, deep in thought, and made no attempt to break it.

As far as she could work out, nobody thought that much about widows and, if they did, they didn't mention them. It was a bit like India, wasn't it, where widows were supposed to shut up and disappear for the rest of their lives? Everyone went on and on about bereaved children, parents and widowers, and of course she could not — would never — deny that coping with loss was desperate for orphans in particular.

But widows? Julia began to believe that the nasty secret in many hearts was that they were a despised breed. Or, at best, they weren't considered wholesome and were, perhaps, even vaguely shameful.

Yet these were the women who had to pick up the pieces and patch them back together again. They were expected to do this unobtrusively, without making a fuss and with no demands.

There were times when she felt so frustrated that she was tempted to run up to the first person in the street, grasp them by their lapels and hiss: 'It's not like that, you know.'

Hearts break.

It was a fact. She had felt hers go when the delegation arrived to tell her about Martin. *It was probably quick. Is there anything we can do?*

No, there wasn't. And all for an operation whose usefulness was being openly questioned by many of Martin's fellow pilots in the RAF. Why had they sent the Mosquito squadrons to bomb Amiens jail on that cold, cold February day? No one she had met could explain its purpose or knew how useful the raid had been.

After they left, she remembered looking out of the window on to the dispiriting Hertfordshire landscape and watching the icy rain fall over the roofs. 'Stair-rodding,' Martin would have said and sent her one of his lovely smiles. *Was he cold? Was he wet? Please, someone, cover him up.* She sat down in those rented quarters and counted the red bricks over the fireplace in order to try to cope with the pain. Not so very long after that, another kind of pain hit her as their daughter slid far too prematurely into the world.

Shock, they said.

Oh, my God, how could she not have protected her unborn daughter?

From then on, during the terrible days that followed, she remembered nothing much with any clarity except for Gus telephoning.

'I'm so sorry.'

'Where are you?' Her voice was hoarse.

'Can't say, old thing.'

'I hate this terrible, bloody, awful war. I hate, hate the Germans. If I got my hands on one, I would kill him.'

Her voice finally gave out.

'Shush, Julia. Shush. Listen to me. Go to Clapham. The house needs someone to look after it and it's your home.'

'Don't cry,' Tilly broke into Julia's reverie. 'Chin up.'

Julia drew in a heroic, shuddering breath. 'Sorry.'

'Feeling more amenable?'

'She's *German*, Tilly.'

'Oh, for God's sake,' said Tilly. 'She's a human being. The real point is that she's not Nella and we are going to have to find some way of getting along with her.' She flashed a smile. ' "The Mede

49

is at his gate! The Persian on his throne!''

Julia had heard this one before. 'Don't tell me. Byron.'

'Byron knew a thing or two.' Tilly's mouth twisted oddly.

She began to pace up and down and the full skirt swung with her movement in a way that had not been seen on women for a long time. 'Tell you what, we should learn German. Show we are willing.'

'Should 'we'?' Julia was appalled at the notion. 'God, no.'

Tilly pointed at Julia. 'Stop it.'

Julia struggled to bring herself to order. Life must continue. Searching for the practical, the comprehensible, the do-able, Julia fell back on the routines which got her through. 'We should start thinking about Christmas,' she said. 'It will take weeks to stockpile the food. Any ideas, Tilly?'

But, actually, she was thinking: *How am I going to cope with my hatred?*

5

On her second morning in the strange house, in the strange country, Krista collapsed and was put to bed by Gus. 'You've been through too much,' he said. 'You need rest. Absolute rest.'

Who *was* she? Her brain was a fog, and her body rendered useless by fatigue and long-held shock. Thus she hovered between life and immobility.

The bedroom door opened and closed at regular intervals and figures came and went. Gus. Julia. Once, Tilly. *How are you? Do you need more food? Should we get the doctor?*

Her sisters-in-law did not want her in the room . . . did not want her in the house and she imagined Julia contacting her friends and telling them about the interloper bride. Krista could almost frame word for word the shocked surprise snaking back down the telephone lines, the letters penned in indignation, the condemnation of Gus, the speculation that she must be pregnant, or practise exotic sexual arts — the implication being that the affront to British patriotism of a German spouse in the family constituted a huge disaster for the Cliftons. *And not only a German but probably not from a good family*, Julia might add.

Where was she?
In Berlin?

She coughed until she thought her lungs would come up.

Her skin burned. Her eyes hurt.

A mad, fragmented tide tossed her this way and that. Her gaze roved around the room and came to rest on an expanse of cold-looking blue wall which turned into a screen over which slid the images of chaos and terror.

Her people, struggling down the highways and byways of her country. Parents and children searching for each other. Former Nazis seeking a hiding place. Families crying: 'Where are you?' And, always, the refugees scavenging for food, for warmth, for shelter.

There were messages on scraps of paper left on burned-out doorposts or wedged under stones: 'Find me at the church.' But, so very often, the church had gone.

Allied troops ensuring Berliners knew they were defeated, elbowing them out of the way, off the pavements. Victors condescending to converse with despised Germans.

No functioning public clocks, no water supply, no cutlery, pots and pans, scissors, shoelaces or soap. All the things that, only a few years before, had been taken for granted. Everyone had dug themselves into their chosen ruin, going nowhere, doing nothing. Berlin was the mother-church of the raped, the starving, the wounded, the mad. It was a citadel of boltholes and rat runs. It was the city of the defeated.

Gus appeared by the bed. 'How are you?'

She peered up at him. 'I am not sure,' she replied. 'But better, perhaps.'

He made her sit up and gave her aspirin then settled her back down to sleep.

She lay flat between the sheets and watched him go out of the door.

What did she know about her husband?

He was thirty-one years old. Before the war he had worked as a criminal barrister. During the war (he was vague about the details) he had worked with a team which had made use of his fluent German 'asking people questions'. Some sort of intelligence capacity, she imagined. Not that she cared too much. As long as he offered a means of keeping alive, she wasn't going to waste her energy speculating.

After the Allies fought their way into Berlin, Gus arrived with his team. Thanks to the years of Sister Elisabeth's tuition, Krista was fluent in English and, after their first . . . *that* . . . encounter, he insisted on securing her a position on his team of interpreters and — pure gold, this — obtaining a ration book.

Being co-opted on to Gus's team meant that, when someone suspected of being a war criminal was captured, she was involved in the interrogation process. The task was to discover any strategic information regarding the enemy, or any plans for a last-ditch insurgency — those crazed pockets of resistance — and to determine if there was a case to answer. Their reports went to the teams who prepared the affidavits.

He was a good teacher. The best. And he taught her how to sift through the language, to screen the words, to observe every facial flicker, every blink of the eye, signals which told their

53

own stories. As the native speaker, he told her, you contribute the extra dimension, the subtleties and nuances.

'Am I betraying my country, Gus?' she'd asked.

'You're helping to put it back on the path.'

Was she?

'I need you to tell me about the culture. I need you to help me to digest the slang, the implied, even the humour. I need to be told of any linguistic tricks, evasions and indicators and to know what secrets lie underneath a 'yes' or a 'no'.'

'Chance would be a fine thing,' Krista remembered replying, deliberately using a German slang word then watching him trying to work it out. 'Why should I help you? You, of all people.'

He looked at her hard and long. 'You want to survive?'

She hadn't reckoned on Gus insisting that he marry her.

Predictably, his army bosses dispatched him back to England with his new and unacceptable wife. She had overheard one of his fellow officers on the team saying: *That's fucked you, Clifton. What did you think you were doing?*

'Did marrying me cause problems?' she asked him. Having some culpability in the situation, she thought she should try to show interest.

'Possibly,' he said. 'With the army, I suppose. But there are other options.'

He declined to specify what.

The fever was dropping. Her mind cleared and the events of the recent past came back into focus.

There had been the train ride from Berlin. Detail by detail, the memory slipped back into place.

Gus was telling her about his pre-war work as a barrister and a picture took shape of a man who delighted in the cut and thrust of arguments, who had pride and didn't much care for convention. 'Basically, I dealt with fraud, racketeering and murder.'

'*Ach so*, you worked with bad people. Berlin was nothing new.'

Krista was seized by a coughing fit. Gus asked if he could rub her back. 'Don't touch me,' she managed to splutter at him. After her chest had stopped heaving, she asked, 'Is there any difference between doing bad things in a war in order to survive and doing bad things in peacetime in order to survive?'

'I can't answer that. I wish I could.'

They stared at each other and Gus blinked first. 'But some things are always unforgiveable.'

The crowded train moved out of the station, leaving behind a pall of choking, gritty smoke. It ground through the flanks of the destroyed city where knots of hollow-faced women and their children, who were crying with hunger, had mounted vigil alongside the tracks.

She felt their want boring into her.

It was inexcusable not to do something. Taking down the travel rations which they had been issued from the luggage net, she waited for the train to stop at the signal and tugged at the leather strap which let down the window. Aiming at a mother with a baby on her hip and small

55

toddler clutching her filthy coat, Krista threw her rations at them.

She was not alone. Many of the other passengers — troops, journalists, civil servants — were doing the same and packets rained down on to the tracks. Manna from the bible, she thought. Only it was 1945. Nothing could be heard above the hiss of the waiting train except the sobbing of the women who were lucky, and the animal cries of those who were not.

Krista turned her head this way and that on the pillow.

Clicketty-clack, went that train. Clicketty-clack all the long, long way to Brussels.

Her mind worked sluggishly, oh so sluggishly, from lack of a proper diet. She was pretty sure she was anaemic too, and longed for the return of her brain's rapid responses, the quick emotions she'd known before the war when she had been strong and positive and the world had worked in a rational way and was mostly kind.

They passed uncultivated fields and ruined towns: a landscape of defeat. Phlegm oozed down the back of her throat. It tasted of the sickness and insanity which was now the lot of her country.

Silently, she said her goodbyes. *Please heal thyself.*

★   ★   ★

After three days of sleeping for hours at a time, Krista felt better. Finally, she woke, still coughing and weak but with her mind washed

56

free of the most distressing memories.

The sheets and nightdress were bunched and tangled, but she knew where she was. She raised a hand and stared at its shape, the skin colour, the feminine oval-shaped nails and an even greater fear raised its head: that she, the German girl, was disappearing. And, what was more, she had to disappear.

Making a huge effort, she turned her head towards Gus's side of the bed. It was empty. With a cry, she rolled over and pressed her nose into the pillow which Gus slept on. It smelled of him and, for a second, nausea rose. It wasn't so much Gus — although it was him as well. It was the smell of men.

Easing herself up on to the pillows, she pushed her hair back from her eyes.

A woman's hairbrush had been placed on the chest of drawers which stood between the windows and she focused hard on that. Whose was it? Hers now, she supposed. Otherwise it wouldn't be there. A hairbrush? She had a hairbrush. It was important to hold on to this precious fact.

Downstairs, a female voice was raised in anger. Julia's?

She fumbled her way out of the bed. *Steady, keep steady*. She edged her way over to the chest of drawers and picked up the hairbrush. It was of superb quality and smooth to the touch, fashioned from ivory with a narrow silver trim and stiff bristles, which age had yellowed a trifle. Obviously, another woman had used it before her. Without any warning, no preliminary sob, no pricking at the eyes, she began to weep big hot tears. It was such a civilized thing, a hairbrush, and now she was in possession of one.

Touching her dry, thin hair, she wondered if it would even grow again. Tentatively at first, then enjoying the sensation of the bristles on her scalp, she brushed it with increasing confidence. After she had finished, she dropped the brush into her lap and remained perched on the edge of the bed.

There was a knock on the door and Julia said, 'Krista, I've got you some clothes.' She didn't wait for Krista's permission but pushed her way in. 'You'll need these.' She held out a pile of folded clothes. 'Here. Cast-offs.'

Krista put aside the brush and took them. 'Thank you.'

'Gus said that you had nothing but what you were wearing.'

A whiff of ancient perspiration, overlaid with soap flakes, rose from the pile which Krista accepted. 'I am grateful. I miss my clothes.'

'You miss your clothes? I miss . . . ' Julia checked herself.

Krista thought she understood. 'I'm sorry.'

'We are all sorry,' said Julia, her eyes agate hard. 'Very sorry. About everything.' She turned on her heel. 'I have to go. I'm making the tea.'

The clothing included a pink Viyella blouse which Krista decided to wear. The colour was pretty enough, flattering to her pale complexion even, but it was well worn, particularly under the armpits, where the material was stiff and matted from another woman's sweat. She fingered the cuff. Which of the two sisters had sacrificed it? She suspected Julia — and gladly.

After dressing, she inspected herself in the mirror.

What a sight. Lips cracked. Hair lifeless. Skin like chalk. Every bit of clothing hanging off her. Stockings wrinkled at the ankles. They would hate her. Of course they would hate her. No one could love someone who looked as she did.

Even Gus?

Having forced herself to walk out of the bedroom, she stopped, ran back in, snatched up the hairbrush and hid it at the back of the drawer with her other bits of hoarded stash.

Julia and Gus were conferring in the kitchen. The wireless was on. Gus looked surprised at her entrance. 'You're up,' he said and pulled out a chair. 'Sit down.'

Krista obeyed and it was only now she registered properly what would be her domain.

The stove was made of white enamel, so old and grubby that it was hard to tell it was enamel. The floor was laid with earthenware tiles of a dull red — a colour Krista disliked. The cold hugged the edges of the room and the windows were misted with damp. In this state, it was not a place where Krista wanted to linger. But those good and elegant bones which she noticed when she first arrived at the house suggested that transformation was possible.

Her imagination rose on tiptoe and soared into a sunny, colourful future.

Clean the windows. Paint the shelves. Place the table under the window. The results would

59

be different from German kitchens. The convent's, her friend Lotte's warm and enveloping one, the tiny space in the flat she had lived in when she worked at the ministry, so cramped that it could house only a gas ring, a basin and the hutch in which to keep cheese.

Home.

'Are you all right?' asked Gus, adding with the flash of sympathy that she had seen him display at work: 'Sadness is not for ever.'

'I am well.'

'Tilly should be down soon,' he said. 'We'll have a celebratory cup of tea in the drawing room.'

'Don't count on Tilly.' Julia poured water into the teapot. 'Anyway, she might not be here. Tilly takes off at a whim; she's usually somewhere in Chelsea. We tease her that she's got a secret life.'

'We?'

'Nel — ' Julia stopped herself mid-syllable. 'I mean Teddy. Tilly hangs out with the artistic types in Chelsea. They all sleep with each other, you know, and don't think anything about it.'

'Sex?' said Gus. 'Good heavens.'

A flush surged into Julia's cheeks, suggesting an innocence which sat oddly with her sly, slightly bitter remarks about an outrageous life in a bohemia called Chelsea. She busied herself refilling the kettle and cutting thin — extremely thin — slices of bread.

Gus turned to Krista. 'Didn't I tell you that Tilly did things her own way?'

From the wireless came a snatch of Beethoven. The Pastoral Symphony. Krista found herself

60

clutching her hands together in her lap. Before a British bomber had dropped his payload on to the convent, a painting had hung by the entrance to the refectory, as it had done for decades. It showed men, women and children streaming over an Alpine meadow towards a distant figure of Jesus, standing with raised arms. Whenever she looked at it, Krista imagined herself breathing the scents of musty lichen spore, the fresh snap of crocuses and gentians, with the Alpine air slicing into her cheeks.

Gus sprang up and switched it off. 'It's hard to listen to music these days.' He pointed to the waiting tea tray. 'I'll take it up. You bring the pot.'

As he edged out of the kitchen, panicky sensations ran up and down Krista's spine. For the first time in months she had made no provision for somewhere to run and hide and she was in hostile territory.

She made herself sit quite still.

The light peering in at the top of the window struggled to make itself felt. Julia busied herself buttering the bread. Every so often, she sent Krista a speculative look. *Stranger. Interloper. Enemy.* She could almost hear Julia's thoughts.

'Were the clothes any good?' Julia ran water into the sink and washed the buttery knife.

The gas under the kettle made a soft popping noise.

'As you see,' said Krista, plucking at a button.

'I suppose clothes are very difficult to get in Germany.'

'Yes. If you need some you probably have to steal them.'

That seemed to get through. 'How awful.'

'In Berlin everyone steals and, after a bit, it becomes ordinary. The Soviets look on it as something that is accepted. It is a way of life for them. One of my German friends told me it was like a physical urge.'

Any softening in Julia vanished. 'Well, not here,' she said fiercely. 'This is England.'

In a grey jumper which had been expertly darned at the elbow and blue-green tweed skirt, with a row of seed pearls at her throat, her new sister-in-law embodied the RAF officer's wife. Krista could well imagine that she did her duty to the men and their families efficiently but with a kind of innocence which she had glimpsed when they first met. Julia *was* a lovely woman, with large, slightly protruding, long-lashed eyes, but she was closed-up, so closed-up.

'Do you mind me asking something? What did you do in Germany during the war? I mean . . . were you . . . ?'

Krista took a gamble. 'I worked in a ministry dealing with propaganda. Gus said not to mention it, but it was a job and I had to keep myself.'

'So you didn't have anything to do with the terrible things we are reading about?'

She thought of the whispers, the fear, the necessity to keep below the parapet. 'I heard some things,' she admitted. 'But we had trouble keeping ourselves safe. Not heroic, I know. But it was like that.'

Julia nodded. 'Only a few days ago I had no

idea of your existence,' she said. 'It seems extraordinary.'

'I understand it must be a big shock.'

'It's no use denying it and we must discuss what happens next.'

'Would it not be better if Gus was here?'

'I think you and I can manage.' Julia sat down opposite Krista. 'I know the world considers women to be idiots.' She arranged the slices of bread and butter on to the plate into a fan shape. 'You must forgive me if I ask you what this marriage is about?'

'About?'

There was a horrible pause.

'I apologize. Forget I said anything.' Julia examined her reddened, chilblained hands, took in an audible breath and spoke more moderately. 'After Martin was killed . . . died, Gus asked me to be housekeeper here. Did he mention that our parents died at the beginning of the war?'

'No, Gus and I have not talked about that sort of thing.'

'I don't understand. You seem to know so little about each other.' Julia seemed increasingly bewildered. 'The house has been in the family for generations so there was no question of selling. I'm grateful to Gus. He gave me a lifeline. It helped me.' Levering herself to her feet, she said, 'But it will be your job from now on.'

'Oh, no, Julia.' Krista sifted through her vocabulary for the words that would build bridges. 'I must not intrude.'

'You're Gus's wife. It will be your duty to run

the house. Not mine.'

'*Bitte!*' Krista's English was disintegrating. 'I don't want to take what is yours.'

'Wasn't this what you wanted? It's obvious you don't know each other that well, and while I still can't figure out what Gus's intentions were, I can imagine what *you* might have thought you would get out of marrying my brother. Perhaps you are . . . ?' She gestured at Krista's stomach. 'You know? That happens in war, doesn't it? A grapple in the ruins. My brother is very honourable. No one more so than Gus.'

Julia could not have been more insulting.

Krista held on to her breath. 'No. I am not having a baby. I cannot have a baby at the moment. My body won't let me.'

'Oh. Oh, I see.' Julia backed down. 'I don't know the customs of your country but in England,' there was the tiniest inflection on 'England' ' — it's the wife who takes over the running of the house. Before the war we had a maid who lived in, plus the gardener, who came twice a week. I don't think that will be possible any more. Tilly and I will do all we can but don't expect too much from us.'

Krista also got to her feet. 'I am sorry you had no warning.'

'Look at you,' said Julia, sharp and bitter. 'Not fit for purpose. One breath of wind and you'll fly away.'

The kettle hissed.

'You see, my husband's dead.' Julia wrapped her arms around her middle. 'He's lying in bits in a French field. Killed by a German pilot.'

The kettle gave a shriek and boiled.

'Please,' said Krista. 'Please.'

Julia's knuckles had turned white but she made a visible effort to change the subject. 'We must get hold of your ration book as soon as possible and I will have to teach you how the house works.' Julia filled up the teapot and said, 'Shall we go upstairs?'

A fire was burning in the hearth and Gus insisted that Krista sit beside it. He handed her a cup of tea and fetched a small table for her to put it down on.

Julia watched this interplay. 'I think Krista should take over the running of the house, Gus.'

'Krista isn't well enough yet,' said Gus.

Krista noted the 'yet'. 'Julia,' she said, 'this is your home. You mustn't leave.'

'I never said I wasn't going to be here,' Julia flashed back. 'But you can cook the meals.'

The weakness and weariness which had been Krista's near-constant companions now took repossession of her. 'Gus . . . Julia, please let everything be as it was. For the moment. I don't . . . ' But the English wouldn't come. '*Ich wollte.*'

'But that's it,' said Julia. 'It's 'for the moment' that I worry about, Gus.' She pushed the teapot over to him.

It was as if Krista wasn't in the room.

'Careful, Julia.'

Julia's wedding ring hung loosely on her finger and she twisted it round and round. 'Let's be honest. Krista shouldn't be here. She should be with her own people. Don't you agree, Krista?'

Twisting, twisting the ring.

'*Julia!*'

'She's German, for God's sake, Gus. We haven't all been at a teddy bears' picnic for the last five years. We've been killing each other. We hate them. They hate us.'

The room was charged with the harsh and vindictive feelings with which they were so familiar. Krista could feel them, see them.

Gus was furious. 'If you want to stay here . . .' He got up from his chair. 'Apologize.'

'*Please,*' Krista begged.

At a loss, she poured out a second cup of the weak tea (she was beginning to realize this was a feature of the housekeeping), and was about to take a large gulp but checked herself and sipped it instead.

'Don't tell me what to do, Gus.'

'Out of order, Julia.'

This was Gus telling them that he was fighting for his wife and would always do so.

Julia gave a smothered sob. 'You may think you occupy the moral high ground,' she flung at her brother. 'But you don't.'

Gus flinched. 'Maybe not.'

Krista looked from one to the other. In another life, she might have been distressed at causing such uproar, but the words of the Red Army soldier whom she first encountered were drumming through her head: 'I swear that I will take revenge as long as my hand can hold a weapon.'

This argument was nothing in comparison. Yet it exhausted her.

The unsettling sensations seeped back. It was as though her knees had been hollowed-out and her heart was struggling to beat. Familiar signs.

She fingered the cuff of the pink blouse that Julia had given her. 'Julia,' she said. 'I understand what you feel about me. I can apologize for my people, if that helps, and for what has happened. But let us be peaceful.'

'What's there to be careful or polite about any more?' asked Julia, and unshed tears glittered in the unforgiving eyes. 'What is there left to live for?' She turned her head away. 'Sorry. I'm as bad as Tilly.'

'Julia . . . ' His sister's grief had touched him and Gus went over and put his arm around her. 'I know what you've had to suffer, Jules. You mustn't think that I don't. Martin's death was terrible.'

His words were gently put and acted as a balm. Julia relaxed against him. 'I must get over him, Gus. I know I must.' She looked down at her hand with the wedding ring. 'At least you never tell me that I'll marry again, which is not helpful. Quite the reverse. Everyone rushes to tell me that it's only a matter of time and another Mr Right will stroll through the door. I don't expect it, even if I did wish it.' Disengaging herself from Gus, she touched the roll of fair hair at her neck. 'You may have noticed there are not so many eligible men left.'

'But you're beautiful,' said Krista impulsively. 'Truly.'

Julia uttered a sound between a sob and a sigh.

'Married or not, we're lucky to be alive.' Gus reached over to the silver cigarette box on the side table. 'I want to deserve my survival.'

This was Gus at his best — the compassionate, thoughtful, generous Gus. Not the other Gus.

Julia pulled out a handkerchief from the sleeve of her jumper and dabbed her wet eyes. 'So be it. I've done enough crying and you're right, Gus.'

She had turned pointedly away from Krista. Even so, Krista caught her expression; it was one of hostility and dislike.

The knocker crashed against the front door. 'Who on earth would that be?' asked Julia but her eyes flew to her brother. 'Oh, Lord, Gus. Do you think?'

'I'll go,' he said.

'Could it be Nel — I mean . . . ?' Julia did not finish the sentence and Krista was seized by a bout of coughing.

Within a few seconds, Gus reappeared in the drawing room accompanied by a tall man smartly dressed in a grey overcoat and holding a trilby hat. He walked with a pronounced limp. His features were neither ugly nor handsome, but somewhere in between. Used to ravaged-looking Berliners, to Krista he looked healthy and fresh-skinned enough. Yet there was an air about him suggestive of a complicated inner life. As she did so often these days, she recognized the effects of destructive experiences made obvious in apathetic bodies and trembling hands. In this man's case, the dead giveaway was a pair of eyes drained of expression.

'Teddy.' Julia whipped to her feet. A huge smile lit up her face, and it was possible to glimpse the young wife who had been so full of life and energy and joy. 'Why haven't you been to see us?' Reaching up, she kissed his cheek. Teddy indicated his leg. 'Of course. I remember you were having treatment out of town. Did it work?'

'Good to see you, Julia.' But his attention was focused on Krista.

'You've come to see Gus, I take it? Let me take your coat.'

He ignored the last. 'Tell me, Julia, what would you think? My lifelong friend comes home from an interesting hotspot and doesn't make any effort to contact me. Very odd, wouldn't you say? Then a letter arrives for Nella.' He smiled but entirely without humour. 'You can imagine, we found the situation puzzling and, since my lifelong friend had not had the guts to come to us to explain what was going on, I thought I would come and find out for myself.'

Gus took up a stance beside Krista, much as a soldier stands beside a comrade. 'This is Krista, my wife. Krista, this is Teddy Myers, my oldest friend.'

Teddy's complexion went a degree paler. 'So.'

'I was coming to see you,' said Gus. 'As soon as Nella got home.'

'You've got a bloody nerve, Gus.'

Gus stood his ground. 'Nella is owed the first explanation, not you, Teddy.'

'Good thinking, Gus, but you're out of date,' said Teddy. 'Nella has already returned. Desperate to come home and get married to you, she managed to blag an early passage on a troop ship, which was tricky because she's got some godforsaken Egyptian bug. She had planned the big surprise but your letter was waiting for her. She's lying in bed very ill and now grieving, with your charming letter on her bedside table.'

Krista heard herself exclaim, 'Oh, Gus.' This was followed by an absurd, and almost overpowering, desire to laugh and she dug her nails into her palms. Hard.

Gus stared hard at Teddy. 'True?'

Teddy nodded and Gus swung on his heel and left the room.

6

,A grim-looking Teddy limped after Gus into the hall. 'Where do you think you're going?'

Gus snatched up his coat and hat. 'Where do you think? I must go and see her now.'

'I'm coming with you.'

'No, you're not, Teddy. Keep out of it.'

Teddy squared up to him. 'How on earth did you think you would get away with this?'

Gus fingered the rim of his hat. 'It's not a question of getting away with it, Teddy. Believe me.'

It was true. Even if he had imagined that his marriage would go down well (which he hadn't), Gus never for a second thought that it was going to be the joyful, easy affair of the sort that those struggling through a war might dream about to get them through.

It was a five-minute walk to the Myers' household and one he knew like the back of his hand.

Five minutes. Five hours. Five days. He was reminded of how, in moments of tension, chronological time went haywire. Yet his feelings of guilt and dread were tempered by a surprising exhilaration that the wretched situation in which he had found himself would soon be cleared up.

The Myers' house was more substantial than the Cliftons', with considerably more stucco and embellishment, but of — to his mind — a

71

clumsier architecture and built in the harsher red London brick of a decade later. The Myers were better off than the Cliftons, employed more staff, ran a car and, in the years when the Clifton children had been in and out of the house on a regular basis, had entertained frequently.

Some time elapsed before Mrs Myers answered the clang of the bell pull. In itself, that was innovation — a maid in a frilled apron had always previously done that duty. Mrs Myers was in her usual uniform of an afternoon frock with a regimental badge pinned on to the front and her hair was permed into grey furrows. She took one look at Gus. 'So, it is true?'

'May I speak to Nella?'

'I'm not going to allow you anywhere near her.' Her light, mannered tone dripped with indignation.

'I think I must insist.'

'You should be ashamed to show your face. Haven't we suffered enough?' This, Gus well knew, was the despair of a mother coping with a wounded son and, now, a jilted daughter. 'After all this time, I thought I knew you, Gus.' She looked one degree away from weeping — an unthinkable breach of her social poise. 'I would never have thought it of you, Gus. *You.*'

Once upon a time her contempt would have cut Gus to the quick. 'Teddy tells me that Nella has got my letter. Is she very ill?' Mrs Myers' features slackened and wobbled. 'I think it would be better and kinder if I faced her.'

'My daughter is suffering,' she said, outraged. 'Really suffering. But perhaps you're right.

Perhaps she should tell you herself just what kind of rat you are, Gus.'

Leading Gus up the stairs to a spacious landing, she ushered him into a bedroom which opened off it. 'Five minutes, that's all.'

Gus had never been into Nella's bedroom and he saw at once that the prettily decorated, rather cluttered room, with chintz curtains and armchair in matching material, suited her. Nella herself was marooned under linen sheets and a green satin eider-down which had half-slipped off the bed. Her eyes were closed, her breathing unsteady and her cheeks flushed with fever. On the bedside table was an alarming array of medicine bottles, an enamel measuring jug and teaspoons. A smell of disinfectant mingled with the frowsy odour of a sickroom.

Before Krista, Gus had been in the habit of running an inventory of Nella through his mind in order to keep the memory fresh. Light-brown hair swept back from a broad, pearly forehead, the perpetually slightly surprised gaze, high cheek-bones. Nella had always blushed easily. Sometimes, dusky pink. Sometimes, red: shocking, painful red. Yet, when he had kissed her for the first time, she had gone quite pale.

At this moment, she did not look any of those things but white, sweaty and ill and his heart contracted. At Gus's entrance, her eyes opened. 'You.'

Mrs Myers hovered in the doorway, flustered and hopeless. 'Darling, I will be downstairs if you need me.'

Gus approached the bed. 'I've come to say I'm

sorry and I hope that, one day, you might be able to forgive me.'

Nella murmured through dry lips. 'I want to know *why*.'

He could not think of anything to say except to offer an unhelpful explanation about the happenstance of war and of how it was possible to be both a coward and a hero at the same moment. And how a man, or a woman, could long for death while fighting for life.

'I am truly sorry.' He considered touching her cheek and knew that he must not.

Tears slid from the corners of Nella's eyes down on to the frill of the starched pillowcase. 'The letter . . . I thought I was hallucinating. I couldn't make sense of it because I remembered our wedding. Then I realized the wedding was the hallucination. From the fever.' Her head moved restlessly. 'I wore the pearl necklace you gave me.' Her eyelids dropped down over her too-bright eyes. 'Tell me it isn't true and you haven't married someone else.'

He took a risk and sat down on the edge of the bed. 'Nella, it is true. And I want you to know that it is not your fault. You were not wanting in any way. I'm so sorry, very sorry.'

'But I want . . . I need to understand.' A sob convulsed the body under the green eiderdown and she hid her face with her hands.

'I'm sorry, too, that you're ill. I know how awful tropical bugs can be. I hope you got good care.'

How stilted he sounded — with no indication of his conflicting feelings.

She muttered from underneath her hands. 'The heat was terrible but they looked after me very well.'

There was an agonized pause. Downstairs, Gus heard the front door open and slam shut and the sound of raised voices in the hall.

'Could I have a drink of water, please?'

Gus filled the tumbler from the water jug, propped Nella up on the pillows and helped her to hold the glass. She drank gratefully, thirstily, gagging a little in her haste.

'What happened? Before I left for Egypt, we were still writing to each other about the wedding.'

He had destroyed all of Nella's letters, except for one.

Dearest Gus,

I always knew there was a chance of separation and now it's happened. I want to tell you that I won't change. I firmly believe that. Perhaps both of us will see some horrors and I have primed myself to be courageous and sensible about that sort of thing. I feel so much more confident with you, dearest G, and, knowing we will be together, I have no fear of the future.

'In the old days, I would have had you drummed out of town,' said Teddy furiously from the doorway, where he had suddenly materialized. 'And got you blackballed from pillar to post.'

'That's not helping,' said Gus.

Before the war, Teddy would never have uttered anything remotely comparable, disliking the practices of clubland and the establishment. The old Teddy would have been far more likely to say: 'Let's live life as we wish. Preferably with lots of sex.'

Flushed and out of breath from his walk from the Cliftons', Teddy lurched into the room and took up a position by his sister's bed.

Mrs Myers reappeared in the bedroom. 'Get out.' She enunciated each word with cut-glass precision. 'And never come here again.' For the ultra-polite, socially adept Mrs Myers, it was shocking language.

'Yes, of course.' Gus bent over and took up one of Nella's hands. 'It's not your fault, Nella. You must believe it.'

Nella turned her head away.

'Don't cry, sweetie,' he heard Teddy say as he left the room.

Mrs Myers followed Gus back downstairs and held open the front door. 'Just to warn you: if you come back you won't find her here. As soon as she can make the journey, I'm sending her down to her godmother to convalesce.' She seemed to fold into herself, like a fan snapping shut, and said, with the falsely bright note which Gus loathed, 'Don't worry. She'll be out of your way.'

The information elicited a pang. Putting Nella on to the eleven-thirty train to London Road, Guildford, to visit her godmother (to whom she was devoted) had been one of their decorous pre-war rituals. In those innocent days Mrs Myers considered eleven-thirty in the morning to be a safe time of travel for a lone female.

Gus headed for the Common. The encounter had been bad but it was done, albeit leaving behind a sump swirling with regrets and dirty secrets.

Once on the Common, and craving the release of exercise, Gus stepped up the pace. Soon the blood pounded in his ears and he was panting. Too many cigarettes, he reckoned, without resolving to do anything about it. Three people passed him in the opposite direction and he snatched a covert look at each. *Moustache. Large black handbag. Greying hair in net.*

Walk. Walk. The impact of his feet on the grass, the movement of his arms, the rise and fall of his chest helped to push back the encounter with Nella.

Dusk was falling rapidly. Disconcerting shapes loomed in and out of it, including the abandoned anti-aircraft base, as he took the path which ran across the grass. The guns had gone but the Nissen huts which used to house their crews and WAAFs were still there and the marked-out area where the WAAF girls had been taken through their drill paces.

A shape loitering by the gun-emplacement footings emerged out of the dark-grey gloom. *Male. No hat. Trousers too short.*

Problem?

They passed each other and Gus's instinct told him it was fine. Fighting a war taught most to watch their back, and Gus was certainly one of them. The kind of work he was doing in Germany meant he had had to refine the techniques which, in the backwash of terror unleashed in a disintegrating nation, was only prudent. In future, too, being professionally watchful would be part of the job.

The future?

Police and military interrogation techniques were impressive but, of necessity, rigidly applied. He had used them when seconded to the now-infamous Combined Services Detailed Interrogation Centre, CSDIC, at Bad Nenndorf earlier in June, and later, after he left there in disgust, to 1 War Crimes Investigation Unit.

Walk. He knew to keep walking. Walking helped to suppress the rise of stomach acid and the drumbeat of exhaustion behind his eyes. He picked his way past a row of allotments and bypassed the trenches which flanked them.

To witness the abuse inflicted by the British on the prisoners at Bad Nenndorf had been a wretched lesson. Yes, there had been some muttering, but nothing had been done. Many said instead: *They had it coming.*

The day before he was seconded out (in reality, kicked out) of CSDIC because he had taken his objections regarding prisoner treatment to a superior, he wrote to Teddy:

We fought the war not to be infected by what Hitler unleashed. Have you escaped? Have I?

He never sent the letter.

But he was not stupid and understood that morally questionable things could be done for the right reasons. It was the conundrum — the hall of mirrors — over which he puzzled. Human nature was unreliable and corruptible, including his own.

He turned homewards but found himself reluctant to face the music. Instead, he walked into the saloon bar of the Windmill pub on the south side of the Common and ordered a pint of beer.

As ever, he was greeted personally by Jeb York who ran the place, a ferrety-looking man who liked to know what was going on. 'Nice to see you back, sir.' The beer slid into the glass and York pushed it over the counter to Gus. 'The last few years haven't been a picnic, have they, sir? But, with a bit of luck, we'll get things back on the road.'

Gus took a long pull of beer and wiped the foam from his top lip. 'You often say that, Mr York.'

Punters were coming and going. Glasses clinked. A man in a pinstriped suit smoked a cigar and its smoky perfume vanquished the customary odour of damp sawdust and spilled beer.

Mr York picked up a cloth and polished the first in a line of glasses. 'I hear congratulations are in order. I hope you will bring Mrs Clifton for a slap-up glass of sherry. On the house, of course.' He picked at a cotton thread smeared over the glass. 'A bird tells me she's not British, if you get my meaning. Some won't like that, you know. But we're all humans, I say. Don't you think?'

An optimistic bubble, small but not insignificant, surfaced and Gus grinned. 'I do think.'

It was late when he returned home, the beer warring in his veins with the whisky he had also drunk. He went straight upstairs and retreated into his dressing room, undressed and emerged into the bedroom, where a fully-clothed Krista was standing by the bed.

'I have been waiting for you.'

Gus tied his dressing-gown belt around his waist. 'Please say what you wish, Krista. I will not stop you and I will listen.'

'Why didn't you tell me about Nella?' she asked, not unreasonably.

'Because we happened quickly.'

'No, Gus. Not that quickly.'

'You're right.' He sat down on his side of the bed. 'I think it was because I didn't want her to become too important. For you, I mean.'

'But she was important. And how could I not find out about her?'

Krista sat down on her side of the bed, only to leap up and begin rearranging the articles on the top of the chest of drawers. Comb. Hairbrush. A glass bowl which used to contain his mother's face powder. 'You are thirty-one, Gus, and handsome. Of course there was another woman.' Opening the top drawer, she stowed the hairbrush in it. 'Why didn't you marry earlier?'

'If anything happened to me, it would have been hard for her.' Gus did not sound convincing. 'We thought we had time.'

'But you knew what war was and what might happen.'

'Yes, I did.' He looked down at his hands clasped between his knees. 'Except . . . you don't really know. But something must have held me back.' He owed Krista honesty. 'I think I was seduced by the adventure of war.' He had wanted love and sex and Nella, of course. Yet he had also yearned for a freedom to be himself — a philosophical freedom — as he moved around its theatres.

Krista turned round and her starved-looking features reminded him of its cost.

'The things that had seemed important didn't any more when the war came. That was the big change.' She closed the drawer. 'We are lucky to be alive.'

Yes, but at a price. Occupying Gus's thoughts — crowding his thoughts — were the phantasms of the violence and breakdown he had witnessed. And, above all, the suffering.

He found himself longing for Krista's touch. Any touch.

In her accented English, she said, 'I think Nella is pretty. I asked Julia, who said she was. She also said that Nella loved you very much. I am ugly and foreign. It is a bad substitution.'

Gus stood up. 'Come here, Krista.'

However softly conveyed, she reacted badly to an order so it took her a few seconds, but eventually they were standing face to face, not touching, but each feeling the faint eddy of warmth which emanated from the other.

'Whatever you think,' said Gus, 'whatever

81

happens, I want you to remember that I married you.'

Krista looked at him. 'You are free if you wish to be.'

He reached out to grasp her shoulder but she evaded him. 'Krista, never say that again.'

'I am a mess and I am a problem for you.'

'Never say that again either,' he said angrily.

'I am the enemy, Gus.'

'Or that.' His voice cracked.

Head bowed, she was silent.

'Do you know something?' she asked in a low voice. 'During all the interrogations we sat through together, hours of them, you kept control of what you felt. You were always very cool, very calculating as you dug away at the defences put up by the prisoners, but always in control.'

The accented voice was light and sweet and he found it incredibly touching that she would say such a thing.

'We'd better go to bed,' he said at last. 'You're not yet well and you need your sleep.'

7

Sarah and Dennis Mackie were Gus's closest surviving relations, Sarah being the younger sister of Gus's mother. She had issued an invitation — actually, a summons — to Saturday tea at their house in Kensington, in order to inspect the new bride. It was written on Sarah's familiar dark-blue, headed writing paper:

I assume Saturday would be more convenient for you, Gus, since you will be at your chambers on weekdays? Please bring Julia and Tilly too. Coral would love to see them.

After lunch on the designated Saturday, Krista went up to her bedroom, where she sat down on the chair by the window and waited for the homesickness which was tormenting her to pass.

'Home.' She said the word aloud, first in German and then in English.

It mattered little that Germany was in ruins. Nor that she had no family there. Nor that Lotte was dead. Each morning, she woke in the bed she shared with Gus thinking she smelled coffee and cinnamon buns, or the fresh, green snap of Alpine meadow grass, or was hearing the guttural brass of the band playing in the park.

Home.

Having steadied herself, she got up, took off her skirt and blouse and put on a sea-green wool dress which Tilly had given her. Because it was cut with a narrow skirt, it did not drown her like the clothes Julia had given her. Its colour reminded her of the dress she had bought with her first wages, all those years back, when Germany seemed invincible and she was still innocent. She had worn it to the cinema on the first evening she had spent with Jan. They had held hands and talked of the future. Jan had wanted to be an engineer and Krista found herself confiding to him her journalistic ambitions.

Jan was dead.

Dressed more or less to her satisfaction, she searched in the drawer for the hairbrush. Its handle fitted snugly into the palm of her hand as it must have done for Gus's mother. As her hair had grown, a halo of soft baby-like hair had sprung up and she struggled to smooth it. Finally, she picked up her hat, the one she had worn when she travelled with Gus from Berlin.

She was here now and, outside, birds were singing.

'Krista, are you coming?' Gus called up from the hall. 'Hurry.'

The Mackies lived in a grand street in Kensington, quite close to the Albert Hall.

'Don't worry,' said Tilly as they descended from the taxi. 'They may hate you but they can't bite.'

Krista envied Tilly's outfit, the swirling black skirt and boiled-wool blouse, which looked comfortable and a world away from the formality of her and Julia's afternoon dresses.

A maid showed them into the drawing room, where two figures were sitting either side of the fireplace in which burned a generous fire. At the entrance of the party, they got to their feet.

Sarah Mackie had a long, bony face, very marked eyebrows, a contralto voice and a large diamond brooch pinned on to her dress. She allowed Tilly and Julia to kiss her on the cheek. 'Hello, dears. Hello, Gus.'

'This is Krista,' said Gus.

'How very nice. Welcome to the family.'

Dennis shook Krista's hand and said, 'I hope you play golf.'

'Dennis,' said his wife, 'don't start. Why should the poor girl play golf?'

Dennis's eyes roved over Tilly, Julia and Krista. What he saw clearly did not please him and he repeatedly picked up and put down the copy of the *Telegraph* which he had been reading until interrupted.

The conversation centred on cricket and arrangements for Christmas. Dennis treated the Cliftons to a minute description of England's disastrous trouncing at some match or other. Neither of them referred to Krista, to the marriage, or to Germany, for which Krista was thankful.

Cricket having been exhausted, the exchanges ground to a halt that defeated even Aunt Sarah, until Tilly leaped into the breach with a description of an exhibition that one of her artist friends was staging. 'He's not interested in drawing or painting as such,' she explained. 'It's the concept.'

85

'Such as?' The question was posed by Coral, Sarah and Dennis's daughter, who had come into the room. A tall, angular girl with a pasty expression and stubby eyelashes, she was wearing an unflattering brown dress and looked cross.

'Oh, hello, Coral,' said Tilly without enthusiasm. 'Well, I'm not quite sure. He's busy rescuing bits of ironwork from bomb-sites and hopes to arrange them into the concept.'

Coral flashed a set of mousy teeth. 'Goodness.' She kissed Julia and Gus and nodded at Krista. 'Hello, you must be Gus's new wife. I'm afraid I have to hurry out again. Is tea soon?'

A kerfuffle ensued as to who should be seated where when tea was wheeled in by the maid. Lapped by starched napkins and a lace-edged tablecloth it looked magnificent, but it became apparent that there was, except for hard-tack biscuits and *ersatz* fish-paste sandwiches, very little of it.

Her mother handed her a cup and Coral drank it down at professional speed. 'I'm helping to rehouse some poor families,' she said, with some smugness. 'It's urgent work.'

'That reminds me,' said Sarah. 'Julia, I want to co-opt you on to a committee I have in mind.'

'No,' said Julia. 'That's not my bag, Aunt Sarah. Not at the moment, anyway.' She gestured vaguely. 'I have to do other things.'

'What on earth would you have to do?' asked Coral. This was said in a cat-which-had-got-the-mouse tone. 'I mean, aren't you at home all day?'

Sarah observed her elder niece thoughtfully.

86

'We'll see about that,' she said.

Coral sat down beside Krista. 'Which part of Germany do you come from?'

'You're not addressing a public meeting, Coral,' said Tilly.

'I am not sure,' said Krista. 'I never knew my parents. But I have lived in Berlin for most of my life.'

'Did you have anything to do with that awful man?'

Again, Tilly intervened. 'I think Coral means Hitler.'

'Coral, don't be childish,' said Gus.

Krista was offered a sandwich and she stuffed it whole into her mouth.

There was an appalled silence, broken by Coral, who whispered audibly to her father, 'Do you suppose manners in Germany are so different?'

Gus got his feet, picked up the sandwich plate and offered it to his wife. 'You must have another one, Krista.'

She shook her head. 'No, no.'

Gus insisted: 'Please, Krista, you must get strong.'

Keeping her gaze locked on his, she obeyed. This time she took only a dainty bite.

Coral transferred her attention back to Tilly. 'Such a pretty skirt, Till, but you do realize there's enough material in that skirt to clothe two people?'

Tilly called Coral's bluff. Leaping to her feet, she fiddled with the skirt fastening. 'If you like, you can take it now.'

'For goodness sake,' said Aunt Sarah. 'Stop it, you two.'

Coral beat a retreat and Tilly called after her, 'My name is Tilly . . . '

Only when the goodbyes were being said did Dennis address Krista directly. 'I expect you are very glad to be in London. We do things so much better here.'

★　★　★

Julia was giving Krista a lesson in the running of the house.

She led her upstairs to check over the linen cupboard and explained that a special towel was always kept for the doctor's visit so that he could warm up his hands in hot water before an examination.

At the top of the house they inspected two empty, awkward-shaped rooms where the servants used to sleep. There was a third one but that was now used by Tilly and the door was closed. 'If the council had its way, we would have a family billeted on us,' said Julia. 'But we seem to have escaped.'

Moving around Number 22, Krista was again conscious of its beauty but also, in the harsh daylight, of its dilapidation. Dust was everywhere. Some walls had cracks and the paintwork needed attention. But, with patience, its life could be reignited, brought into order, given a new lease.

The pantry, leading off the kitchen, smelled of must and old pickles and Julia showed Krista how the food was kept under dampened terracotta covers. In the adjacent storeroom she pointed to the near-empty shelves and said, 'So many things are unavailable still.' Her voice sharpened into hostility. 'We had our first sighting of oranges in the High Street the other day. It was so exciting that people were dancing outside the shop. Odd, isn't it?'

This is what your country brought us to.

'But nice?' suggested Krista.

Julia now conducted Krista into the scullery down the passage from the kitchen. Shiny with moisture welling between the grouting, the red floor tiles looked treacherous. Stacked on the shelves were tins of polish, a bottle of Jeyes Fluid and a packet of soda crystals. A cake of lye soap sat in a zinc dish in the butler's sink and the acrid combination of disinfectant and cleaning fluids filled the small space.

'We hang the washing out here.' Julia tugged at the door. The wood was swollen and took a bit of force but eventually yielded.

Following Julia outside, Krista inhaled tangy, autumn air which still held traces of scent from the plants which had survived in the battered back gardens. The remnants of flower beds, a neglected lawn and, at the bottom of the garden, a shed had also survived. Avoiding the mud and worm casts, Krista went to take a look. It was almost derelict with mould sprouting over the window glass. She scratched off a patch with a fingernail, and peered in and spotted a hoe, ancient seed packets and a watering can minus its spout.

'Are you coming, Krista?' shouted Julia.

Fallen leaves peeled away under her feet as she made her way back. In the next-door garden, the sun was slanting through the branches of a sycamore tree. She glanced up at it. It looked sturdy enough. Soon the cold weather would lock down, but — and she liked to think about this, *needed* to cling on to the idea — the rooted resistance to extinction would mass underneath the garden's winter skeleton, biding its time until spring. And then microscopic stirrings of life, a burst of growth and the first snowdrop, the first crocus would happen.

She went back into the house.

In the scullery, Julia rolled up her sleeves and pulled on a pair of protective cuffs. 'We must deal with the washing, I'm afraid.' Having threaded the shaft of a wooden panel into the handle of the lid covering the washing tub, she lifted it off, releasing a stink of dirty, sudsy water. Inside, there was a staggering amount of tangled laundry. 'Help me get this lot out.'

Picking apart the sodden knot of shirts, trousers and night-wear was hard work and the smell in the steamy scullery initially made Krista gag. She and Julia took turn and turn about at the mangle, one of them feeding the sopping clothes through the rollers, the other rotating the handle.

Mangling was heavy work, too heavy for Krista, who succumbed to a bout of coughing, and Julia ended up doing most of it. 'When things were normal, this was Martha's job. After she left, my parents managed to employ an ex-lady's maid. She was furious at having to take a position which she considered beneath her. It didn't work out.'

'But it was work.' Krista swapped places with Julia. 'Work is better than no work.' With an effort, she turned the handle. An initial rush of energy helped her. Then it disappeared, leaving her weak-kneed. 'Sorry,' she said and stepped back.

Julia straightened up and kneaded the small of her back with her fist. 'Perhaps you don't mind the hard physical stuff. A girl like you?'

There was an insult buried in the question but Krista wasn't sure of its purpose. On the train, Gus had explained that the English were a little tricky about who came from which section of society and how they should be treated. 'It's nonsense, of course,' he said. 'But I should warn you.'

'Are you asking if I come from a bad or poor family?'

Julia busied herself with folding a damp shirt. 'No,' she said. 'I was merely . . .'

'Julia,' Krista cut in. 'Did Gus love Nella very much?'

Julia let the clothes rack down from the ceiling and indicated that Krista should help her drape the mangled clothes over the slats. 'Yes, I think he did. Obviously, he changed his mind.'

It required the two of them to haul on the pulley to raise the rack up to the ceiling. Shirt sleeves and trouser legs hung down from the slats like wet stalactites.

Julia's enmity was like a hostile grip on her

91

shoulder, but Krista pressed on: 'Will you tell me about Nella?'

Julia secured the rope around the cleat. 'When Gus went off to war we thought everything had been arranged between him and Nella. Nothing was said to us. It didn't have to be. The pity was, when Gus came home on leave that last time, they didn't get to see each other. Nella had been posted to the Middle East. After that, he left to work in Germany where he met you. So, apparently, everything had not been arranged.' She made a final adjustment to the rope. 'You must have bowled him over.' Her tone dipped into malice. 'Sometime you must tell me about it.'

'Is Nella your friend?'

'More Tilly's. But I would have welcomed her as a sister-in-law.'

Julia was obviously unwilling to discuss it further. Tilly might be a better bet if Krista wanted to find out about Nella. 'I apologize for asking you these questions but I am concerned.'

'Really?' Julia pulled off her cuffs and rolled down her sleeves. 'I'm sure there's no need.'

'I am so sorry about your husband.' This was something Krista felt she should say.

'Don't . . . ' Julia twisted the discarded cuffs into a tight ball. 'Don't talk about my husband.'

Krista tried again. 'I am sorry about him.' She tried to put the right words in the right order. 'I understand a little. There are so many lost in Germany as well.'

'I know.' Julia was checked and, for a second, it was as though they understood each other. The moment of shared empathy vanished. 'I try to understand. But I lost someone who I loved more than my life.' She poked a stray strand of hair back into place. 'And there's no need to tell me others also did. I *know*. But it doesn't make it easier or more acceptable.' She turned on the cold tap and swished water around the sink. 'Sometimes, I want to be dead too and . . . ' She stopped mid-sentence, as if she was astonished by her own words, and fled from the scullery.

By now, damp had seeped into her shoes. Krista turned off the tap and wiped down the draining board. Then she stowed the soap in the dish and swilled out the tub. She wiped her hands, buttoned up her cuffs and returned upstairs.

That morning, Gus had left without saying his usual goodbye and this small omission succeeded in triggering the old terrors. Was no goodbye significant? Was it a bad sign? Back home, where she worked in the ministry of information translating the propaganda broadcast by the British Broadcasting Corporation into German, she had become a past master at interpreting tiny pointers from her superiors. They all had.

Judging and interpreting the smoke signals was a skill in which she had grown wise and corrupt. Unlike poor Heidi who had left it too late to run and hide. Heidi's brother had voiced anti-Hitler views and everyone knew that, as a consequence, the supervisor reported Heidi's comings and goings to the secret police. One sunny morning, she was hauled out from the

93

ministry typing pool and vanished into the *Nacht und Nebel*, which they all knew about but never mentioned.

Where to go, if she had to flee the house? Where to go in this strange country, with these strange people?

Taking refuge in the drawing room, she took up a position by the window. It had started to rain and the watery light painted the elegant room into an autumnal watercolour of fading greens and ochre. The curtains in here were made of thick, yellow woollen material which, given the formality of the room, introduced a homespun note. The rough weave was pleasant to touch. When she ran her hand down one of them, puffs of dust rose like tiny geysers.

She imagined beating the dust out of them and pressing them until they hung in proper folds. She imagined washing the window frame and polishing the glass until it gleamed.

In Berlin they were starting from the beginning. There was no choice. Brick by brick, stone by stone, the city would have to be rebuilt by anyone who could work — women mostly, because the men were dead, wounded or mad. None of them knew where the next meal would come from, but build the city they would.

On the Common she could see the allotments and the pathways. She knew that, beyond those, was a confident-looking bandstand which she had seen when she had first arrived.

Bandstand. Germany.

Ach, the music in Germany. The bands, the concerts in the park, the singing.

94

Don't cry.

On the edge of the Common closest to the house was a clump of trees, two of which were mature beeches. A squirrel cavorted on the lowest branch of the largest one. 'You're lucky,' she informed it out loud. 'In Berlin you would have been eaten.'

Only then did she notice the figure standing by one of the beeches.

Seemingly obvious to the drizzle, she was a slender woman of medium height who was standing quite motionless, her gaze fixed on the house. She was wearing a headscarf tied under her chin and held a handbag hooked over one arm. Even through the rain it was possible to see that her winter coat was of vivid blue, the kind of astonishing, uplifting blue that sang out of medieval paintings and was impossible to ignore in the sea of drab.

The woman dabbed at her eyes with a handkerchief and then, in a gesture of grief and hopelessness, buried her face in it.

The rain began to fall in earnest and the lights visible across the Common were being blotted out. The woman put out a hand to the tree trunk to steady herself, walked over to a car parked near the trees and got in. The blue coat was swallowed up.

8

Gus walked along the Embankment past Westminster Bridge, on to Waterloo Bridge and turned into the station. A boat train had just steamed in. Passengers in tow, the porters ferried luggage across the crowded concourse. Quite a few of the men wore demob suits and some — coming in from the battlefronts in the East and Europe — still wore uniform.

Gus made his way to the newsagent by Platform 3, where he was greeted by the man behind the counter: 'Nice to see you again, sir.' He bought a copy of the latest *Vogue*.

'Hello, Gus.'

He swung round. 'Nella. I thought I might see you here.'

Nella set down her case. Dressed in a grey suit with a fur tippet, with her hair hanging loosely under a grey velour hat, she looked sallow-skinned and shaky. 'Were you wanting to talk to me?' A tiny ray of hope lit up her face. 'How did you know I'd be here?'

'I got Tilly to find out when you were going down to your godmother.' He held out the *Vogue*. 'I thought you would like the usual for the journey.'

She glanced at the cover. 'Do you imagine I'm going to forgive you because you've given me a magazine?'

She really did not look at all well and Gus was

96

concerned. Checking the time on the station clock, he said, 'You need a cup of tea. There's time.'

He picked up her case and offered Nella his arm. She refused and they walked separately over to the cafe by Platform 13, where Gus commandeered their favourite table by the window.

The interior of the cafe was dim but everything was well scrubbed and a vase of harsh-pink dahlias had been placed on the counter. The girl behind it nodded to them. 'Hello, there.' Her red lipstick and the red-and-blue headscarf wound around her head in a turban offered some cheer.

Gus ordered a pot of tea for two and lit a cigarette. A brass band was playing rousing martial music in the station concourse. A livid scar marked the face of the trumpeter and the cymbals player had a wooden leg. The man passing the hat around had lost an arm.

Nella folded her hands in her lap and refused to look at Gus. Instead, she watched the band, her eyes wide with what he took to be pity. Eventually, she said, 'Thank God the war is over.'

Their tea arrived and Gus poured it out. She tried to lift the cup but her hand was shaking and she used both to manoeuvre it to her mouth. 'I can't believe that everything we shared has gone.'

'It was nothing you said or did, Nella. That's what I wanted to impress on you.'

'Should I believe you? It's just I keep thinking

97

about that evening before you went. That awful restaurant. You had just been told that you were going somewhere secret. I was frightened. You were going to do things in which I had no part. Of course, you weren't thinking about me because you had whatever it was to worry about. I said what I said because I was hurt and — I see now — I wanted your attention.' Her shoulders lifted in a tiny shrug. 'Childish of me, but sometimes you say things for all the wrong reasons. And they're not true.'

'None of that had anything to do with it.'

The confession was a stumbling one. 'I think about you all the time, Gus,' she said. 'I can't help it.' There was a tiny splash of tea on her chin. Gus hesitated before reaching over and wiping it with his handkerchief, and she permitted him to do so. 'When you've been abandoned . . . ' Gus tried to protest. 'Let me finish. When you're abandoned, when you're tortured by something, the mind gets stuck in a groove. I discovered that, lying in bed.'

Steam was accumulating in gritty clouds under the station roof. A porter shouted. Nella traced the shape of a heart on the table top. 'I sense you have changed. A lot.'

'I have, but it doesn't mean I didn't — don't — care for you.'

'Ah, that . . . ' she said with evident disbelief, turning her head away.

The band in the concourse struck up with 'Nearer my God to Thee'.

He had so often thought about the coming home, when he had expected to be greeted by

98

Nella. It was to have been the culmination of the dreams of the war years. He had envisaged minutely the emotions and contentment of stepping back into his old life. During the dead periods between the battles, he had longed for very simple things: the smell of hawthorn blossom and the sound of a blackbird singing on a June morning.

'Even Teddy tells me that he doesn't recognize you any more.' Nella made a visible effort. 'He said you changed after you went to Germany. You never actually told me where you went, Gus. Or anything about the work, really. Since I was out in the Middle East and unaware you were busy betraying me, I have to take my brother's word for it.'

This much he owed Nella.

'I was co-opted to work for the outfit dealing in war crimes, in which capacity I visited one of those camps which you will have read about.' Nella gave a little gasp. 'After that I was sent to Bad Nenndorf, which was another experience that affected me badly, and then to headquarters in Bad Oeynhausen. From there I went to and fro, mostly to Berlin, and writing was difficult.'

'Not that difficult, Gus.' She tapped her fingers on the table. 'All you need is a scrap of paper and pencil.'

What was there to say?

Take Berlin where, among others, Gus had interrogated a general who had ordered babies to be shot and a lieutenant who had made a speciality of killing civilians by the dozen. He hadn't been fussy about how. It wasn't possible to interrogate such people, people as far removed from decency as anyone could imagine, without being infected by their poison.

The band's brass notes floating over the station hubbub sounded clear and true.

'Teddy's right. It's true that I saw and heard some life-changing things.' The tea was disgusting but he drank it. 'It's ironic because I deal in language,' he said in as light a tone as he could muster, 'but, in the end, I found it almost impossible to describe to anyone who wasn't there.'

'We at home suffered too,' she said.

He leaned over the table. 'Nella, even Teddy didn't have to face anything as evil as what happened in those camps and his experiences were bad enough.' His face was close to hers and her sweet and familiar scent drifted past him.

'And that's what I hate about all this,' she said, her mouth tightening. 'This competition to see who has suffered most.'

Her hand hovered over Gus's. Then she removed it.

'I know about the unspeakable suffering, and anyone with an ounce of humanity feels terrible about it too. But it does not make my mind obedient. I can't help, or stop, what I'm thinking and feeling about us. About you.' She spoke with an eerie calmness that Gus found unnerving. 'Before the war, I would have died rather than admit it. No well-brought-up girl would ever admit to, or discuss, their feelings like I'm doing now.' Her voice dropped. 'What *did* happen in Berlin, Gus? I know you. I know you wouldn't have abandoned me without a good reason for that girl. You're not that sort of person. Something tells me so strongly . . . ' She tapped her chest in the region of her heart.

He was alarmed at how close Nella had edged to the truth and distressed by her obvious misery.

'Do you ever think about?' she continued. 'We . . . Well, you know.'

'Yes.'

On that shimmering summer's day, Gus had taken a rug from the car and they spread it under the trees in a place with a view of a cornfield fringed with poppies at its edges. Any worry that someone might come upon them had been overridden by the urgency and physicality of the moment. It had been so easy and simple and innocent.

'I cry myself to sleep thinking about that time. Not that I sleep much at the moment. Grief is exhausting. It doesn't let go of you even for a second. But I hope you remember that time, Gus.'

Of course he did. But it had become irrelevant. What happened then had been placed behind a plate-glass window for him to view from time to time. Nothing more.

And, if he was truthful, he thought more about the stench of bodies that were trapped under buildings and couldn't be reached, and the women staggering around the ruined city with hungry children and pitiful possessions.

'Where did you find Krista?'

The girl behind the counter was drying up the cups and saucers. There was a lot of clattering and she sent him a cheeky smile.

Where? What? How?

Not long before the war broke out, he had talked with Teddy. A luxurious, easy conversation of the kind enjoyed by trusted friends.

They had been drinking. Beer, lots of it. And he had peered at Teddy's flushed, happy face through a haze.

'The past, old boy,' said Teddy, 'is what actually happened. History is what we choose to remember and what we choose to write down.'

He argued back. 'What we remember is not necessarily a choice. We remember what we can remember.'

The Nella who was sitting opposite him was so much smarter than the sweet and pretty girl who once lay down willingly in a field in the hot sun and to whom he had promised to return. He chose his words with care.

'I found Krista in the ruins of a convent in the Charlottenburg district. She and others had had a dreadful time.' The half-lie came surprisingly easily. 'The Soviets had spilled over from their sector and were hunting down deserters and raping indiscriminately.'

Nella picked up her handbag. 'A starving girl must have been hard to resist. And, yes, I can understand. One look from a starving German girl and you forgot about me.' The bag clicked shut.

'I know I behaved badly to you, Nella, and I am sorry, so sorry.'

Her gaze was stony. 'I never knew how useless the word 'sorry' is.'

'But Krista is my wife.'

Nella froze. 'If only you knew how much that hurts.' She repeated it in a whisper. '*Hurts.*'

Her chair screeched along the stained floor. 'Go away, Gus. Leave me alone.' She snatched up her gloves. 'I don't want to see you. I don't want to speak to you.'

With that, she picked up her case and left the cafe, disappearing in the direction of the platforms. Gus stopped only to pay the waitress and went after her. The crowd on the concourse was dense and partially obscured by a cloud of smoke billowing across it. He elbowed his way through and found her sitting on a bench, smoking a cigarette. She looked defenceless and beaten.

He stood in front of her. 'I didn't know you smoked.'

'There's lots you don't know about me.' Nella blew the smoke over his head. It was an angry gesture, and full of contempt for him. Fine. That was fine.

She turned her head away. 'Gus, if you thought something had happened which was so awful that you felt you couldn't live with me you should have tried to explain. I would have listened, understood perhaps, and we would have got married and I would have done everything to make you happy. We could have done our best to live normal lives.'

Her cheeks had flushed and he was concerned that the fever was returning. 'Could you come back to the ordinary after Cairo? Could you forget the heat, the smells, the otherness?'

103

'But I *am* ordinary.' Nella threw the cigarette down and ground her shoe over it. 'I would have thought everyone would crave ordinary after what has happened.'

Gus sat down and captured one of her hands. 'I truly regret causing you pain.'

Her hand rested in his and he had to suppress the urge to run his finger across the soft, tended palm.

As he used to do.

'Gus,' she said in a low voice, 'our homes have been bombed by Germans. Teddy is lamed. I know we are supposed to be a Christian country but we have a duty to hate them.'

If he was honest, Gus felt relief at the smallness of Nella's view because it gave him something to dislike. He released her hand. 'If we want to stop another war happening, we can't think like that.'

'Did you learn to love the Germans while fighting them?'

She shot out the question with a venom which was quite new to him.

An inaudible announcement came over the station's tannoy and passengers surged towards a platform. The band had played its last hurrah and was packing up the instruments. The cymbals player lurched slowly towards the exit.

There was nothing else to say. Gus accompanied Nella to the platform and the waiting Guildford train. Hunting for change, he found some pennies, paid for a platform ticket and walked her to the First Class carriage. 'Would you like me to stow your case?'

She shook her head.

'I hope we can be friends sometime in the future?'

Her coat hung loosely over her diminished frame, giving her an extra vulnerability.

'Here . . . ' He handed her the *Vogue*.

'I gave you my virginity and, in return, I get a magazine. Of the two of us, who had the best deal, do you think?'

'Please take care of yourself. Tropical bugs can stick around.'

'At least something will stick around.' What she said next disturbed him: 'You were, and are, my great love, Gus. I don't know what is going to happen from now on but I know I won't change.'

★ ★ ★

Outside Waterloo Station, Gus took the bus to Victoria. It was forced to take a detour as it made its way up Victoria Street.

'It's the water main, sir.' The conductor was gloomy and fed up. 'It's been threatening for months. Now it's gone and done it. Place is awash.'

Indeed.

He closed his eyes for a moment or two and the sense of being out of kilter with life resurfaced. This was something he often felt these days. He was missing his friendship with Teddy. So much of what he had taken for granted about it — the camaraderie and loyalty, the certainty that each would be there for the

105

other — had almost certainly been killed off by his marriage.

The bus ground onwards in stop-start fashion. The plush on most of the seats was worn down to the warp and the straps to which people clung did not look a hundred per cent reliable. A young and tired-looking woman with a baby perched on her knee sat beside him and he caught the whiff of poverty and stale milk.

A man in a gabardine mac seated three up from him had got on at the same stop. The nondescript mac, and the hunch of his back, suggested strongly to Gus that this man did not wish to be noticed. Even after so short a time in his new calling, Gus had developed an instinct for the feint and counter-feint of tailing and he was not surprised when the man in the mac got off at the same stop.

If he was a tail, he wasn't very good at it. Maybe that was the point? Gus was also aware that the methods employed by his new bosses were opaque, if not baffling.

Maintaining a normal pace, Gus turned in the opposite direction to the one he wished to take and snaked around the streets which flanked Rokeby Street. He did not look back but, having noted that the heel of one of the man's shoes was badly worn, he listened out for the shuffle and clump of an uneven walk.

Ten minutes later, he turned into a street with a terrace of town houses. Built by a Georgian grandee in the eighteenth century, they were tall and elegant and mostly unscathed from the bombing.

Footsteps! Soft. Careful. Slightly uneven.

To continue or not? It was possible the tail was there to stake out Gus's movements. In which case, which lot would it be? The organization for whom he now worked? Or the other lot, which was likely as they hated each other? On the other hand, the Soviets were very busy watching everyone.

Keep the pace natural and the shoulders relaxed.

Possible reasons for being tailed?

There were quite a few. In fact, he reflected grimly, he had gone about accumulating an impressive list. One, the work in army intelligence, which included the interrogations of captured German army personnel and those suspected of being war criminals — any one of these could have resulted in a vendetta. Two, he was now working for the secret services. Three, he was married to a German who had cooperated with the British and there would be some who would have it in for Krista, via him. All it would take would be a telephone call from Germany to a contact in Britain. Four — and admittedly this was far-fetched — he had submitted a report on what he had seen at Bad Nenndorf to the Foreign Office, and, if they had sight of it, this would have earned him the hatred of his former CSDIC bosses.

The baldly laid-out list had failed to convey the disgrace of how the prisoners had been treated:

1. insufficient clothing;

107

2. intimidation by the guards;
3. mental and physical torture during the interrogations;
4. they were kept in solitary confinement for days at a time with no exercise;
5. they were confined to punishment cells, not for any offence but simply because the interrogator was not satisfied with their answers;
6. during the winter they were deprived of certain articles of clothing in the punishment cells, had buckets of cold water thrown into the cell and were forced to scrub the floor for long periods;
7. they were assaulted and man-handled;
8. medical attention was grossly inadequate;
9. food was insufficient . . .

He still thought about all that and it haunted him.

He slowed and the footsteps slowed.

The Soviets were pretty nasty. However, if it were the British security services watching him, it would be a simple matter to get them off the scent by operating in the evening. The joke in secret circles ran that the MI5's surveillance teams knocked off on the dot of five-thirty and their chaps in trilbys and light-coloured mackintoshes all buggered off back home to Watford or Beckenham.

Not for the first time, he concluded that working in the Army Intelligence Corps during the war had been straightforward compared to what he had now got himself into. Interrogating prisoners of war had not been, and would never be, like running a cake stall but the army rules and procedures around the conduct of it were clear.

There would be no more such rules to safeguard procedures. At a stroke, his life had become more ambiguous and, in case he was in danger of forgetting, more interesting in every way.

Gus stopped to retie a shoelace. Within a few seconds, the man with the uneven footsteps had passed him.

Clean-shaven. Tow-coloured hair.

Gus turned round and retraced his steps. Teddy would have appreciated how ridiculous this farrago was, and he imagined discussing it over a late-night whisky. *The absurdities,* Teddy would say.

Ducking down a side street, he waited a couple of minutes before setting off again in the direction of the house further down the street.

Waiting on the doorstep to be admitted, he admired the writhing branches of a wisteria which grew above the front door. The door opened and Gus went in.

The house's interior suggested it was lived in by owners who favoured expensive antique furniture, black-and-white marble floors and an unimaginative oil landscape or two. This dull, but reliable, decor hopefully did its job of persuading the casual observer that it was a private house.

Gus was ushered into a panelled room overlooking a garden resplendent with box hedging and a trimmed laurel tree. The man he knew as James Minet was sitting at a desk covered with closed buff files. In the corner was a secretary at a much smaller desk that was almost completely covered with boxes containing index cards.

Minet was dressed in his usual fashion, which bordered on the raffish. If his demeanour suggested a man who would prefer to be drinking at the club, that was to underestimate him. Minet was famed for the intensity which he brought to his job.

He was searching through the drawer of a filing cabinet and did not look round at Gus's entrance. The secretary, a pretty woman with fluffy dark hair, cocked a sympathetic eyebrow.

'A couple of things to discuss, Clifton.' Minet finally turned round. 'For the time being, we want you to work on documents. Rather a lot of them. A hell of a lot of them, actually.' He paused. 'They have been captured from former German intelligence and security by the team working on industrial espionage. We need a report on German methods and their data. We need to know the gaps in our knowledge.' He sounded more than a little sardonic. 'For next time.'

Gus understood this was entry-level stuff and part of his initiation into the service. While he worked on the documents, they would watch him and assess. And watch Krista, too.

What Minet and the other chiefs wanted to

disinter were technical details on secret weapons and industrial technology. The Germans excelled in those subjects and, however holier than thou they thought they were, the British would do their best to secure an advantage in this over their so-called allies.

Minet offered Gus a cigarette from a heavy, silver cigarette box embossed with a coat of arms. Gus shook his head. 'There's a tug of war going on between London, Paris, Moscow and Washington, all of whom want to get their hands on the information. Naturally, we want to suck it dry first.' Minet lit up. 'But the Soviet threat is increasing. Anyone who thinks differently is mad and, in the future, we will also need every scrap of German intelligence and expertise on Communist networks and their methods. That's where you will come in eventually.' He balanced his cigarette on the rim of the ashtray and the smoke dissolved in grey curls. 'However, your old unit in Berlin have indicated that they need you back for a month or so in order to wrap up some cases. Apparently, you are good at the interrogations.' Minet added, 'You must be good if they're asking for you, considering you're a trouble-maker.' He sounded surprisingly sympathetic. 'I gather it was a shocking state of affairs at Bad Nenndorf.'

'It was.'

'No one denies it. They just don't want it broadcast.'

'I can't be alone in concluding that one should not allow poison in the system. Or . . .'

111

Minet raised an eyebrow. 'Or?'

'Or in oneself.'

Minet stubbed out his cigarette. 'Tricky thing, a conscience. You will have to learn to manage it.' He lit a second one. 'You will keep your eyes and ears open in Berlin for us. In future we may put you in place there too. We need someone to run the sources, someone who knows the ropes.' Minet's expression was neutral. 'But we are not quite there yet.' Gus took that to mean that Berlin would be crucial.

'You must leave the law. As far as I can ascertain, it won't miss you.' He seemed amused at his own joke.

'No, I don't think it will.'

Gus looked back on his work with his army unit with reasonably justifiable pride. Having spotted a blockage in the flow of information between the cryptanalysts, translators and the intelligence analysts, none of whom were fluent in German, he decided to do something about it. Quite apart from anything else, the challenge of knocking heads together appealed to him.

'It's a holistic approach,' he had explained to one of his (bone-headed) bosses.

'I don't care if it's Christ on an elephant. It had better work,' was the reply.

It had.

Facing Minet across the desk, he realized that this use of his initiative was probably responsible first for the hand clapped on his shoulder by a stranger in a trilby who said his name was Haynes, and then the invitation to apply to a branch of the diplomatic and consular services which no one had ever heard of. The office spooks must have reasoned that this was someone who was capable of pulling together seemingly random pieces of information and finessing them into place.

He nodded.

'Resign from your chambers. With many regrets, of course, and the suggestion that your experiences in the war have proved a little too much. For the time being your new cover is in banking. That has already been arranged. A merchant bank in Half Moon Street. They know never to ask questions, and they arrange suitable job titles and happily send people abroad.'

Minet stood up and went over to the window.

'Did you put a tail on me?' Gus addressed his back.

'Not necessary, Clifton.'

'Someone was on to me.'

'If you have been noted,' Minet had briefed Gus when they first met, 'they will be watching.' He'd added, 'And you have made some enemies, I think.'

Minet nudged the half-open shutter at the window a fraction. 'Everybody tails everyone else. Our sister service tails Labour politicians and, now they are out of government, our Tory friends. Just in case they are too cross about being kicked out of office by a grateful British electorate. We tail the Soviets. In return, they tail us. It's a glorious party. We'll send a car next time.' He turned round to face Gus. 'Just be ready to go when we want you to go. It could be in a couple of weeks.'

Gus wished he had accepted the cigarette. 'My wife isn't up to it yet.'

'I'm sorry,' said Minet. 'That's how it is.'

'Look,' Gus said, observing Minet's heavy frown, 'there's no point sending her when she's still broken.'

'You should have thought of that when you married her.'

★　★　★

It was as Gus could have predicted.

When he got home and informed Krista in the privacy of their bedroom that she would be going back to Berlin at some point, she turned chalk-white. 'When?' she got out between stiff lips.

They were talking in rapid German — the language binding them into an ever-tighter circle.

'We have a few weeks' grace.'

He wished that he knew her better, for he had no idea whether he had said the right thing or the wrong thing. Gus wanted to stroke the pale, soft skin on her cheek and wished fervently too that they had a common history to call upon in moments such as this one. *Do you remember when we had that picnic . . . when we danced . . . when we listened to that piece of music . . . when we had that row?*

The sore on her bottom lip was healing and her lips had a delicate, fresh-pink tinge. 'I am just beginning to settle here and to forget the homesickness. Every day, I tell myself that this is my home now.' She turned to Gus. 'I am going to plant some narcissi bulbs in a pot. They will flower after Christmas.' A hand clenched. 'I wanted to see them flower.'

9

Tilly discovered Krista on her knees in front of the kitchen dresser, polishing it with a rag. 'You shouldn't be doing this.'

Krista sat back on her heels. 'I wish to. It looks better. Yes?'

'It certainly does. Much better.'

Krista struggled to her feet. 'Gus says I have to be normal. And I asked myself what is normal, and I decided that making a kitchen nice is normal.'

Her skin was looking a little less transparent but a blue vein still filtered up one temple. It was a face of hunger, Tilly decided, but that of a survivor, too.

'You're the mistress of the house now,' she pointed out. 'And you must do what you want, but you shouldn't overdo it.' She gestured to the window over the sink; it was letting in some autumn sun. 'Gus mentioned that your coupons have now been given the go-ahead and you should pick them up, and I've offered to go with you. But I insist we go for a walk on the Common first, and that, I assure you, is a perfectly normal thing to do.' She added shrewdly, 'Gus would approve.'

The two women set out. Tilly was wrapped in a black cloak which she had unearthed from a pre-war sale of theatrical clothing and with it she wore a yellow wool beret threaded through with

116

violet ribbon; Krista was in her brown serge coat and felt hat.

'You look very wonderful,' she told Tilly. 'Beside you, I am a brown bird.'

Tilly burst out laughing. 'Once we have the coupons in your hot little hand, I'll take you clothes shopping. Julia's cast-offs won't do.'

They skirted the trenches and allotments, Tilly leading the way at a brisk pace. Very quickly, Krista became breathless and Tilly made her stop and rest on a bench which happened to be beside a trench. Since the end of the hostilities, these had been allowed to erode and, in many, the roughly dug earth sides were caving in.

'It would be a good place to bury a murder victim,' remarked Tilly.

Krista seemed nervous and jumpy. 'Would not you be seen? Here is very public.'

'Often the best way to get away with things,' said Tilly. She turned to look over the Common that she knew so well. 'When I was little, I used to think that giants, goblins and spiders from an evil kingdom lived in those trees over there and I was too frightened to go near. Julia and Gus laughed themselves sick about it. Gus was the worst.'

After a moment, Krista said, 'I cannot believe Gus was unkind.'

'Think again.'

Krista's gaze was fixed on the trees; they appeared to be soothing her.

'I'm glad they survived.' Tilly glanced at Krista. 'London got a right old battering, but not as bad as Berlin, I think.'

Krista's breathing was returning to normal. 'You want to know?'

'I wouldn't have asked otherwise.'

Krista indicated the milk cart and horse plodding peacefully around the north side of the Common. 'That is not a sight you see any more in Berlin. It is so ordinary and it is so beautiful and sort of . . . kind.'

Tilly thought about this. How simple and clear things had become. And, at the same time, how black and muddied.

'What did you do in the war, Tilly?'

'Nothing brave.' Tilly was a little hesitant. 'I was part of the team studying photographs and postcards. I would take a bet that I know more about the Normandy coastline than the people who live there. Ask me about the *Plage Menadie*. Go on.'

Krista was amused. 'Tell me about the *Plage Menadie*.'

'It's a nudist beach. We had the photos of it. One man was in a very strange position indeed. Very strange.' She grinned. 'Why, oh why, can't I blackmail him? I would be set for life. What a strange, half-lit existence it was. Very intense. Very silent. Excellent for the poetry, though. *Horizon* have just told me that they will publish a couple of my poems from then. Which is good, Krista. It means they think I'm good.' Her eyes glowed at the thought. 'I'm told by people who have been there that you heat your houses much better in Germany. Certainly they did when I lived in Switzerland for a bit.'

'Yes, we do.'

'Blood, tears and sweat. We've all had to put up with those. But we had bloody cold houses to boot. You know, you mustn't mind if people are less than friendly. It's the shock. It's not who you are. It's *what* you are.'

They headed down the path in the direction of the High Street. Tilly stole a glance at Krista. She was planting her feet carefully, one in front of the other, her expression serious but not sad. Every so often, she stopped and checked the path behind her. Anxious? Searching for something? Under that dreadful hat, her cheeks showed some colour whipped up by the fresh air.

'Hello, Miss Clifton.'

Tilly looked round. 'Hello, Tommy.'

Sixteen-year-old Tommy Garfield lived at the end of the terrace. He and his sister had recently returned from Wales, where they had been evacuated and remained for the duration. Only the other day, Tilly had bumped into his mother, who complained that both children had picked up Welsh accents.

'You've come back grown up, Tommy.'

His mates in tightly belted mackintoshes and flat caps laughed at that one. They were older-looking than Tommy and looked more aggressive and street-wise.

'This is my new sister-in-law, Mrs Clifton.'

Tommy had mean eyes, an uncertain expression, a gash of a mouth and a moustache of fine black hair on his upper lip. The nervous smile with which he had greeted Tilly switched into malice. 'You're the German.' He sounded faintly Welsh and out of his depth.

119

One of the youths, the taller, bunched his hands into fists. The other spat a gob of phlegm on to the path.

'Tommy, have you lost your marbles? Apologize at once.'

Unsure and nervous, Tommy searched for an anchor — and found it. 'My mum says if she had her way she'd line you up against the wall and shoot you. My dad says Mum is right.'

One of the other boys stamped a boot down on the tarmac. A woman trudging along the path pushed past him. 'Get out of the way,' she said. He swore at her.

Krista looked as though she had been punched and Tilly knew she had to defuse the situation. 'You go ahead, Krista, and I'll catch you up.'

Krista obeyed. With a prickle of apprehension, Tilly saw the other two fall into step behind. Krista quickened her pace. They quickened theirs. Krista broke into a run. They ran. Outraged, Tilly turned on the boy. 'Call them off, Tommy. Stop them. *Now.*' He shifted from foot to foot, hoping to emulate a fighter's stance, but failing. 'Germans started it, Miss Clifton.' The Adam's apple in his thin, still-childish neck was working like a yo-yo.

The taller of Krista's pursuers scooped up a stone and took aim. '*Stop them!*' Tilly screamed. Tommy shrugged. Krista cried out, clutched her ribs and skewered to a halt while Tommy's friends legged it in the direction of the Common's north side and disappeared into the distance.

120

Tilly rounded on Tommy. 'I'll have the police on you.'

He raised sullen, indifferent features. 'I didn't do nothing. They did.'

Tilly grabbed at him and caught him by his shockingly thin shoulders. She shook him as violently as she dared. 'I'm going to report you.'

Tommy's face was practically in hers and she caught hostility, boredom and the whiff of poverty. He smiled nastily and dropped his voice. 'Me and the boys are going to get rid of the Krauts if they are stupid enough to be here.'

He resisted her grip but Tilly's anger lent her extra heft. In this way, pushing and grunting, they reached Krista.

'Are you hurt?'

Krista's eyes were watering and she was biting her lip. 'It hit my ribs. Just give me a minute.'

Tommy ducked and Tilly heard his shirt rip under an arm. 'Oh, Christ,' he said. 'Mum will kill me.'

Too bad. 'Krista, Tommy here is going to say sorry.'

'Nah,' he said. 'Krauts deserve what's coming.' Spittle flecked his chin. His small eyes reflected the easy hatreds that gave him a purpose.

'Please. It is all right. He did not mean it.'

In the distance, a car sounded its horn.

'You are disgusting, Tommy. And ignorant. Do you hear me?'

He shifted from foot to foot: ready for the off, ready for the fight. With whom? With what? At the same time, in his youth and uncertainty he was almost laughable. Pitiable, even. 'Talk away,

121

Miss Clifton. It won't change my mind.' He focused on Krista. 'As my dad would say, keep an eye out, lady.'

'If you don't stop it,' said Tilly, 'I'll tell my sister-in-law about the time you wet your trousers in the street.'

A brick-red flush smacked into his cheeks. Backing away, he raised a fist. Then he was gone, legging it down the path in the direction his friends had taken.

Tilly tried to take Krista's arm and felt it go rigid. 'You mustn't mind.' She groped for something compensatory to say. 'Boys of his age are stupid.'

'Not that stupid,' said Krista, who was trembling 'Believe me, I know.'

'I'm taking you home right now,' said Tilly. 'Forget the coupons.'

The wind in the trees had got up. The autumn afternoon was dying and Krista was shaking like a leaf. How bad this war had proved to be, unleashing the darkest responses and desires, even in children.

'If anyone else gets at you, Krista, try to make fun of them. The British hate that.' Krista's shoulders sagged, bending under the weight of whom and what she was. 'At the best of times, people prefer their own tribes. This isn't the best of times.'

Krista's expression was closed and inscrutable. 'Do not tell Gus, please.'

'I think I should.'

Krista stopped abruptly. 'Tilly, it is important that he does not know. Please.' Her eyes shifted over Tilly's shoulder. Searching. Checking.

For what?

'All right,' Tilly said reluctantly. 'But only this once.'

★ ★ ★

Tilly and Krista were waiting in the registration queue for the coupons. It was the following day and their shopping, in string bags, rested at their feet.

They were in a makeshift office which had once been the tram depot on the High Street. Seriously bomb-damaged, it was doubtful whether the depot itself would ever be used again but some of the outbuildings were still usable and these had been commandeered by the ministry.

The room was dirty and unswept. Of course it would be, thought Tilly. Black-out tape, peeling and sticky, partially obscured the windows and half the chairs were damaged. A tense, grim atmosphere pervaded the queue of grey-looking and shabby applicants shifting slowly up towards the two desks where the clerks were sitting. The war spirit had snapped and been replaced by a dispirited vacuum of no expectation and ever-more-restricted diets — the weekly bacon ration had just been cut from 4oz to 3 and cooking fat down to 1oz. *Threadbare. Exhausted. And everyone smells because there is no soap.* Except, Tilly was quick to note, for a couple of naval ratings in uniform in front of them; they looked smart and well fed.

123

The first naval man was called up. A couple of men in the queue looked at them with suspicion and not a little confusion. Tilly had a good idea what they were thinking. It was the forces who were supposed to have been the ones to bear the brunt of the war, not the civilians. But it hadn't worked out like that. Not at all.

For the first time, Tilly felt serious apprehension for Krista. Barring accident, and accidents were happening in the post-war city, she and Julia would have to deal with the problem of sheltering Krista until such time as Britain rose from the ashes and everyone loved one another again. Had Gus considered what Krista was likely to encounter, yesterday being only one example? It wasn't going to be fun. Feelings ran deep, hatreds especially so. Even Tilly's careless, boho friends voiced them. There had been such violence and brutality on both sides, and decency and comfort had been cut away. No one was the nicer for any of it.

Krista was clutching the handbag which Julia had given her far too tightly. In the everyday camouflage of a brown coat and headscarf, she resembled most other women in the room. *Everywoman* — that eternal figure. Whereas Tilly, who spent her life fighting that image, had today got herself up in an old army-issue coat with the facings and insignia removed and an overlarge grey scarf. The outfit was completed with rubber plimsolls normally worn by schoolchildren, but she reckoned they looked chic. She knew perfectly well that the outfit shrieked, 'Look at the unconventional and daring me,' and would be criticized. But, as with so many other things these days, she didn't care.

A heavily pregnant woman with a toddler trailing behind came in and sank down into a chair and closed her eyes. Her toddler yelled and ran around the room. Her eyes snapped open. 'Shut it, Charlie,' she called out.

'Your system of rationing is very fair, I think?' Krista had the good sense to whisper.

Tilly moved closer in order to hear what she said. 'I don't think everyone sees it as fair,' she whispered back. 'And it's hated.'

'But it shouldn't be,' said Krista. 'Without it, there can be no order. Which is what happened to us in Ger — ' She cut herself off.

Tilly could not but endorse this view. 'You're right. There, did you ever imagine a Brit would concede that the enemy is right? Does that make you feel better? It should do.' She smiled in what she hoped was an inviting manner. 'We can discuss it later in a more private place. Tell me more about yourself, Krista. We know so little.'

She fiddled with the strap of the handbag which was, Tilly noted, very worn. Julia really should have given her a better one. 'You know about the orphanage and the convent. That is all there is to it. My parents died when I was very young.'

'Poor you. Raised by terrible old penguins. Hell in black and white.'

Krista stared straight ahead. 'When I was young, I hated them. Then I saw them differently. They educated me, Tilly. Fed me. I cannot think of them in that way now.'

Tilly felt a little shamefaced. 'What was . . . '
She checked to see if anyone was listening to
them both. 'What was your country like? We
were — we *are* so insulated here.'

'Most of us believed what we were told.' Krista
opened and shut the brown handbag in a restless
way. 'Seems hard to understand now.'

The second naval man was called forward to
one of the desks.

'How your countrymen swaggered to begin
with,' Tilly said matter-of-factly. '*Hateful*. If we
were honest — and we're too smug to be honest,
but if we were — the Brits were fascinated by the
certainty. Yet things change and now we are the
ones who swagger, which is equally unattractive.
Did you ever doubt what was going on?'

'Not to begin with. It was difficult to see
through what we were being told by the party
chiefs all day, every day. In the end we did, of
course, and we had to keep our doubts hidden.
Very secret. Or terrible things would happen. We
thought we had built the country on good rock.
Aber, we had not. We had not even built it, let
alone on sand.'

Tilly pulled a face. 'Don't use German words,
Krista. Best not. If you can manage it.'

Krista flushed. 'Sorry.'

Tilly rooted in her coat pocket, produced a
scrap of paper and a pencil and wrote: 'rock,
sand, belief'. She would have liked to have put
her arm around Krista but there was something
in her rigidly held posture that told her the
gesture would be rebuffed.

Krista was watching the clerks at the desks

126

who seemed overworked and flustered. 'At the ministry, after everyone had fled or been killed, I ran the office.'

'Good grief.' Tilly was genuinely surprised. 'You don't look old enough.'

'Oh, yes,' said Krista flatly. 'I was old enough.'

What Goebbels and his propaganda machine had got up to was increasingly well documented. 'Don't tell anyone about your work in the ministry. Please.'

The two women exchanged a look. The beginning of a complicity, perhaps? And an acknowledgement that they understood how, once unleashed, spite and prejudice hung around.

Krista poked her foot at one of the string bags. A potato rolled out and under the chair and she bent down to retrieve it. The handbag dropped off her lap, burst open and a hairbrush and a notebook spilled across the floor. Snatching up the brush, Krista stuffed it back into the bag. 'Sorry, sorry.'

The notebook was straddled, spine up, and Tilly rescued it. Inside, the pages were covered in closely written German script. However, the word 'Gus' leaped out at her. For some reason, a finger ran unpleasantly up her spine and she raised her eyes to Krista. 'You write? Like I do?'

'It's a diary,' said Krista. 'Mine.'

So, secrets? Hidden knowledge? Things Tilly should not know?

'Would you like to hear some of it?'

Tilly edged her chair closer to Krista, who read out in an undertone, translating as she went. ''Today, at the ministry, I learned that a British bomber crew has a life expectancy of little over a month. That statistic keeps us going.''

'I see,' said Tilly, thinking of the pilots who used to drop into her unit.

Krista continued. ''My apartment in the Charlottenburg is in ruins. Lotte and I have decided to make for the convent as the word is that it is still standing. I can't think of anywhere else and the Sisters know me. Lotte and I have discussed whether we would kill anyone who tried to harm us. Lotte said she couldn't, but I wonder. There is so much we don't know about ourselves.'' Krista turned to another page. ''After the bombers came, I helped to carry the sick and the wounded into the chapel, which is still standing. The Sisters are trying to keep the hospital going but they are dying, too. Lotte has no strength left.'' Her voice faltered as she repeated: ''Lotte has no strength left.'' She inhaled a breath. ''The lay workers have long got out and I helped to clear away the worst of the debris which was blocking the door to the makeshift hospital. The patients are dying from wounds and neglect. Two of the Sisters died from their burns. Typhus has arrived. I try to pick the lice out of their veils but it is hopeless.''

'Go on.'

She turned to the last page. ''Germany is finished.'' Pain crackled through her voice. ''The Soviets have reached the Oder. We are panicking. We pray that the Allies get here first but we do not think our prayers will be heard because our troops are retreating westwards. They would prefer to surrender to the Western Allies than to the Soviets . . . '' She looked up at Tilly. 'Enough, I think.'

'And Gus? Where is he in all this?'

Krista closed the notebook and turned enormous, but unreadable, eyes on Tilly. ''Today, Gus brought me a tin of spam.'' She was quoting from memory. ''That was a special day. He rescued me.''

'What is Gus to you?' asked Tilly in a low voice. 'You don't love him. I can tell.'

Krista took a little time before replying. 'I hope I will love him.'

'I hope so, too,' flashed Tilly, and she could not resist adding wryly: 'Since you're going to be together a lot.'

It took patient negotiation to get Krista's details recorded. The clerk who dealt with her insisted on examining her marriage certificate in detail and then conferred with his colleague as to whether one issued in Berlin was valid. By now regretting she had offered to help Krista, an increasingly bored Tilly did the talking. Finally, it was done and Krista was asked if she required a green ration book or a buff one.

Bewildered, she looked at Tilly. 'For God's sake, the green one is if you are pregnant.'

Krista shook her head. 'Not the green one.'

After supper that night, when Krista and Gus had gone to bed, the two sisters found themselves by the fire in the drawing room and Tilly told Julia about the diary. Julia sank down into a chair and buried her face in her hands.

129

'I'm glad they suffered. Glad. *Glad.*'

★ ★ ★

Tilly got on the bus to Chelsea and sat looking out of the window. She wanted to persuade herself that the colours she was seeing were as vivid as colours had seemed before the war.

They weren't — which was part of the problem. The sheen and radiance that had once impressed themselves on Tilly had dulled. Rusted. Turned sour.

For some, the war hadn't been so bad, and for Tilly it had brought change and camaraderie and arcane knowledge. Not many women — not many *people* — knew about the work in which she had been engaged: searching for enemy aircraft factories, for V weapons and camou-flaged aircraft hangars.

The litanies of Imagery Analysis, which members of her unit recited as they peered through the stereoscopes at reconnaissance photographs, remained with her, and they would do so for a long time. Was she looking at trees? *No.* Were the trees fakes? *Almost certainly.* Did they hide a panzer division? *Probably.*

It had been, in its curious way, very exciting.

'Sir, I think I've found something . . . '

'It had better be good, Clifton.'

It was good. She had spotted in the latest photographs just in from the reconnaissance boys that part of a mountain top had altered shape. On examination, it looked as though it had been shaved off to make a platform. Then,

130

peering deep into the grey fuzz in the background, she had also spotted an aircraft being winched up it. Tilly had found a secret aircraft factory.

While the senior officer phoned through to intelligence, he fixed his attention on Tilly and she knew he would ask her out for a drink.

Putting down the phone, he said, 'Clifton, you're as sharp as a tack.'

Quite how Tilly had fetched up in Imagery Analysis was a mystery — it was usually the boring geographers and academics who snaffled what were perceived as the cushy jobs — but it was fortuitous. She'd been selected after a series of stringent eye tests, for only a certain type of sight qualified. It had suited her. To her surprise, it had been the solid working practices of the outfit which had helped ground her.

She thought she was climbing towards the
   sky to heaven
And making good progress
Amazed at how quickly she was passing
   the obstacles
Tree roots, scree, rocks and sodden earth
Until she realized
That she was falling head first
And the slope up was, on looking closer,
   the one down

The work in the unit had been extraordinary; both feverish and disciplined. After the reconnaissance pilots came in, the film was processed and she and the other interpreters got to work

131

with their stereoscopes. Speed was of the essence. They rolled the film over a desk which was lit from underneath, checking the pilot's trace and the data relevant to the area. Was this patch of woodland what it appeared to be? Or was it providing cover for a Panzer division? Was a farm shed really a farm shed or did it hide a rocket factory or a manufacturing base? (The Germans had been good at hiding their small industries.)

Some of the pilots were keen — like Jack and Ben. Often, they looked in on the team to see the fruits of their work. A tiny shiver of pleasure went over her at the memory of Ben, but he had buggered off in the end. They had been so nice: brave and, sometimes, when they were frightened, careless of other's feelings but the kind of men who appreciated women's company. Even so, it would have been a big mistake to have fallen in love with them. Anyway, Tilly had craved the freedoms and licences which men had and she had helped herself. One of her lovers, a big, blond, Danish airman, had been scathing about the British. 'You make such a deal of sex. It should be as simple as eating and drinking.'

Tilly thought about the comment, agreed with it, put theory into practice and it had worked. For a while.

The bus reached the King's Road. Tilly descended on to a pavement pocked with holes and made for the World's End, where she turned into a smaller street and headed for a stucco house at the end.

She rang a bell at the side entrance. After a

132

few minutes, slightly unsteady footsteps could be heard on the other side. The door opened.

'Oh, it's you,' said a male voice.

'Hello, Marcus.'

'Have you brought any booze?'

Tilly held up a half bottle of whisky which she had found in the cellar of Number 22 and stolen. 'Ta-dah!'

Soon, she and Marcus, whose hair was growing shaggier by the second, were ensconced in the studio hut at the bottom of the garden, and Marcus was giving orders to Ned, his assistant, who was assembling pieces of salvaged, rusted ironwork into a sculpture.

The sculpture looked frightful — but maybe that was its point. Instability, ugliness and the incomprehensible all rolled up into one. *Plus ça change.* The studio, which Marcus was renting for peppercorns, was damp and mouldy and, now that it was late October, pretty cold, but Tilly was content to sit back on the sagging sofa with Marcus and sip whisky from the tumbler.

The sadness Tilly could never quite shake off was creeping through her — that black dog, *cafard*, whatever she chose to call it, which waited always to pounce. Sometimes, Tilly visualized it as a fanged animal with a ruff of flecked fur. At other times it was a rope around her neck. 'There is so much we don't know about ourselves,' Krista had written. That was right. You never knew. Who would have thought that Gus would have dumped Nella and married the enemy? Still, her brother was — had been — the barrister who never let on what he really

133

thought. He would never have stood up in court and said: My client is a disgusting murderer. Or: My client is guilty of the most terrible neglect of their spouse.

Or: My client gave her child away.

Marcus stopped shouting instructions and fumbled in his pocket. 'Got 'em,' he said, and pulled out a bottle of pills. 'Bennies.' He shot a look at Tilly. 'You look as though you could do with one.'

At the end of the war, Tilly had expected to dance on its corpse. She had expected to pluck its devils — the fears, anxieties and tiresome privations — from her spirit, like feathers, and watch them float away. But it hadn't turned out like that.

'Let me have a try.'

Marcus was watching Ned as he struggled to balance a long, thin, rusty strut upon a second strut. Without saying anything, he proffered the bottle in the palm of his hand.

Tilly took it.

10

It was 9.30 in the morning and a queue had formed outside Evans's Bakery in the High Street. Krista slotted herself behind a mother who, with a baby in her arms, was failing to keep her toddler under control.

Each day, she had set herself the task of exploring a little more of the area. Each day, the layout of the streets was becoming more familiar and her orientation more sure. On her way to the baker's, Krista had crossed the Common, felt the sun on her face and admired a dahlia in a front garden. Lotte — darling Lotte — would have appreciated these small triumphs: the successful navigation, the enjoyment of the flowers and Lotte could never get enough sun.

The queue, which was substantial, was composed mainly of women wearing shabby overcoats and headscarves, like those in front of her. Most of them looked exhausted and the exchanges between them were subdued.

Queuing and waiting. Waiting and queuing. It was true of Germany and it was true of here. That's how the populations were controlled, she reflected, and while she queued and waited she rehearsed Julia's instructions. On this, her first solo shopping outing, she wanted to obey them and to please her sister-in-law.

'I've indicated the order you must follow,' said Julia when she handed over the list. 'First, the baker.' She had numbered the items on the list. 'Second, the greengrocer. Then the chemist and the butcher. I'll give you the directions. Try to remember the order in which you should do it.'

Did it matter which shop Krista visited first or last?

Apparently, it did and she couldn't work out if this was a quirk of Julia's nature or something to do with the complicated class system, which Gus had warned her about. Whatever the explanation, buying the bread came before the meat, the vegetables before the chemist. Julia also told her that she did not need any money. Each of the shops kept a book, an account which Gus paid off at the end of the month. 'We have thirty days' credit with the tradesmen,' Julia explained. 'They deliver every afternoon. Don't carry it back yourself. Only the bread. I hope you don't mind me mentioning this, Krista, but carrying the shopping isn't the done thing. By us, I mean. I know Tilly does, but that's Tilly. It's something I thought you would like to know. There are ways things are done here . . . ways that we must observe. How can I put it? As Gus's wife, you have a position to maintain.'

The queue shuffled on. The bakery was tiny and the door into it looked unsafe on its hinges. Sacks of flour were lined up under the window and there was a dusting of the stuff all over the floor and windowsills but it was warm and smelled of new bread.

Eventually, Krista reached the counter and held out her coupon to the man she assumed was Mr Evans. 'One loaf, please.' Her accent cut like a knife through the mutter of the queue and betrayed her.

If the reaction had not sent prickles of fright down her spine, it might have been funny. The assistant whipped round from the bread oven, where he was slotting the paddle under the latest bake, and said under his breath, 'She's a Kraut?'

Not again, thought Krista. *Please.*

The tension rippled between the assistant and Mr Evans and infected the queue.

'A Kraut?' A large woman behind Krista shifted her basket from one arm to the other. 'Here? I'm not sure about that.'

Krista squared her shoulders and concentrated on Mr Evans, who looked like a reasonable man. 'I am German. But I am here to buy a loaf of bread.'

A strapping lad, fair-haired and pink of cheek, the assistant had eyes as blue as Hitler would have wished. These narrowed into aggressive slits. 'A *Kraut?*' he repeated. Like Tommy's, the words were unwholesome, but, unlike him, he was wholly adult.

'I am German,' Krista repeated, and her insides had turned to water. 'And I have come to buy a loaf of bread.'

Mr Evans looked exhausted and irritable. 'Shut it, Ken.'

'Will you be serving the *Frau*, Mr Evans?' Ken slid the loaves off the paddle on to a shelf and spread them out to cool.

The baker retrieved a loaf and wrapped it. He glanced at the waiting queue and lowered his

137

voice. 'I'll have you remember this is a Christian country.'

'I don't care if we worship pink elephants, we don't want them here.' Ken touched his left cheek where there was a livid scar. 'They owe me.'

'We're not fighting them now, in case you hadn't noticed.'

Ken picked up the paddle and held it in a rifleman's grip. 'The boys and I . . . ' He checked himself.

'You're not in bloody Italy now,' said Mr Evans, 'so do as I say and shut it.'

Blue-eyed Ken had probably fought his way up the spine of Italy, and relived it over and over again. She knew the type. It was the same with the men and boys returning to Berlin from their units. Battle had turned them into professed disciples so versed in fighting, so steeped in its assault and violence, that they could do nothing else.

His angry gaze met Krista's as he slapped another batch of bread on to the shelves. *And look what I came back to,* said that look.

The atmosphere in the bakery had turned poisonous. Her own anger stirred and something in her urged: *Fight.* But she knew she must leave.

Mr Evans handed a loaf to Krista and she surrendered the coupons. The baker checked them over and noted in the book the difference in what was owed. After that, and having done his bit for Christian charity, he turned his attention determinedly to the woman behind

Krista in the queue.

'Shoot 'em,' said a man shuffling in through the door. A female voice behind Krista said, 'We don't want you in here again.' Her companion tried to shush her. 'I will speak up, Madge. We've the right.'

Krista left the shop to the accompaniment of Ken's valedictory insult: '*Heinie.*'

As she passed him on the way out, Krista noticed that the man in the doorway was missing an arm. The head-scarfed women inching forward in the queue who had overheard the exchange refused to look at her.

She bit her lip hard. She was sorry, very sorry, but it was a fair bet that all those English men and women queuing for bread would not for a second consider that, to Krista, *they* were the enemy.

There was a light touch on her shoulder. 'Listen, love . . . ' A woman had followed Krista out of the shop. 'You mustn't pay attention.' She was young, almost a girl, kindly looking and her grey coat was very shabby. 'I can see that all that nonsense got to you. It's bound to. What you need to do is visit old Herr Laube in his bookshop. He came over after the last war. He'll tell you what's what.' She pointed up the street. 'It's by the railway arch on the right. Go and see him.'

'Thank you,' she managed to articulate.

The woman smiled. 'My brother was fighting in Germany and a villager gave him water when he was wounded,' she said. 'You don't forget.'

They parted company.

Did that stupid Ken think that she wouldn't mind? After the German calamity — the sickness and insanity which was her people's and, by inference, *hers* — would a few names called out by a bully matter? *Kraut, Hun.* 'You can be as rude as you wish,' she muttered to herself. 'I don't mind. *I understand.*' She picked her way along the High Street in Julia's cork-soled, cast-off shoes. 'But remember . . . remember that we Germans are capable of answering insult for stupid insult.'

Her German blood beat in her ears. Someone in her country had given water to a wounded soldier. That was enough for her to know.

Basket slotted over her arm, she continued walking, searching for the shops which Julia had instructed her to visit. 'Only go into Roxton's the chemist, mind,' she said. 'Not Townsend's. I don't trust that man. He's short on the measuring out.'

Despite encountering differing reactions to her nationality — the chemist was efficient but clearly unfriendly — Krista made good progress and she was cheered when the woman in the flowered overall in the hardware store put a tin of floor polish with the rest of her order, ready to be delivered, with a polite 'Good morning', and the butcher wrapped up their regular order of beef chine with an equally polite, 'I hope it's to your liking.'

'We have the left-overs from the Sunday roast on Mondays,' Julia had said. 'Tuesdays we have cottage pie. Wednesdays, mutton.'

She'd added that there was no need for Krista

to have ideas about alternatives. The menu had been in place for years. 'And *that is that.*'

Only when she had followed Julia's instructions to the letter did Krista allow herself to search for Herr Laube's bookshop, which she found sandwiched between a hardware store and a place which was selling old mattresses. The shop had a narrow frontage. The window needed a clean and some of the books displayed in it were singed at the edges. Krista tried the door but it was locked.

Her disappointment made her realize how anxious she was to speak to someone from her own country. Just to say a '*Guten Morgen*' would help.

Krista watched the flow of pedestrians, buses, horses and carts make their way up and down the street as she waited for ten minutes or so just in case. Many of the shop fronts remained boarded up. A group of workmen clustered around a hole in the road. A redundant poster hung soggily from a hoarding. It read:

Forward Together. Join the Army.

Fragments of the paper peeled into the gutter.

Traffic was building along the High Street and she abandoned the wait. Walking towards the Common, she passed on her left the defunct tram depot. In the forecourt a Punch and Judy man had set up his tent and children were clustered around it, jumping up and down to beat the chill. Punch was having the time of his life, hammering his opponents and calling out,

141

'That's the way to do it.'

Krista joined a motley audience: mostly silent mothers and children released for a small moment into another world. 'Bit late in the year for this,' said one. 'Anything for a bit of fun,' said her companion.

Punch hit the baby. *'That's the way to do it.'*

The jumping, skittering children shrieked with laughter.

The bread turned out to be surprisingly heavy. God knew what had gone into it. Chalk and dust? It was a common enough scam. Good bread made life bearable and to debase it was horrible. The longing to be back in the convent kitchen, smelling the spices and aromas as a meal approached, gripped her. Rye bread. Pickle. Her favourite *Apfelpfannkuchen*. Even when the war was at its height, the lay Sisters who ran the kitchen managed to keep it in sweet order. At the worst of times, Krista had dreamed of having a kitchen like it.

At the end, the struggle to be normal had been impossible. Still, she and Lotte had managed to keep the vegetable patch going all through the summer of 1945, which had been vital to the survivors. The memory of those vegetables, their colours and shapes and smells, would remain for a long time: the many shades of green, some luminous, the swollen yellow-ochre squashes and the purple kale with its inky-black heart, the sharp, sappy smell of new growth and the rot with its hint of the sewer. Hard or soft, pulpy or decaying, scattered by explosions or thrown on to the compost heap, they were predictable in a

142

way nothing else turned out to be.

A bus lumbered along the road, crammed to the gunnels, followed by a horse and cart going at a fair lick, its load of barrels swaying with each strike of the horse's hooves. In the distance, a girl in a draggled, blue knitted outfit sat on the front steps of a house, listening to her mother shouting at her.

A couple of boys ran past her, followed by a puppy of indeterminate breed. It halted and pattered back to Krista, wagging its tail. She stooped down to stroke it. It was warm and solid and happy and, for a moment, she felt the same. Watching it dash back to the children, she put a hand up to her cheek.

Her skin felt gratifyingly smooth. There had been times when a rash had crawled over her face and neck. *Berlin maquillage*, Lotte had called it; she had been troubled by the same complaint and they had grieved over their ruined complexions.

Today, Krista was wearing another of Julia's cast-off jumpers and a tweed skirt. It was too large at the waist and had a trick of swivelling around her body and bunching at the hips. Neither the colour nor its style suited her and the jumper needed darning at the elbow.

To the north, the sky was turning a bruised plum colour. Used to clear, crisp, shudderingly cold winter days, Krista's spirits sank. Grey was London's uniform — grey streets, grey houses complete with grubby white paintwork and rooms painted in grey distemper. It looked and felt like a city which, having used up all its

143

energies, had nothing to spare.

As she attempted to cross the road, she looked the wrong way and only narrowly missed being hit by a bus. Safely on the pavement again, she paused to steady herself. Glancing back, she noticed a woman waiting at the kerb; she was wearing a coat of vivid blue that Krista was pretty sure she had seen once before.

The path on the Common ran parallel to the south side and, hampered by the shopping, she dawdled along it, halting every now and again to shift the basket from one arm to the other.

Then footsteps sounded from behind. Krista stepped aside to be overtaken by the woman in the blue coat, who looked neither right nor left as she passed. Krista noted an abundance of light-brown hair under a black felt hat and high heels made of expensive-looking crocodile. She was setting a rapid pace, her black leather gloves clenched tightly in one hand. Soon she was well in front, heading in the direction of the air-raid shelter at the opposite end of the Common.

Back at the house, Krista wrapped the bread in a tea towel and stowed it in the tin, then went to report her progress to Julia, whom she found ensconced in a chair in the drawing room. A fire had been lit and a newspaper lay on her lap. She did not look round when Krista came into the room.

Krista sat down on the edge of the sofa. 'I've brought the bread back.'

Julia pulled herself to attention. 'Thank you.'

Krista smoothed down Julia's cast-off skirt, which still felt unfamiliar, and focused on the mirror above the fireplace.

Was she safe? When would Lotte's beloved face cease to patrol her dreams? Would she ever be forgiven for the things she had done in the past?

Her thoughts felt so physical — like tangible presences in the room — and she wanted to grab them and to stuff them away in a sack.

'Krista, I've managed to get someone in to do the cleaning,' said Julia. 'She works for the vicarage and the vicar's wife very kindly agreed to share her. She has respectable references. Her name's Ada, if I remember correctly. Two mornings a week. Will that suit you? I said it would.'

'Thank you,' said Krista.

Julia was no longer overtly hostile but neither was she warm. 'Perhaps you think I should have consulted you? I did think about it but it seemed to me that you wouldn't know the form, or what to ask.'

It was going to be hard settling here. Harder and trickier than she had imagined when she had said yes to Gus's proposal. 'No, of course,' she answered in a deceptively gentle manner. She knew all about surviving hostility: stealing from friends, tearing clothes off a dying man's back, eating a neighbour's dog.

One had to be realistic and cunning. If she was versed in the tricks of survival she understood, too, that her reserves were low and her armoury meagre. Julia and Tilly held the advantages, the main one being confidence. With their bony, well-bred features, their glittering blue eyes and

145

long limbs, their English beauty, they exuded ease and assurance, and the reason for that was simple: they belonged.

'It's difficult for us,' said Julia and there was a thin smile stretching her lips. 'We will get used to one another, I'm sure.'

'I want to do what is best for Gus and to make him happy.'

'I can't argue with that.'

There was a bristly pause before Julia changed the subject. 'It's a pity about the garden. Once upon a time it was my parents' pride and joy. Do you like gardens? Maybe that's something which you are interested in?'

Krista slipped over to the window.

Roses in pale-washed tea, ruffled peonies, spiky lavender and small, bright-black berries on ivy. Recollecting these beautiful, beautiful plants prodded into life an appetite so sharp that it was almost painful — but she welcomed its discomfort because it meant she was beginning to be normal.

'Yes, I am.' She swallowed. 'Next door will have a lot of clearing up to do, with the wall and the rubble.' Julia did not respond and she tried again. 'At least the tree is still there.' The sycamore growing at the bottom of Number 24 was clearly a survivor. But what a dull, ugly tree it was. She checked herself. Surrendering to nostalgia for the graceful cherry trees and poplars of back home would do no good.

'Julia, what did your parents grow?'

Julia lowered the newspaper she had picked up. 'Fussy things,' she said. 'Marigolds and

146

alpines. I never much liked what they had. Mind you, I was only a child and not interested.' She added, 'My mother was fond of lavender. Every year she made lavender bags for us to put in the drawers.' She reached for her cigarettes on the table beside her, lit up and inhaled thoughtfully. 'We don't do any of that now. Filling lavender bags is only a memory.' She tapped ash into a silver ashtray. 'Krista . . .'

'Yes.'

It struck Krista as odd that Julia was unoccupied at this time of day. No darning or knitting. Was it usual for Englishwomen to sit in drawing rooms in the middle of the morning?

'Krista. The clothes you're wearing. Do look on them as yours. I don't want them back. And about lunch. There's some cold meat and pickle in the larder. We shall have to make do with that.'

* * *

Gus was a rotten sleeper. Since Krista didn't sleep well either, she was alert to his every toss and turn. Sometimes, he abandoned the double bed for the camp bed in his dressing room.

Winter was coming in fast. Each night the temperature in the bedroom plummeted and the cold air made her nose ache, which did not help her cough.

Hardly luxurious, the bedroom nevertheless had a peaceable atmosphere, perfectly in tune with its purpose: to shelter the intimacies of a man and a woman who had elected to be together. From time to time, on opening the

147

wardrobe or a drawer, she caught a hint of her mother-in-law's lavender, which was curiously reassuring.

Her memories of the convent were not ones on which she wished to dwell but, for some reason, a few were particularly persistent. Such as: being in the cloister watching the grey and white of the nuns' robes undulate with the movement of their disciplined bodies as they filed in to chapel. The singing: that rarefied, frustrating plain chant and the whispered incantations of Lauds and Nones, the farewell to the light at Vespers.

The bombers got them in the end. The chapel and the white cross on its roof went up first. The Sisters, the poor Sisters, stumbled out from their hiding places. Some were bloodstained, or badly burned; others were too shocked to speak.

'I'm losing track of time,' she recorded in her charred notebook.

I've found a source of fresh water from a pipe in the next-door garden and I made Lotte and I douse ourselves twice a day. I didn't tell the Sisters. Should I have done?

Had she been guilty of gross spite and negligence in not telling them of that precious water supply?

She and Lotte had sometimes talked over their childhood. More often they had talked about what was to come. After the Soviets arrived and, terrified that Lotte was dying, Krista had made her listen to a vision of a future which she had

148

confected for them both.

Children . . . daughters (she didn't want boys) . . . racing into the bedroom and demanding to be taken into the bed. She, Krista, presiding over tea in the garden on a hot afternoon, her hair arranged in a roll like Greta Garbo's, and wearing a dress which had been made by a dressmaker to her instructions. Lotte would be the loved and frequent guest at these times. She had a clear picture of herself walking through the house last thing at night, stopping to check the occupants of the bedrooms. One head. Two heads. Three?

She held Lotte as she was dying. 'Do you remember, Lotte, when Sister Eva gave us a lollipop and we shared it? Yes? Do you remember when we rowed out on to the lake and it was so silent and still? You said it was the most beautiful, happy day you had ever had?'

Whispering stupid things to Lotte, cradling her as her breathing stuttered to a finish, attempting to cushion her body from the hard floor, she lied as she had never lied before. She told Lotte that when she woke up she would be warm and loved. Above all, loved.

That was then. *Think of now.* What was good, what was true, what was beautiful?

She could sense that Gus was awake. 'Are you all right?'

'Yes, are you?' he replied.

'Thinking about the past. But also the future. Gus, I know your position was damaged when you married me.' She placed a hand on the expanse of sheet that lay between them. 'I know

149

we cannot discuss the work but you were good at that job. You liked it and I'm sorry if I have ruined it.'

He turned towards her. 'My security rating was compromised.' In the dark his voice was companionable and confiding.

'That goes without saying. But the war is over and I have been asked to do other things which will involve you.'

Her sigh was a mix of relief and apprehension. 'I'm pleased that I am not too big a problem for you.' She grabbed her pillow. 'I will try not to be anxious about it.'

There had been no question of love. That would be impossible. Anyway, Gus couldn't love her, not the real Krista at any rate. No one could. The real Krista was dead. Or, rather, she was so deeply hidden that it could be argued that she no longer existed.

Her fingers were cramping. 'I am frightened about Berlin.'

Her feet slipped to the floor and she stood up, stumbling over to the chest of drawers. Grabbing the hairbrush, she held it to her chest.

Berlin.

Gus got out of bed and took away the hairbrush. 'Krista, don't. You are safe here.'

She was tired, oh so tired. She should tell him that she appreciated his kindness: buying her the black-market gloves, ensuring that she had a seat facing the engine when he discovered that acute anaemia made her nauseated a lot of the time, making sure she was warm enough. She knew it pleased him to make such gestures, even if she

150

felt that she was not worth it.

He replaced the brush on the chest of drawers. 'Krista, understand something. You saved me and now I must save you.' He did not touch her but his breath played on her shoulder. 'Come back.'

Obediently, Krista got back into bed. The sheets were now cold and gooseflesh ran up her thighs. How would she — who regarded herself as an expert on surrender — react should Gus touch her bare flesh, whisper to her of his desire?

Go roaming, she instructed her mind, *as the soldiers queued up to take her. Go where you will not notice what is happening to you.*

Walk the Alpine meadow studded with tiny spring narcissi, through which you once walked on holiday from the ministry. Evergreen moments. Think of it as migrating to a different country, where your mind is as free as the scents of summer rising into the sky. Does it matter if your body is invaded? Is wounded?

In the corridor outside the bedroom a floorboard creaked. Automatically, she stiffened. How would she escape? Through the window?

The now-ingrained reflexes kicked in. *Run, hide . . .* But never, even at her most frightened, had Krista prayed, which was what the Sisters had exhorted them all to do. 'I will pray only when peace returns,' she had told them. 'And perhaps not then.'

A scene was playing itself out in her mind. As it did. Always.

They were in the chapel — or what remained of it. She and Lotte grabbed each other's hands

151

so tightly that the bones cracked, and watched as the marauding soldiers lit a fire on the once-beautiful marble floor. Louts. One of them, a small wiry man with a mean mouth, searched for something among the stones with a rifle butt.

Lotte whispered, 'They're no different from the Soviets.' It was true, because they had the same hot, hungry eyes.

Most of them were drunk and clutched bottles. Yet another man stumbled in from the road outside. An officer. He was tall and dark, with an expression in his eyes which told her he had seen most things. Violence, death, brutality.

He was also very, very drunk.

11

Aunt Sarah never wasted her words and, in early December, Julia was summoned over the river to the back streets of Chelsea. 'It will do you good and take you out of yourself,' she informed her niece briskly down the telephone.

'Glad to see you look less mopey,' was her greeting when Julia presented herself at the soup kitchen which had been one of her aunt's more inspired ideas. Coral hovered in her mother's wake and the cousins dutifully clashed cheeks.

'How's that ridiculous sister of yours?' asked her aunt. She had never had much time for Tilly.

Julia's loyalties surfaced strongly. 'Tilly is *not* ridiculous, Aunt Sarah.'

Her aunt gave her a shrewd look. 'No?'

'It's those peculiar clothes,' said Coral. 'I always think they give the wrong impression.' She faltered a little under Julia's gaze. 'Not very elegant, anyway.'

Julia assessed Coral's dreary brown dress which emphasized — oh, so unfortunately — her cousin's thick waist and not very slender calves. 'How would you know, Coral?'

Coral fiddled with her hair; in her sole concession to vanity and fashion, it was set in meagre little waves which reminded Julia of the skin on elderly meat stock. 'No need for that tone, Julia.'

The soup kitchen had been set up in what had

153

once been a printer's premises and the smell of soup warred with traces of printers' ink. It was truly disgusting, thought Julia. But she hadn't reckoned on the additional stink of unwashed bodies and dirty clothes, which succeeded in overpowering all other odours as the recipients of the soup queued for their portion.

Alongside Coral, Julia worked hard: washing bowls, ladling out the lentil soup, cutting the rationed bread and government-issue cheese into small portions, and discovered there was something soothing in its mindlessness. A dulling of expectation, punctuated only by her acute pity for some of the poor souls who were clearly only just clinging on to their lives and sanity.

Every now and again, Coral emitted a gusty sigh designed to draw attention to how hard she was working. 'It's so purifying to be doing good,' she remarked cheerily at one point, easing a very small slice of the cheese on to a plate. 'Don't you think? You must be pleased that Mother and I insisted you snapped out of yourself. Otherwise, one can become very . . . well, a bit selfish.' She lowered her voice. 'Father and I were only saying the other day how wonderful your forbearance is. Not everyone could put up with what Gus has done.'

No, thought Julia bitterly. Not everyone could. And she disliked Coral all the more for holding a mirror up to her.

Coral continued in her up-beat voice. 'So that's why Mother and I thought it would be nice for you to meet some people.' She nudged Julia. 'Francis over there would love a word, I'm sure.' Julia just stopped herself from saying something unforgivable. Francis was sixty if he was a day, with a vile moustache and a hangdog expression. Then Coral produced her *coup de grâce*. 'He won't mind that you live in Clapham, Julia. Truly. Nobody minds about that sort of thing these days. Not everyone can live in Kensington or Mayfair.'

Julia was absolutely sure that her mouth was drawn into a snarl. 'Shut up, Coral.'

However fast Julia worked, Coral was always ahead of her: washing more bowls, cutting more bread, carrying more pots from stove to table. It was a race to sainthood in which Julia competed hard, cup of tea for cup of tea. 'You're slacking,' she had the satisfaction of saying at one point to Coral, and she was rewarded by a scowl settling over her cousin's saintly expression.

At the end of the session, an exhausted Julia turned down Aunt Sarah's invitation to tea and set off for the bus stop with Coral's valedictory comment in her ears: 'We'll make a tea-pourer of you yet, Julia.'

The Number 19 bus lumbered over Battersea Bridge and stopped halfway across. Julia looked out over the river. Fog was creeping across it, and the hoot of the barges floated through the murk in ghostly fashion. This, then, was the underworld as it would be, she reflected, watching the fog wash over the buildings, many of them broken, rendering them both insubstantial and ominous in the same breath.

It was going to be a pea-souper and she hoped she would get home before it set in.

A man and woman were walking over the bridge towards the bus. His arm was around her waist and she was talking nineteen to the dozen. Absorbed in each other, they approached and passed the window out of which Julia was looking and she saw that his hand rested on her buttocks.

The painful lump which she tried to subdue fought its way back into her throat. Unable to resist, she turned to watch their retreating figures. The hand on the girl's buttocks was so suggestive of a sexual intimacy, an easy and sensual one, and she felt a sharp, almost forgotten, sensation in her pelvis.

She pressed her balled-up fist hard into her stomach. Inside, she felt chilled, crabbed and a hundred years old. Sex was not something she allowed herself to think about and she had dug the subject into a deep, dark grave in her mind.

Yet, and yet, during the rest of that bus ride home, Julia could see nothing else but the man's hand resting on his girlfriend's buttocks.

★ ★ ★

Walking home from the bus stop, Julia's thoughts beat out in time to her steps.

Bereavement was a thing to itself: a new country to travel through, and her companions were grief and pessimism. Taking repossession of her childhood bedroom in Number 22 and its narrow nun-like bed, it was if she had never been the 'divine Mrs Orville', never heard any of his friends whisper an aside to Martin: 'My God,

156

you're a lucky man.' The chaps in the mess had been very good to her after it happened. Of course they had. Then things changed. Nothing was ever said, but she knew that they no longer included her in the RAF family. How could they? She was a reminder of death, which they could not permit themselves to consider, and it was her business to go away. They had other things to do than to worry about Julia's diminished authority and dwindling importance.

Imagining Martin's anguish as he died was a torture. Had he managed to think about her during his last moments? Julia supposed not — dealing, as he must have been, with the dreadful situation of the Mosquito screaming to earth. Selfish though it was, it would be so comforting to know that he had gone into the darkness with her image in his mind.

Back in the house, she deployed her usual tactic of concentrating on the practical. She made a couple of telephone calls, wrote out a shopping list to give to Krista and checked over the house for any new cracks. Two extra ones had appeared in the ceiling in the drawing room and these she dutifully logged for Mr Forrest.

Julia and Tilly (who was on leave) had been at home when the bomb fell and a pretty terrifying experience it had been, too. After the dust had settled, Mr Forrest had come round with his clipboard to notify them that he would be undertaking an inspection of the houses adjacent to Number 26. He would, he informed Julia in his charmingly unofficial manner, be submitting a report to the special council committee. What does *that* do, Julia wanted to know. Mr Forrest had been vague but he thought the special committee had been set up at the behest of the government to help out on acute housing needs.

Shrouded by the boiler suit he wore to protect the well-cut grey suit underneath, he returned a few days later and made a thorough check on the ruined Number 26 and the damage done to the others. He was a good-looking man but far too thin, and his fingers sported nicotine stains which Julia could swear were bigger each time she met him. He had already warned Julia that many bomb-damaged houses were listed by the local councils to be demolished. 'The government has issued instructions to rehouse the homeless.' To Julia, the policy seemed short-sighted. 'Doesn't turfing people out of their damaged houses make them homeless too?' she enquired. Then, realizing that she had been lacking in sympathy, she hastened to butter him up. 'You mustn't worry about us, Mr Forrest, when you have so much to do. My brother will organize the repairs when he returns.'

She directed as sweet a smile at him as she could muster. A dazzled Mr Forrest wrote down something in his notebook, which had several pieces of paper stuffed into it, and snapped an elastic band around it. 'Mrs Orville,' he said, and she couldn't make up her mind whether it hurt her or pleased her to hear her married name, 'while your brother isn't here, I must trouble you to keep records of any new cracks and any new changes in the house. Your safety may depend on it.'

'Records?'

'Very easy to do, Mrs Orville, and I can help you out at any time.'

In Mr Forrest's report it was now recorded that Number 26 was a write-off: its monument a pile of concrete and twisted girders, topped by a bath which had landed upside down in the garden. Numbers 28 and 24 were badly damaged, the explosion severely weakening the back wall and roof of Number 24. Numbers 22 and 30 had escaped with minor damage.

After the dust had settled, the sisters picked their way into the Johnsons' house and it had been a ghastly experience. In the hall, a grandfather clock lay face down, partially buried by a slurry of overcoats and jackets which had been tossed from an oak cupboard. In the front room, plaster dust sifted over broken china, cutlery, a teapot and a pot of mustard whose contents had been flung against the wall. The basement, which was partially flooded, had turned into a dangerous labyrinth. God knew what was floating in the black water.

'The death of a house,' said Tilly. 'We shouldn't look. It's too private.'

'Thank God they weren't here when it happened,' said Julia.

After a couple of weeks, the Johnsons had returned to salvage what they could and then went to live with their daughter in the country. The house was now empty.

On one of Mr Forrest's later visits, Julia confessed what she and Tilly had done, and he was horrified. 'These houses can be death traps.

Reports are coming in, too, of the homeless using them for shelter and there've been some nasty incidents, even a murder in Tooting.' He had laid a hand on her arm and she had shivered from the unexpected masculine contact. 'You must take care, Mrs Clifton.'

Mr Forrest's penchant for visiting the Cliftons had not gone unnoticed by Tilly, who teased Julia that Mr Forrest had more on his mind than derelict houses. 'Perhaps he is moved by the sight of the beautiful widow?' she said.

'It's the cake he's after,' said Julia.

Tilly shot her a look. 'If you say so.'

Tilly's insinuations were almost laughable, but they brought Julia up short. Women like her — the widow — did not admit that they were interested in the subject of sex. They didn't. They couldn't. And they had to pretend to themselves that the subject was dead to them. No one (not even Tilly) spared a thought for the women like Julia, starved of lovemaking. And that was not to mention the affection, companionship and the regular salary which had made married life so attractive.

★ ★ ★

Julia hunted down Krista in the scullery and addressed her appallingly thin back. 'Here's today's list for you. You did well last time, but there were one or two things.'

Krista turned round, her eyes looking like enormous frog-spawn. 'I'll go later,' she said. 'I wanted to finish this.' She held up a large earthenware flowerpot from which she was brushing layers of dirt with a wire brush. 'I am going to plant it with a . . . how do you say?' She gestured to a bulb lying beside the flower-pot. 'That.'

Julia hastened to nip any rebellion in the bud. 'We do the shopping in the morning. Always.'

'Oh.' She seemed amused and Julia wondered if she was secretly laughing at her. 'Leave the list on the kitchen table, Julia. I shall go when I have finished this.'

Her English was really *very* good and, for some reason, that irritated Julia even more. She felt her jaw tighten in the way that was becoming almost habitual. 'I see.'

A couple of hours later, she watched Krista let herself out of the front gate. Grudgingly, she acknowledged that the girl could not be called faint-hearted.

Julia went into the bathroom to remonstrate with Tilly, who planned to go out — 'Julia, darling, Marcus called. There's a Christmas party. I'm off on out' — but not before running a deep bath.

Recently the bathroom had developed a permanent damp smell. There must be a leak, Julia thought for the nth time. But no one could locate it, and plumbers were impossible to find. Making things worse, the steam from whatever hot water there was made the distemper rain down like snow. The basin, which had been put in at the turn of the century, was a huge thing with a moulded depression for the soap, and brass pipes which sported green rims at the

161

joins. The black line painted around the inside of the cast-iron bath was still there from the war — a reminder of the national effort to beat Hitler — and flecks from it had a habit of flaking off into the bath.

Tilly was lying in an indecent amount of steamy water.

'You realize you've pinched all the hot water.'

Tilly's hand brushed against the lick of pubic hair visible between her legs. 'It's a bit sparse, don't you think?' She meant the pubic hair. 'But no one so far seems to mind.' She patted it. 'You'd better look spruce,' she added wickedly. 'Just in case.'

'Tilly!' Julia busied herself with folding a towel over the rail. Her hand curled around the rail and her knuckles whitened. Now a dam had been breached, she could not ignore the subject.

Her friend Muriel had fallen for an Italian officer while her husband, Robert, was on active service abroad, and she got pregnant. Muriel begged Robert to forgive her, which he maintained he did — but he strangled her all the same. The all-man jury spared him the death penalty by opting for manslaughter, not murder. Had they thought about the baby who had died with Muriel? Apparently not. Julia still felt sick and angry about it.

The last Julia heard from Muriel was when she phoned Julia. She sounded absolutely desperate. 'Why did I have to let Rob down? I didn't mean to. I love him. I must have been mad.'

Groping, as she appeared to be, towards an understanding of the disconnection between faithful, romantic love and a purely physical, sexual life, Julia was beginning to understand. Slippery, burning desire was so insistent, so *present*.

'Don't look like that, Jules. Sex is perfectly normal.' Tilly stopped the tease. 'Don't worry, I'm not on a sex spree.'

Julia made a face. 'Do I envy you, Tilly?'

'God knows. Just because I've had a few lovers, Jules? No, probably not. No, no.'

Tilly sounded a touch blue and Julia's heart sank. She switched the subject. 'Have you seen Nella at all? She will be hating people talking about her and Gus. You know how private she is.'

'She's still convalescing on and off with her godmother. Comes up for a day or two and then goes back. But I think she'll be back permanently quite soon.' She sploshed about a bit in the bath. 'Would it have been easier for her if Gus had been killed, like Martin, do you suppose?'

Julia flinched. '*Tilly.*'

'At least you can mourn the beloved with no strings attached, if you see what I mean. If you're angry, it's with the Germans, plus there's none of the humiliation which Nella must be feeling.'

She was truly shocked . . . yes, yes, she was. But a tiny part of her acknowledged that her sister had a point. 'Tilly, that has to be the worst thing I've ever heard you say. Gus could have all too easily got himself killed.'

Tilly ignored that one. She was good at ignoring anything she didn't wish to answer or reckoned was inconvenient. She sank further into the water. 'Nella loves this house. That will be hard for her, too.' Lifting a foot, she jabbed a pointed toe at the green mould on the bath tap. 'She can have it. As far as I'm concerned, this place is a mausoleum.'

'Your skin's wrinkling,' said Julia. 'Where are you going?'

'World's End. Is there a choice? Gus looks half-dead, his bride looks like a ghost, you're furious and Marcus phoned and said, 'Hey up, old girl, there's a party.' What am I do? 'Hey up' I shall go.'

It crossed Julia's mind that Tilly could have included her too. She perched on the edge of the bath. 'If you had a choice, Tilly, what would you like to do?'

Tilly did not hesitate. 'Go to Italy. And you know something? I'm going to get there. Somehow.'

Tilly's escape plans were part of family lore.

'Ha, ha,' said Julia.

'Not joking.' Tilly stood up and reached for the towel.

Julia was taken aback. 'You will take care to look after yourself?' These days they were all thin but Tilly was especially so. Even her breasts had shrunk.

'Precisely for what, Julia? I have no job, no money except for the bit Ma and Pa left us, which wouldn't keep a gnat in gin. And no skills, apart from an ability to look down a stereoscope at a photograph and say in a polite, but urgent, voice, 'Sir, there's a possible tank by the tree.' It's not going to get me far, is it?'

164

'What about your poetry?'

A closed expression crept over Tilly's face. 'That's my business.'

'That's odd,' said Julia, standing up. 'You used to talk about it a lot.'

'That was before.'

Tilly sounded odd and as if she was angry with herself. Some time ago, the sisters had talked over Julia's bereavement and the stillbirth of the baby and of how Julia felt that life was almost too much trouble to live. It was then Tilly confessed that she understood absolutely. 'It's the *cafard*, Jules.'

Julia was bewildered. 'But you've got no reason to feel like that.'

'But that's the point, Jules. It has no rhyme or reason.'

Tilly sloshed the draining water around the bath with its flaking Plimsoll line. 'Do you think our boring diet is sending us mad?'

That was the normal Tilly speaking and Julia left her to it. Not long after, she heard the front door open and close.

★   ★   ★

Was everything so pointless?

Did she care if the grate was cleaned out or the bedrooms dusted?

With Martin, she had thrown herself into housekeeping, pondering joyously over menus for the dinner parties they gave. Would Constance Spry's egg mousse do for the Squadron Leader or should she splash out on

165

Beef Wellington (surely the reference to a victorious warrior would be appreciated)? She had become faintly politicized, confiding to chosen friends how shocked she was at the derisory funding allocated to the RAF. 'After all, it's mounting Britain's front-line defence.' However, Martin had had to shut her up on that one: 'Darling, do you wish to bugger my career?'

But that was all over and done with. Her baby was stillborn, love was finished and, shoehorned into the restrictions of widowhood, she had nothing much to occupy her.

Instead, she speculated about her brother and his wife. Strange bonds and compromises existed between men and women but she knew enough to know those two did not love each other and there was a mystery attached to the marriage. This led her to consider: did she not have every right to find out about the woman at the centre of it and who had invaded their family?

In this spirit, and with only a small pulse of shame, she pushed open the door to Gus and Krista's bedroom and went inside.

Time hiccuped and peeled away.

Her mother was lying in bed, a slight shape under a grey knitted rug, a plait resting on her shoulder. Her father was standing in front of the small mirror, a hairbrush in each hand, brushing both sides of his head simultaneously. Her mother's work basket was on the chair, spilling over with darning wools, her father's shoes arranged in a neat row under the window.

These details were as hard-edged as an etching, which Julia found curious because she could not have been into her parents' bedroom more than a dozen times during her childhood.

It always amused Martin whenever she described her childhood. The flatness and dullness of walks on the Common, nursery teas and the occasional outing to the zoo to look at equally flattened and dulled animals.

As children, the Cliftons had been well looked after and comfortable, yes. But there had been no encouragement to be curious. No exhortations to be good at something, even an activity like skipping. No sunlit days of childish adventure. No roaming had ever been allowed during the girls' skimpy schooling in the nursery on the top floor. (Gus, of course, had been sent away to be educated.)

It was only when they grew up that the siblings began to enjoy themselves and the outings with Nella and Teddy had become a feature. Those Julia remembered as golden.

The room was tidy, bleakly so. Gus had never gone in for clutter and nor, it seemed, did his wife. Not that Krista possessed anything much with which to be cluttered.

One of them, Krista probably, had pulled taut the chenille bedspread (a ghastly thing it was, too) and draped it neatly over the corners of the bed. Both the pillows and the worn towels on the rail had been precisely positioned. The towels looked damp, a perennial problem.

The chest of drawers was tall and unusually narrow. Family legend had it that it had gone on campaign with Wellington's army when he was chasing Napoleon around Spain. Who knew? As a child, Julia had longed to find out but never did and, now, she no longer cared.

Why was she doing this underhand, mean-spirited thing? God only knew. But she was.

Julia opened the top drawer. Inside were several pairs of Gus's socks and a stack of handkerchiefs. The next drawer down contained a brassiere — foreign-looking — two pairs of knickers and a folded pair of darned stockings.

After her parents' death, she and Tilly had bundled up their parents' clothing. 'We are not keeping any of it,' said Tilly. 'However bad the shortages. There are limits. Look at Mother's awful coat. It must be a hundred years old.' At that time, Julia had gone along with Tilly. Post-Martin, and having learned that to rid oneself of a dead person's clothing was another form of death, she might have been more reluctant.

The sisters had cleaned out the drawers but neglected to reline them with paper. Easing aside Krista's underwear, Julia exposed bare wood streaked with dust and, poking out from under the threadbare brassiere, the corner of the charred notebook.

Snooping should be anathema to her, she told herself. It *should*. It shamed her but, but . . . oh, God . . . she was enjoying the illusion of power.

She picked up the notebook and leafed through it, and the torrent of German appeared to slide away under her fingers. Repulsed, Julia put it down. How dare Krista? How dare she have this in the house?

Were human beings intrinsically evil? She had

never thought about it in depth. But, now, faced with the newspaper reports practically every day she knew she must. 'As far as I am concerned, you can forget the building of a new Jerusalem, Mrs Orville,' Mrs Evans had said to Julia last time she had been in the bakery and discussing the latest horror in the papers. Her worn face wore an adamantine look. 'Four walls and roof is all I ask, with a door I can shut on the world. And shut it, I will.'

With Krista in their midst, that would not be possible. They couldn't shut the door on a depressed world.

The smell of the notebook on her fingers sickened her — it was the smell of war and death. Sliding it back into its hiding place, she encountered a hard object wrapped in material. Her trespassing fingers traced a handle, a metal muzzle and, in a separate piece of cloth, a couple of small, hard, pointed objects.

Surely, it wasn't?

It was.

She drew it out. A gun barrel now nested in the palm of her hand, a totally alien object. She did not have the remotest idea how to use it, which was ironic, considering how well she was — had been — acquainted with aircraft guns.

Close-up killing was a different order of experience.

With a terrifying clarity, she pictured herself pointing the gun at Krista, her finger trembling as it sought consummation with the trigger. She heard the bullet tear the air apart as it travelled into Krista's chest. *That is for Martin.*

'What are you doing?' demanded Krista from behind her.

Julia whipped round. Krista stood in the doorway, her cheeks faintly flushed from the exercise, her hair flattened against her skull and her sharp, starved shoulder blades sticking out from under the pink blouse.

'Looking through your things.' She indicated the gun. 'As you can see.'

'You have no right.'

The guilty breath hissed into her lungs. 'I need to know if there's a gun in the house.' The intensity of her hatred melted her self-control. 'You're wicked to bring it into the house.'

'*Ach so?*'

The German was intended to be insulting.

'Does Gus know you have a gun?'

'*Yar.*'

'Are you a spy, Krista?'

For someone as ill-looking as Krista, she proved to be surprisingly strong. She stalked up to Julia and her hand circled Julia's wrist in a tough grip. 'I could ask the same of you,' she said. 'Are *you* a spy, Julia?'

'How dare you?'

'But you were doing something that a spy might do. I know about these things. In Germany we were all spies.'

The gun dropped from Julia's fingers to the floor. 'I'm an honourable person.'

Krista shrugged as if to say: *Prove it.*

'I don't normally do this sort of thing. I'm an Englishwoman.'

What on earth had made Julia say what she

did? *An Englishwoman*. How stupid could she be? In a flash of the surreal, she pictured herself sitting on a park bench waiting to be contacted, as she had once read in a novel, moving down shadowy streets, surrendering truth for evasion, principle for safety, smoking endlessly to soothe queasy nerves.

She raised her eyes to Krista, aware that her earlier sensation of power had been an illusion. But also, shockingly, in that moment she knew that she was capable of murdering Krista.

Krista picked up the gun. It appeared to sit easily, familiarly, in her hand. 'By the end, there were a lot of weapons lying around in Berlin. All over the place. Men were killing themselves everywhere. You could pick them up beside the bodies.'

'My God,' said Julia. 'Did this one . . . did you?'

'I stole it from a Russian. A living Russian with whom I had to make friends. I felt sorry for him afterwards. He would have got into trouble from his sergeant for losing his weapon.'

'God knows what you got up to.'

The lids closed down over the huge eyes. 'Julia, you know nothing. *Nichts*.'

'Don't speak German to me.'

'Sorry. I forgot. You are an Englishwoman.' The irony was wounding and meant to be.

'Guns are not permitted in England.'

Again, the shrug. 'It is mine and I will keep it.'

'Gus can't allow it, surely?'

Krista's expression did not alter. 'Julia, you do not know the circumstances.'

171

'I'll speak to him.' Julia's control of the situation was vanishing.

'Do what you wish.' Krista turned away from her and folded the pistol up into the material. 'But, if you do bother him with this, I will say that I found you in here, looking through our things.'

Gus's reaction to Krista telling him that Julia had been going through their things would make the situation in the house much worse. Much worse.

Krista's breath exhaled with a soft hiss. 'Can I take it you won't be searching through my things again? Or should I lock the drawers?'

'What were you going to do with it?'

Krista turned on her. 'What do you usually do with a gun?'

Blushing painfully, Julia backed out of the room.

12

Gus had been summoned to meet Minet at his club.

Since their previous encounter, Minet had not been in touch and Gus knew this meeting would be to give him his orders. It had only been a matter of time.

It was a clear morning, but very cold, with an occasional glimmer of sunshine. He set off from the bank in Half Moon Street and headed for Pall Mall, taking a short cut through a bombed-out street. In one of the houses, the front door had been split almost in half and torn blue blinds were moulded against the shattered window panes. He stopped to take a look.

The house was too modest to have been designed with a hallway and the door opened directly on to a room. Inside, plaster dust smothered ruined furniture and terrifying glass shards were pinioned into the back wall. Oddly, several of the pictures — cheap prints of railway posters — were still hanging more or less straight. A doll lay on the floor, its head blown off and its skirt lifted up, exposing fat pink legs.

Further on, he passed the nightclub which Teddy, Nella and he had often visited during the war years. That had been the fun time and, despite the war and the bombs, the easy time.

He missed Teddy and the deepness of their

173

friendship. Their differences, too. The disagreements. The solidarity between them.

Gus's father had a clear moral code. 'Play straight and the world will play you straight in return' he used to say. For a time in his life, Gus had believed it, too. Teddy, though, had never subscribed to the idea and did his best to talk Gus out of his innocence. 'It's the crooked and privileged who net the spoils, Gus,' he said, believing as he did that the British were the most class-ridden society in Europe and that the toffs always won. He was right.

Teddy was a partner at a successful firm of solicitors that handled high-profile corporate matters and made money by the fistful. Gus had ended up in a mid-ranking chambers as a criminal barrister, working long hours. Not that it had ever been an issue. Gus had chosen his career with his eyes open, but he allowed Teddy to treat him to expensive dinners from time to time.

Growing up, they told each other most things — until the war, when both of them changed and that early intense intimacy was lost. Gradually, they relied on humour to communicate.

'My Italian medal', as Teddy referred to his leg wound. 'Got it chasing dark-eyed, sultry *signorinas* in sunny Italy.'

The real story emerged only in scraps which Gus had some difficulty piecing together.

Shot up during the ferocious assault on Monte Cassino in Italy, Teddy had been left on the mountain slope for a day and a half before the

174

medics picked him up. Infection had set in by the time he had reached the operating table. 'Look at it this way, Gus, if you can from your comfy billet . . . Downside, I have a leg that's as unreliable as a witch's tit. Upside, I was spared some of the worst fighting. Not that that would mean anything to bum-on-cosy-seat you.'

This was, as Gus (and the British) later discovered, taking understatement to its finest point. The Italian campaign had been hellish.

'But I got to look at Piero della Francesca's *Resurrection* in Sansepolcro. There we were, filthy animals, gazing on it. Shall I tell you something, dear friend?' Teddy's eyes narrowed, a sure sign he was hiding emotion. 'It made me cry. The world was in ruins but Christ was rising. You haven't lived, Gus, until you've seen it.'

In the midst of the stink and terror of bombardment, and the slog of battle, Teddy had gazed on one of the world's great paintings. 'Lucky old bugger, you. I'm deeply envious.'

'Don't worry.' Teddy's hand was resting on Gus's shoulder. 'The only thing that matters, Gus, is the lucre.'

For once, Gus, who could usually read Teddy's mind, was unsure if he was joking or not.

Before she was posted to the Middle East, Nella helped to nurse Teddy. Whenever Gus managed to snatch leave, he joined her and the two of them had often sat beside a sleeping Teddy's bedside and discussed the future. *When it's over.* After Teddy got back his appetite, they dined together. Either Gus brought over his coupons and they fixed a simple meal or, when

Teddy was mobile, they decanted uptown. Except for rare occasions, the food tended to be unspeakable but there was gin and music to be had in the Piccadilly nightclubs. They had gone, they had danced. They had drunk.

The wind was cold now and Gus quickened his pace.

Spilled milk.

Minet's ultra-traditional club was to be found plumb in the heart of London's clubland. Its interior had the mucky, as-yet-to-be-cleaned-up look of many of London's buildings but it still felt solid.

Gus was handing in his coat and hat to the porter when he felt a tap on his shoulder. On turning round he was confronted by the uniformed figure of Bunty Phillips, one of his superior officers at Bad Nenndorf, a hard man with whom he had clashed.

'I just want you to know that you're a fucker, Clifton,' Phillips said pleasantly enough. 'Got it?'

Before Gus could answer, he walked out into the street.

Gus gazed after his retreating figure and almost smiled. If he had got a man like Bunty Phillips on the defensive then something had been achieved.

In the room where Minet waited for Gus a fire burned in an ornate Victorian fireplace, the seating was upholstered in leather and the conversation was hushed.

After greetings were exchanged, Minet drew him into a corner where two armchairs were set close to each other, and ordered the drinks. 'We

176

can be private. Members can be trusted not to listen.'

Gus wondered whether he really believed that.

Whisky arrived in cut-glass tumblers and Minet waited until Gus had taken his first mouthful. 'How's the new position working out?'

'I have an office, a desk and a very good safe, and they leave me alone. Perfect.'

'And progress?'

'From what I've seen in the documents, it was as we suspected. The German military science is hugely impressive.'

'Superior to ours, actually.'

'Radar, ballistic missiles, detection systems and a plethora of secret weapons. They are all meticulously documented.'

'Yes, they would be.' Minet sounded very dry. 'Of course all the material will be sent to the boffins but we . . . ' he tapped his chest, ' . . . we need to know before then if there is anything we should act on at once.'

'Not so far.'

This appeared to satisfy Minet. There was a pause which Gus knew better than to break. Eventually, Minet continued, 'You're off.'

'I didn't imagine that I had been summoned for a drink.'

'Berlin, I'm afraid. The pair of you.'

'Both?'

'As I warned you. For two reasons. One, we need her skills. Two, you can keep an eye on her.'

Minet did not add that they would be watching Gus too.

He gave Gus one of his shrewder looks. 'You

177

rarely find the purely principled working in this business. Most of us have other motivations. Especially the hurt or damaged. The watchers have to be watched.' He spoke with the lightest of ironies but Gus was not fooled. 'Apart from anything else, the state needs to be sure that the huge amounts of money it expends on the service is well spent.'

Gus reapplied himself to the whisky, thankful he had warned Krista that the pay-off for her new life would come sooner rather than later. 'Will it be at all dangerous for my wife?'

'For God's sake,' said Minet. The question had irritated him. He extracted a silver cigarette case from his jacket and pushed it over to Gus. 'What do you expect?' He lit his cigarette, then observed the burning tip for a few moments before drawing on it. 'Nowhere in Europe is safe. It's a mess. Refugees. Utter breakdown of law and order. Retribution. Disease. Take your pick.'

'The immediate job?'

'Back pro tem to the unit, as I told you. The Americans, Soviets and British have been scouring Europe for suspected war criminals and you've already worked with some of them. Anyway, in Berlin, the Allies are now responsible for trying in their respective zones all those suspected of those crimes. As you know, a central registry, CROWCASS, has been set up to assist the United Nations to deal with prosecutions and to coordinate the information.'

The act of briefing had restored Minet's equanimity. 'There're plenty of cases to choose from and also plenty of old scores are being settled. However, our lot have netted in a female who we have reason to believe ran the women's section in one of those God-awful death camps.' There was a pause. 'Auschwitz, in fact. We have to deal with her and it's been decided that you're the man to do the job.'

Gus decided to take a cigarette. 'That's why you need my wife.' It wasn't a question.

'This woman was captured in a barn near Bremen. She says she was a farm worker. Her papers are in the name of Gretl Helger. Almost certainly forgeries, but good ones. We think she's Gudrun Kreutz, who is on the staff rota for Auschwitz, but we haven't got it out of her yet. I'm afraid she was beaten up a bit by our boys when they arrested her so the medics are patching her up. But she will soon be ready for questioning.'

'I see.'

'Your job is to establish that she is who we think she is so the legal chaps can assemble their case, and we're not ultra, ultra fussy about how you get it. Only a little fussy.' A raised eyebrow sent several messages. 'Your wife will be there to assist the interrogation. She will understand the linguistic nuances better than you. She will also be there to stave off any accusations of sexual bullying. Tedious. But there we are. Technically, it has to be done by the book.' He paused. 'And you and I both know that is vital. Bad Nenndorf has tarred us. Badly.'

Both men were silent.

'Since your wife must know which side her bread is buttered on, we think it will work well.'

The implied threat was no surprise but Gus thought he would give it one more try. 'Is there no one else who can do it?'

Minet ignored that one. 'That was the deal we made in order to get your wife back here and we've carried out our side of the bargain. It's over to you now. God knows why you married her.' The look he sent Gus was a probing and not necessarily friendly one. 'But you did and we can use it to our advantage. For the time being. If her feelings need soothing, tell her she's in on quite an act. If her health is bad, we have doctors. The Germans are calling our operations over there 'government by interpreter' and they're not wrong. But, if she doesn't play ball, then we may have to think again.' He reached down to a briefcase by his feet, hauled out a file and handed it over. 'So far, *your* track record is good, Clifton.'

Minet never gave a compliment without an ulterior motive and Gus concluded that the case had been given top priority. He accepted the proffered file. 'How long do I have to crack this woman?'

'As long as it takes. You will be given transport and a comfortable billet. If anywhere in Germany can be said to be comfortable. Both of you will be uniformed. It's easier that way to get through the zones, et cetera.'

'When?'

'Ideally, tomorrow. These people have a way of killing themselves but I think we have to give it another few days to get her on her feet. Shall we say a week? Don't delay, Clifton.'

180

'Understood.'

'The file contains the latest dos and don'ts for survival in Berlin. Don't get ill and keep out of the nightclubs. You can pick up something nasty.'

Gus thought he was being dismissed but Minet had one more bullet in the armoury. 'A word to the good, Clifton.' His smile did not suggest the milk of human kindness. 'The other lot are still hysterical about embedded Nazi spies over here and the need for de-nazification of anything that moves. Your wife will be a target for their poking around. It might be an idea to get rid of her if you want to progress. It would be best not to have a weak flank in the future.' The smile had become icy. 'You could always leave her behind in Germany.'

★　★　★

Gus is being driven through the ruins of Berlin, which is to skirt the foothills of hell. It has the effect of making him hyper-aware of his own body — of the muscles twitching over the bones, of his feet cramping from cold in his army-regulation shoes, of the beating of his heart.

Next.

He is seated at a desk in a room whose meagre lighting barely pierces the gloom, facing a man whose body is so painfully arranged on the chair that it suggests he is injured. Beaten up by the guards? Does Gus mind? Almost certainly, this man has been instrumental in sending thousands to their deaths.

Stop. He has no proof.

Gus arranges his files. The vocabulary of any interrogation has to be carefully chosen.

Sitting beside Gus is a sergeant, pencil at the ready to take down the transcript.

The interrogator's qualifications must include: 1) a broad knowledge of the cultural and historical background to the country; 2) excellent speaking and listening skills. But the most essential requirement is the last: 3) loyalty — otherwise who knew what could be ignored or deliberately mis-translated?

'Did you not ever question what you were doing?'

'I was obeying orders.'

'Would you obey the order to kill your mother, or your wife, or your children?'

The prisoner shifts and grimaces with discomfort. 'If I believed it was right.'

'Ah, so you believed it was right to send certain categories of persons to their deaths?'

The prisoner's smile is laden with sarcasm. 'Won't you be doing the same? I am in a category of which you disapprove and you will be sending me to my death. Granted, with a lot more process, but the result will be the same.' He continues: 'You are arguing that I was wrong to have obeyed orders. But, consider this: the behaviour of those who gave the orders was approved by the population. Times change. The majority now approve of your orders . . .'

Clever, clever. The prisoner is verbally dextrous and uses irony.

This was a familiar dream. Or was it more

182

precise to call it a memory because it was played in the no-man's land between sleep and full consciousness?

It was morning, almost light, and he was in bed with Krista beside him. Krista was a restless sleeper and, when the nightmares came, she often cried out. At those times, Gus reached over and gathered her unconscious body to his — for she seldom woke — and did his best to cradle her. Sometimes, he pressed his mouth to her bare shoulder. Sometimes, he brushed the hair back from her slender neck. Sometimes, he murmured into her ear, 'You are safe.'

That probably wasn't true any longer. Cautiously, he rolled over to look at her. A hand tucked under her chin, Krista still slept, her newly growing hair fanned out on the pillow. He watched her for some time, getting to know a little better the shape of her skull, the nape of her neck, the quick tempo of her breathing.

The sleeping Krista murmured something in German and shifted closer to Gus, and he yearned to pull her to him and for them to make tender, triumphant love. That would be his and Krista's defence, a bulwark. *I will defend you*, he would tell her. *Guard you.*

His thoughts travelled along less-than-cheerful lines. Optimism and certainty had all but vanished in the vacuum that resulted after such a collective act of violence as the war. The fighting had ended, but also it had not. Europe was a boiling soup of different conflicts, and what had happened during the past five years had made completely sure there were many, many reasons

183

not to love one's neighbour.
Or to love oneself.
That, too.

★   ★   ★

In the afternoon, Gus went into his study and dropped down into the chair. Opening up Minet's file, he read the first paper from the pile of carbon copies it contained.

It began with a general overview.

Germans are being expelled from the Oder and Neisse (now Poland), from Czechoslovakia, Hungary, Romania and Yugoslavia. The question of where these people are to go is of utmost urgency. Many German cities are rubble and refugee camps are overflowing. A significant proportion of these people, having lived away for several generations, feel no real contact with the Motherland and are severely depressed and desperate.

Understood.

On first entering Germany, Allied troops were warned that they would have to deal with robust German resistance. This proved not to be the case. In fact, the women had taken control of local organization and, although frequently in extreme need, often homeless and frightened, they proved instrumental in the clearing-up.

When the knocker on the front door sounded, Gus was deep in military statistics and ignored it.

The sound of singing startled him. He had forgotten that Julia had warned the household that the local church was sending out carol singers. In preparation, she had changed into her best dress and swept back her hair with a pair of tortoiseshell combs which had belonged to their mother, and set out glasses and a jug of orange squash in the hall.

Gus heard Julia call out with an excitement rare for her: 'They're here!' Abandoning the file, he took himself into the hall.

A hatted and muffled group of ten or so singers was ranged on the steps, including the vicar, who looked in a bad temper. His wife was clearly struggling with a nasty chesty cough and Athene Yannis, the child of non-English-speaking Greek parents, who insisted she was British through and through, was singing flat.

An icy blast roared into the hall as they progressed through 'O Come All Ye Faithful'. As they tackled the third verse, and to Gus's surprise, the group was joined by Nella and Teddy, who added to the volume.

'Come in and get warm,' called Julia as it finished. 'Have a drink.' The frozen carollers filed in, with the Myers bringing up the rear.

'Hello, Nella,' said Julia, her appalled gaze flicking to Gus. 'Should you be out in this cold?'

'Teddy and I thought we would join in for half an hour or so. Otherwise, it wouldn't be Christmas.' Nella stepped on to the Turkish carpet in the hall. 'We all want Christmas to be like it was.' She sniffed. 'I remember the smell of the polish you use,' she said, and her eyes were pink-rimmed and watery from the cold. 'I love it.'

Teddy hauled himself over the threshold and took up position beside his sister. A wary smile fixed on her mouth, Julia handed around the orange juice and a plate of biscuits. 'Hello, Mrs Thomas, that was lovely. Have you been practising?'

There was a hundred per cent take-up on the refreshments and there was much discussion as to which carol should come next.

Nella was jittery and dabbed continually at her watery eyes with a handkerchief. Teddy leaned on his stick and there were dark shadows under his eyes. Banished was his formerly long, floppy hair. In its place was a short back and sides, and his suit under his thick coat was a conservative three-piece with a subdued blue tie.

It was obvious to them that the milk and honey which had flowed between the trio in the old days had been cut off at the source. Their youth had been compromised, along with the glossy skin, thick hair and the vitality they had taken for granted, blasted away as the guns opened fire across Europe.

Nella put down her glass on the tray. 'Gus, the book you lent me before you went away — I'm returning it.' She waved Hemingway's *For Whom the Bell Tolls* in front of him. 'I'll put it back. I know where it goes.'

Gus followed her into the drawing room. In

the hall, the carol singers struck up with 'O Little Town of Bethlehem'.

The curtains had not been drawn and a frost-rimed night unfolded in the area illuminated by the street lamp. Behind the road stretched the black expanse of the Common where, over on the north side, some lights were visible. Nella pushed the novel back into the glass-panelled walnut bookcase between the windows. 'There.' She touched one of the glass panels and said, without looking round at Gus, 'That's the last thing I will ever do for this house.' She stepped back. 'I was always fond of that bookcase.'

'Nella,' Teddy interrupted from the doorway. 'Don't talk to Gus without me.'

'Nella can speak to me in private, if she wishes,' said Gus.

'Teddy knows everything about us.' Nella sent Gus a hurt little smile. 'You never minded before.'

In the past, the perfect understanding between them had appeared so simple and desirable. Now it flashed across Gus's mind that this tight-knit triangle might not have been ideal for a marriage.

The chorus in the hall swelled and moved towards the final notes.

'We must go.' Nella looked up at Gus.

'Nella would like a bloody apology, Gus,' said Teddy from the doorway.

'You didn't mention that when we met, Nella?'

'I've been thinking things over,' she said, 'in the way that one does.'

Teddy's grey eyes reflected a cold, dead light.

187

'If this were Italy, I would kill you for dishonouring my sister.'

'Teddy, don't,' said Nella. 'There's no point.'

She pushed past him and rejoined the group in the hall.

Teddy did not move. Five seconds ticked by . . . fifteen . . . his stillness conveying a menace new to Gus. 'Don't think this is the end of it between you and me,' he said eventually, then he limped out of the door.

The carol singers were launching into the first verse of 'Silent Night'. Julia was singing away but Nella wasn't. Trapped by the large number of carollers in the hall, Gus and Teddy were forced to stand beside each other.

The first verse was sung more successfully in some parts than others by the diligent carol singers (the Reverend Thomas's baritone was variable). The carol seemed to be having a calming effect on them and, for a second or two, Gus and Teddy were shoulder to shoulder.

Then Teddy moved away.

At the beginning of the second verse, Mrs Thomas was rendered speechless by a choking cough, leaving the higher registers underrepresented. To the accompaniment of coughing, the group struggled on.

'*Christ, der Retter ist da!*'

A female voice took up the slack. A true lyric soprano, with diamond notes in it, it faltered, strengthened, then sang with passion and abandonment.

'*Christ, der Retter ist da!*'

Nella gasped audibly. Gus turned round and

188

looked up. Krista was standing on the landing, and singing.

The Reverend Thomas looked aghast. His wife was embarrassed and Athene was clearly furious.

The old words, the old tune . . . Krista's voice climbed effortlessly ever upwards, to vocalize the promise that peace and happiness were possible.

Nella closed her eyes.

Gus found himself clutching at Julia's hand. 'I had no idea,' he said under his breath.

One by one, the singers fell away, leaving Krista to finish a German carol about peace and stillness and birth, in German, on the first Christmas since yet another war with Germany had ended.

For that half-minute or so, nothing else could be heard but the voice and the music. Krista was crying as she sang the final note.

Afterwards, the carol singers said their farewells and filed out of the door. Teddy drew Julia aside and talked to her for a couple of minutes before following them. Last to leave was Nella, who cast a final look around the hallway. A section of her coat hem had come down at the back, denting her trademark elegance, and there were obvious tearstains on her cheeks. 'Goodbye.' Her fingers rested on Gus's arm for the fraction of a second.

Her jasmine scent, mixed with the rose face-powder she favoured, was achingly familiar. Leaning over, he kissed her on the cheek. 'Goodbye, Nella.'

Julia closed the front door and leaned back limply against it.

189

Gus took the stairs at speed, joined Krista on the landing and seized both of her hands in his. 'Wonderful, wonderful,' he said. 'Why didn't you tell me of this extraordinary thing you can do?'

For once, she did not resist his touch. 'You didn't tell me she was beautiful.'

★　★　★

'I do not wish to go to Berlin,' said Krista. 'They will kill me.' She was pacing up and down their room. 'But yet I want to go home.'

Gus paid her the compliment of not telling her she was exaggerating. They both knew she wasn't. The majority of the reports he had read narrated in clinical detail incidents of retribution all over Europe. Incidents of the kind which came under the heading of what the French called *épuration*.

She sat on the edge of the bed that she had made up so neatly, hunched in on herself. 'It will still be cold, so cold.'

He looked around at the bedroom's uninviting blue paintwork. 'It's not so warm here. I'll see to it that we have proper army-issue overcoats,' he said sitting down beside her.

'I'm frightened, Gus.'

'Not with me.' At that, she shrank away from him — which was no less than he could expect. 'Please try to reconcile yourself to what happened to you and trust that we can keep you safe.'

'It is not possible, Gus.'

190

He realized that it would be better to stick to practical matters. 'Going back is part of the deal, Krista. You're needed.' He outlined the advantages. 'It'll be difficult but we'll be comfortably billeted and fed. It won't be like you remember. I'll take care of you. I promise.'

At that she seemed to quieten. 'Gus, you have a talent for tenderness.'

It was a strange compliment but it moved him more than anything he could think of. 'Do I?'

'Yes.'

He looked down at his hands clasped loosely in his lap. 'Well, that's a beginning.'

'I know . . . ' Krista made a visible effort to pull herself together. 'I know that we Germans are not permitted flags any more, no songs, no uniforms. You think of us as nothing. We are no people. Being back in Germany will be strange because I was used to the opposite. And it will be strange for you because it is the Communists who you now have to fear and to worry about. Not the Germans.'

'If we can crack the interrogation, we won't be there for long.'

'But, afterwards, there will be another one. And another.'

Krista was almost certainly correct but he chose not to pursue it. 'We must take plenty of disinfectant. The reports say that cuts and abrasions don't heal well. The dust is infected.'

Krista got up and opened her drawer. 'Infected dust,' she murmured. 'That seems appropriate.' She searched around at the back of it. 'We'll take the gun.'

Her back was still frighteningly thin. 'Yes, take it.'

'I hope you know that I will do my best, Gus.' Snatching up the hairbrush, she said, 'I will hide this before we go. I wouldn't want to lose it.'

Suddenly, Gus felt weighed down by the enormity of what he had taken on. How was he going to cope with the fragile Krista? There were — there must be — ways and means of dealing with such damage and he would do his best to search them out. But it was miserable for both of them, and there were times when he thought he wouldn't manage. 'No one will steal it here, Krista.'

She held the brush to her chest.

'When . . . when are we going?'

'At the end of the week.'

★ ★ ★

On the day they were due to travel, Gus carried the suitcases downstairs, bumping into Julia as she emerged from her room. She was dressed in her going-away costume of flecked green tweed and holding a black felt hat with a small feather. Seeing his sister look so nice was cheering.

'I recognize that outfit. I thought you reserved it for very special occasions only.'

She held up an arm. 'Fraying at the cuffs. But Martin liked me in it. He often asked me to wear it.'

'I'm sorry you and Tilly might have to have Christmas on your own,' he told her as they went down the stairs.

192

'I am too,' said Julia. 'You've only just come back. But that, I suppose, is the hush-hush life of yours.'

'More or less.'

She checked her image in the mirror hanging in the hall. 'You are so mysterious these days but it can't be helped. Nothing is the same, actually. People aren't the same. They've seen and heard too much. Maybe . . . maybe . . . ' She shot him a look. 'Maybe they've done things they can't escape?'

Gus refused to take the bait.

Julia inspected the flowerpot on the hall table which Krista had planted up and from which a green spear was emerging. 'Poor Mrs Bloxham's son has come back from the East and he's gone half-mad. He was in a Japanese prison camp, you know. He spends his day gazing out of the window, and has terrible tempers. Or he cries. Mrs Bloxham can't get any medical help for him and she's at her wits' end.' Gus realized that Julia's chatter was, in fact, a diversionary tactic. 'Actually, Gus, I've been meaning to tell you . . . '

'What?'

Julia did not quite meet his eye. 'Nella and I are going to meet to talk things over. I thought it would be a nice thing to do.'

'Yes, it would,' said Gus.

Still, Julia did not meet his eye. 'She also said that Teddy might join us. But only might. He's busy with his new line of work.' She was on the defensive. 'You don't mind? You wouldn't think it disloyal?'

193

Gus set down the suitcases by the front door. 'Of course not. What's the new line of work?'

'It's with the local council. Councils have been ordered to build a million homes between them. A *million*. Think of that. He says they will have to levy compulsory purchase orders in order to do this and he will be dealing with the legal side. I think it's a good idea if we all meet. Don't you?' Looking rather self-important, she added, 'I'll see what I can do to heal the breach.'

13

Krista clasped the ferry rail, knuckles whitening with the effort of keeping her balance. Her headscarf was tied extra tight but strands of hair kept whipping across her face, which did not help matters.

They had escaped from the saloon, where knots of men in uniforms of one sort or another were drinking noisily, smoking and playing cards. After a bit, Krista had become agitated. 'The soldiers . . . do you suppose they know I'm German?'

'Don't speak. Just show your papers, if asked. Remember you are Christine Clifton,' said Gus. 'All right?'

Even in the bulky ATS uniform, she was still way too thin and frail, he noted, but she had improved vastly since he had first set eyes on her. She had none of Nella's lushness but, if she was thin and snap-able, a fire burned in her. An obduracy which, he was beginning to understand, would not allow her to give in.

Spray lashed across the deck and caught her on the cheeks, making her laugh. Gus offered his handkerchief. She wiped her face and tucked it back into his greatcoat pocket. 'Thank you.'

The gesture was almost intimate. Gus leaned over the rail and allowed the wind to buffet him. One day, the two of them might do something as ordinary as go on holiday. He pictured them motoring along the French roads in a two-seater, stopping to inspect a chateau, or a church, and discussing menus which were so very different from English cuisine that they were an education in themselves.

The wind gusted harder as Belgium loured into view. It had the grey look of a hard winter when the cold has been anchored over the land for some time. 'Home is over there.' Her voice struggled against the roar. 'I have almost forgotten what it is like.' She concentrated on the flat Belgian shoreline. 'Gus, I wish it had not been my country that was responsible. More than anything, I wish that.'

The deck heaved under their feet and the wires threaded between the rail struts thrummed as if demented. It was becoming impossible to hear properly and he hustled Krista inside into a quieter area of the saloon, then fetched two brandies. 'Listen to me. Every so often a tyrant, or tyranny, gains an upper hand. Humans can be monstrous wherever they are. How the monster is vanquished varies, I suppose.' Krista sipped her brandy. 'Your country will be in trouble for some time but not for ever. Hitler won't be the last.'

Krista looked down at the floor. Was she listening? Who knew? Gus could never be sure.

Predictably, the train journey was long and difficult, and both were exhausted by the time they arrived at the Lehrter Stadtbahnhof. Waiting for them was a black Mercedes outfitted with leather upholstery and a lingering smell of cigars. Nothing much had changed since they had left the city and the British driver had his job cut out as he nosed the car in fits and starts through rubble-littered streets to the hotel in the Charlottenburg district.

Krista was glued to the car window. Every so often, she murmured, 'Oh,' and 'Oh, no.' At one point, she said, 'I can't bear to think of the bodies under that rubble. Smashed and burned.' Her hands clenched together in her lap. 'The smell must be terrible.'

Quite a few of the ground-floor windows were missing at their hotel and a piercing draught blew through the lobby. Mercifully, the windows of their room on the third floor were intact but brick dust lurked in the corners and the tap on the basin yielded up water only intermittently.

'Sorry about that, sir,' replied the duty sergeant when Gus asked if there was any chance of a bath. 'We're working on it.'

They dined in the makeshift dining room on ham with cabbage and a suet pudding tasting like cotton wool, washed down with a passable Moselle which Gus suspected had been snaffled by their lot from the American NAAFI. Gus wouldn't have minded another bottle but, on asking, it wasn't forthcoming.

A couple of khaki-clad officers sat two tables away talking quietly. They were making inroads into a second bottle and the younger one was turning a brass cigarette case round and round between his fingers.

Gus said to Krista, 'Does it feel familiar?'

She glanced around the damaged room. 'Funnily enough, it does.'

197

Krista seemed nervous and jumpy as they got ready for bed. For extra warmth, she put on a pair of men's thick flannel pyjamas which were far too big. Rolling up the sleeves, she said, 'Gus, I know we have talked about it. But being back here . . . means I will be betraying my own people.'

He had half-expected something like this. 'You did it before.'

She concentrated on the sleeve she was tackling. 'I was using you and you knew it. Thanks to you, I am no longer hungry or . . . ' The confession was halting. 'You have made me your wife and given me a home. But that has given me time to think things over. The work you do is important but, sometimes, I don't think I can do it. Sometimes, I don't think I can bear it.'

He thought of what Minet might say. 'You can't get out of it.'

She searched his face. 'No? But *you* must know that deep down,' she tapped her chest and switched into German, 'deep down it goes against what is natural.'

'It doesn't matter what we feel. If justice is not done we don't have much.'

Who would blink first?

Krista did. 'Justice, yes.'

'Then you won't be betraying your people because you will be doing the right thing.'

'That makes you sound very simple, Gus, and you are not simple. Or stupid.'

Her eyes were as haunted as never before. 'I can't make you do anything, Krista. But you will be helping to put things right.'

'Based on hatred. Hatred of Germans,' she pointed out, adding in a low voice, 'and self-hatred.'

You could always leave her behind in Germany.

Aware that Krista's rebellion could be tricky for both of them, Gus said coldly, 'You can decide not to cooperate, that's up to you. You can decide to abandon this. But you must understand that I can't ever help you again. Never see you, even. You would be abandoned by us and left here to fend for yourself.'

He spoke more harshly than he had intended and terror flickered across her features. After a moment, he said, 'Let's go to bed.'

As customary, they kept a space between them. He thought of how he had placed his mouth on Nella's breast that time they went into the fields on that still, warm day, and of the contrast between her willing surrender and the hostility exuded by the shivering body beside him.

'Sometimes, I can't remember what actually happened,' Krista said into the darkness. 'I wake up and I try to think of that night and my mind is blank. I prefer it that way.' She turned on to her side away from Gus. 'I will cooperate,' she said. 'Don't worry.'

In the middle of the night, they were woken by shouts and the sound of heavy boots pounding down the corridor. On investigation, Gus was told by the same duty sergeant that it was a raid by the Soviets looking for Red Army deserters. It happened a lot, apparently. 'All

199

sorted now, sir,' he said.

★   ★   ★

The interrogation was to be held in the Spandau district in a medieval town hall which had, miraculously, managed to survive the bombing. It had been chosen as a site for the interrogations because its original architecture and history had nothing to do with Hitler's Reich.

It was arranged that they should be driven there an hour earlier than necessary. Gus wanted to introduce them both to the war-crimes staff, and to make contact with the representatives from Haystack, a group dedicated to hunting down Nazis. Haystack men were not men to be messed with and he wanted them to brief him.

On the walls of the room allocated to the interrogation teams were pinned up photographs of SS guards and administrators, with names, ages and distinguishing characteristics. There was also a list of suspected war criminals which had been published by the UN's War Crimes Commission. A team of secretaries and translators stood by to prepare the affidavits after the interrogations had been completed. These would be sent for assessment by the prosecution service before the legal teams got to work.

He had no doubt that the upcoming interrogation would test him — perhaps to the limit. As with most things, preparation was the key. To this end, he called in all the information available on the death camps, including Auschwitz. He had read through the file on 'Gretl

Helger' in a meticulous fashion and concluded that, during initial questioning, she displayed psychopathic characteristics, as opposed to plain stupid or violent ones. Rereading his text books on the subject, he brushed up on Henderson's *Psychopathic States*, in which it was argued that psychopaths usually possessed a certain level of intelligence, exhibited antisocial, or asocial, behaviour throughout their lives and were difficult to influence by whatever means. In short, ran the conclusion, they are unable to adjust to ordinary existence and there is no cure.

On that basis, Gudrun Kreutz — if it was she — was almost certainly a clever misfit. But that was not a proof of guilt.

Presupposition and prejudging were traps waiting for him. In this work, the mind had to be clear of preconceptions; plus, an almost infinite supply of patience was mandatory. Shuffle forward. Snaffle a hint from here. A hint from there.

Gus arranged the desk, the lamp and the chair in which Gretl would sit at the angles that suited him best. He planned to sit opposite her and just to the left, which would keep him in the shadow. Krista would be to his right and sitting a little back, the duty sergeant on his left; a stenographer would be positioned under the window.

The team waited.

On the dot, the prisoner was led in. Good God, Gus thought, taken aback. What had he expected? A female thug? Instead, they were faced by a tall, almost elegant-looking woman, with a beautiful complexion and reddish-blonde hair tied back with a ribbon. She was dressed in overalls, liberally splashed with mud. An unhealed scar slashed across her cheek and her right wrist was bandaged. She held her head up and did not cringe.

Having ascertained that she was reasonably comfortable, but not too comfortable, Gus adjusted the desk lamp. It was important to illuminate her face — not enough to dazzle her but sufficient to allow him to register changes of expression.

It began.

'What is your name?'

'Gretl Helger.'

'Where did you grow up?'

'In Bremen.'

'What role did you have during the war?'

'I was a farm worker.'

This was risible. Gretl Helger was no farm worker.

'What are the crops grown on the farm?'

'Before the war? Or during? It changed.'

The discussion of crops took time, as did the response to Gus's request for the prisoner to supply the names of the people she had worked with.

The hours crawled past. Once or twice, Gus looked over to Krista, who had noted down a couple of words.

'Are you married?'

'My husband is dead.'

'When you were arrested you had four diamond rings and other items of valuable jewellery in your possession. Can you account for these?'

'They belonged to my grandmother, who gave them to me before she was killed by British bombs.'

'Her name?'

No hesitation. 'Hedwig Essen.'

So it continued.

Gretl was stone-walling: flat, hard, unbreakable. A fine sheen of sweat coated the stenographer's forehead and the sergeant had taken to pacing up and down at the back of the room.

Nothing. *Nirgends.*

At the end of the third hour, Gus ordered a break. The prisoner was led away while he and Krista were conducted to a room down a panelled corridor to where soldiers, on catering duties in a makeshift canteen, were working the tea urn and plates of sandwiches. The room smelled as though it had not been aired for centuries and the steam hissing from the urn did not help matters. On one wall, there were traces of an old fresco, and, on the opposite wall, the remnants of a faded blue-and-red banner, possibly one that had belonged to a trade guild.

Gus downed a cup of tea and Krista accepted a sandwich. 'It's good to taste German bread again.' She held the sandwich so tightly that the filling was in danger of falling out.

He reached over and loosened her grip. 'There're plenty more where those came from.'

The sandwiches weren't brilliant but they would do. Gus bit into a second. 'Am I right, Krista? She says she was born in Bremen but she pronounces some words with a Munich accent.'

'Correct,' she said. 'I've listed the words.'

He chewed thoughtfully. 'A Munich accent doesn't make her guilty.'

He could see Krista thinking, *hear* her thinking, as she tested the cooperation she had promised him. Some crumbs had dropped into her lap. Licking her finger, she vacuumed them up. 'Push her more about where she was brought up.' As they left the canteen, she added, 'Question her about her husband.'

The corporal manning the urn stared openly as Gus took hold of Krista's hand. She tried to pull away but he retained his hold. 'Krista, this woman is clearly well tutored in being questioned, or is very bright. Possibly both. So we should structure the next session differently. Use surprise. When I push a file over to you, that's your cue to take over.'

Five minutes later, they were again confronting Gretl across the desk. The short break seemed to have refreshed her and she seemed composed, almost tranquil.

'What was your husband's name?'

'Joseph.'

'I don't believe you.'

'What can I say?'

Gus placed his forefinger on the buff folder and slid it over to Krista.

Krista placed her hands on it. 'Where did you get married?'

Gretl's head snapped up and, for the first time, her composure was rattled. '*Mein Gott*, are you German?'

204

Krista ignored the question. 'Where did you marry?'

'A German . . . ' The prisoner's voice lashed at Krista. 'How long have you been a traitor? Always? Or just to save your skin?'

'Answer my question.'

'Can you sleep at night?' Gretl peered into Krista's face. 'By the look of it, you don't.' She stopped and said abruptly, 'I would like a cigarette.'

The sergeant looked at Gus, who nodded. A packet was produced, a cigarette extracted and lit and given to the prisoner. Gretl inhaled luxuriously, deeply.

'Pay attention,' said Krista.

Gretl leaned forward and breathed out a storm of smoke into Krista's face. 'That's for traitors.'

The sergeant snatched the cigarette away and stamped on it.

'No more cigarettes,' Krista said quietly.

'A German and you do this?' Gretl's eyes beamed malice and a hint of triumph. 'Aren't you ashamed of betraying your country? These people are our enemies.'

Krista squared her shoulders. Her face was calm. Gus felt the stirring of pride for he knew that, if he placed a finger on the bird-like wrist resting on the desk, the pulse would be beating hectically.

'I have friends on the outside,' said Gretl. 'Remember that.'

There was always danger that an interrogation could slip away from the interrogator. 'Shut up!' Gus spoke so violently that the sergeant jumped.

At a stroke, the atmosphere in the room became electric — which was what he had intended. Gus turned to the sergeant. 'You might have to keep her in check,' he said in English. The sergeant took up a position behind the prisoner's chair. She tried to spit at him.

'No, you don't.' Before she could blink, the sergeant had slipped his arm around her neck and pulled back her head so the tendons in her neck sprang into bas-relief. 'No, you don't, missy. And don't think I won't hesitate to go further.'

The prisoner's startled cry sounded very loud in the room.

Gus signalled for the sergeant to release his hold.

'Are you going to protest at this treatment of your own countrywoman?' she demanded of Krista.

'Make them wait,' Gus had instructed Krista when they discussed their strategy for the interrogations. 'Make them wait until they are begging for someone to say something. Very often they talk then.' What he hadn't told her was that subjects in interrogation usually broke quicker when a woman was asking the questions. It was also the case — apparently — when women did the torturing.

The best of pupils, Krista held the moment in suspension. Cherishing and stroking the silence.

The seconds ticked by.

'No,' she said eventually. She slid the buff file back to Gus.

A second prearranged signal which meant that

206

Krista wanted to think.

'Take her back to the cells,' Gus ordered the sergeant. 'We'll start again tomorrow.'

★ ★ ★

Driving back to the hotel, the driver of Gus and Krista's car took it very slowly down the Charlottenburger Chaussee. Passing the Königs-platz, the car approached the British attaché's apartment on their right.

Gus disliked this point in their route. It was the place where, however hard he tried to avoid it, the past intruded on what peace of mind he enjoyed.

Once so massive and well-guarded, the frontage of the convent came into sight, the stone arch and its doorway reduced to a skeleton of what they had been. Without warning, Krista pointed to a side street which flanked the building. 'Gus, tell the driver to turn down that street.'

'Krista, don't.'

'*Please*.'

In her agitation, she had clutched his arm and did not remove it instantly. Placing his own hand on hers, Gus gave in. 'If you must.' He instructed the driver to do what Krista asked. The car eased its way into a small cul de sac along one side of which ran the bombed-out convent building with the remains of a belfry at its far end.

'Can I have five minutes?'

He glanced at his watch and consulted with the driver. 'Only five.'

Krista pushed open the door and the bitter air invaded the car's interior. Moving fast, she disappeared through a modest wooden door set into the convent's wall. When Gus caught up with her she was kneeling in the centre of a courtyard beside a stone statue on a pediment. The statue was so badly damaged it was impossible to say what it had once been.

'Help me, Gus.' She was scrabbling in the frozen earth. 'I want to take something from here in the garden back . . . home.' There was terror and yearning in her voice and gestures. 'Help me.'

The expensive gloves he had given her were being ruined. Dropping down beside her, he seized her hands. 'Krista, this is not sensible. It's too cold. We can buy plants in London.'

She pulled away from him. 'The Sisters gathered here in the summer at the times they were allowed to talk to each other. Sister Elisabeth . . . she was the gardener . . . planted it up with aromatic plants. Herbs and things.' She looked wildly around. 'Everything for the Sisters had a symbolic meaning which they tried to teach us, the children, so we could carry them on. Trees, plants, the seasons, death. I now see it was important to have those meanings . . . not just for the nuns. But now those meanings have gone because . . . ' Krista bit down on her bottom lip in the old way and said in German: 'Because we're all dead.'

He stared into her agonized countenance and he knew what she meant. After all and after everything, war had taken away the power to believe and, in his case, his ability to worship God. Any god.

Krista was brushing away the snow, leaving a circle of frozen earth.

'What are we looking for?'

'Anything that lives. That's the important thing.'

He glanced up. Windows set into three walls surrounding the courtyard revealed roofless rooms behind them. One wall had remained more or less intact but most of the doors hung on their hinges. Wind swept through the ruined spaces and the stones and burned wood cracked in the cold. The certainties and order which had once been rooted here were gone.

Ripping off his gloves, Gus dug his fingers into the earth. *Earth as hard as iron.* Then he struck gold. A tiny sprig of thyme was fighting for life under the ice blanket. 'Wait,' he said. All official cars had been issued with shovels and he went to fetch theirs.

It took an almighty effort to dig it up but, finally, Gus managed to disinter a small root from which the sprig was growing and handed it over to Krista. The palm of her hand cupped it protectively, possessively.

'Thank you, Gus.'

14

It snowed again during the night, an icy dusting, and the wind blew in razor-sharp gusts which slowed down whatever traffic was moving.

Stiff and exhausted, Gus and Krista rose and dressed as quickly as possible, drank a cup of tea and got into the waiting car. At the CROWCASS headquarters, the team assembled and there was much talk of the cold and demands for tea 'n' wads. At ten o'clock precisely they filed into the interrogation room.

Today, Gretl was looking rumpled and any suggestion of elegance had vanished. Sweat stained her overalls under the arms and the smell of it slid into their nostrils.

Krista opened the proceedings. 'According to our records a Gudrun Sholt married Pieter Kreutz in June 1942. Is that you?'

'I've never heard of these people.'

Krista removed a newspaper clipping from the file and pushed it across the table. 'Read it,' she said.

Gretl glanced down and — for a second — extreme emotion registered on her features before they settled back into their perpetually mocking cast. 'My eyesight has deteriorated.'

'It's the notice of a marriage,' said Gus. 'Dated 13 June 1942. We think it's yours.'

Gretl shrugged.

Krista looked down at the clipping and

extemporized. 'It says here that the bride was expecting a child for the Fatherland.'

'No, it does not.' As the words rattled from her, Gretl realized her mistake.

'So you do know this clipping,' said Krista. 'You know what it says.'

Gretl retreated into silence.

Krista held the line of questioning. 'You are an intelligent woman. How was it possible to kill so many people at, for example, Auschwitz?'

Gretl did not blink. 'How do I know? Except that, being German, I know that we can deal with technical things very well. Killing people could be said to be a technical problem.'

Unemotional. Matter of fact.

Gus's stomach tightened. 'But you agree that many people have been exterminated?'

Gretl did not bother to look at Gus. 'If you say this is true, then I must believe you. But I knew nothing about it.'

'Now that you do know, as we all do,' asked Krista in the same level voice, 'how do you feel about the moral position?'

The prisoner stared at the stenographer and sweat glistened at her temple. 'The moral position is that we have to obey orders.'

Krista took her time rifling through the papers in the file. The tension mounted. 'Please remove your wedding ring,' she said finally.

The lids fell down over Gretl's eyes. 'It's stuck. Been like that for years.' She held up her right hand, displaying a grimy, frayed bandage that partially obscured the ring.

'You refuse to remove it?'

211

'I can't.' She tried to pull the bandage down over the ring.

It was a curiously protective and yet unsettling gesture. Encountering the prisoner's gaze, Gus was disconcerted to discern a hint of pleading. 'Please do as you have been asked.'

Gretl pressed the corners of her mouth down and was silent. Gus swung his lamp around and shone it at her. The face which looked back at him was bitterly hostile. But there was — just, and for the first time — a hint of fear. 'No problem,' he said quietly. 'We can cut it off. If necessary. Sergeant, do we have a set of pliers?'

The sergeant couldn't have been happier. 'I'll fetch some, sir.'

Outside, the winter's day had darkened and the circle of light thrown on the figure in the chair appeared the more intense. Gus glanced down at his papers. 'Eight hundred thousand estimated victims at this moment. Twenty-eight thousand children.' He looked up. 'According to our research that is a conservative estimate of the number of dead at Auschwitz I and Auschwitz-Birkenau. We have yet to verify the totals.'

'Not my business,' she said flatly.

'Have you got those pliers, Sergeant?'

The prisoner tensed. Looking over to the window, she focused on the patch of light framed in it.

'Sergeant . . . '

Krista gave a tiny gasp.

The sergeant took up a stance beside Gretl, seized the hand with the ring and tussled with it. The pliers slipped. The prisoner exclaimed. A thread of scarlet appeared.

'Sergeant . . . ' It was a sufficient warning, and he kept his eyes fixed on Gretl, who blinked but did not flinch. Again, the sergeant applied the pliers. Blood slid down on to Gretl's stained overall.

'All right.' She tugged at her finger. Slowly, slowly, she eased off the ring, smearing blood over her hands as she did so.

Ignoring Krista, she placed it in Gus's outstretched hand.

'Thank you.' Gus held up the ring and examined it. He read out the engraving: ' "Pieter and Gudrun, 13.6.42".' Placing it on the desk between them, a small gold circle, he said, 'So the papers were correct, Gudrun.'

Something like a sigh escaped from the prisoner — a sound full of regret, perhaps repentance?

Gus produced a paper from his file and pushed it over to Gudrun. 'Could you tell me what that is?'

She gave it a cursory look. 'A payroll?'

'And the underlined name?'

' "Gudrun Kreutz, née Sholt",' she read reluctantly, angrily.

'And the name above?'

' "Rudolf Höss".'

'For the record,' Gus addressed the stenographer, 'Rudolf Höss is the former commandant of Auschwitz.'

By now, Gudrun would be working out her options and wondering how soon Gus would spring the trap. He kept his voice level. 'It is no

213

use denying that you worked at Auschwitz.'

She glanced at Krista, then at the window.

'We have the payroll.' Gus was quiet but insistent. 'The sooner you admit it, the sooner this can be over for you.'

There was no way out from the corner she was in and she knew it.

Gudrun said, 'Yes, I was employed there.'

'In what capacity?'

She fixed Gus with an angry look but answered calmly enough and with a hint of pride. 'I was supervising the women's section.'

The sense of relief in the interrogation room was palpable. A foot forward, thought Gus.

Krista sent him a tiny smile and Gus handed over the ring to the sergeant, who attached a label to it.

Gudrun watched him. 'Will I get it back?'

'No.'

Anguish registered — but only for a second.

'Bandage her up, Sergeant, if you would.'

An hour's break was declared and Gus escorted Krista into an inner courtyard for some air. The ancient beam over the doorway was fire-damaged but the studded doors opening on to the courtyard and a wooden-pillared loggia carved with medieval figures were more or less intact.

The cold cut into the exposed skin on their faces and hands.

Lighting a cigarette, Gus paced around.

A trio of soldiers idling by the entrance stamped their feet and swung their arms. One of them was telling a joke.

'My girlfriend is a suicide blonde. Do you know why? Dyed by her own hand . . . '

It wasn't particularly funny but it was good-natured.

Gus felt his circulation speed up and the ache in his knees iron out. He returned to Krista, who had lit a cigarette but wasn't smoking it. Instead, she watched the ash burn.

'That was clever,' he said. 'What made you think of the ring?'

'Simple. For many women it would be the last thing they would abandon. It was worth taking the chance.' She had elected to wear her wedding ring on her left hand and glanced down at the brass band which was the best Gus could find at the time.

'I promise to get you a proper one.'

She shrugged.

'So,' he said, 'we've got her pinned down as supervising the women's section. Now, the details.'

'I will go through the files again,' said Krista. 'Before we go back in.'

Gus smiled down at her. 'Good. So will I.'

They made for the door. One of the soldiers shouted out, 'Hey, miss. Germans are not allowed to talk to the British.'

Returning to the interrogation room, Gus found two extra observers already seated. They identified themselves as George Talbot and Robert Cadogan, names which were clearly fake but it didn't matter. Gus knew they would be from Minet's team.

Gus steepled his arms, resting his elbows on

215

the desk. 'You agree that you're Gudrun Kreutz who worked at Auschwitz I and Auschwitz-Birkenau supervising the women's section. What did this role entail?'

She had had time to think.

'To ensure the welfare of the women prisoners.'

'Detail the duties.'

'Provision of rations and health care.'

'According to the records, the women's section, Section Bia, was set up in March 1942 and in August 1942 was moved to Auschwitz-Birkenau and run by women members of the SS. As we have established, you supervised the women's section so I would submit that you were a member of the SS.'

Silence.

Talbot and Cadogan listened intently and took notes. Once or twice, they asked Krista for clarification of a word or phrase.

'How many people did you have working for you?'

'Possibly fifteen. It varied.'

'Were you aware of the gas chambers?'

'No.'

'Did you have anything to do with the trains which came in?'

'No.'

'If you were at Auschwitz-Birkenau it would have been impossible to avoid them.'

Gudrun spoke clearly and fluently. There was no obvious repugnance when Gus read out descriptions of the mass killing. There was no irresolution either, merely a polite, closed desire

216

to respond to the questions as briefly as possible.

Yes, it was true she had been employed at the camp to deal with insurgent and criminal females who were causing trouble in the prison population. It was her opinion that the camp had been well run and there had been every effort made to treat the prisoners humanely according to the rules, but, sometimes, it had been impossible and measures had been taken. Obtaining sufficient provisions had been an ongoing battle but she and her staff had gone out of their way to ensure that the prisoners received regular food and clothing.

From time to time she touched the place on her finger where her ring had been.

'Look at these, please.' Gus spread out a montage of black-and-white photographs which the Allies' photo reconnaissance unit had taken on first going into the camp. Scenes of such horror: human beings barely alive, heaped bodies, block houses, mountains of shoes, piles of hair and luggage.

Gudrun glanced at them. 'If this is a true record, then it must have taken place in a part of the camp I knew nothing about.'

Cadogan lit up his fifth cigarette.

'Let's go over this again. Were you aware of the gas chambers?'

'No.'

'Either in Auschwitz I? Or in Auschwitz-Birkenau?'

'No.'

Endless patience, cunning and stealth were

necessary. He knew from experience not to drop the reins until the very last moment.

The hands on the clock ticked round. The stenographer was exhausted and the sergeant jumpy; Talbot and Cadogan were growing restless and Krista's cough sounded more frequently. It was late afternoon and regulations stipulated that they must stop after six hours.

Gudrun was dextrous — no backtracking or hesitating, only a precise repetition of the answers she had learned by heart. She possessed a hard, obdurate determination to survive and the ability to maintain the smokescreen. 'The prisoners under my care were well treated. It was a point of honour.' And so on. The lips in the good-looking face moved and spoke with an apparent desire to tell the truth.

That was always the worry: being led by a talented liar into the wrong belief, which resulted in the wrong questions being asked.

'What did you know about the crematoria at the camp? Surely they were used if the women under your care died?'

'Others dealt with the disposal of bodies.'

'And how were they disposed of?'

'I have no idea. I did not ask.'

Cadogan was watching her like a lynx. Talbot, he noticed, was watching Krista.

The notes on Gudrun in the file spelled out a deprived upbringing until the war. Then she had seized the opportunities and used her looks and wits to secure a position. Having been at the bottom of the social heap, it was a fair assumption that she relished her new power.

218

A different tack was necessary. Sliding a map of the camp over to Gudrun, he asked her to point out where her office had been located. Gudrun jabbed down a finger, its nail rimmed with blood. 'How interesting,' observed Gus. 'The crematoria, or the gas ovens as we might as well call them, were approximately quarter of a mile from where you have identified your office, and in direct line of sight.'

Gudrun shifted abruptly.

Bullseye?

No, not there yet.

'No one will believe that you didn't know what was going on in the buildings so close to where you worked.'

'It's the truth.' Gudrun still had herself under control, her voice contained and unemotional. 'I concerned myself only with my charges.'

'Or that you did not know any of the personnel who worked in the crematoria.'

Again, she touched her ring finger.

'I did not. I knew no one. I didn't know anything about crematoria.'

'You did not exchange any kind of information with anyone?'

She shrugged. 'We were very busy. There was no time for contact with people like the Geheimnisträger.'

Sitting beside Krista, Gus heard her tiny intake of breath. She closed the file in front of her, which was a signal they had agreed between them. He hesitated for a second. Had Krista got it right? Should he risk jeopardizing the balance of the interrogation? He nodded.

219

Krista said quietly, 'You used the word '*Geheimnisträger*'.'

There was a flash of understanding, followed by anger, then, once again, fear. 'Did I?'

Krista turned to the onlookers and spoke in English. 'Gentlemen, this is a word which, translated, means 'bearer of secrets'.'

She addressed Gudrun. 'What was the secret?'

'How should I know?'

'We have sworn testimony that this group of people were also known as the '*Sonderkommandos*'. Would you agree?'

'If you say so.'

'According to reports, the *Sonderkommandos* were the units which disposed of the corpses after gassing. That was their sole task. They were kept apart from the rest of the camp. That was the secret. If you were aware of their existence, it therefore follows that you knew there were gas ovens.'

'Not necessarily.'

'The *Sonderkommandos* were generally put to death after three months. But some of them managed to preserve a record of what had being going on.' Krista opened her file and produced a small black-and-white photograph.

The packet containing this particular piece of evidence had been delivered the previous day.

'This was found buried in the ruins of the crematoria by one of them who must have been very brave. Could you describe what you see?'

Gudrun's eyes flicked over it. 'Naked women.'

'What are they doing?'

'Going through a door.'

'And who is standing by it?'

Gus intervened. 'The door has been identified as leading to the shower room where the gassing took place.'

'Who is standing by the door?'

Krista's German flowed, clear and inexorable.

There was no way out for Gudrun. She cleared her throat and a kind of defiant pride coloured her answer. 'I am.'

The truth.

'So you will not deny that you knew about the killings in the camp and were instrumental in them?'

Gudrun's ringless hands clenched together. 'Question yourself, rather. What did you do to help the Fatherland? It's people like you who have brought about Germany's defeat with your disloyalty. You're the one who is guilty and deserves to die.'

'Please answer the question,' said Gus.

Krista rose to her feet. The uniform of a First Officer in the ATS which she had been allocated was far too large. She had done her best to hide it by rolling over the waistband but it hung loosely from her body.

She held up the photograph and pushed it in front of the once-elegant blonde. 'Can you deny it?'

Gudrun looked down. She looked away. She looked hungrily at the packet of cigarettes lying on the table in front of Gus. She fixed her eyes on Krista. The two women stared at each other — but Krista did not yield.

'No,' Gudrun admitted at last.

'Take her back to the cells,' said Gus in English. 'The case will be prepared for the trial.'

Krista repeated the order in German.

The sergeant ushered Gudrun out of the room. At the door, she turned round and spat at Krista, 'You *will* pay.'

★ ★ ★

Over a dinner of some sort of stew and the ever-present cabbage, Gus took solace in the bottle and even Krista was persuaded to have some.

She observed the wine in the cheap glass. 'How will I pay, do you think?'

'You won't.'

She ran a finger over the wine label on the bottle. 'You don't know what it's like out there. Anything could happen. Anything does.'

He urged her to drink the wine, which was a meaty burgundy (stolen, no doubt), and she took a mouthful. Over the rim of the glass, she said, 'I love your optimism, Gus, but it is only optimism.'

That night, and just in case, Gus checked the soldiers were on sentry duty downstairs; he locked the bedroom door and barricaded it with a chair. When they were driven to CROWCASS headquarters the following morning, he instructed the driver to take an indirect route.

At the headquarters, Gus was informed that he had been allocated two more cases, neither of which had a time limit — 'Just get a result'. Neither looked as tough to crack as the Kreutz case had been, but complex enough for Gus to judge that the interrogations would take it out of both Krista and himself.

His concern for Krista deepened and he blamed himself for underestimating the damage to her. From time to time in England, she had nightmares but, since arriving in Berlin, they were frequent. Awakening from them, she was almost always speechless with a fear which she wouldn't discuss.

'Go away, Gus.'

Go away.

He couldn't sleep easily either. Sitting up very late, he wrote his reports by the light of an inadequate bulb. Once, in the small hours of the morning, he looked up to find Krista watching him. She didn't say anything, but her huge eyes were unblinking and the most troubled he had ever seen them.

'Go to sleep, Krista.'

'If circumstances had been different, Gus, could I have been that woman?'

Gus thought he understood what she was trying to say: *You are writing up the case notes of the guilty but I am the guilty one, too, aren't I?*

'No,' he replied. But actually he wasn't sure.

And she knew that he was equivocal.

'No, listen. Gus, I know. I could have been in a different place, having to take what was on offer there, rather than the job I did fetch up with.' Krista had planted the thyme in a tin can begged from the NAAFI and put it on the windowsill, where it acted as a magnet. 'The so-called Ministry of Public Enlightenment and Propaganda was bad enough, but because it was easy and sheltered I was lulled into thinking that Hitler was acceptable. I went along with it. I helped to create the lies that went out. Later, of course, I learned; but I am haunted by the idea that if things had been really bad for me I would have ended up like Gudrun.'

'You would never have done what she did.'

She stared at him. 'Did you ever think you would do what you did?'

'Don't.' The instant he said the word he regretted it. 'Not now, Krista.'

'But we should, Gus.' She shifted restlessly. 'It is always there.'

He realized then what a threat the figure of Gudrun was to their fragile accord. 'Yes, but not now,' he repeated.

Krista lay down, pulled the sheets over her shoulders and closed her eyes.

He couldn't wait to escape Berlin. The stink of the ruined city was disgusting enough, but the stench of vendetta, hopelessness and guilt was just as pungent.

The final case — a particularly nasty one — was wrapped up by the end of the second week but Gus was told they were not free to go home yet. 'I'm afraid you're going to have to kick your heels here over Christmas,' Gus was told by the officer commanding the unit. 'Take a day or two off while we sort it out.'

A day later, he handed in his report to the authorities and gave a verbal debriefing to Cadogan (who would relay it to Minet). On the way back to the hotel, he instructed the driver to drive Krista and himself around the city.

'You'd like to see it, I think.' He took a risk and touched her hand. 'It might help.'

She did not look at him. 'You are very kind, Gus.'

The driver branched off in the direction of the ruined Reichstag. 'Look at the shadows,' said Krista after a few minutes. 'I've never seen anything like them.'

The jagged shadows thrown across the streets were created by the sharp, blistered outlines of what remained of blasted buildings. Creeping about in those ink-black patches were what looked like animated bundles of rags. Scrabbling. Ferreting. A woman searched in a dustbin at a street corner, her head so deep into its cavernous belly that she almost disappeared. In this area of the city, not many walls were wholly intact and these were covered by the edicts issued by the military government. Whenever the car slowed, children emerged from nowhere and surrounded it. 'Chocolate,' they called. 'Chocolate.' Turning into Wilhelmstrasse, the driver encountered an impassable ridge of heaped rubble, on top of which was silhouetted a line of women — the *Trümmerfrauen* — passing buckets from one to another. Most of them looked dangerously thin. All of them looked cold and hungry.

'*Schrecklich*,' Krista said under her breath.

The driver backed up the car but they didn't make it very far. Roadblocks and rubble saw to that. In the end, Gus instructed the driver to drive west to the Wannsee Lake, where he knew that Krista had enjoyed going.

225

During the night, an inch of snow had fallen and now, in the late afternoon, it was beginning to freeze. The driver had to take extra care on the slippery road, but eventually they drove through the pines and drew up by the lakeside.

Gus told the driver to give them half an hour, then he went around to the passenger door and opened it. 'Come.' He held out his hand.

The air was bitingly cold, whistling down into the lungs. The dark pines stood out against a white, glistening landscape and the slate-grey water. For a while, they walked along the beach and then headed towards a clutch of trees growing down to the edge of the lake. Shoulders hunched, gloved hands thrust into her coat pockets, Krista walked rapidly, which pleased Gus as it was a sign of her restored health. Every so often, she halted, shaded her eyes and searched the expanse of water. For what? Memories? Gus strolled on and reached the tree line.

He turned to watch Krista.

His breath streamed from him. Here, away from Berlin, the world was painted in white. Frost had traced a wedding-cake icing on the pines and the undergrowth glittered with it. Silence was enfolded into the scene, bringing relief to his tired senses. Nothing had changed here, and thank God for it. The grey lake and grey sky, the attitudes of the frozen trees, the silvery glint at the water's edge; these were elemental and had always been thus. Despite what had been thrown at it, he thought, the land was holding its own. It would endure.

He raised a hand to wave at Krista.

Behind him, something — twigs, a branch? — snapped.

There was a crunch, a slither of feet on frozen mud.

The old fighting instincts kicked in. Bending his knees, he swung round, fists tensed. Almost immediately, a starved-looking, shaven-headed youth launched himself on to Gus, his right hand with two stiff, forked fingers aimed at Gus's eyes.

'*Drecksau*,' he hissed. 'Give me.'

Gus stepped to the right, brought up his arm and chopped at the back of the youth's head with the edge of his hand. No good. The youth faltered for only a moment then he was at Gus again, fingers stabbing, ever stabbing towards Gus's eyes.

'*Blödes arschloch . . .*'

Without further thought, an enraged Gus kneed him hard in the groin and, with a scream, he went down. But, within seconds, he was trying to rise to his feet. Gus kicked him hard and he sprawled, winded, on the ground.

'I will kill you,' the boy snarled through phlegm and tears streaming down his cadaverous face.

Gus whipped out Krista's pistol, which he always carried on outings. Fury, fear, the it's-him-or-me instinct fuelling his actions, the trained reflex . . . He raised his hand and prepared to bring the butt down on the youth's head.

'Stop it.' Krista was hanging on to his arm. 'Stop it, Gus. Remember. You said never again.'

Oh, Christ.

The youth lay on the ground, snorting and gasping. Krista knelt beside him, uttering a

227

stream of German. 'I'm sorry, I'm sorry.'

Digging into her pocket, she produced a *Reichsmark* note and stuffed it into his hand. 'Forgive us.' Then she ripped off her scarf and dropped it over him. 'Run, Gus.'

She fled after him.

Back in the car, he ordered the driver to get away as fast as possible. Twisting round to look out of the back window, he saw nothing except that glittering, peaceful expanse.

He had been wrong: nothing had healed. Certainly not him.

Never again. Say it over and over, yet it was there — that black, hard, violent reflex taught him by conflict. He'd hoped it had been buried.

Krista was slumped against the seat and he didn't attempt to speak to her until they were back in the hotel. He instructed the driver not to report the incident as no harm had been done.

Gus hustled the silent Krista up to their room, where she walked straight over to the window. Clutching her greatcoat around her shoulders, she looked down on the few vehicles managing to crawl up and down the street.

'Krista,' Gus moved towards her but she turned away from him. A puff of dust shook free from the tattered muslin hanging at the window.

'Don't touch me.'

After a while, she asked, 'Did you think nobody would notice if you killed him because he's a German?'

'It was him or us.'

'He did not need to be hit again,' she argued stubbornly, angrily.

He thought he understood what she was getting at. 'I would never hurt you, Krista, if that's what's worrying you. I promise.'

She turned on Gus. 'How so? You promised never to be violent again. I believed it. But I saw you. You were out of control.'

Except for the drip, drip of the tap into the cracked basin, it was quiet in the wrecked, dispiriting hotel room.

Krista spoke to herself, not Gus. 'What am I doing?'

'You agreed to marry me because you wanted another chance. You wanted to live. I offered it. Most people in your situation would have taken it.'

But bringing Krista back to Berlin had opened a can of worms and he wasn't, as yet, sure how to deal with it.

'Krista, I promised to protect you and I will.'

'My safety is not so important. Even though I make a fuss about it.'

Gus inspected the bruise which had sprouted over his knuckles and wished he had a drink.

That bloody tap wouldn't stop dripping.

'Gudrun Kreutz . . . She was right. I am a traitor to my country, whatever it has done. If my country is guilty, I am guilty.'

Gus sat down wearily on the bed. 'Nonsense.'

'I have such strong pictures of it in my mind: happy people eating good food in undamaged houses, children with dogs running through meadows. These pictures tend to have a lot of sunshine. But something happened to us in the war. We returned to being animals and everything is in shadow.'

A drunk soldier clumped down the corridor outside their room, singing 'Away in a Manager' — reminding them that this was Christmas Eve. *Happy bloody Christmas.*

The greatcoat slipped from her shoulders to the floor. Gus did not stir. Krista picked it up, dusted it down and draped it over the chair. Gus could see clearly the outline of her body under the ill-fitting uniform: the terrifying curve of her hip bone and the still-savage semicircle of her shoulders. 'One of the men, one of your men that night called us a bunch of shameless whores, didn't he?'

She went over to the tap and tried to stop the drip.

He knew precisely to what she was referring. 'You know I don't . . . ' The words were dragged from Gus. 'I don't remember anything.'

'I ask myself all the time why I married you.' Krista sent him a tiny smile. 'And you're right; I wanted to survive, I suppose.' She picked her way with care. 'But, sometimes, I'm not sure of anything.'

He patted his pockets for his cigarettes. *Happy bloody Christmas.* 'You're free to go, Krista. Any time. I won't fight you. We can do a deal.'

'Yes, maybe.' She looked bleakly around the awful room. 'Maybe, I should.'

'I could arrange papers. Get you some ration books.'

Krista clung on to the chair as if her legs could no longer hold her. 'Do you want me to?'

Did he? The thought of Krista no longer in his

life was, to his surprise, truly painful.

Leave her behind.

She slipped to the floor and, head bent, began to sob in great gasps. 'Leave me.'

'Stop it, Krista. Stop.' He bent over and dragged her to her feet, pulling her body roughly against his, and she collapsed like a doll against his chest. He whispered into her ear, 'Don't waste yourself on grief.'

'I should go. Leave you to marry Nella and live the life you were supposed to have.'

At a stroke, regrets lost their sharpness to be replaced by an urgency to make this . . . what was here with Krista . . . work. He pressed his cheek against hers and felt her tears on his face. 'Forget Nella. She's gone.'

Krista looked up at him.

'Truly.'

Leave her behind.

'It's you and me, Krista.'

She gave a small sigh and buried her face in his shoulder. 'One of the soldiers, a Soviet, told me that when you are wounded you very often don't feel it at first. It's numb and you think everything is fine. No pain. No fear. It's only afterwards, sometimes a long time afterwards . . . ' She wiped her wet cheeks with her hand. 'But you would know about that, I think, Gus.'

'I do,' he said through stiff lips.

'I knew you would understand. We do have that.'

Somehow, they were lying together on the bed. Longing to be normal, hungry for contact, Gus kissed her neck and the inside of her wrist. She

231

turned her head towards him, exposing the nape of her neck and he kissed that too.

The only thing that could help — the sole thing — was contact between two people.

He gathered Krista to him and all the elements in his life that had unravelled began to knit together again. 'Look at me.' She turned her head. 'Let me,' he said. 'It would be a beginning. A sign of trust. But you must also forgive me. That is the only way our life together is going to be possible.'

'Forgive . . . ' The word sighed from her pale lips.

Krista was stirring up his deepest, and most complicated, responses. Guilt had proved to be as bitter and destructive as thwarted desire, and yet, incredibly, it seemed to have yielded a sweetness.

'Gus?' She said his name with more tenderness than he had ever heard before. It moved him deeply, nudging to the surface the feelings that he hardly dared acknowledge.

Very carefully, he unbuttoned the regulation blouse which swamped her, revealing the pearl-white body underneath. She permitted him to and then she put her arms around his neck and drew him down.

'Gus.'

Much later, he was woken by Krista tugging on his arm. 'What is it?'

Her body felt as fragile as a flower against his. But it was warm and living. His wife.

She kissed his shoulder. 'Happy Christmas.'

15

Most people tried to do something about celebrating that first Christmas after the war. *We've beaten that bugger Adolf and what's not to like?* Tilly had been touched by the efforts made to decorate trees with anything to hand — old ribbons and cardboard Father Christmases. Mr Evans baked a dough Christmas tree and put it in his window; the butcher made a paper crown with 'Happy Christmas' written on it and stuck it on a sheep's head.

At Number 22, Julia, Tilly and the Mackies, who had agreed to venture across the river, ate a Christmas lunch of lamb chops and carrots and — joy — a fried onion. They rounded it off with a suet pudding made with raisins ('*Where* did you get those?' Tilly demanded) and bottled plums which Julia had unearthed. They had lain forgotten in the cellar for some years but tasted fine, with just a touch of acidity.

Post-meal, Julia put a match to the fire in the drawing room. They all sat around it and listened to a concert on the wireless while Uncle Dennis smoked half a cigar and Coral darned socks for the poor.

'Do you think we could play charades? Have a bit of fun?' muttered Tilly as she and Julia brewed acorn coffee in the kitchen. 'Or would fun kill them?'

Julia positioned a starched cloth on the tray

and laid it with the coffee cups. 'If you suggest it and we have to watch Uncle Dennis attempting to wuther for *Wuthering Heights* again, I'll kill you.'

Tilly flung open the cupboard which contained their precious store of drinks. One bottle of sherry. One half bottle of gin. 'We need help.' She poured a generous slug of sherry into a glass and took a large swig. 'Here,' she said, handing the glass to Julia. 'Fortify thyself.'

Julia took a small nip and frowned as Tilly disposed of the rest.

'I can't help thinking of your poor mother,' remarked Aunt Sarah cryptically as she put on her coat ready for the perilous journey back to Kensington. Tilly cocked a less-than-affectionate eye at Coral, who was tying up the laces on her clumpy outdoor shoes, and rather thought that, when it came to mothers to be pitied, the boot was on the other foot.

'I take it you are referring to Gus marrying Krista, Aunt Sarah?'

'A Kraut. After everything we've had to go through.' Uncle Dennis anchored his hat on to his balding head.

Tilly heard herself say, 'Krista is very nice and I think you should all be more open and welcoming,' and shut the door on their offended figures. She slumped back against it. 'Do you think I've caused a rift in family relations?'

To her surprise, Julia laughed. 'Who cares?' She held up a finger. 'Do you remember Mother's favourite saying? 'Better to marry a Jewish person than a Catholic.''

234

'God knows, then, what she would have made of Krista.'

Her mother's dreary sayings were frequently a way of expressing her terror that Tilly was becoming 'difficult'. Shortly after her seventeenth birthday, Tilly was dispatched to finishing school in Switzerland in a bid by her mother to head off at the pass these so-called 'difficulties', with lessons in deportment and menu planning. After that, it was off to Florence to look at paintings. 'A mistake,' said Gus. 'It will leave her with a taste for foreign men.'

Cunning Gus. Of course he knew what would happen to her. Tilly had departed English and returned a European with Europe's wine and culture thrumming through her veins. How could anyone fail to fall hopelessly in love with what the continent had to offer, she demanded of her family?

It was an affair of the heart that endured even after the European togetherness was blown to smithereens by a former corporal from Austria.

Gus understood. He had been in Heidelberg for only a couple of weeks before he, too, went irritatingly native; he returned after a year having undergone a sea change. How he tyrannized the family with German phrases and a (phoney) passion for *Bratwurst*. Tilly still possessed the photograph taken in the murk of a Munich *Bierkeller* which showed the now-thoroughly-assimilated Gus sitting at a table with a group of men — mostly blonde — all attacking steins of beer. She had studied the image with the same intensity that, later, in the unit, she studied the

235

bridges, roads, woods and rivers shown up in the reconnaissance photos. His absorbed 'otherness', which she did not recognize, taught her that, however close they might be, other people were unknowable. 'If you loved it so much, why did you come back?' she asked him.

'Politics,' was the terse reply.

With the end of the war, the sense of common purpose had vanished and there was nothing, absolutely *nothing*, nice, or evenly remotely European, to be enjoyed in England. As the new year of 1946 struggled into being, Tilly wondered how they would cope with the endless flatness of the peace.

January came and went and Tilly's forebodings were proved correct. Life was dull, unutterably dull.

Gus rang twice, each time to say that his and Krista's return had been postponed. Julia took the first call and Tilly the second, holding the receiver tightly as she tried to imagine what Berlin looked like these days. 'Conditions are pretty frightful here . . . ' Gus's voice splintered down a variable line. 'The weather is awful and the zones in the city make getting around very tricky.'

'So when are you coming back?'

'God knows,' he said. 'A week or so.'

Not so long afterwards, Tilly came back from spending the night on the sofa in Marcus's studio, to find Julia in the hall putting on her coat. 'Church stuff?' she asked flippantly. 'Doing good?'

'*Church* stuff?' Julia looked appalled at the

idea. 'No. What good has the church been to me?'

Considering the Reverend Thomas had made time on several occasions to visit Julia in her widowed state, this was unfair. But her sister had a point. With an unshakeable, if sweetly conveyed, conviction that women had been put on earth to serve men, the Reverend Thomas did not channel a deity who was of comfort to his female parishioners.

Julia added, 'And God is useless.'

Tilly did not wish to look over the cliff into the dark depths of Julia's despair any more than was necessary (her own had to be dealt with first). 'Agreed. We don't bother with God.' A piece of fluff had been caught up on the collar of Julia's coat and Tilly whisked it off.

Julia's mouth twitched. 'Last time he came here, the Reverend was more concerned about you, Tilly. Apparently, what you get up to in Chelsea has been spotted by the parish harridans. They're worried for your immortal soul. And your social standing.'

'How would that lot know about what I get up to?'

'Goodness knows.' Julia tied a scarf around her neck. 'Just as long as you're careful. Is it cold out there?'

'Careful like you oh, big sister? And, yes, it's freezing.'

'I'm a widow, remember, living off my brother. I have to take care what I say. What I do. How I behave.'

Julia's lovely features betrayed nothing as she

now put on her hat but Tilly knew her well enough to know she was still seriously put out by Gus's marriage.

'Whatever you imagine, you're not relegated,' she said impulsively, touching Julia on the shoulder. The rough wool texture grazed her fingertips. 'Who are you going out to see?'

Julia tucked a strand of hair up under the hat band, decided against it and patted it down on to her shoulder. Keeping her face averted, she adjusted the hat brim to a jaunty angle over her face. The message was unmistakeable: *Don't pry.*

'Tell me.'

'Tilly, you're going to drive me mad.'

'You drive *me* crazy, Julia.'

'And what do you think you do to me?'

Faintly, faintly the shades of two girls in smocked lawn dresses slipped into the space between them. Having been urban children, the ghosts did not skip through poppy-and-cornflower-strewn hayfields, but took the form of serious little children who went for conservative walks on the Common.

But search as they might for the traces of their old selves, neither of them would find them in the other — or in themselves. Both of them were older and thinner, with fatigued bodies, and both of them perceived things differently.

' 'Fess up as to why you're being so secretive.' Tilly barred the way to the front door.

Julia gave in. 'I'm going to meet Teddy and Nella.' She took a final look in the mirror and stepped away. 'After Gus left, I met up with

238

Nella. We agreed that the families should try to make it up. But we need to take it gently and Teddy's going to arrange a lunch at his mother's. Meanwhile, we thought we would have a nice tea at the Ritz.' A trace of guilt crept across her face. 'So that's what I'm doing. Just like old times. Teddy's been very sweet, considering. Actually . . . ' She turned back to the mirror for a last adjustment to her hat. 'It was Teddy who sent over the raisins for the Christmas pudding.'

'How on God's good earth did Teddy get hold of raisins? And why give them to us now he hates us?'

Julia ducked Tilly's question. 'I hate everybody, too. We make a fine pair.' She peered at her sister. 'You look a little rough, Tilly. Are you taking care of yourself?'

Peace was supposed to have brought new energy and a quickening of Tilly's creative life. It hadn't done anything of the sort. On the contrary, more often than not, she felt sluggish and useless.

Up. Sticks. Go. To. Italy — where she felt her heart belonged. Dante knew all about that.

. . . *Tu lascerai ogne cosa diletta*
più caramente; e questo è quello strale
che l'arco de lo essilio pria saetta.

Tu proverai sì come sa di sale
lo pane altrui, e come è duro calle
lo scendere e 'l salir per l'altrui scale . . .

. . . You shall leave everything you love most:

239

this is the arrow that the bow of exile
shoots first.

You are to know the bitter taste
of others' bread, how salty it is, and know
how hard a path it is for one who goes
ascending and descending others' stairs . . .

Ascend 'others' stairs'. Up and up, towards the
sky.

★   ★   ★

Gus and Krista did not return until the end of
February, arriving chilled to the bone. Julia was
out and, after the clatter and fuss of their arrival,
they sat in the drawing room and Tilly served
them tea and thinly sliced bread with a scraping
of butter. Both were grateful for Tilly's attention
but fatigued and subdued.

'Was it terrible in Berlin?'

'Yes,' said Gus. 'And it wasn't easy. But I had
Krista.' He smiled at his wife and she sent a tired
smile back at him.

Tilly later reported to Julia, 'Something has
changed between them. They look quite normal
for a recently married couple.'

Once again, Number 22 was crammed with
the family and it was, Tilly reflected grimly, a
nightmare as they jockeyed around each other
and tried to make their communal living work.

'Others' stairs,' she muttered more than once,
and she even went so far as to look up the trains
to Italy — at best a hugely complicated journey.

240

Instead of packing her bags, Tilly continued to put herself out to be nice to Krista. 'I believe in being European. Inclusive,' she told Julia, who laughed in her superior-sister way. Tilly fished around for another reason to hang on to to prove how civilized she was being. 'If we are decent people, we should do so anyway.' Again, Julia laughed, and not particularly humorously.

One afternoon in early March, Tilly persuaded Krista to accompany her up to the Troubadour cafe in Earls Court.

The days were lighter now, but the previous month's spiteful cold had given way to a dampness which soaked macs and trickled down collars.

'Please let it be summer soon,' Tilly prayed, for she sensed the black dog was stirring and she needed to quieten it with heat and light.

She led Krista into the Troubadour's smoky, crowded bar area and secured them a table. In a corner, a lone guitarist strummed away and sang under his breath. Not very well, it had to be said.

'That's Pete,' Tilly informed Krista as she bore two large G&Ts back to their table. 'He's depressed.'

Krista raised an eyebrow. 'Who is not?'

Tilly liked her better for that riposte.

The G&Ts were warm, and the juniper tasted bitter and disgusting. Whoever had bought it had chosen the wrong black-market deal. She took a second gulp and observed Krista over the rim of the glass. 'Welcome to my world. This place is stuffed with pansies, painters, poets, ponces . . . most of whom are off their heads. Yet . . . ' She

241

held up a finger. 'We are united in not wanting anything to return to how it was before Hitler shook us all up.' She turned her head and called out, 'Is that right, Pete?'

Pete did not miss a beat. 'That's so, Tilly Clifton.'

A lot of people were talking at the same time. Then they weren't, and Pete's dirge-y strumming fell into the hush.

Evidently, the gin met with Krista's approval for she took an enthusiastic mouthful, which amused Tilly. 'Did they teach you to drink gin at the convent?'

Tilly could almost see Krista thinking: *Is she a friend or not?* 'The convent taught me a lot of things.'

Tilly ran up a possible tally. 'Wimples and disciplines? Silence and ridiculous privation? What on earth could a convent possibly be useful for?'

'Sister Elisabeth taught me my English. She had been brought up in England but entered the order when her fiancé was killed in the trenches. She made me look at the map of the world. 'See how pink it is. You'll need to speak their language.' She and I spoke English every day before the Grand Silence. For years. She died in 1941. I don't think she could face it all again. By then I was working in the ministry but I went to her funeral.'

'I like the sound of Sister Elisabeth.'

'It is strange. I hated much of my time there. But now I miss it.' Krista looked down at her almost full glass and pushed it away. 'I am sorry.

I think I have had enough.'

Tilly was struck by the way she articulated 'I am' instead of 'I'm'. That extra care with those words indicated that Krista had to think before she spoke, a feature which set her apart from those with mouthfuls of words tumbling out. The delivery boys, the shopkeepers, the bus conductors . . .

'Did any of the Sisters survive?'

Krista scrutinized Tilly, obviously choosing what she was willing to confide. 'No.'

'I'm sorry.' And she truly was.

'By the end, nobody bothered with funerals. Both men and women were killing themselves or dying. Everyone was looting and drinking bad alcohol, which probably killed them faster than anything.'

The gin was making Tilly feel odd. Detached and — somehow — cut off from emotion. Even so, a flash of empathy for what Krista and the Germans had experienced got through to her. 'Enough of all that. It's,' she looked around at the room, 'it's poetry time.'

A tiny bit unsteady from the gin, she trod over the floorboards to the microphone in the corner.

No one paid much attention but there was nothing unusual in that, and Tilly read out her two latest poems. The first, 'The Tree in My Garden', described the seasons of a tree. She followed that with 'Cloudless', a meditation on the limits of freedom.

Do you see how these simple gulls are
  floating

243

high in the turbulent air?
Playing with the wind
with that freedom we long for?

After a while the audience grew restless and Tilly said into the microphone, 'Bored with me?'

A youth in tight trousers and with a goatee beard called out, 'Utterly, darling.'

Tilly was grinning when she rejoined Krista, who was looking pale and reflective. 'Not bad,' said Tilly. 'I'm usually booed off sooner. I got my favourite one in.' She ran a finger around the inside of her empty glass and licked it. 'It came to me as your country and mine were killing each other. At the time, I was studying photographs and postcards of the French coastline.'

'Stop it.'

'What?' To her surprise, Krista seemed to be furious. Blisteringly so.

'You make it sound like a joke. What happened. But it is *not* a joke. It was not.'

'Hey,' said Tilly.

'It is so like you English. Make fun. Pouf — and nothing matters.'

'Good Lord, you have a temper.'

Her words acted as a check and Krista's face cleared. 'Sorry,' she said. 'Sometimes . . . '

'Yes.'

'I can't help it sometimes. Being angry.' She raised her eyes to Tilly's. 'The strange thing is I am not normally. I was not an angry person before.'

What would be the words to pin down the

intensity reflected in that face, with the neck and chin pulled taut? 'Tell me,' she invited.

Krista shrugged. 'It's nothing. Please don't worry. I think it is the result of a bad diet.'

'It seems everything is the result of a bad diet,' said Tilly drily. Reaching over, she picked up one of Krista's gloves, intending to admire it.

In a flash, Krista had snatched it away from her. 'Those are mine.'

Wild? Animal? No, feral was better. The best word to use.

'Sorry. I didn't mean . . . ' Tilly's eyebrows climbed up her forehead. 'What on earth have you been doing with them? They look expensive.'

A stillness crept over Krista. 'I dug something up. I wasn't thinking about the gloves, which I should have done.'

'It doesn't matter.' Tilly scanned her sister-in-law's troubled face. 'Do you feel more settled with us?'

At that, Krista gave a smile, which transformed her. 'You have been sweet, Tilly. I am grateful.'

'I hope we are friends.'

'I hope so, too.' Krista picked up her glass, endeavoured to take a second mouthful and put it down hastily. 'Tilly, I have to go. I am not feeling so well. A little sick. The gin, I think.' Clutching the gloves, Krista got to her feet with an obvious effort. 'I am grateful that you have been so kind.' She glanced around the smoke-wreathed room. 'But I am tired and I want to go now.'

'Don't let me stop you. You can catch the bus

from the opposite side of the road to where we got off.' The gloves *were* intriguing. 'Where did you get the gloves?'

'Gus bought them for me.'

'Haven't seen a pair like that for years. He must love you.' She leaned over to Krista. 'Can I have your gin if you're not going to drink it?'

'Of course.' Krista stuffed the gloves into her bag.

Pete had resumed his plaintive plucking. 'He isn't very good, is he?' she said.

Gin always made Tilly reckless. She reached out and touched Krista's arm. 'Did something happen with Gus in Berlin, Krista, during the war? He's a good man, and a sweet brother, but war is what it is.' She felt the drumbeat of the past sound in her ear. 'Things happen.' If she wasn't careful, she was going to cry and she slugged down another mouthful of gin.

Krista's haunted features glowed with deep emotion. She moved away. 'Please, Tilly.' And again there was the suggestion of anger. 'That is enough. But thank you for taking me out.' At that, she pushed her way between the barflies and the bodies clustered in the middle of the room and disappeared, leaving Tilly with a thumping heart.

Eventually, Tilly's chest returned to normal.

As she smoked a couple of cigarettes in quick succession, heated, disturbed thoughts sifted through her mind. Oh, bugger my life, she thought, nobody needs me. Would it be good to be needed? In that half state between sleep and consciousness, she had occasionally dreamed of

246

being married and having children, a serene epicentre of fecundity and domesticity. Usually, when she woke up it was to dismiss the idea.

Tilly had spent a great deal of her childhood puzzling over how to get her elder brother and sister to treat her as if she mattered. What a waste of time that had been. Far more profitable had been her determination to think differently from the other two — to the point of contrariness. But at least it meant that she had held her own. Also, the gloss acquired in Switzerland and Florence had given her that extra veneer of superiority.

A tall young man at the bar was staring at her. *Bugger off.* He was wearing a demob suit, was tie-less and his shoes were laced in different colours. Was it the handsome profile (spoiled by a slightly weak-looking chin) and the abundant dark hair? Was it the louche look, combined with a hint of humour, that made her return the stare?

Contact of sorts having been made, he walked over to Tilly's table. 'Hello, would you like to buy me a drink?'

'Not really.' She was cool. 'But what were you having?'

'I like a good gin.'

There was a touch of the East End in his accent.

'So do I.'

'I'll get two then.' He smiled down at her. 'The name is Neville.'

That was a beginning and it would do.

16

Julia was sorting a box of cast-off clothes which had been placed in the foyer of Chelsea Town Hall. She was wearing her overcoat and gloves and wished she had brought her scarf as well because there was no form of heating whatsoever inside.

A fit of coughing forced her to stand upright. Walking down the King's Road from the bus stop, she had run into a demolition gang working on a bombed house. The air was bad and the whiff of decay and gas hadn't been so pleasant either. She had hurried past but not before inhaling what felt like a lungful of dust, then stumbling into a deep puddle.

However, Chelsea Town Hall seemed reassuringly solid as she ran up the steps to the double doors and let herself in. Like so many London institutions, it had been built in a confident, blustering era and its layout and decoration, reflected in its vaulted ceilings, marble columns, wood panelling and ironwork, were embodiments of that optimism. Today, it was filled with teams of commanding-looking women in impregnable tweed skirts and jackets in shades of blue, green and heather. They were organizing a sort-out of clothes into a row of labelled cardboard boxes destined for the needy families crammed into the houses down the King's Road.

Along with Coral, Julia was on Aunt Sarah's

248

team. 'Lovely to see you, darling,' her aunt said as she kissed her on the cheek. 'This is just the sort of thing to get you going again.'

Was it? Julia felt bleak at the prospect.

She looked around at the busy women. They all seemed so purposeful, so keen to do some good and, from the bottom of her heart, she wished that she was cut from the same cloth instead of just pretending to be.

Coral sidled up. 'Do you like my blouse?' She pointed to the cuff which had a minute edging of lace on it. It was actually very pretty and it was a long time since women had been able to obtain clothes with any kind of unnecessary ornamentation on them, let alone lace at the cuffs. 'I do,' replied Julia with a touch of envy.

The clothes smelled and some of them were in bad condition. But they had to do. She shook out a girl's cotton dress that was missing most of its buttons and had a rip under one arm. But it couldn't be thrown away. It would have to be mended, washed and pressed. You couldn't but pay tribute to the spirit which had put this operation together — and Julia's admiration encompassed her aunt, of whom she was fond.

Aunt Sarah and Coral were packing up men's trousers and jackets into one of the boxes. Coral, Julia noted grimly, worked fast and efficiently. Coral would. Julia's parents had admired her cousin and she had been frequently held up as an example to the Clifton sisters. *Very bad tactics*, said Tilly. Over the years, Julia had striven to like her — 'Why bother?' asked Tilly — but had never quite managed it.

As she was thinking these less-than-charitable thoughts one of the helpers, a thin, elderly man whose trousers were far too big for him, came over to consult Coral. Watching her deal gently and respectfully with him, Julia found herself shamed into feeling a flicker of respect.

Aunt Sarah now turned her attention to the children's clothes. 'Julia, I'm counting on you taking some of these back to wash. We can't give them to anyone in this condition.'

Julia's heart sank. 'Aunt Sarah, I'm afraid we haven't much help at the moment.'

Aunt Sarah folded up a pair of trousers which had oil stains on the knees, and a beige-coloured cardigan. 'Would you like me to come over and see what's what? Organize you?'

Coral said, 'I could come, too. The more the merrier.'

'Good Lord, I wouldn't dream of it.' Julia back-pedalled hard. 'Of course I can cope.'

'Doesn't the German girl pitch in?' asked Coral.

The question was not friendly. Her feelings doing an abrupt volte-face, Julia found herself in the position of defending Krista. 'Krista isn't in the best of health.'

'That's all you need,' said Coral, with considerable satisfaction. 'Having to run around after a German.'

'You know, Coral,' said Julia tartly, 'you should do something about the blouse. It's a little tight.'

★　★　★

250

Both sisters were finding it hard to adjust with the house full.

'Lucky I have bolt-holes,' said Tilly.

Julia's mood was not improved by this and she found herself fretting over stupid household things which, anyway, were now Krista's and Ada's business.

'Stop it,' said Tilly. 'It's up to Krista now. Leave her to get on with Ada. Do something else. Nobody thanks you.'

Tilly had been sharper about the situation and it became clear that Julia's efforts were not so much unappreciated as simply not noticed, which was worse. Furthermore, Krista may still have been in poor health, but she was more prepared to fight her corner. Many times Julia asked herself why she crossed swords with her new sister-in-law. Was it because she felt usurped? Or was it because each time she looked at Krista a voice in her head said: *Martin died?*

She set her teeth and resolved to take Tilly's advice.

She was doing fine until she bumped into Krista on the landing on the top floor. Krista was carrying an armful of the most worn blankets.

'Where are you taking them?'

Krista replied that she was going to cut them up for dusters. 'I've been through them. They really are no good.' Her accent was marked, which meant she was tired.

'They're good enough.' Julia attempted to take the pile away from Krista. 'You've no idea how difficult it is to get blankets.'

'Yes, I know,' said Krista. 'But you cannot save these ones. Truly.'

They faced each other. Because Krista's shoe had a slight heel, their eyes were more or less dead level, which Julia found particularly disconcerting. Close to, Krista's skin was beginning to turn a healthy pale instead of a deathly pale. There was a beauty creeping in, washing life into the skin and turning the coppery hair lustrous.

Julia heard her mother's voice issuing through her mouth. 'We'll cut them up and put the sides to the middle. Like we do with the sheets. I have a sewing machine. If we ever get someone to live in again then they can have them.'

Why had she said that? She made it sound as if these people didn't deserve proper conditions.

At that moment, the hatred Julia felt for her sister-in-law almost burned her up. It was hatred of a depth and intensity which she prayed later she would never again experience.

'I suppose you must do as you wish.'

Still clutching the disputed blankets, Krista made to go downstairs. *So be it.* Julia leaned back against the banister to allow her to pass.

'Don't do that,' Krista cried out. 'The rail is loose. You could fall. I nearly did when I came up here.'

Perhaps as a result of the bomb, a couple of the spindles had worked free and the rail was unstable. What with everything else, it had slipped Julia's mind. 'Thank you.' The words were grudging . . . mean.

Sounding in the attic above the two women

252

was a scutter of feet.

Julia looked up. 'Mice are everywhere these days. We must send Gus up with poison to get rid of them.'

So, Julia went about the daily chores: the daily round, the daily cycle of memories. And she tried not to feel vengeful. But what had Gus done to the family? *What had he done?*

Come on, Julia.

Her turmoil was the result of the fear that she was struggling to keep walled up. The fear that, widowed and without much education, there was nothing to justify her existence.

Oh, God, she thought. War had changed her warm, red blood into a cold and spiteful brew.

What was she going to do about it?

★　★　★

The lunch at the Myers' house which Nella and Julia had discussed at length was, at last, happening. More than a little apprehensive, Julia made the short journey between the houses. She did not blame Mrs Myers for not wishing to see the Cliftons. But Nella had insisted, and apparently Teddy had, too, and she had agreed.

'Hello, Julia.' Nella greeted her perhaps a little warily, she thought. 'Mother will be down in a minute.'

Teddy stuck his head around the door of the drawing room. She hesitated. Should she get up from her seat and kiss him, as of old? But Teddy solved the problem. He limped over to her,

253

reached for her hand and held it tightly.

She took back her hand. 'Teddy, we're still living on the memory of the raisins. Thank you again.'

'We're old friends,' he said. 'Aren't we?' He signalled a wish to be magnanimous. 'We must make sure we don't forget it.'

Julia gave a sigh of relief. 'In the circumstances, you are more than generous.'

Nella said, 'It's very boring but the maid has left and we can't get another one. You're going to have to make do with my cooking.'

She left the room. Julia glanced down at her hands in her lap. 'Nella's being heroic.'

'My sister is magnificent. She always was.' Teddy steadied himself on the back of a chair. 'We are all heroic.'

Julia glanced around the room. She had always admired the Myers' Lalique vase in the shape of a shell, and the Colefax and Fowler upholstery in reds and greens. Once upon a time, she had imagined that she might choose similar material for her drawing room.

'You in particular must miss your old life,' Teddy added unexpectedly. 'Apart from anything else, having a position and a home.'

'Oh yes, I do. The companionship. The fun . . . and . . . '

Teddy was regarding her with a dispassion that made her nervous.

'Married life,' burst from her lips and, realizing what she was implying, she felt the colour flame into her cheeks.

Teddy raised an eyebrow. 'Of course.'

'I mean . . .' Julia did not know which way to look.

'Married life,' he repeated, as if chasing a new train of thought. 'There's no need for explanations.' He smiled. 'Don't look so stricken.'

Nella called out, 'Lunch, Julia,' and Julia got to her feet.

Teddy caught her arm. 'I can hear Mother coming downstairs so I'll be quick. Meet me for a drink tomorrow at seven o'clock at the Blue Feather in Greek Street.'

'Soho?' A prickle went through her. 'I couldn't do that.'

'Yes, you could.' He released her. 'I know you better than you think and I've every expectation you will be there.'

Julia went to bed totally resolved that there was no way she would ever meet Teddy in such a place. When she got up the next morning, she decided the opposite. Life was too short, and too serious, to give up on and, after all the agony, she was not going to.

Greek Street was stuffed with people, many of whom did not look very respectable, especially some of the heavily made-up women. Unfamiliar with Soho, which was notorious, Julia had one or two anxious, and extremely self-conscious, moments trying to find the Blue Feather, terrified that she would be taken for a tart.

The pub was noisy and smoky, very crowded and done up with red plush and an overabundance of horse brasses tacked up on the walls, interspersed with prints which veered close to the indecent. It was not the kind of place to which Julia was used to being taken.

Martin. A lump rose into her throat but vanished almost as fast as it arrived.

Teddy was pleased to see her and fussed over the drinks but he also seemed on edge. 'Cocktail to your taste?' he asked.

It was so sad how Teddy had changed, she thought. He was no longer the fun-loving, easy-to-talk-to person he had been. Gus had said so, too. She sipped her gin cocktail; it was eye-wateringly strong. 'Lovely.'

There was an awkward silence. An olive had been speared on to a cocktail stick and added to her drink. Olives still seemed so strange and foreign, and not knowing what else to do with it, she twirled it around the glass. 'Teddy, what's the real reason for this meeting?'

The dead eyes registered amusement — and, suddenly, the old Teddy was back. 'We've always got on, Julia. I thought it would be nice.'

His tone was pleasant, almost gentle, and she settled back on the banquette. On close inspection, there were more than a few traces of the good-looking and debonair man from the pre-war days but he did look older — and her heart twisted. Would Martin have looked much older at the finish? Would she have had to support a man whose courage had almost run out? Whose nerve had gone? Probably. It happened. She knew that. She had seen it several times. Yet, dealing with a burned-out pilot would have been a role that gave her purpose and meaning and she would have tended to him gladly. Lovingly.

'Do you remember taking me and Nella to the theatre? Ages ago. It was very hot and I was terrified my dress would be ruined. You bought us both a fan. Mine had a picture of a Spanish dancer on it. It was before I met Martin.'

Was she gabbling?

Teddy rotated his glass between his fingers and the signet ring he wore on his little finger caught the light. 'I hope you're feeling better, Julia.'

It was on the tip of Julia's tongue to reply that it was obvious that Teddy had not suffered a bereavement, otherwise he would not have asked the question. But his sympathy, the slight hesitancy, made her think better of it. Even if you hated your husband (and she had loved Martin beyond words), you would never really feel better, merely different. It was a question of enduring in the best way possible. 'If you mean, am I coping? Well, yes.' She allowed a heartbeat to elapse. 'Sort of.'

Teddy got the point — that was always part of his attraction. 'Of course one's changed.'

Julia concentrated on her drink. 'The outlook is a bit bleak. Gus . . . Well, you know all about that. It's difficult.' Teddy's expression had been sympathetic, but at the mention of Gus it changed and she glimpsed something else seething underneath. 'Don't look like that, Teddy.'

'Like what?'

'Really angry. Murderous, almost.'

He shrugged.

'Is there anything I can do to make it up?'

'Not really. But you could keep in touch with Nella. She needs support.'

'I will. I am. So will Tilly.' She popped the olive into her mouth, bit down and recoiled from the tartness. 'Teddy, I wanted to say . . . ' She quailed a little. 'It would have been wonderful if Gus and Nella had married. We all get on so well and we understand each other, and Krista is . . . Krista is a stranger.'

Teddy said nothing. Julia looked down at her glass. Good Lord, she had finished the White Lady. Teddy beckoned the waiter and ordered a second. The cocktail had made her bold. 'Also, speaking selfishly, it's difficult for me. Living in the house. But,' she dropped her voice, 'I've nowhere else to go.'

Teddy did not reply immediately. Then he leaned over to Julia. 'You'll marry again, sweetheart. Someone as lovely and good as you.'

Lovely and good.

An extraordinary idea stormed into Julia's mind and, for a second, it made her breathless. 'Like you, Teddy,' she said, and corrected herself: 'Not the lovely bit, but good.'

He smiled his enigmatic smile. That was attractive enough, but it was the flash of vulnerability she imagined she caught that made it doubly so, and the quivering, needy bits of Julia were prodded into life.

Teddy understood her. The notion was so powerful that she felt the stirrings of erotic response. Teddy needed looking after, too. Her thoughts whipped along: *Teddy needs a wife.*

258

'Is the leg still painful, Teddy? Do you need more treatment?'

'Probably. But it will be expensive.' He sounded as though the subject did not interest him very much. 'You expect to get shot in a war. It's lying around on the battleground waiting to get seen to which is the real trial. There was a chap beside me who was much worse off. I think he died.' He reached over and readjusted the overlarge glass ashtray on the table in front of them. 'The bombardment from the Jerries, who were occupying the buildings higher up the mountain, was relentless and it was touch and go if the orderlies would get to us. My toes had gone numb and when I could see my leg swelling I resigned myself to losing it.'

Julia winced.

'After a while I became quite reconciled to the idea. Then I wondered if I was going to live at all and I looked up into the sky, which was the bright blue you only get in Italy, and thought: I might as well die in the spring. It was May, you know.'

Strange responses were shifting deep in Julia — pity and the deepest concern, and anticipation, all mixed up with a curious breathlessness.

'It's funny, Jules.' He used the old nickname. 'I miss the war. I thought I longed for quiet and peace and I do, I really do. But I also long to be back in the excitement and determination of it all. It grows on one. It gives one a purpose.'

This was like the times when she had tried to read articles in Tilly's so-called intellectual magazines and was left feeling totally at sea and angry at herself for being made to feel stupid. 'Teddy, you . . . ' She groped for the words. 'You can't mean that.'

Teddy checked himself. 'I didn't mean to wallow. Time to look forward.' He raised his glass.

Was he attractive? In the past she hadn't noticed, especially after she met Martin. Face to face with the Teddy of now, she sensed a darkness and turmoil in him that made her take note.

'I like to hear about what happened,' Julia said. 'I don't have Martin to talk to and it helps to know what you all felt.' She decided to take the bull by the horns. 'Teddy, you will forgive Gus, won't you? It would be truly awful if we all fell out. We must make the best of it, and without you as a friend life would be bleak. You won't take it out on him?'

'You mean I shouldn't demand an eye for an eye?'

She wasn't sure if he was joking.

More people were arriving at the Blue Feather and the area around the bar had filled up. Julia found herself transfixed with envy of a woman wearing a full, glossy, midnight-blue skirt and she felt weak with the desire to get her hands on something so beautiful.

Teddy's gaze rested on the bottles gleaming behind the bar. 'Julia, you asked me if there was anything you could do. There is one thing. Would you . . . could you . . . entertain someone for me?'

260

Julia did not understand. Then she did. 'Oh,' she said.

'Only for this evening.' Teddy was turning his glass around thoughtfully. 'This chap is a friend of mine and wants some feminine and intelligent company for a couple of hours. You told me that you were missing fun and going out and I thought of you.'

Her disappointment was so intense that she found it almost impossible to speak. 'I thought you and I were spending the evening together.'

He lifted his eyes briefly to hers. 'We are.' Again, the practised twirl of the glass. 'But the idea of you meeting him has just occurred to me. You would be helping me a lot. He's someone with whom I may be doing business. Don't worry; he'll make sure that you get home all right.'

Did solicitors do business in this way? Julia wasn't sure. 'I see.'

'Funnily enough, he seems to be here. Let me introduce you.' He raised his hand and beckoned.

She was utterly bewildered. 'Teddy, wait. What do you want me to do?'

It was too late. A man detached himself from a noisy group around the bar and came over. 'Evening, Teddy.'

At first glance, Julia thought he looked rather dashing. He had a fine-featured face and very blond hair swept back from his forehead.

Teddy introduced them. 'Stephan, this is Julia. Julia, this is a good friend of mine.'

Stephan lifted one of Julia's hands to his lips

261

and kissed it, and Teddy melted away. A few seconds later, he was enveloped into a group standing by the door.

Sitting down beside Julia, Stephan snapped his fingers at the waiter and ordered a whisky. He didn't ask Julia if she would like a refill.

'Unusual name,' she ventured at last.

'German blood somewhere, way back.' He smiled at Julia. 'You look worried.'

'I don't mean to.'

By the time they had finished their drinks, Julia felt better. Stephan was both polite and a good conversationalist and they talked about the war (of course) and, less predictably, horse racing, about which Julia knew little but managed to keep her end up. After a while, Stephan declared that they needed dinner and asked if Julia would join him. Shortly afterwards, they were seated in an Italian restaurant which was decorated with fishermen's nets and Chianti bottles. Having never seen anything like it, she exclaimed over the decor, which amused Stephan. 'You need to travel more.'

They dined on chicken served with an excellent, and foreign-tasting, tomato sauce. It was so good that Julia determined to find the recipe.

'Let's go.' Stephan paid with a twenty-pound note and such a large denomination caused some problems. Julia was intrigued. Twenty-pound notes were rare. As he counted out the tip, he asked casually, 'Do you prefer your place or mine? I'm afraid mine is very much a

262

bachelor's lair. I only keep a room in a mansion block for when I'm in town.'

Julia's heart thumped. 'I think there's been some mistake.'

It was as if a light had been switched off. Stephan's pleasant expression darkened. 'Aren't you making a mistake? That was the deal.'

Julia swallowed, and demanded through dry lips, 'What deal?'

'Oh, come on. You know perfectly well.'

She faltered. 'I thought I was here just to keep you company.'

He shrugged. 'What on earth made you think I was dispensing charity? I haven't spent a good deal of money just for the pleasure of your conversation. I made the arrangement in good faith.'

'What do you mean 'good faith'?' A ghastly thought took shape.

His eyes narrowed. 'Never mind. I can see you are an innocent. Let's just say that dinner was expensive.'

Julia grabbed her handbag. Her heart was now beating so fast that it was in danger of bursting through her dress. Teddy wanted her to sleep with other men. But why? 'I didn't know.' She felt unworldly and unfathomably foolish.

Perhaps it was the sight of her genuine distress that softened Stephan, and he said in a more moderate tone, 'You should sort things out with Teddy. Otherwise, things could get nasty.' Slotting his wallet into his breast pocket, he added, 'For the record, it's not that outrageous. Men want certain things and often they are

263

prepared to pay for them, fair and square. It's a reasonable bargain. Straightforward commerce.' He placed his hands on the table and got up. 'What's wrong with that? The church and moralists would have you believe that plenty is, but it's worth thinking about.'

'Actually . . . ' She was desperate for a coherent opinion. 'Women aren't always averse. When married, you know . . . ' She was too shocked to be articulate. 'What I mean is, it's very clinical. I don't think most women like that sort of arrangement.'

He beckoned for his coat to be brought over. 'How curious. I have found the opposite to be true.' His smile pitied her. 'You should take a good look at yourself, Julia. If the heat in this kitchen is not for you then it would be best to get out.'

With that, he abandoned Julia at the table where, poleaxed by rage and humiliation, she sat on until she pulled herself together and asked for a taxi home.

★   ★   ★

Having spent an uncomfortable, restless night, she telephoned Teddy first thing at home to demand that she came to see him after he returned from work. He had agreed, reassured her that neither his mother nor Nella would be around, and was now propped up against the fireplace while she berated him from the sofa.

'How could you? How could you use me like

that, Teddy? How could you be so disgusting . . . ?' She beat her hand down on a cushion. 'Is this your way of getting back at Gus?'

'Darling Julia, you've got yourself in a terrible muddle. There was nothing sinister or wrong in what I arranged.'

She was dizzy and light-headed from lack of sleep. 'What you were doing was . . . ' Her arm crept across her stomach. 'I can't believe it.'

Teddy seemed genuinely bewildered. 'I thought you might like Stephan. Pleasant company, a meal and some drinks. Nothing more nor less.'

'You were selling me.'

'Don't be so ridiculous.' His gaze was cold and steady. 'You don't seriously think?'

'Yes, I do.'

'Julia — ' Teddy sounded very concerned — 'I think you misunderstood what Stephan said. If you were as shocked as you say you were, you probably weren't taking in what he said properly.'

The blood crept up into her cheeks and she looked away. 'Perhaps I did misunderstand.' She heard him give a faint sigh and felt treacherous at having doubted him.

'In my defence . . . ' Teddy said as he moved away from the fireplace and came and sat down beside her. 'What is my defence? There is no need for my defence, dear Julia. More to the point, did you encourage him in any way? You're experienced enough to know that some men take advantage if they can. They are not always honest, or honourable.'

Any blame was sliding from Teddy. Perhaps

265

she had made the most terrible mistake? Perhaps she had said something which had led Stephan on?

'I did not encourage him on. Not in that way.' Her blush felt painful. 'The only person I could possibly love . . . after Martin.' She lifted her gaze. 'I mean . . . ' What did she mean? What was she thinking? 'All that's finished,' she said.

Teddy raised an eyebrow. 'If you say so.' He seemed to be all kindness and concern. Reaching over, he unlocked Julia's clenched fingers, turned her hand over and traced a circle in her exposed palm. 'Since we are talking about these matters . . . ' He allowed a small pause to elapse. 'Julia, what happened last night is not so sinful, you know. Sexual satisfaction is not a crime. Discreet fun is not a crime. A lot of people agree, more than you would imagine.'

His finger continued to trace soft circles around her palm and she said, 'I can't sleep with someone on the basis of a dinner.'

'Are you so sure?'

Teddy's question drove a sharp, doubting nail into Julia.

He bent down and kissed her on the cheek. 'Think it over.'

Think it over.

17

Krista hunched over the lavatory and, once again, lost her breakfast. After a few minutes, she felt well enough to sluice her face in the washbasin and to return to the bedroom.

Six weeks back from Berlin and it was becoming a constant. At first she thought it might be a stomach bug which she had picked up in Germany, where germs were rife. Then she was pretty sure she had eaten a piece of bad meat from the butcher which had flattened her for some time. On good days, the nausea was just about tolerable. Other days, she collapsed like a rag, retching and gasping.

She had been beginning to feel better and so this episode was a setback. She went and laid down on the bed.

Think of good things. Funny things. Growing things.

The thyme in the tin can had been transported back to Clapham, wrapped in pages which she tore out from *The Practical Manual for British Officers and their NCOs Working in the German British Zone.*

1. Do give orders.
2. See that these are carried out promptly and punished severely if not.
3. Do play your part as a conquering power and keep the Germans in their place.

That journey to London had been much better than the previous one. Gus had snaffled a half bottle of whisky from the NAAFI and, to ease the hunger pangs after they had eaten their rations, they drank it in slugs and talked incessantly about food.

'We'll have to stop,' said Krista after Gus gave an almost unbearable description of *boeuf en daube*. 'We'll drive ourselves mad.'

'I will if you will.'

They laughed companionably, catching each other's eye.

How different the taxi ride to the house from the station had been this time — feasting as she did through the window on a spring panorama, and staring so hard at the colours that they spilled into many shades.

How delicately the daffodils presented themselves in the gardens, and how fresh and vivid the spectrum of greens unfolding on the Common. As a child, she had imagined she could listen to the hiss of leaves expanding and buds crackling open, and those old habits of mind persisted. Was it possible? Maybe. She thought of feeling petals brushing against her fingers, of smelling apple blossom and damp earth, and of the sight of tiny narcissi trumpeting the arrival of spring.

Something immensely fragile and barely there began to take root in her chest. It was too soon to call it hope. And too soon to call it optimism. But it was there.

Gus poked his head around the bedroom door. He took one look at her and ordered her to make an appointment with Dr Lawson.

'What can he do? This is the result of what happened during the war. Starvation has repercussions. If I have a bug or food poisoning, it settles in for the duration.'

He stood over her on the bed. 'Are you listening to me? He can keep an eye on you. That's what Dr Lawson can do.'

'It will be expensive to see him? It is nothing. It is my body readjusting to what happened to it. You know that.'

'Krista, look at you.'

Krista got out of bed. Despite her thickening hair, she knew from the bathroom mirror that she was paper-white and puffy-faced. However, if she was still thin, she was positively plump compared to what she had been. 'I'll make an appointment.'

'Good.' He dropped a kiss on to her cheek. 'My car has come. I'll be late for dinner.'

She patted his lapel. 'It sounds so normal, Gus. A man warning his wife that he will be late home.'

Gus grinned but, she noted, he was already moving towards the door. 'It does.'

At ten o'clock, Krista set out for the doctor's surgery, which was on the north side of the Common. She had a sketchy map with her, drawn by Tilly, and stopped at intervals to consult it. After a while she grew uneasy. A sixth sense told her that she was being watched.

'Listen,' Gus had warned her, 'the Soviets will try to penetrate our intelligence services. It is possible, just possible, they might want to use you.'

Yet the Common appeared perfectly normal. An odd ray of sun struggled through grey clouds, mud from the disintegrating trenches was trampled into large areas of the grass and an obstruction in the road had caused the traffic to bunch up on the north side. A few late commuters hurried towards the entrance to the Underground and shoppers headed for the High Street.

According to Tilly, there was a network of underground bunkers under the Common. 'God knows *what* went on in them.' Krista found the idea both compelling and repulsive. So much in Germany had gone on under the surface that she distrusted the very notion. The gap between the hidden and the open was always dangerous.

What was she expecting?

A malignant succubus to fly down out of the sky and scoop her up?

She quickened her pace, the feeling of being watched fell away, and by the time she reached her destination she was concentrating on other things.

At the surgery the practice nurse conducted her into the doctor's room. Dr Lawson wore a conservative three-piece tweed suit and too much hair grease. He was writing a prescription and did not look up as Krista sat down in the chair opposite him. Half a minute ticked by. Eventually, he blotted his work and asked Krista what he could do for her. While Krista explained, he took notes, then he asked for her medical history, plus some searching questions about her periods and bowels, which she

270

answered with no hesitation.

Dr Lawson professed surprise. 'You're very open, Mrs Clifton. Most of my young wives find these sorts of questions hard to answer.'

It was not a compliment.

'In Germany we like to be frank.'

She caught the dislike that he tried to mask. 'You are still recovering from a prolonged experience of want. That will have put a great strain on your systems.' He made it sound as if Krista's predicament had been her fault.

Whatever his feelings, Dr Lawson was a professional. He made a thorough examination, asked for a urine test and told her to return in two weeks' time. It could be one of three things, he said, which included advanced anaemia. 'You have some injuries,' he added.

'Which?'

'Which might give you problems later. But there are procedures which can deal with them.'

He did not ask how they had occurred and she wasn't going to tell him.

'And,' He did not look at her. 'These flashbacks you describe, and your nightmares, are no doubt associated with your experiences during the war. They may have laid down a neurological pattern. But I doubt they are long-lasting. Once you have settled into your domestic life, you'll find you will be as right as rain.'

When she arrived back at the house, Tilly was hovering in the hall in her outdoor things. 'Where have you been? Oh, never mind. I want to take you somewhere.'

She looked particularly colourful and her cheeks were flushed. Dragging Krista out of the house, she banged the door shut and said, 'Oh, help. Do you have the key?' She tapped her head. 'I was forgetting. It doesn't matter. There's always a spare key kept under the stone by the steps, which no one else knows about except Nella.'

'Where are we going?'

'To a bookshop. It's about time you read some English books. I've been meaning to take you there for some time but you keep coming and going.'

She set a cracking pace and Krista had to beg her to slow down. 'Sorry, sorry,' Tilly said.

Krista hadn't been here long but already the High Street was changing and commercial life was getting under way. Intriguingly, it seemed to consist of repair shops — cobblers, electrical repairers, a dolls' hospital. A pen hospital? Had Krista read that correctly?

Many of the women thronging it were still thin and pale, with dingy clothing and unwashed hair. No one had enough soap to wash hair regularly, although Krista had determined to hoard enough to wash hers as frequently as possible. Most people's teeth required dentistry and she had, as yet, to spot a pair of stockings with no darns in them, let alone a pair of nylons.

The bookshop turned out to be Laube's, the one that had been recommended by the kindly woman in the baker's queue and which had been closed when Krista originally visited it. The same volumes were still being displayed in the window.

This time there was an 'Open' sign on the door.

Tilly pushed open the door and the bell rattled. Surrounded by ledgers in green covers, a man sat at the desk. He was elderly, a little worn, clean-shaven and had probably been once very good-looking. 'Good morning.'

His accent was unmistakeably German and, on hearing it, a dam broke in Krista. Homesickness overpowered her. Sinking down into the chair in a corner, she covered her face with her hands.

'Krista! Don't. There's no need,' said Tilly.

Krista pulled herself together and said, '*Guten Morgen.*'

At the sound of his language, Herr Laube at first looked wary, then defensive. About what? Her? His being German? Then he smiled. 'How unexpected,' he replied in German, the gentleness of his tone inviting her to share their common bond. 'But how delightful.' It was clear that he would have liked to have continued speaking in German, but courtesy to Tilly prevented him and he switched into English. 'How can I help?'

Tilly knew precisely how. 'My sister-in-law should read some English books. Novels, I think, and some poetry. We have some at home but we need something modern. I don't think *Pride and Prejudice* will quite do the trick.'

'I have a couple of novels.' Herr Laube moved towards the shelves, which were stuffed with a mixture of new and second-hand books but he located two volumes unerringly. 'There you are: *The Death of the Heart* and *A Handful of Dust*.'

273

He laid them gently in Krista's lap.

She glanced at them. 'The last novel I read was *All Quiet on the Western Front*. It was banned, you know, by Hitler because it was not war-like enough.'

'There is no war in these novels,' he said.

Tilly had moved off to the poetry section in the back of the shop.

'Where do you come from?' asked Krista. 'Why did you come? Tell me, please.'

Herr Laube was reluctant. 'Koblenz. In the early thirties. My wife and I saw the way the wind was blowing.'

'And was it easy?'

He looked sadly at Krista. 'No, it has not been easy. Why would it be? But if it has not been easy, it has been safe, in a manner of speaking. Yes?' He gestured at the window. 'Be careful, please, coming here. When the war came, they questioned me a lot. They still watch me.'

'They?'

'The British state. Very often a man is out there with a notebook.' This was uttered with a glint of humour. 'I imagine what he is writing. 'Subject opens shop. Subject dusts books.' Do you think that would be helpful?'

Krista laughed.

'But you will be all right, I'm sure.' Herr Laube had resorted to a startling stage whisper. 'The English may be awful but they are also kind. Look at me. Most people don't remember where I come from.'

He was lying and she knew it, but she was touched by his efforts to reassure her.

'I do not want to forget.' She fingered the books. 'Which should I read first?'

'*A Handful of Dust.* It is a book to shock. All about the English upper classes.'

Tilly emerged from the back of the shop holding a well-thumbed magazine. 'Wonderful, a back copy of *Horizon*. Herr Laube, will you let me know if you get any more of these? How much do we owe you?'

Krista took Herr Laube's advice and tackled *A Handful of Dust* first. It was funny and sharp but she was bewildered by the author's dislike of women. She also thought, as she told Gus when they were getting ready for bed, that some of the behaviour in the novel was quite mad. 'The main character is very passive,' she pointed out. 'His house is falling down and his wife is silly and he doesn't do anything about it. Am I supposed to admire him?'

A tousled Gus emerged from the dressing room in his dressing gown, a much-loved, grey wool one which made him look ridiculously young. From it poked his legs in striped pyjamas which, she had learned, were also much treasured and much repaired. 'It's a satire.'

'Oh. I think I might try something else, then. More real.'

Gus moved around quietly, opening and closing a drawer, adjusting the curtains. Her thoughts drifted pleasurably. Who could have painted this utterly normal domestic interior scene? Vermeer? Yes. Only he could convey the inner stillness and quietude of this particular moment.

275

She could not resist it. 'Are the English so unfeeling?'

'Certainly not,' he replied gruffly.

'Oh, but I think they are,' she countered, and hugely enjoyed his outrage until he realized she was teasing him.

★   ★   ★

She was not feeling any better when she returned to Dr Lawson's surgery for her appointment. Seated across his desk from her, he tapped his fingers together and confirmed a diagnosis.

'You don't seem pleased, Mrs Clifton,' he commented. 'Aren't you?'

'Yes, I am pleased,' she answered but she may as well have substituted 'dumbfounded'.

She chose a route back across the Common. It had rained while she had been in the surgery so the ground was slippery underfoot and she opted for the least muddy path. The foliage on the trees was now well advanced but not yet luxuriant enough to screen off the war detritus of metal and wood and heaps of soil still littering the turf.

Someone *was* following her.

The feeling was so strong, so concrete, she did not need corroboration.

Who? Why? Krista made a slow inspection of the people in her line of sight, searching for the kind of figure who had become so familiar to Berliners. Men in trilbys and, very often, long leather coats, who moved slowly.

She was shaking. Fright? Elation? This is England, she told herself, which was not much use: she had grown too used to anticipating the worst.

Turning for home, she caught sight of a woman wearing a blue coat and brown felt hat walking towards her. Her high-heeled shoes were highly polished, and almost certainly clipped her walking pace. Under the hat brim a quantity of light-brown hair was drawn back from her face and allowed to fall down over her shoulders. She was pretty and soft-looking and very feminine.

Krista unlatched the gate to Number 22. As she drew closer, the woman in the blue coat slackened her pace and Krista recognized her. Stepping back on to the pavement, she called out, 'You are Nella, I think? You came to the house with the carol singers.'

The woman shifted a package tied up with string from one hand to the other. 'I am.'

Krista found herself gnawing her lip in the old way. 'I want to say I am sorry.'

Nella raised her eyebrows. 'Don't try to make this into a polite exchange.'

'Have you been following me?' asked Krista.

'No,' Nella replied flatly. 'I live two streets away and I've been walking up and down this road all my life.'

'Yes, of course,' said Krista.

The other woman backtracked a little. 'But, yes, in a way I have followed you.' She gestured to the Common. 'I saw you the other day, walking towards the doctor's surgery. I couldn't help wondering . . . ' She cut herself off. 'Wondering why I lost out to you.'

'Take a look.' Krista spread her arms wide. 'As much as you wish.'

A drop of water fell on her face. An English spring rain was beginning to fall.

'I want to know why you came here.' Nella's cheeks were also wet. She wiped them with the back of a glove.

Krista was horrified. 'Please,' she said. 'You will ruin your beautiful gloves if you do that.'

Nella pulled them off and dropped them into her bag. 'It won't end well, you know. This marriage.'

'You do not know that. No one knows that. And you have no right to say it.'

'My brother could make trouble for Gus,' Nella said. 'In all sorts of ways. At the club, for example. In the places where men meet and which they consider important.' She glanced towards Number 22. 'You know, Teddy and the council are working together on plans for new buildings. Houses will have to be demolished. Teddy has a lot of influence over that.'

The threat was crude, almost laughable, but also saddening. It was being made by someone for whom making threats was so obviously unusual.

'Are you saying what I think you are saying?'

The rain was gathering in earnest and both women were shivering. Nella shrugged.

Krista was very polite. 'I know about threats. You do not frighten me. And you have no right.'

'For sure, I don't. But who's going to know? You won't tell Gus because he would have to confront Teddy, and you and I both know that

Gus confronting Teddy is not a good idea.'

Having receded, her nausea was creeping back. 'Gus and Teddy were very close?'

'Sewn together,' said Nella.

The rain slid under Krista's collar, pooling in the gap between her breasts, and the ends of their hair dripped. 'We're getting wet,' she said.

'Yes, we are.'

Neither of the women moved.

'Gus married me. I am sorry for your pain, truly sorry, but it is done and I did not know about you.'

Nella searched in her handbag, found a handkerchief and dabbed it over her face, leaving a faint imprint of face powder on the cotton.

'I hope that you find someone else.'

Nella gave an outraged gasp. 'And you should go back where you belong.'

In the distance a small boy and a girl ran over the Common, shrieking as they kicked up puddles. A woman hurried after the children, shouting for them to be careful.

'I think I must say goodbye.' Krista let herself in at the gate and went up the front steps.

Behind her, Nella raised her voice. 'I'm sure papers could be easily arranged if you agreed to go without a fuss. Your family in Germany would have you back.'

Krista turned round. 'But I have no family.'

'Ah. But you must have someone. You could live with them until things become normal again.'

Nella had followed Krista up the steps, her feet in the high heels unsteady on the wet stone.

The expression in the soft and disarming eyes was pleading and desperate, and tears began to roll down her face. 'Gus loves me,' she said. 'I know he does. He can't love *you*. I know him through and through. You *don't*.'

'I do know him.'

Nella stared at Krista. 'You know nothing about Englishmen.'

Once again, Krista was back in the rubble of Berlin. Vicious cold gripped her so tightly that she was breathless. Her stomach, so empty it was feeding on itself, craved food, and yet it didn't. She remembered folding her arms across her rattling abdomen when Gus and his men piled into the chapel. *Again? Do men never stop?* He and his men were drunk and she knew from experience that it would be useless to shout: *I am too sore and used. Too used.*

'I know enough.'

The trick was to endure, and by enduring you became stronger than they were. Krista had learned . . . Lotte had learned . . . that nothing distinguished one set of warring men from another. Whatever their stripe. They were one and the same animal. Whichever reasons and pretences they offered — political imperatives, defending oppressed nations, defeating a tyrant — what they did came from a primeval urge to demonstrate their power.

Could she possibly confront the kind, pretty Nella with what she knew? Could she tell her that in order to survive you would do most things? And that rape was too commonplace to comment on? In all likelihood, Nella would

280

know nothing, believe nothing, of what Krista could tell her about drunken men in wartime.

With her hand on the door, Krista thought about unspoken truths and spoken ones and how to choose which was appropriate. 'But even if I wanted to go back, I cannot. Not now.'

'I know Berlin is occupied by the Soviets, but you can return to the Allied area, I'm sure.'

Krista turned round. 'I do not mean that.'

'Then what do you mean?'

She had the power to chase a beaten Nella away, and it was sweet. But she also had the power to withhold. 'Never mind.'

Closing the front door on Nella, she waited until she heard her footsteps die away and then sighed with relief.

★　★　★

'Don't stop.'

Gus appeared in the door of the garden shed.

Singing a snatch from a Verdi mass, Krista was lining a cardboard box with the remnants of *The Practical Manual for British Officers and their NCOs*. It was — absolutely — the best use for them. Later, she would plant the box with seeds.

Restoring order had been fun. Next to be sorted were the shelves; they were still littered with redundant seed packets, broken pots and fertilizer powder. None of those were salvageable and, although she found it hard to throw anything away, she had managed to build a throw-out pile of the heavily damaged seed trays and pots. This had released sufficient space for two people — just — to crowd inside.

'Keep singing,' said Gus. 'Please.'

Smiling at him, she sang the next ten bars. Gus leaned back against the shed wall and closed his eyes, remaining in that pose after she had finished. 'I imagine you learned to sing like that at the convent.'

Massed lit candles. Musty incense. Female voices climbing ever higher. The shudder of the singers' bodies in their grey-and-white robes. Sopranos singing of God's omniscience.

The familiar images chased through her mind; unloved, and yet truly mourned.

'Yes, I did.'

Gus pushed himself upright. 'Julia tells me you were looking for me.'

It was late in the afternoon and she guessed Gus had been drinking, something which she had learned to expect when he went off to meet the boss in London's clubland. The question pushed its way past her lips. 'Gus, are you going to continue to work for these people?'

His expression darkened. 'What's bothering you?'

She addressed her next remark to the space above his left shoulder. 'Only that those sort of people never let you go. In Germany, once they had their hooks into you, that was it.'

'Tell me about it.' Gus was impatient.

She punched the last bit of the *Practical Manual* down into the box. 'I *know* those people. Everyone did. They do what they want. They kill if they want.'

The silence imposed by terror was unforgettable. So, too, was the torture of anticipating the worst and the secret people were past masters at spinning it out. Everyone had had friends or acquaintances who had brushed up against them, and their techniques. Some anticipated the outcome and took their own lives.

'You can't back out now,' he was saying. 'Nor can I. Don't desert, Krista. We will manage.' It was a question. 'Between us?'

His appeal made her feel ashamed of having stirred up the questions, especially now. 'Do not worry, we will manage,' she conceded. Nudging the discard pile at her feet, she asked, 'Can you help me clear this stuff up?'

Gus surveyed Krista's handiwork. She had decided to keep a fork, a rake, a shovel and a spade, two trowels and a hand rake which was missing a couple of its tines. These she had cleaned and oiled and stacked against the shed wall. There was also an antique blowtorch and a metal wall sign which advertised Smith's garden tools: 'Horticultural providers'. Unusually for her, she stumbled over the words as she read them aloud.

Gus picked up the sack which he had found lying in the road outside the house. 'Shall we use this?'

Taking a deep breath, Krista tipped the rubbish into it. *There.* She had thrown things out. Gus laughed. 'That wasn't so bad, was it?' He grabbed the neck of the sack. 'Pass that twine and I'll tie it up.'

She didn't do as he asked. Instead, she held up the pot of thyme, which she had replanted into one of the intact flowerpots. 'Gus, you know you

283

sent me to Dr Lawson? He has told me something very . . . very unexpected. I . . . we are having a baby.'

Gus dropped the sack and shards of earthenware bounced over the floor of the hut. 'A baby? When?'

'In the autumn. September, I think.'

He grabbed her by the shoulders and she smelled the brandy on his breath. 'But you must have known for some time.'

'No,' she replied simply. 'I did not understand my body.'

She tried to read his face. Delight? Shock? Disbelief?

'But this is wonderful! Wonderful,' he said. 'I can't quite take it in.'

She clung to the 'wonderful' as reassurance. 'Dr Lawson says it is possible that my bones have suffered and I was anaemic but it does not seem to have mattered in the end. I suppose I have been so much better fed.'

'Just give me a minute,' he said.

She squeezed past him and wedged the flowerpot with the thyme into the patch of earth which, earlier, she had dug and raked over. It was sufficiently sheltered by the shed and the herb would have a head start. 'It would make an interesting study, how food affects us. I mean, I never thought about food in that way before the war.' She was trying to fill the awkwardness. 'Professor of Food.'

'Nutrition would be the term, I think.' Gus sounded shell-shocked.

She was crouched down with her back to him.

'Are you not pleased, Gus? Tell me.'

He pulled her to her feet. 'Look at me. I am pleased, so pleased I can't express it adequately. It wasn't something I had been thinking about. That's all.'

She clung to his hand. 'I will do my best to produce a good, healthy baby for you.'

'And for *you*. And you will.' He turned over her hand and inspected the palm; it was streaked with dust and soil. Tiny hemp filaments clung to her skin. 'I will help you. We will all help you. Julia. Tilly. Especially Tilly.'

She thought about the baby-fat little arms, tiny clothes and demands and remembered the bundles of rags moving around the ruins of Berlin shouting for chocolate.

Do you remember, Lotte, when Sister Eva gave us a lollipop and we shared it? Do you remember when we rowed out on to the lake and it was so silent and still? You said it was the most beautiful, happy day you had ever had.

Her throat caught. 'I did not think it would be possible to ever have a baby.'

Gus smiled: slightly drunken, tender, delighted. 'Apparently, it is.'

They went back into the shed, cleared up the mess and tied the sack with the twine. Gus carried it around the side of the house and stacked it by the front wall where the refuse men would collect it.

18

Pete warned Tilly about Neville. 'He's got form, darling. It's said, and who knows, that he did for the husband of one of his lovers. Body found in the river. Nothing's been proved, but the rumours stick around.'

Did that make Neville more touchable, or less? These days many had killed. In their planes, with their guns, in their ships, or in their hearts as they sat in their homes with one thought on their mind: *We must beat the enemy.*

He proved to be an astonishing liar, so good that she was filled with admiration. 'Why bother not to tell the truth?' she demanded when she discovered that, far from being the son of a milkman as he said he was, Neville was the illegitimate son of a well-known peer. Even so, he was never going to be on *Tatler*'s social list. So what?

'Darling, you're not with the times. None of us are allowed to be well-bred any longer. You have to come from the gutter to get anywhere.'

She laughed. 'I agree it's more interesting. But I won't believe anything you say from now on.'

A mistake. Neville looked thunderous and vanished for a couple of days, which affected Tilly more than she expected it to. (Eventually, she tracked him down to a dive off Brewer Street and told him that, in future, he could tell her what he pleased and, if she didn't believe him, she would keep quiet.)

Neville's second lie was his declaration that he had fallen in love with her on sight. Not only did he declare his love. He also claimed that Tilly was the woman he had been searching for all his life. Listening to it lit a small flame of happiness deep within her but, true to her undertaking, she did not question him, even when she discovered that Neville also slept with men. There was one thing, however, which could not be ignored.

'Why did you tell me you were thirty when you're only twenty-five?'

'Because. At thirty you sound less of a sponger.'

'No, you don't.'

Neville kissed her. 'Despite everything, Tilly. You are an innocent.'

A silent cry went up in Tilly's heart and she struggled for control. After a minute, she managed, 'Now I'm convinced the sexes are totally different. No woman would *ever* add five years to her age.'

Tilly spent a lot of time in Neville's digs off the King's Road (abandoning Marcus, who didn't like it). Or, rather, in his studio, which in Neville's case was a flexible term as not much creation of any sort went on in it. Many of her friends were horrified by him and they were right to be. However charming and sexy he was, Neville *was* a sponger.

Tilly didn't care. 'Let's just get through the days,' she said.

'No problem with that.'

Between them, they managed to become

287

thoroughly and happily unhealthy in a very short space of time, overdoing the gin and the Bennies, to which Tilly had become attached, and never bothering to eat or to sleep properly. She knew she ran the danger of damaging her mind, her moods, her well-being, but she didn't much care.

One morning, Tilly woke up feeling so bad that she thought she was dying. Rolling over, she prodded Neville awake. 'We've got to get away. To the country or something.'

Neville opened an eye. 'Don't do nature.' He fell back into sleep, waking up a few minutes later. 'Where do you suggest?'

She recollected the trips she took into the country when she was in Florence. 'Pete knows someone, who knows someone, who has a house in Italy. We'll go there.'

Neville groaned. 'Adam and Eve stuff?'

'It's in a remote valley in Umbria somewhere.' She was a bit vague about where but that was easy to solve. 'It's been empty since before the war because no one could get there. Obviously.'

'That settles it. It will be unliveable. Think bird dung and beetles, Tilly.' He rested a proprietorial finger on her thigh. 'You won't like them.'

'Possibly the Partisans lived in it.' Tilly was thoughtful. 'Apparently, they can be quite violent. Or were. It hasn't any electricity but it does have running water.'

'Well, that's all right then.'

'Listen to me. If we can get there, it's cheap. Think of the summer. Nightingales and olives.'

'And peasants who will think you're a whore. And dogs. Horrible dogs. Anyway, you can't cook, Tilly.'

'I can.'

'If you call making a cup of tea cooking.'

Tilly slapped him playfully on the stomach and he pulled her to him.

It was early morning for them and the lovemaking was unsubtle but delicious. Halfway through, he asked her: 'Why do you want to go?'

Because she felt that she was now the ghost of herself? Once upon a time she had been unafraid, now she was mired in shivery fear and self-loathing. There was nothing brave about her. Nothing admirable either.

She wanted to step lightly over brown, summer-dry earth. She wanted to immerse herself in the aromas of thyme and marjoram. She wanted to forget.

Like a drowning person gulping for air, she yearned for the remote Umbrian cottage shimmering in the heat, where she would be free from the demons massing in their battalions in her mind.

and hear, perhaps, distant buzz of talk
rise through the chestnut trees, the *paysans*
sun-wrinkled, square, exchanging pleasant-
    ries
beside spruce carrots and plump aubergine

'Tilly?'

His whiskied breath caressed her cheek.

She moved restlessly under him. 'Get on with it, darling.'

Being sick into the basin in the Ladies at the Troubadour was a relief. It got rid of the weight sitting in Tilly's stomach and cleared her head, which meant she was lighter and better able to keep on top of things.

'All right, darlin'?' enquired Jackie, a girl with whom she had struck up a conversation before bolting for the lavatories. 'Best out, I always say.'

Unable to speak, Tilly waggled her fingers at Jackie.

'Brandy settles the stomach.' Jackie went into a cubicle, banged it shut and urinated.

Tilly raised her head. Was Neville around? It all depended. She liked it when he was there but survived more than adequately when he wasn't. 'The sun doesn't shine out of your arse,' she told him. 'God, no,' he replied with a grin.

Poetry. Bennies. Gin. Troubadour. More Bennies. More gin. Sex somewhere along the line. She and Neville were enjoying themselves to the hilt and he had promised some new stuff he was going to give her when he had got hold of it. He didn't know quite what it was, but he had been told it was good. For a little while longer it was going to be fun. After that, she would behave herself. But not yet.

The days, then the weeks, had clattered by since she had met Neville. To her surprise, Tilly was tranquil, at moments even happy — something which she never felt she would feel again — and the black dog was in its kennel. So, it went on.

Now summer was almost here. Granted, a milksop kind of early summer, the kind in which England specialized.

> The blaze and crackle of Italy
> Does not singe the sodden rolls of English
>   green.

It certainly didn't.

She wiped her face with her handkerchief and, digging into the pocket of her green skirt, she found her comb and tugged it through her hair, which fell lustrously back into place. Lucky Tilly. Her hair never failed her, and she was well aware this wasn't fair on the good girls with bad hair who behaved themselves.

There was one small cloud on the horizon. The urge to write appeared to have left her and she could not summon it back. It was temporary, she promised herself. *It was*. And she needed to believe it because the terror of not having poetry in her life was too great to contemplate. Not that she went on about it. Certainly not to Neville, who got bored by that sort of thing. He would never understand that, without poetry, the world seemed out of whack. But why should he? There were plenty of things that she didn't understand about him.

The face looking back at her from the meagre mirror was drained but composed. Feeling more normal, she took herself back into the bar and settled herself into her seat.

'How about that drink, darlin'?' said Jackie. 'You did say.'

Clearly, Jackie was a professional cadger and had spotted Tilly from the off. What the hell? She pushed three shillings across the table. 'On me.'

She had not been back to Clapham for a week, having fled from the house where they had to jostle to use the bathroom. 'I can barely tolerate her,' Julia had muttered in Tilly's ear, meaning Krista. 'I shouldn't say this but everything she does undermines the way I've been doing things.'

'Julia, calm down. You'll get wrinkles.'

'We're being pushed out.'

'That was likely to happen when Gus married.'

With her arm clenched across her middle, a tense, indignant Julia pointed to the Common through the window. 'It's strange to think there's hardly a house intact and people are living stacked on top of one another like sardines.'

'You realize you've just made the best argument for being very, very nice to Krista?' said Tilly drily.

'Where would I go?' Julia scratched a fingernail down the window pane and it gave off a thin, nerve-grating screech which dried up the inside of Tilly's mouth. 'Martin's pension is tiny.'

'You're the wifey type, Julia. You'll get married again. I guarantee it.' She had slipped an arm around Julia's surprisingly narrow waist.

'I miss . . . being married. Companionship and . . . you know.'

This was a surprising admission from her buttoned-up sister. 'You mean sex?'

Julia went red. 'It's difficult without . . . when

you have got used to it . . . to think that you might not have it again because there are no eligible men left.'

Tilly's lips twitched. 'You can take a lover.'

'*Tilly!*'

'Don't be so stuffy. It happens all the time.'

Julia grasped the curtain so tightly that the curtain rings rattled. 'Sometimes, I dream that Krista is dead.' She looked at Tilly. 'And the awful thing is that, when I wake up, I wish it were true.'

Tilly was a little shocked. 'For heaven's sake, talk to Gus and see if you can sort out something.'

Long ago, in the days when Gus wore short trousers and Tilly smocked dresses — the era of seaside holidays, slabs of Wall's ice cream between wafers, and tree-climbing — Gus had always been the one to turn to. He was the brother who stood up for his sisters: a very young knight in armour. One never-to-be-forgotten time he fought the street bully, who had tripped up Julia. Gus's bloody nose had been a badge of honour and talked about for weeks.

Actually, on his good days, Neville reminded her a bit of Gus.

Tilly got up and asked for some water at the bar.

It hurt to remember the three of them, small, flitting ghosts of memory, and the innocence and solidarity they had surrendered to adulthood.

Busy reminiscing, she did not notice Gus until he touched her on the arm. She jumped. 'What

293

are you doing here?'

Since their return from Berlin, Gus was looking much better. He dressed more casually than normal, his hair shone and his skin had a new glow. 'Krista's sweet-talked the fishmonger into selling her some extra cod and we thought we should all share it.'

'*Krista* did? Gosh, peace has broken out. Any special reason?'

'Perhaps,' said Gus.

Tilly peered at him. 'How did you know I was here? No, don't tell me. It was your wife. I should never have lured her to my den.' She shrugged. 'No good deed ever goes unpunished.'

Gus grinned. 'That's better.' He hooked his arm under Tilly's. 'Krista instructed me to fetch you back in a taxi.'

Why not? Tilly gathered up her bag. 'I'll just leave a message at the bar to tell someone where I am,' she told Gus.

He looked enquiring. 'Anyone I know?'

'No.' Unsure of many things except this one, Tilly was going to keep Neville private.

The daylight hit Tilly's retinas unpleasantly as Gus hailed a taxi and bundled her into it. The interior smelled of leather and cigars, suggesting the rich and easy life. Tilly huddled in one corner and Gus sat upright in the other.

'Quite like the old days,' she said, thinking of the times after Julia had got married when she and Gus would find themselves at the same parties and come home together.

'Do you miss those times, Tilly? I do.'

From under her lids, Tilly studied her brother.

294

Despite the new, healthy look, she had an idea that he was more troubled, more serious. She couldn't put her finger on what exactly but her instinct told her strongly that something was going on. Julia had also changed, and how on earth Tilly herself had developed her own blend of rebellion and predisposition to excess she could not say. With parents like theirs, it was almost impossible for the girls not to have ended up donning the twinset and pearls and marrying a suitable man in order to live a blameless life of bone-deep boredom. Oops a daisy . . . she checked herself. That was more or less exactly what Julia had done.

Gus was questioning her in his old sweet and reassuring way. 'What are you playing at, sis? Trying to kill yourself?'

'Don't be stuffy.' To her horror, tears sprang into her eyes. 'I'm making a life for myself, actually. You are, too, though God knows what you get up to in your work.' She glared at him. 'As for Julia, well, it's poor Julia, but I expect she will find something to do, or someone to marry and, pouf, all will be well.'

'You should know by now that I don't mind what you do. You could perform stark naked at the circus as far as I'm concerned, so long as you are happy.'

'Truly?' Tilly was delighted. 'Gus, you always were a darling.'

He took up one of Tilly's hands and dropped a light kiss on to it. 'Julia tells me Coral is worried that you are being ruined.'

Tilly snorted. 'I think Coral means that she is

worried that she's *not* being ruined.'

Gus laughed companionably. 'Most people are not adventurous and it can make them spiteful if they see someone who is.'

The green spaces of Battersea Park rolled past the taxi window. There were new lines on Gus's face, most markedly running from nose to chin. If she squinted, she could imagine those lines deepening and sharpening, incising into his face, and that was how Gus would look when he was old.

'I do love you, Gus,' she said.

The taxi driver drew to a halt at a junction and Gus leaned forward and peered through the taxi window.

'Gus, what is it?'

A four-door Austin had drawn up alongside them, driven by a dreary-looking man in a bowler hat. Otherwise the road was almost empty.

Both cars eased left at the junction. The Austin idled beside them for a few more seconds before cutting in front and pulling away with a grinding of gears. The taxi driver swore.

'Are we being followed?' asked Tilly, who was beginning to enjoy herself. 'You are acting as if we're in a bad film. I like that.'

Gus brushed whatever it was aside. He sank back on to the leather upholstery. 'If someone *is* following us, he certainly drew attention to himself, which is the cardinal sin.'

The malicious imp unleashed in Tilly was, by now, doing a merry dance. 'By the way, did Julia tell you she's been seeing Teddy?'

'She did.'

'Teddy invited her out and introduced her to a friend. She came home reeking of fags and booze.'

'What are you talking about?'

He sounded furious. Too late, Tilly realized she should have kept her trap shut. Put it down to the Bennies, she thought wearily. They left the brain as flat as a pancake. Oh, what the hell, she thought. 'Teddy took Julia out and she was wined and dined by one of his friends. I got it out of her.'

The taxi halted and Gus searched for his front-door key. They got out and walked up to the front steps.

'What's our Julia doing with Teddy?' asked Tilly.

'They were always friends.' He pushed open the door. 'Are you seeing Teddy?'

'I've met Nella for tea. These days, I find Teddy a bit creepy. He's a walking bomb. So wrought up he's ready to explode. I steer clear.'

Tilly went up to her room, and thought despairingly of the next few days during which she would sober up, get clean of the pills and try to sleep properly. All excellent objectives until boredom slithered into view which, she knew very well, it would. She also knew that excess did not do precisely what it said on the tin. If she was strictly truthful — if — each time she indulged and went on a bender, the satisfactions were harder to achieve. Or, rather, less satisfactory, which meant that the excess in itself became the imperative. Having analysed this, she

297

found it to be true. However, the experience was still sufficiently novel to remain enticing. Her dabblings played brilliant havoc with her mind and forced her to think of unthinkable things which had nothing to do with her present existence. This out-of-world venturing was what she craved, as much as she craved the sensation of the drugs crawling through her body and making her forget everything: past, present and any thought of the future. The minute any of it didn't work, she would give it all up, cash in her coupons and buy a tweed skirt, perm her hair and retire to live a blameless existence.

Tilly's bedroom was under the eaves and reached by a flight of stairs from the landing on the second floor. Occupied formerly by Martha, who had been employed and grossly overworked for years by their mother, it had been left empty when their housemaid had made her dash for freedom. Having informed the Cliftons that she had got a job in a munitions factory — 'Where they pay a decent wage, Mrs Clifton, unlike some, and wild horses will not tempt me back' — Martha walked out and Tilly had claimed the room which was larger than the other two up there. Cold in winter and stifling in summer, it was not easy either to occupy or to manage, and she was sure it was haunted by the ghosts of past exploited housemaids, but it gave her privacy.

The room was as she had left it, which meant it was strewn with paper and clothing. Julia said she was heading to slutdom. Yes and no. When the muddle became too much, Tilly merely

298

scooped up a handful of the stuff and squashed it into the studded leather chest on the landing which took care of the problem temporarily.

This was her chosen eyrie, and from here Tilly could look down on to their garden at the back, and next door's garden too.

She glanced at the hole that had been blown in the party wall with Number 24. As ever, it was an ill wind: the damaged bricks and masonry scattered over the back gardens like dolly mixtures offered up images of destruction that found their way into her poetry.

Yes, it was strange. She lingered more over the images of destruction now than she had ever done during the war.

> The hinge rusting in the grass
> Belonged to the door
> That opened and shut into my heart.
> Until the bomb dropped into my life
> And blew it apart

Tilly slept for most of the afternoon and woke just before dinner time. With an effort, she got herself down to the bathroom and stuck her face in a basin full of cold water. Having dressed in an ancient, green cotton frock (which she would never wear outside the house) and shoes which could only be worn indoors because they had holes in their soles, she took herself downstairs and joined the others who, because it was a warm evening, were in the garden. Gus had carried out the kitchen chairs and they sat and drank sherry.

Since she had last been home, a flower bed had been dug by the shed. 'Who's the gardener?' asked Tilly.

'I am,' said Krista. 'I am looking forward to growing plants.' Tilly inspected the dug area, which cannot have been more than three feet square. 'It is a beginning,' added Krista, registering that Tilly was not that impressed.

Julia held her glass to her chest. 'Why the fuss, Gus?'

Gus got up and refilled their glasses. 'I . . . we . . . have something to tell you both.'

Krista appeared to be absorbed by the small herb-like plant growing in the new flower bed. Good Lord, thought Tilly in an inconsequential way, noticing that her eyelashes had grown astonishingly and almost feathered her cheeks. She had put her hair up, too, which was very pretty.

'Well?' There was a pause. 'Are we waiting for the seven days of creation to take place?' Tilly demanded.

'You might have guessed,' said Gus. 'But Krista and I are going to have a baby.'

No.

Tilly felt her eyes widen and heat crawl up her body. 'A baby? When?'

'Late September.'

'Julia . . . ' Tilly searched for something, anything, to say. 'Your mouth is open. A fly will get into it.'

'Is it so surprising?' Gus looked from one sister to the other.

'Late September.' Tilly grappled with the

300

calculations. 'But you must have known for some time.'

'We have and we kept it quiet.' He exchanged a look with Krista and a message passed between them. 'Because of Krista's health. And also we just wanted to enjoy the news ourselves.'

With a beatific look on her face, Krista echoed Gus: 'We wanted to make sure it was well on its way because it might not have been straightforward.' She smiled broadly and, for the first time, Tilly got a hint of what the real Krista — a normal, lively Krista, a beautiful Krista? — would be like. 'I hope you're pleased.'

At bedtime, back in her room, Tilly sank down on the unmade bed and made herself sit quite still with her hands in her lap.

Her stomach lurched queasily and it hurt to breathe as if she had broken a rib in a fall. Then she was inhaling air in great gulps.

Words came and went. She tried to grab them . . . tried to pin them down, but they were expert escapologists. Certainly the ones she used to build a skin over hidden things:

Now that you have gone,
I am a fragment of light that does not
    reflect.

Even the straightforward ones — jealousy, anger — vanished into the sump of her hot, tired brain.

After a while she managed to stand up and throw open her window, calculating that if she stood with one hand on the sill just so and with the other hanging on to the frame just so, she could stay upright.

It was twenty-five years since there had last been a baby in the house: her. Her fingers inched over the sill's paintwork, dislodging tiny specks of grubby white. Such a long time, a generation, in fact. The house would have forgotten what it was to have one under its roof. Houses held memories and could embrace, or reject, those who lived in them. They could also obliterate.

A tiny breakable skull was taking shape in Krista's starved-looking abdomen. How easy it would be to crush it. Tilly imagined the tiny veins forcing their unfurling branches through the foetus's flesh, the formation of a nail, a toe, an eyelash. She thought of it thrashing in its watery uterine ocean, entirely safe and cosseted.

No, not wise to think about those images. Don't make the mistake of thinking about them.

The major in charge of their unit, whose name she couldn't remember, had been nice in many ways — strong and determined (which Tilly liked) and very clean, except for the lightest tang of male sweat. Like they all were, he was under duress.

They had holed up in his quarters with a half bottle of gin and some grenadine. Not the best mixture, but who cared? He had put a record of Joe Loss's orchestra on the gramophone but had neglected to wind it up properly so there was a terrible screech. They were drunk, but not too drunk, because they managed to get their clothes off and to get on with the business.

Afterwards, he had gone the whole hog and

got roaring drunk. When Tilly enquired about his wife (a mistake), he had lashed out and hit her at the corner of the eye. 'Unnecessary,' she had told him. 'I don't want to see you again. I was only being polite.' The bruise on her face had been interesting and she had lied like a trooper to all and sundry that she had fallen off her bicycle.

Were there consequences of the night of gin and grenadine?

Tilly's nail dug ever harder into her flesh. A pinpoint of pain around which the sinews corded in protest.

She would never task any man with the consequences, especially not the hitting major. It was nobody else's business but hers and, if she had to contemplate the idea of witnessing the results being carried out in a slop bucket, then that was her cross.

'Up you go, dear,' Mrs Jakes had said, indicating that Tilly should get herself up on to the kitchen table.

Tilly regarded the scuffed table top. 'Is it scrubbed?'

'Cleaner than a baby's bottom, if you'll pardon the reference,' said Mrs Jakes.

A baby's skin. Soft and untouched. Innocent.

Tilly had turned away. Could she? Would she do it?

Now, with a cry, Tilly examined her tortured hand. It sported a red crescent. The humiliation she'd endured then had been bad enough. There had been worse to come. The pain which she now experienced was of a different order and it could never be dulled by drugs or by time and she had grown to understand that both guilt and grief were past masters at holding on.

There was a knock on the door. It was Julia trussed up in the green satin dressing gown which had been part of her trousseau. 'What do you think of the news?'

'Someone has to produce the next generation.'

Julia uttered a sound between a gasp and a cry of anger. Pressing a knuckle to her mouth, she bit down on it.

'Don't, Julia.'

'Martin and I so nearly managed,' Julia picked at a seam in the dressing-gown sleeve. 'I don't want a baby in the house. I don't want to be reminded . . . ' She stopped and forced her voice into a softer modulation. 'Tilly, I'm turning into a monster. How could I say such things? Where has my kindness gone?'

'Where everyone else's has gone,' said Tilly acidly. 'Go away, Julia. It's too late for all this.'

Obediently, Julia made for the door, the dressing gown undulating in a green cloud behind her. Placing a hand on the doorknob, and striving to sound civilized and generous, she said, 'Forget what I said. Of course we want a baby. Of course we do.'

'If you say it a third time, we might convince each other,' said Tilly.

Tilly knew, Julia knew, the words made no difference.

I don't want a baby in the house.

★　★　★

304

Tilly tried to sleep but the images which had plagued her since the war returned sharpish behind her closed lids. Planes downed in flames. A foot poking out of the rubble by St Paul's. The grainy, secret reconnaissance photograph of a bridge spanning a canal. Sex up against a wall with that chap she had worked with from Reconnaissance — a crude but effective-for-the-moment antidote to the bloody awfulness that was going on in the world.

The images from the present were less clearly etched. Funny that. It was as if she wasn't that interested in life as it had become.

19

Teddy telephoned Julia. 'Are we friends again?'

Julia took the call in Gus's study. 'Never not, Teddy.'

'Come and have a drink with me at the Blue Feather next Tuesday? We can talk things over.'

Would she? There would be no ambiguity this time. If she went, she would be entering into a compact with Teddy. She wasn't sure quite what that compact was yet but she was sure there was a risk that it would lead to her changing from a virtuous woman into one her mother would not have had in the house.

Terrified at the implications, she flung herself into the work up at Chelsea Town Hall and even managed to be polite to Coral. As she sorted and packed, Julia interrogated her motives and herself. Do you want to be good? Yes. What do you need to do to be good? Her gaze rested on Coral: so energetic, so certain, so . . . unbearable.

How to be good? Be nice to Krista.

Returning from the latest of these penitential trips, she searched out Krista and discovered her in the garden trying to train one of her mother's surviving roses up the wall with some old string and rusty nails. At Julia's approach, Krista turned a laughing countenance to her. 'This is so difficult.'

Julia held out a package that she had brought

306

back from Chelsea. 'I thought you would like this,' she said, hoping that Krista would not realize that she had done it out of a guilty conscience. 'It's hardly worn but your colour, I think.' She shook out a pretty yellow cotton dress which was sufficiently roomy to accommodate Krista's growing stomach.

There was a moment's silence. 'But that is so kind of you, Julia,' said Krista with a catch in her voice. 'It's lovely.'

On the Tuesday evening, Julia found herself putting on a dress, fixing her hair in a chignon and taking particular care with her lipstick.

Before she knew it there she was again in a hubbub in a packed Blue Feather. Teddy pushed a ten-pound note across the bar towards Julia. She stared down at it. 'What's that for?'

'Get yourself a dress, sweetheart. A nice one.'

To say that Julia was surprised was an understatement. 'I can't accept it.' Teddy rolled his eyes. 'Teddy, women can't . . . don't accept presents or money like that except from their husbands or fathers.'

'And their lovers,' he interjected. 'Would you like me to oblige and then you could take it without worrying?'

She stared at Teddy, hope flaring, and her senses quickening in the newly familiar and disturbing fashion. 'Don't joke. Please.'

'Sorry.'

Was he making fun of her? Sometimes, when faced with enigmas like Teddy, Julia felt that she had never married, and never run a household, or a social life, or acted as a mentor to other

307

ranks' wives, so stupid and ill-equipped did she feel.

Her initial excitement was now replaced by a slightly desperate sensation which took over whenever she was reminded of her situation. Martin was gone and, instead of living a nice, normal married life, she was halfway obsessed with a man who hated her brother in a horrible, unwholesome kind of way.

'I hope I haven't offended you.'

Could Julia believe a word of what Teddy said these days? It was becoming harder than ever to reconcile the Teddy from before the war — the witty, beautifully mannered friend — with the watchful, far-less-benign man sitting on the bar stool beside her.

'Teddy, you are getting better, aren't you?'

'The leg's a problem. It keeps me awake. Is it written on my handsome features?'

The words were said lightly but she knew him well enough to know that he minded a great deal about his injury. 'Not at all,' said Julia hastily, adding, 'anyway, we all look different. Older.'

'Don't be silly.' He touched her chin. It was a lingering, almost erotic, touch. She tensed, waiting for something. Anything. Instead, he said, 'I've been meaning to grill you again about that evening with Stephan. He's disappeared out of the picture, which is a little puzzling as we were engaged in a project together.'

'We had dinner and then he suggested we went to either his place or mine.' Julia looked down at her lap. 'When I said no, he got angry and told me in so many words . . . that I was a bore. It's not often you get propositioned so quickly and directly. I agreed to have dinner with him mainly to please you, as he seemed to be an important business contact. Am I right?'

'Yes.'

'You must have had an idea if he took real offence?'

Teddy seemed impatient with the question. 'No, not for sure, as I told you. But I have an insight into how other men's thoughts might run.' Julia felt an unfamiliar sensation creep up her spine. Teddy raised his eyebrows. 'When men come to London they look for diversion.'

She said as calmly as she could muster, 'But I'm not a prostitute.'

Teddy was genuinely taken aback. 'Nobody said you were, you idiot. But we're grown-ups now. Men like sex and think about it a lot. Why shouldn't women be the same? Why shouldn't both sexes enjoy it? Why should we not be open about it?'

She felt hot, confused, embarrassed — and as if she was sitting in front of Teddy with no clothes on. Nothing in her childhood, or her marriage, had prepared her for such a frank and open conversation.

'Have you been talking to Tilly? She says things like that.'

'Tilly knows a thing or two. *You* might not see it yet but I'm doing you a favour, Julia.'

A large doubt insinuated itself at the back of her mind. 'Teddy, are we really friends?'

'Despite your brother, Julia, we are.' His breath smelled of the gin cocktail.

309

'You're not setting me up as a sort of revenge because you've fallen out with Gus?'

For a moment, he looked so angry that she shuddered inwardly. 'Have you been reading too many thrillers, Julia?'

Yes, she *had* touched on an element, a partial truth, and she persisted. 'You are furious with Gus. I know you are. Look at me, Teddy . . . ' Teddy did as he was bid and she peered into the eyes which, these days, never expressed much. 'You're going to have to forgive him, Teddy. I hate the situation and I don't like Krista very much, but there may be a good explanation. I don't know what went on between them in Germany but something did. Gus never talks about it.' She grimaced. 'Actually, no one ever talks about anything. Maybe that's the way we survive.'

Teddy leaned towards Julia. 'I agree. To survive we have to change and not look back. You will. I will. I have every confidence.'

Their faces were almost touching and her skin goose-fleshed in a way she had almost forgotten. 'Gus has been an idiot,' she said.

'Hatred is quite useful, unless you allow it to dominate,' he remarked.

'Oh, Teddy . . . '

'Give me a kiss, Julia.'

With a gasp, she reached up, intending to kiss his mouth. At the last moment, Teddy turned his head and her kiss landed on his cheek.

The strange sensations deep in Julia burst into flame.

'Teddy . . . ' She reached for a future, and the

words flying from her possessed an unstoppable momentum. 'Teddy, why don't you marry me?'

Horror and disgust flashed across his features, as plain as day.

'Teddy, *don't* look like that.'

Teddy reached for the chunky ashtray on his left and pulled it towards him.

She heard her voice drip with greed and supplication — and hated herself. 'I could care for you. I'm a good housekeeper and hostess. I would be an asset.' Her voice trailed to a halt, embarrassment making her speechless.

At last Teddy looked up from his prolonged contemplation of the ashtray. 'Sweet Julia, it's not possible.'

'Why?'

'Because.'

She eyed up the banknote that still lay on the bar. 'But you would like to make me go to bed with other men?'

'Sweetheart, there is no 'make' about it.' Teddy picked up the banknote and folded it. 'If the idea bothers you then we needn't have any dealings.'

'I thought . . . ' But she knew better than to continue. *I thought you and I . . .*

He glanced at Julia and she imagined she detected pity and even regret, but she also saw absolutely no hope.

Again, the unreadable smile. 'There's no need for us to discuss this any more.' He reached for his stick. 'I'm going to dinner in Piccadilly. Why don't I get you a taxi and you can drop me off?'

That was all she was going to get out of him. When he kissed her goodbye in the taxi, she

311

proffered only her cheek.

Teddy noted the gesture. 'Julia, let's be clear. Remember I told you that you *are* both lovely and good. I wouldn't deserve you.'

What? Why? How? The questions were like bees buzzing in her tired brain. What had happened to Teddy, her brother, to everyone? None of them understood each other in the way that they used to.

He placed a paternal hand on her shoulder and Julia thought she would die of misery and humiliation. 'Why don't we forget all about this?' he said. 'It never happened. You needn't do anything. I'm not for you and, if you prefer, we won't even see each other again.'

No Teddy. No life, other than the one in Clapham. No Blue Feather. No anticipation of anything, other than a permanent coldness and yearning. The idea was numbing. Deadening.

'But I should emphasize that you wouldn't be selling your soul, Julia.'

The pros and cons — her needs, her morals, what she expected of herself — spun around the centrifuge in her head in a chaotic muddle. Somehow, she had to retrieve the situation and make sure that she resurfaced from the bottom of the pond to which she had sunk.

Huddled into the gloomy interior of the taxi, she was full of wonder that she was even entertaining the idea of discarding her morals and her upbringing, as easily, it seemed, as stepping out of her fraying, green satin dressing gown.

'Shall we be seeing each other, Julia darling?'

Teddy was waiting.

Wordlessly, she held out her hand. Teddy placed the banknote in her palm and folded her fingers over it. She experienced an extraordinary sense of unreality, as if she had dropped into someone else's body.

Teddy picked up her other hand and kissed it. It was almost as if he was greeting her for the first time. Perhaps he was? Perhaps he was welcoming her into the discreet, exclusive, Teddy Myers club?

'What do you want me to do?'

He levered open the taxi door. 'Meet a friend.'

'Stephan?'

'Someone else this time. Be at the Ritz this time next week.'

★ ★ ★

In the drawing room at Number 22, Julia was closing the shutters. A few lights sifted through the summer dusk from the other side of the Common, which was no place to be at night for a woman. People had been murdered there, including a man who, local gossip had it, had been an anarchist.

What would all the boys in the mess, stiff with fatigue and nervy from a sortie, have made of that? She could hear the jeers, the anger, the ribaldry. *Give him a one-way mission.*

A man skulked past the house, wearing a flat cap pulled down over his forehead. Idly, she tracked his passage and watched him until he disappeared suddenly — which was odd. It

313

crossed Julia's mind that he had ducked into the bomb-damaged Number 26.

She slotted the iron bar into place and secured the shutters. It had been a warm day but it was a little chilly now. Having laid the fire earlier, she lit a match and applied it to the kindling and balled-up newspaper and drew her chair close to the fireplace.

In the bedroom upstairs, Krista was moving around. A chair scraped along the floor.

The sewing basket was on the floor by her feet. She selected a card of beige wool, threaded up the darning needle and set to work on a pair of Gus's socks.

These days her wedding ring was so much looser and it slipped around her finger as the needle went in and out. Bloody darning. Still, she wasn't doing a bad job. Every so often, she looked up, trying to sort out questions around her future. How ill-prepared women — women such as she was — were to face adult life. They knew so *little*.

The door drifted open and Krista entered, wearing the yellow dress. 'Oh, you have Gus's socks.'

Julia kept her voice level. 'In a bad state, I'm afraid. I think I've managed to rescue them.' She lifted them up for inspection.

'It is very kind of you.' She sounded reasonable. Sweet, even. Julia noticed that a brown patch had appeared on her face just above the left cheekbone. 'But it is my job to mend Gus's socks.' She held out her hand. 'Please.'

Did Julia care? Why would she wish to darn

socks when she could be with Teddy in a bar somewhere? Somewhere nice.

'Please.'

Krista's German accent grated on her inner ear — the finger-nail down the blackboard.

Please.

It was the accent of the tyrant who had raged through Europe, and it lived here, in this house. Her new sister-in-law's expression was determined and — God help her — concerned and, for a terrible moment, Julia thought she was not going to be able to stop herself slapping her.

She handed over the socks. 'I was only trying to help.'

There was a second's pause, more marked than the previous one. It was like being in a film, Julia decided, where all sorts of things are conveyed silently and it is the shadow on the wall, the flick of an eyebrow, the stealthy tread that tells the real story.

Krista took the chair opposite Julia. 'Julia, I want you to know that I am grateful to you and I want to make your brother comfortable and happy.'

'Good.' Julia was at her most acid. 'But I'd be surprised if Gus wishes you to labour over his socks. Ada should really be doing them. I was only passing the time.'

There, yet again she had managed to be both nasty and snobbish at one and the same time. She squinted at Krista, who seemed at a loss and there was something immensely satisfying about being out-and-out awful. Then there wasn't. 'Forgive me, Krista. I spoke rudely.

Stupidly. It's just . . . '

Krista cocked an eye at Julia. 'Perhaps you would like to say that you wish you were darning Martin's socks?'

Krista's ability to read her caught Julia on the raw. 'Not darning his socks exactly, but yes.'

'I am so sorry,' said Krista. 'Truly.'

'So am I.'

Both of them meant it.

★ ★ ★

The following evening, Julia sat on a stool with her elbows propped up on the bar at the Ritz. She was wearing a new dress — the product of Teddy's largesse. Bought at Debenhams, it was so boned and stiff that it bordered on the uncomfortable but she took comfort in its fashionably fuller skirt, the grey-green colour which suited her and the envy it would induce.

What would Gus make of this? What would Martin say? A voice in her head asked: *Does it matter what anyone thinks? Aren't you your own woman?*

'Are you Julia?' The voice had a Yorkshire accent.

She swivelled round. 'Yes, I am.'

Reasonably tall, with light-brown hair and eyes of nondescript hazel, he was dressed in a rough tweed suit which looked out of place in this London hotel. 'Michael Hebden,' he said, extending a hand. After a moment, Julia took it and he sat down on the stool beside her.

There was a bit of fuss ordering the drinks,

316

which was quite useful because it diffused the situation. Clearly, he was not a man to whom the waiters instantly responded and he was forced to signal several times before he got in the order for two dry martinis.

But he had an open face and his smile was genuine as he raised his glass. 'This is very pleasant. I've been starved of good company.'

'Do you live alone then?'

'No.'

A wife? Almost certainly. The lighting was too dim for her to make out his expression. 'What do you do?'

'I'm working on a business which will make pre-cast reinforced concrete.'

It sounded very dreary. 'So you are starting up?'

'Right first time.' The Yorkshire accent thickened. 'Getting a business up and running. Houses need to be repaired and built and pre-cast reinforced concrete is the stuff to do it with.'

Julia's mind had gone blank, probably with panic, and she struggled to say something sensible. 'There will be plenty of work, won't there? Half of London is in ruins.'

'That's why I'm here so often. To try to persuade the powers that be that I have the product they need.' Julia did not react and he continued: 'Business in this country is old-fashioned in so many ways, with lots of red tape. Particularly if you are dealing with local government. We need to shake it up. This country needs to get a grip on its industry very

317

quickly if we are to survive.' Cocktail in hand, he gave forth on the plans for his business's expansion.

Pleasingly direct, she thought. Energetic. Nice? Michael Hebden brimmed with vigour and she was enjoying the whiff of Yorkshire bog and peat and heather.

Out of the corner of her eye, Julia clocked that Teddy was also in the bar. She hadn't expected that. He was talking to a young woman in a clinging, red cocktail frock. Her mouth tightened.

'Am I boring you?'

Her attention had wandered and she pulled herself to order. 'No, of course not.'

Michael Hebden wound up his paean to the necessities of house-building in a post-war country. 'I *am* boring you.' The hazel eyes narrowed. With amusement, she concluded, which was nice. 'But spare a couple of seconds to think about it. Concrete is the foundation of the future of this country. Get it right, Julia, and there are fortunes to be made.'

Like many, she had never viewed concrete in that light. 'I'm sure you're right.'

There was a short, awkward pause.

'How about we find a bite to eat?'

Teddy had moved to be with a little group of both men and women. Suddenly, she was consumed by panic. 'Thank you, but I'm not sure.'

He wasn't having that. 'Don't worry. I won't take advantage of you.'

How curious. Michael Hebden seemed to

318

understand her ambivalence, to approve of it, even. That made it so much easier.

She waited for her coat to be fetched.

The bald facts were that Teddy was using her for his own purposes and she had agreed to go along with it. Through the cigarette haze she caught a glimpse of him talking away to the group clustered around him. Did he care what happened to her? What if this man was violent? She panned through her memory trying to recall something she had read in the paper earlier in the summer. The news had been full of the details of two violent murders which the reporter had described as 'acts of animal savagery'. As the commentaries at the time had pointed out, it was notable that both these girls had been murdered by a man whom they had met only once.

Had Teddy abandoned her completely? Almost as though he read her thoughts, he looked over his shoulder in their direction and nodded at Julia, as if to say: Mission accomplished.

The girl in the red dress touched his arm and he transferred his attention back to the group.

It was ridiculous to feel quite so apprehensive. She was a grown woman, yes. Married and experienced, yes. Here with this man of her own free will, yes.

A woman squeezed past them, leaving behind her a trail of scent, cheap and eye-watering. Her companion was smoking a cigar, which had a much nicer aroma, deep, rich and expensive. She thought of the alternative to not having dinner with Michael Hebden: picking her way down the platform at Clapham Common Tube, the hideous wind that always hit passengers as they emerged on to the street, the walk home with grit and stones rasping underfoot, her solitary room in a cold house.

'I was thinking of Claridge's,' said Michael. 'Does that appeal?'

He draped Julia's coat over her shoulders, pressing down on them lightly. The gesture had a touch of authority, possession almost, to which she did not object. She slotted the strap of her handbag over her arm. 'Claridge's would be lovely,' she said.

Wearing a pretty dress, ensconced comfortably in a taxi (for which she did not pay), then escorted by an agreeable waiter to a table gleaming with glass and silver, and given a menu to browse through, she had no reason to regret her choice for the evening at that moment.

By the end of the meal, which was the best she had eaten since before the war, it was crystal clear what Michael Hebden expected from her but also that he was prepared to pay for it in kind. At one point he excused himself to make a telephone call. Left to observe the waiters' trained movements as they moved from table to table, Julia recalled with aching regret her wedding night. How awkward, but how lovely it had been, filled with silliness and teasing. How what had happened between them had altered everything — and yet, paradoxically, nothing had really changed beyond Julia herself. How surprised she had been on waking the following morning to discover the world remained as she had left it the night before.

'Sorry about that.' Michael returned to his seat and interrupted her thoughts. 'As we were discussing, I come down to London every month. Hotel life is a bit bleak and I like interesting female company.' The hazel gaze fixed on Julia. 'But with no strings.'

'I see.'

'Do you? I like to give my companions a good time. Good food, music, theatre, whatever is agreeable. Will you think about it?'

Julia was lulled. Her stomach was full and the wine had warmed her. If she was prepared to sleep with this man, *she* would be taken to places she could not afford and, by the sound of things, in reasonable style.

Why not?

Later, in the well-appointed hotel room, Michael unhooked the back of her stiff dress and helped her ease it to the floor. Conscious of her less-than-exciting underwear, Julia stepped out of it.

He bent over to kiss her naked shoulder.

She glanced over to the bed where the pink satin eiderdown and sheets had been turned down by the maid. 'Michael, I've only ever been with my husband,' she said simply.

'I can tell.' Michael sat down to take off his shoes. 'But I think we'll do well enough.' His voice was rough-edged but, at the same time, sympathetic, and the combination was attractive and soothing.

Wishing desperately that the lights were dimmer, Julia held her slip up against her torso. Would anyone who knew her — the figure who

321

so often stood at the window, the impeccable, fragile widow in her darned clothes — ever imagine that she would be doing this?

'Michael, do you have a wife?'

'Yes.' The answer clipped back at her. 'But you mustn't worry about her. She's all right with this.'

Her slip felt cold between her fingers. 'Are you sure?'

A naked Michael came over to Julia and drew her down on to the bed. 'Shall we stop talking?'

What happened under the pink eiderdown was, surprisingly, not so very bad, if a little clinical. And it was a world away from the hot, impatient desire and ignorant tenderness with which she had welcomed Martin. For one thing, it doused the insistent physical yearning which had been plaguing her, although (apart from Tilly) Julia would never admit that to another living soul. For another, Michael proved to be considerate and pleasantly matter-of-fact, which helped to defuse her embarrassment.

There was only one problem, if indeed that was what it was. While she was enjoying the sex with Michael, Julia — and she was floored by this and simply did not know how to deal with it — found herself thinking of Teddy. What if it was his body moving above hers? His masculine smell in her nostrils?

Afterwards, Michael Hebden confessed further to having not only a wife but also two daughters who attended a Quaker school; he was a stalwart of the local golf club and his wife had made their garden into a local talking point.

These were all the ingredients, she thought, of a settled, stable life, and he was possibly jeopardizing it?

Looking pleasantly satisfied, he turned his head on the pillow to face Julia. 'Shall I contact you when I next come down?'

Martin was dead. Her life was slipping away and her future was bleak.

'Yes,' she said. 'I'd like that.'

★ ★ ★

It was astonishing how she was managing to go about her daily life. It was astonishing what she was learning about herself, not least that she could live on several levels at one and the same time.

Julia was aware that to those around her she looked perfectly normal. On the outside, she was the same tidily dressed, conservative widow in a tweed skirt and flowered blouse. On the inside, she was red and raw from thinking, and wrestling with the contradictions of her desires and emotions. Sometimes, she gave herself a pat on the back for having managed to wriggle for a moment out of her present existence, which she found so suffocating.

But there was, of course, the backlash, and, sometimes, she loathed herself.

Kneeling beside her bed, she tried to summon back the childhood habits and to pray for forgiveness for her sin; but she discovered what she had suspected since Martin's death, that God had slipped out of her reach. He was somewhere else, looking after those who still had their husbands, sons and brothers.

What worried her not a little, but also intrigued her the most, was the ease with which she had cast aside her upbringing and her training. It was as if that particular skin had been flayed off her, exposing the most primitive of behaviours of whose dangers she was only half-aware and which she had certainly never before been called on to control.

She rested her chin on her clasped hands. Where was her courage? Up there? She raised her eyes to the ceiling. Or here and now, and at her disposal?

★   ★   ★

Ada worked for two days a week at Number 22. These were welcome but, with the whole house to clean, there was not much time left for her to tackle the extras.

Past caring about those housekeeping details, Julia was no longer plagued by acute anxiety about them. Fresh air was creeping in, bringing a coolness and detachment. Even so, she suggested to Krista that they could help out Ada by taking over the cleaning of the silver. 'You and I,' she added, 'can do it in the kitchen. It won't take that long. We could . . . ' She paused as she recollected how her hungers had been subtly, and not so subtly, assuaged. 'We could have biscuits with our coffee.'

Early on a Thursday morning, Julia and Krista sat down at the kitchen table. With a cup of *ersatz* coffee at their elbow, they worked quietly together. The silence was not completely tension-free but neither was it hostile.

Once, when reaching for the polishing cloth, Julia dropped a knife and it clattered on to the tiles. Seated at the opposite end of the table, a pile of folded dusters and a tin of Goddard's silver powder in front of her, Krista asked politely, 'Do you need help, Julia?'

Picking up the knife, Julia's hand was not quite steady. 'No, thank you.'

Having cleaned and polished the teaspoons, Krista eased back against the hard kitchen chair, a movement which exposed the now-noticeable bump of her abdomen.

Julia averted her eyes.

Restoring the knife to its pile, she concentrated on the next one. 'We should be starting to get together some baby things,' she made herself say.

'I would value your advice.' Krista put down her rag. 'Very much.'

Julia spat on a stubborn discoloured patch and rubbed furiously. 'Of course I'll help.'

There was a stack of fish knives awaiting their turn. Krista picked up the first one. 'Perhaps you wish that this baby was not coming.'

Julia's head snapped up. 'Don't be silly.'

'Or that it wasn't Gus's?'

'Of course not.' Guilt that her feelings had been so obvious made Julia extra sharp.

The smell of Goddard's powder sifted through the kitchen.

Krista held up the fish knife to the light and

inspected it. 'But I feel that you and Tilly wonder about the baby. Am I right?' She sent a sharp, hard look in Julia's direction. 'Gus is the father.' Julia flinched. 'But I know you lost your own baby. I understand. I know it is difficult seeing me.'

The knife Julia was polishing now shone within an inch of its life and she laid it with its fellows. 'I can't talk about it.' She grabbed whatever was to hand — a serving spoon — and began to rub frantically.

Krista hesitated. 'Can you not say anything about it? I would like to listen.'

Could she? By now the spoon was burnished into an almost blinding brightness.

'I can listen,' Krista repeated. 'I know about losing someone. We are the same in that way.'

'Really!' escaped from Julia.

Krista flinched and Julia felt ashamed. 'Sorry, Krista.'

Krista applied herself to a fish fork.

It was then Julia heard herself say, 'It's like having a brick wall in my mind and I can't walk past it. I can't climb over it either.'

There was a pause and Krista's eyes shone with emotion. 'Please go on, Julia. I was the same, you know. How to make sense of it?'

'I knew that pilots were in acute danger and it should not have been so much of a shock when Martin was killed. But it was. If I had handled it differently, been strong, like you, maybe our daughter would have lived. Or maybe she wouldn't and something else was wrong. But I feel it was my fault and if I hadn't been so

326

. . . You can imagine.' She pressed a hand to her trembling lips. 'I would have her now and I wouldn't be envying you, Krista.'

There. Her confession.

A peace stole over the kitchen.

Krista began to say something but Julia held up her hand.

'Don't. I'm . . . just don't.' She blew a dusting of the Goddard's powder on to the newspaper. The action created a tiny hiss over the paper. 'Have you booked in with the doctor and midwife?'

'They are very expensive.' Krista returned to the fork.

Julia was startled. 'Krista, Gus will pay, of course. Promise you will do it. It's important.'

The fork gleamed. Krista placed it alongside its companions and reached for the cutlery roll in which they were kept. 'I know it has been difficult for you to welcome me. But I want to thank you.' She slotted the cutlery into the roll. 'I am glad we have had this talk.'

The softly accented words died away. Building a bridge that Julia should have begun to construct months ago.

She uttered a short, ashamed laugh. 'Yes, I'm glad, too, because it seems to me that, like nations, if we don't talk to each other, we'll end up killing one another.'

20

Earlier Krista had read *The Death of the Heart* by Elizabeth Bowen. Herr Laube had informed her it was a novel about what really went on below the surface of everyday life. Although, like *A Handful of Dust*, she did not like it much, she did relate to the strange, awkward, orphaned Portia, the sixteen-year-old heroine.

'It is not a very warm book,' she remarked to Herr Laube in German. 'I haven't learned anything about the English.'

Herr Laube was trying to reconcile the accounts in one of his green ledgers and apparently failing. 'Speak in English,' he said, without looking up. 'It's safer.'

'Can you recommend another one?' Krista switched obediently into English. 'Tell me where to look.'

'If you will wait a moment.'

While she did so, she wandered from shelf to shelf. Idiosyncratic, to say the least, smelling of paper and ink and — a little — of must and dust, Herr Laube's shop had peacefulness written into every nook and corner. It was the most unlikely place for healing to take place but it had.

Tutting, he scrubbed out a number from a column and rewrote it in another one. The pile of bills and receipts near his elbow was dislodged and Krista was not quick enough to prevent the papers spilling on to the floor.

'Would you like me to do that?' She stooped over awkwardly to pick them up. 'I used to be in charge of an office.'

Herr Laube sent her a look which said: *We may be the same nationality but don't presume.* But he must have thought twice and, after a moment, he pushed the ledger over to her.

Krista glanced at it. 'You have entered two things twice over. Shall I sort it out?'

It did not take long. As she was finishing, Herr Laube did one of his stage whispers. 'Don't look now but the man with the notebook is back. Standing just under the bridge. On the other side of the road.'

She knew the form: don't acknowledge, just lose them. As she emerged from the bookshop, she stopped to adjust her shoe. Easing upright, she took in a beige mackintosh, dark moustache and a pair of large feet in brown lace-ups.

They were the trigger for anxiety to course through her.

She was late for the ministry. Her shoes made a clicking sound on Wilhelm Strasse, telling onlookers of her rush to get to work. She stopped to tighten the strap and the man behind her came to a halt, too. When she moved off, so did he.

It wasn't the first time. What have I done? What have I done?

Sitting down at her desk, understanding dawned. She had been friendly with Heidi, who had been taken away. Typewriters clattered, the door to the office of her immediate boss opened and shut. With a shudder of pure fear, she huddled over her work.

She turned on her heel and made her way as quickly as her increasing bulk would allow her down the High Street in the direction of home. She was not in Germany now and, in a few minutes, she would feel better.

In return for her help, Herr Laube had insisted on presenting her with a free copy of a novel by P. G. Wodehouse, which he told her was very funny, and she accepted it on condition that he would allow her to come back and help him out with his book-keeping. Deciphering the Wodehouse took Krista several weeks. Initially, its humour entirely escaped her and she found it rather silly and childish. Then she caught Gus laughing out loud as he read it and forced him to explain.

'But what is so funny about a pig and aunts?' she wanted to know.

'They are not funny in themselves,' he told her. 'It's how he writes about them.' When she frowned, he said: 'The English love a joke, especially a social joke, and terrible, bullying aunts are considered funny.'

'It is not about real life.'

Gus tossed the book back to Krista. 'That's its point. Its glorious point.'

'Did you read any novels when you were in Germany?' she asked.

'*Berlin Alexanderplatz* by Döblin,' he replied. 'It did not make me laugh.'

'No, but it made you think. Thinking is more useful to human beings.'

'So does P. G. Wodehouse, my sweet. It makes

you think how absurd some things are. And laughter is very useful.'

There was no accounting for it, she thought, reapplying herself to the text. Little by little, she began to 'see' something of what the fuss was about. But not entirely.

It was a relief to move on from pigs and aunts and she embarked on *Jane Eyre*, which offered yet another experience and one to which she related better. Familiar with German castles, Gothic tales and stories of dark, witch-infested forests, she could make sense of the wild Yorkshire landscape and the brutal Mr Rochester.

A string of warm, sunny days saw Krista's health and strength improving. The baby was growing and she got into a habit of talking to it. Occasionally, when drifting off to sleep, she could have sworn she heard a tiny voice responding through the watery echo chamber of her womb. The idea was mad but it gave a moment or two of delighted content.

Thus she was appalled and not a little despairing when, as she sat on a bench on the Common and read about Jane's encounter with the mad first Mrs Rochester, a voice said in her ear: *You thought you had your body back. But you don't.*

She dropped the book.

It took only the smallest pinprick of memory and, once again, serge uniform scraped against her inner thighs and stinking breath was in her face.

Ask any German woman after the city fell and

they would probably understand exactly what the soft sibilant voice was suggesting. Spotting a female — child, girl, woman — alien soldiers, mostly Soviets, gave chase. Some submitted. Some fought with fists and nails. Some fought with their minds but the damage was the same. There was the option of suicide which, by then, no longer repulsed Krista. She had seen too much of it. Rather, she had a respect for the rationality of the act.

There's an interloper inside you.

'Nice morning.' An elderly woman with two heavy-looking string bags passed by the bench where Krista sat.

She knew now that the struggle was on to dissociate her growing baby from the contamination of that past. To keep it quarantined from the images which flashed and tormented and which hid in the underground cells of her brain. From the memories which existed to drag her backwards.

'Yes, it is,' she replied. 'It is.'

Reapplying herself to Charlotte Brontë, she refused to listen to the voice and, gradually, it grew fainter and died. Its absence permitted her to thrill to the story of Jane tramping over the moors as she fled the bigamous Mr Rochester, only to find herself living with the sisters of the oddball and fanatical would-be missionary, St John Rivers. Fanaticism again, she thought. I know about that.

Jane Eyre was a more complicated read than the others and it wasn't until mid-summer that she managed to finish it. 'I am not sure about the conclusion,' she confided to Herr Laube. 'Why would Jane wish to end up with a bad-tempered man like Mr Rochester?'

For once, Herr Laube broke his own rule and replied in German. 'Power,' he said. 'After all those years as a nobody, Jane is now powerful and rich.' He glanced around his chaotic and overstocked shop. 'We would all like to be that, I think. Jane makes a big effort to pretend not to be the one in charge, but she is. She is very cunning.'

Krista opened Herr Laube's current ledger, revealing a spider's web of entries. 'So, to be a successful Englishwoman you must be rich and married to a man who is almost totally dependent on you.' To speak so freely in German was such a relief. 'I love your shop, Herr Laube. It's a place of tranquillity.'

Immediately, he took refuge behind his usual formality and reverted to English. 'I am pleased to be of service.'

As she paid for a copy of Nancy Mitford's *The Pursuit of Love*, she noticed the man with the notebook was there in his usual position, writing away. She knew exactly the entries he would be writing up:

10.52 Suspect enters bookshop. Suspect is
     wearing yellow summer dress and straw
     hat.
11.15 Suspect talks to shop owner.
11.30 Suspect writes in shop owner's
     ledger.
11.45 Suspect selects and pays for book.

11.50 Suspect leaves shop.

Could anything be more clumsy and unsubtle? But she was aware it greased the nuts and bolts of surveillance and the report would be housed in a hidden archive. As a veteran of a secret state, she hated the idea.

Out on the pavement, she hovered while she summoned her resolution. What would be the consequences and would they harm Gus? The baby fluttered, which decided matters. Thinking of its future, Krista walked over to confront the watcher with the brown lace-up shoes. On close inspection he looked to be mild and rather bored.

'It is a waste of your time, you know,' she told him. 'Herr Laube and I may be German but we have no harm in us.' She nearly added: *The war is over and Germany has no interest in what the British get up to any more*, but realized that this was a political statement which would only provoke his handlers.

His astonishment was painful. Almost farcical.

She finished by saying, 'You are very noticeable, you know.' This, she well knew from Gus, was the biggest insult she could pay him.

From the corner of her eye, she caught sight of an anxious Herr Laube putting up the 'Closed' sign and pulling down the blind.

Gus roared with laughter when Krista confessed to him, then sobered. 'Who do you think he was? Describe.'

Krista obliged. 'He wore brown lace-up shoes. Big ones. Highly polished.'

'He's from the other service then. Our lot would never wear brown shoes.'

'Is this class again?' she asked.

'You're learning. It's nonsense, of course.' He ran a finger down her cheek — both questioning and tender. 'You should have told me about him before. But you must take care. It might have drawn the wrong kind of attention to you. Those goons don't have a sense of humour.'

She turned her face to his and he gently traced the outline of her mouth. 'It's all healed,' he said, meaning the sore that had plagued her in the early days. 'And now you are beautiful.'

Out of feeling for her, perhaps, Gus had not given the real reason why he had told her to take care; it was, as she well knew, because her position was still precarious.

★ ★ ★

If uncomfortable at times, particularly the painful breasts and back ache, the changes in her body were fascinating, and lately the butterfly that beat its wings against the walls of her uterus had turned into an acrobat.

On her visits to the doctor's surgery, the practice nurse was never unprofessional in her manner, yet Krista knew that she was kept waiting before she was called in to see the doctor, and for longer than was usual. On one occasion the nurse called out to a waiting room filled with patients, '*Frau* Clifton.' Krista did not move and continued to read about the trials of Linda Radlett's love life. There was an answering

335

echo from one or two of the patients: '*Frau?*' Their voices rose like scandalized question marks.

The nurse repeated, '*Frau* Clifton?'

Krista looked up. 'Do you mean *Mrs* Clifton?' she asked calmly.

Neither could Dr Lawson be accused of neglecting his duties. His questions were as thorough as his examinations. Doctors, said Julia, needed towels because the practice was to warm their hands in hot water before an examination. But Dr Lawson's were as cold as ice.

For much of what Dr Lawson insisted on calling 'the run-up to the finish', Gus was working flat out and she saw him only late in the evenings and early in the mornings.

However, on one of the evenings they did manage together, Gus had shown her Mr Forrest's report.

Roof unsettled by the bomb which landed two doors along and tiles dislodged.

It then listed a number of issues which needed attention. In the final paragraph, he had written:

It is possible that the foundations of Number 22 have been compromised by the bomb mentioned above. They should be inspected on a regular basis.

Mr Forrest turned up one afternoon while Julia was out. 'I was hoping to see Mrs Orville.'

336

He seemed very disappointed.

Krista got the message. 'I will make a pot of tea,' she said and led him down into the kitchen.

Seated at the kitchen table drinking the tea, he said, 'You have made it very nice here.'

Recently, Krista had organized for the windows to be washed — fancifully, she saw them as portals into the soul of the house. The floor had been scrubbed; how many had trodden over it? Every pot and pan had been scoured and burnished by Krista herself. Scandalizing Julia, she had insisted on hanging bunches of dried thyme from the top shelf of the dresser and the air was faintly scented with thyme and sage.

'There's been so much destruction,' Mr Forrest continued, 'and it is nice to see it being put right.'

She straightened wearily in the chair. 'You mean destruction by the Germans?'

He was horrified by his gaffe. 'On both sides the bombing was disgraceful. It was nothing more or less than tribes at war. Like you get in very remote places, or Italy in the Middle Ages.' His features were creased with distress. 'The sights I have seen. They are sadder than anything you can imagine.'

'I think I know,' she said.

He sucked down the final dregs of tea.

'Just plain old murder of ordinary people, I call it.'

She refilled his cup. 'Then we must concentrate on making it better and you are doing very good work, I know. Do you not think that this house is a jewel and could be more so? The rooms are beautifully proportioned, the stairs so elegant, and I love the way it is designed to let the light in. I love the plasterwork in each of the rooms and have you noticed the patterns are all linked? The architects took great care when they designed it. We must do everything we can to repair it.'

Mr Forrest seemed reluctant to comment. After a while, he got to his feet and said he had to go.

'It was very peculiar,' she commented to Tilly when she made an appearance. 'At the mention of repairing the house, Mr Forrest went silent and yet he talks a lot about everything else.'

'Perhaps he was cross that Julia wasn't there.'

★   ★   ★

Shortly afterwards, Tilly telephoned Krista at the house and asked if she was likely to be coming up into town. 'If you are, I thought it would be fun to meet at the National Gallery. Or, at any rate, what's left of it.'

'What a lovely idea,' said Krista.

'I thought so too and it'll be a change for you to look at some paintings. Good for the baby!' She gave a funny little laugh.

'Tilly, that is so nice of you. I had thought . . . '

Lately, Tilly had been odd and distant and had been spending long periods away from the house.

'You had thought what, Krista?'

'Maybe I had offended you.'

Again, there was the funny little laugh. 'Of course not.'

When Krista lumbered into view from the Underground station, Tilly waved to her from the steps of the gallery. In a bright-green blouse and tight black skirt, she looked as exotic as ever. But when Krista got up close, she saw changes. Tilly's eyes were hollow, her skin drained and she had lost weight.

However, it was the familiar Tilly who tucked her hand under Krista's elbow and guided her up the steps and into the gallery. 'They've brought back a lot of the paintings, you know. They had to be hidden in remote Welsh valleys and things while it was all going on,' she said. 'I expect you did the same in Germany.'

'I expect we did,' Krista admitted.

'It must be hard.' Tilly's voice was soft and caring. 'You must miss Germany.'

Krista had developed a new trick to subdue homesickness. When it threatened, she counted backwards from twenty in English. 'Yes. I miss mountains. The beer. A lot of things.' She added, 'But only from time to time.'

Tilly gripped her elbow so tightly that it veered on the cruel as she steered Krista towards the first gallery. 'There's lots we still can't see and the rooms need a massive clean. But there's enough on show to cheer us up and we should celebrate that life is returning to normal.'

Together, they scrutinized two unremarkable landscapes, a stiff portrait of an Elizabethan courtier (which meant nothing to Krista), a populous river scene and a viciously bright pre-Raphaelite painting of a girl expiring by the side of a muddy lane. It was entitled: *The Outcast*.

'Why is she outcast?'

Tilly read the piece of paper which they had been issued on entry. 'Apparently, she has had a baby without being married and no one will take her in.'

Krista stuffed a fist into the hollow of her back, which was aching. 'Poor girl.'

After a while, Krista realized that there was a purpose to this visit. Walking into the penultimate room, Tilly said with some excitement: 'Ah, here we are,' and she led Krista up to the painting that dominated one of the walls.

It was a Nativity, large, tender and luminous. Mother and baby were arranged in an ornate stable with an anxious Joseph keeping an eye on a group of wealthy-looking burghers who were peering in through the window. A greyhound with a jewelled collar was coiled up on the straw in front of the tableau. In a blue cloak with gold trimming, the Madonna regarded the baby in her lap with a thoughtful, almost quizzical, look. Plump and alabaster-skinned, his gaze was fixed on his mother's.

'You're the spitting image of the Madonna.'

True, there was a likeness, in the shape of the face and large eyes.

'I thought it would amuse you,' said Tilly.

Krista drank the painting in. Each line of it, every nuance of its palette, its composition and sensibility, suggested home. The subdued blues and greens and worldly reds, the textures and

340

architecture. It was of her place and of her people.

Twenty, nineteen...

'Lovely,' murmured Tilly. 'See the way the baby is looking at his mother. So touching.' She consulted the paper. 'It's from Northern Germany so I thought you would like it. Late fifteenth century.'

The Madonna's cloak reminded her of Nella's coat.

'I bet you would like to go home.' The suggestion was voiced very sweetly to Krista: a sympathetic sister-in-law being nice to a homesick sister-in-law?

Krista felt a burst of affection for Tilly. 'One day, perhaps. At this precise moment, it would not be helpful to anyone.'

'You could always go, you know.' Tilly was concerned. 'You're not stuck in this country any more than I am. I'm thinking of moving on. You could, too. If you wanted to.'

'Take a baby to Germany now?' The baby in the painting was beautifully plump — so important in a time of want. 'Tilly, that is a very bad idea.'

'Maybe you're right.'

Tilly led her over to the next painting: *The Flight to Egypt*. It was by the same artist. In this scene, Mary was on a donkey, holding the baby, and Joseph walked beside her through a desert towards a city far away in the distance.

They absorbed it in silence.

'See,' Tilly dropped into Krista's ear, 'people do leave if they feel they have to.'

341

The day had turned hot and clear by the time they left the gallery. Krista got down the steps without too much difficulty and paused at the bottom to get back her breath. The baby kicked away. 'Ouch,' she said.

'What?'

Krista grinned. 'There is a game of football going on inside me.'

'Let me.' Without waiting for permission, Tilly pressed her hand on to Krista's belly, her fingers splayed across the stretched cotton. *Possessive. Intimate.* Krista did not like it very much and moved away.

'I think you should sit down. Over there by the fountains,' Tilly said.

The stone ledge on which they perched warmed their thighs. Trafalgar Square was thronged with people enjoying the warmth. Admittedly, their clothing was drab, but if things had been bad in the past and probably still would be in the future, this glorious day at least was giving them a breathing space.

The two of them felt easy sitting together in the sun. 'You're not in any pain?' asked Tilly. She drummed her fingers on the stone. 'No twinges?'

'Not at all.'

Tilly focused on a puppy leaping around a small boy with a ball. 'Nice,' she said. Her breathing sounded a little odd to Krista. 'All being well, that will be you soon. Funny, though.'

'Funny? Is it funny?'

'You and Gus are not like a normal couple. When you first arrived, I asked myself if there was any connection between the two of you at

342

all. Like Julia had with her Martin, I mean.' Tilly opened up her bag and rooted among the contents which, Krista noted, included a volume of poetry. 'You don't have to stay together, you know.'

'Tilly, that is . . . ' Krista would have liked to have said 'outrageous' but she was so dismayed that her English temporarily deserted her. 'Bad.'

'Got you.' Tilly extracted a pill bottle from the bag. 'Oh, come on. We're adults. I only want to help you both. Gus is very dear to me. Very loved.' She unscrewed the bottle top and shook a pill into the palm of her hand. 'And I'm growing fond of you, too. What I wanted to say was this: don't be stuck for no good reason.' She inspected the white oval pill on her spread palm. 'There are lots of secrets from this war. Many will never be known.'

Krista began to feel uneasy. 'What are you taking, Tilly?'

Tilly grinned. 'Just getting through the day.' She tossed the pill into her mouth and swallowed. 'I thought it would be helpful for you to know that you aren't stuck, Krista. You can always take action.'

The stone under Krista's thighs suddenly seemed too hot. First Nella, now Tilly.

Tilly retrieved her cigarettes from the bag and lit up. 'I don't wish to pry. I *hate* prying. Enough people do it to me so I know what I'm talking about. But I sense you're not completely settled.'

Krista opened her mouth to protest but Tilly cut her off.

'Why would you like it here? Terrible old

343

England, full of prejudices and hatred of foreigners. Ignorant, also. If we are told that Germans have horns on their heads, we believe it. Anyway, now that you have, or so you tell me, conquered my brother's heart, you will have cottoned on that we are as dull as ditch water.' She blew a stream of smoke away from Krista. There was a dreamy, detached look in her eyes and the pupils were huge. 'As you say, if you did return to Germany, you couldn't take the baby. But you could . . . you could leave it behind.' Her cigarette glowed red. 'It would have the best of care and love, you know.'

She sounded exaggeratedly concerned, which Krista found disconcerting.

'I don't know what you are trying to say.' She struggled to her feet. 'I'm going home.'

Tilly stubbed out the cigarette, jumped up and said, 'Stupid me, you must be tired. I'm going to put you in a taxi this minute and you will go home and rest.'

It was as if the conversation had never taken place.

★ ★ ★

Am I being watched?

The conversation with Tilly stirred up the old terrors and they winged in. They were hard to fight. In the privacy of the bedroom, Krista sat on the bed, folded her arms and bent over as far as she was able.

Be silent.

Life here was good. It was possible.

344

There was no reason to swivel round at the sound of a footstep too close behind her. This wasn't Berlin. This was plain old, exhausted, shabby London, with agents who clocked off at five-thirty.

She and the unborn baby were safe.

Getting up from the bed, she went over to the drawer where she kept the notebook, took it out and opened it, smoothing the pages flat.

Recently, I have become expert in the insignia and the big, fair Ruskie is a major. Anyway, he insisted on showing me his papers. It seemed important to him. He stalked around the ruins of the refectory, which I had commandeered for my bedroom, and told me how to stuff cardboard into the holes in the walls to keep out the draughts. After a bit he unbuckled his belt, threw it down and hooked his jacket over a beam. Then . . . then, he looked at me as if to ask permission.

While this was happening, I could hear the cries from the kitchen area, where I knew Lotte was, and the chapel, where some of the Sisters had fled. There was no permission being asked of them.

'Please,' I said. 'I am very sore. Please be gentle.' Do you know? He was. I didn't expect a Ruskie to be kind. And, in the morning, he sang in a gorgeous tenor voice. I cried.

Some pages further on, she had written:

There was a row of women with their backs to the wall in the market. Ordinary women with homespun clothes, which were as respectable as they could be in the circumstances. Beside each woman was a pile of tins. The soldiers pushed forward, dropped a tin on the pile and the perfunctory jogging of haunches ensued. Nobody was enjoying themselves. It was just an exchange of goods. A female body for a tin of spam.

'Never again,' she said out loud and folded her hands over her belly. 'Never again.'

21

Krista and Gus were getting dressed in their bedroom when Gus announced quietly, 'Krista, the work I'm doing has to be speeded up and I won't be around as much as I would like.'

'But not in Berlin?'

Gus selected a deep-red tie from the rack and slotted it around his neck. 'Actually, yes, in Berlin. But not before the baby.'

She reached up to knot the tie. It was a little thing she did for him which had become a habit with them. 'Haven't you done your bit?'

'With the mess Europe is in, I don't think we'll ever have done our bit.' Gus rested his hands on her shoulders. 'They wanted you to go, too, but I told them you were pregnant and that put paid to it.'

'For the time being?'

'For good, if I have anything to do with it. But I must warn you that they may send you back in the end.' Krista grimaced. 'It was the deal. We need information, as much as we can get. The picture is now very different and the Soviets are going to give us hell.' He reached for his jacket. 'I wasn't going to mention it. Then I realized that they might approach you without telling me and you needed to be briefed.'

She raised a quizzical eyebrow. 'And you would trust me not to tell them that my husband was letting me in on confidential matters?'

347

'Sadly, everyone is just as jumpy in peacetime as they were during the war.' He pulled down his cuffs. 'Would you tell?' he asked softly.

She moved closer to Gus until their bodies were almost touching. 'Probably. Almost certainly, in fact.'

He grinned. 'If I'm away, you'll have to be clever and careful. I know how difficult it's been for you, settling here. I know many people dislike you on principle. Then they get to know you . . . ' His voice deepened. 'But you have one big advantage, Krista. Everyone wants to forget about the damn war and never wants to hear another word about it.'

'How ruthless nations are,' she remarked. 'And how greedy of their citizens' lives. Yours, mine, any nation.'

He made a face in the mirror. 'My bosses will demand their pound of flesh and I can't disagree with that, Krista. It's a question of what I can negotiate. Do you know any Russian?'

'Very little. In the ministry we had to look at transcripts of Russian broadcasts.'

'I think we both should brush up on it. It will help.'

She touched him on the shoulder. 'You mustn't worry about us.' She meant the baby.

He caught the reflection of her in the mirror and turned round. 'Don't stop.'

'What?'

'Smiling. It suits you.'

'Then I won't.'

She stood on tiptoe and peered over his shoulder, and the mirror threw back the image of both of them. Reflected in his eyes was a question: *Is redemption possible?*

Then Gus laughed and tapped the tip of Krista's nose with his finger. 'You have been . . . are kind to me, Krista.'

She breathed him in. His particular scent was becoming so familiar: a hint of tobacco, a hint of the cologne with which he patted his face after shaving. She liked it very much.

★ ★ ★

Gus predicted correctly and was working flat out. Most evenings, he did not return home until late. Krista occupied herself with the house, with visiting Herr Laube, working in the garden and organizing clothes and equipment for the baby.

The sunny weather had broken and the temperature varied from day to day, suggesting autumn was on its way.

One afternoon, the doorbell rang unexpectedly.

Krista went to open it. A man stood on the doorstep and she recognized him as Teddy Myers.

His eyes rested briefly on her belly. 'I don't think we have ever been properly introduced but can I come in?'

'Gus is not here,' she said.

Teddy doffed his hat, revealing features that appeared harsher and thinner than when she had seen him all those months back with the carol singers. 'Can I speak to Julia?'

349

Ushering him into the drawing room, she went to find Julia. On learning that Teddy was in the house, Julia gave a start. 'Are you sure it's Teddy?' She touched the coil of hair at her neck. 'Will I do?'

'Yes.'

'Quite sure?'

'Julia, are you all right? Does Teddy bother you?'

Julia cast her such a ferocious look that Krista shrank back. 'Teddy is a family friend. And could I ask that you don't join us?'

The words lashed Krista, making it clear she was not wanted. Heaving herself as fast as she could back up the stairs, she grabbed a jacket from the coat stand. She would be leaving Teddy to kick his heels in the drawing room but she didn't care. She let herself out of the house.

A couple of early falling leaves had sifted down on to the bodywork of the black car which was parked outside the house. In her agitation, Krista hurried past and only vaguely registered that the driver was a woman.

As she stood at the roadside waiting to cross, the same black car drew up alongside her and stopped. 'Krista,' called Nella through the open passenger window. 'Get in.'

'Why on earth would I do that?' replied Krista, struggling to fasten her jacket over her swollen belly.

Nella got out of the car. In a navy-blue felt hat and costume suit, she seemed calm and looked very pretty. 'You seem agitated. Is anything the matter?'

'I am fine,' said Krista. 'What about Teddy?'

'Teddy can manage the walk. It will probably help him cool off. He's still so angry with Gus. Swearing dire vengeance and setting the council on him. It's rather wonderful to have someone fight your corner so fiercely. I didn't think he would.' Nella reached behind to the back seat for her handbag. 'I spotted you rush past the car.'

Krista shifted to face Nella, and the feelings of paranoia that she had battled so hard rose to the surface. She blurted out: 'Are you here to gloat? Or criticize? Or what?'

'None of those things.' Nella grimaced. 'When I was in Cairo I was in charge of an office. A small one, I agree. Now it appears my function in life is to drive my wounded brother around.' There was a hint of anger. 'Teddy wanted a word with Julia. We were passing the house. It was as simple as that.' She put up a hand and pulled off her hat, shaking her hair free. 'But I can't pretend that I'm not tempted to spy on you and Gus.' The corners of the pretty mouth turned down. 'Wouldn't you be drawn to watching the man you thought you were going to marry with the wife that took your place? It could become a compulsion. It makes a good story. Don't you think?'

'If you say so,' replied Krista.

Nella's voice shook slightly. 'A warrior went away to war leaving behind a girl to whom he was promised. But he met a girl from an enemy tribe and married her instead.' There was a glimmer of a malicious smile.

351

Krista flashed back, 'You must let Gus and me be.'

Nella ignored her. 'The warrior brought her home but the tribe never accepted her. And, in truth, she was ill and,' Nella flicked her eyes up and met Krista's, 'it was said she would never get better in the strange land.'

Krista pressed a shaky finger to her lips. 'That is a wicked thing to say.'

'It's only a story,' said Nella. 'No harm in that.' She paused. 'No harm at all.'

'But there is.' Krista finally got the jacket to do up. '*You* go home, Nella.'

For a second, Nella looked defeated. Shrunken, even.

As fast as her pregnant state would permit her, Krista fled over the road and on to the Common.

The sun was beginning to set. Filaments of light spiked through the tree canopy. Having got to know the Common, Krista realized it was best to stick to the path rather than to strike out across the sward where the trenches and ditches were treacherous.

Footsteps sounded behind her and, desperate to be alone, she broke into a half-run.

Panting, she tried to make for the church spire poking through the clump of trees directly ahead. To her right, there was a huddle of temporary houses erected during the war, which Gus had said would be coming down. A couple of women with cigarettes in their mouths stood outside their front doors, folding up grubby-looking sheets.

Her belly weighing on her bladder put a brake on her speed and the tendons in her groin twinged in protest.

Someone grabbed Krista's sleeve and tugged hard.

'Stop! You'll . . . ' Nella was out of breath. 'You'll harm the baby.'

The exertion had made Krista's head buzz and she put a hand up to her temple. Seeing this, Nella gripped her other arm so tightly Krista thought the bone would snap.

'Krista . . . ' Nella's lipstick had smudged. 'The baby.'

'My baby doesn't concern you.'

'It's Gus's baby. Of course that concerns me. Anything about Gus concerns me.'

The warrior brought her home but the tribe never accepted her.

'*Grüss Gott,* you are mad. All of you,' Krista whispered.

Nella guided Krista towards the nearest bench, which happened to overlook one of the trenches. 'Sit down, Krista. I order you.'

Krista eased herself down. Thankfully.

'What on earth were you thinking?' Nella was looking down at her, a big question mark in her eyes.

Krista took in a shuddering breath. 'Listen to me. Whatever happened between you, Gus is now married to me. It may be that he still thinks of you in the way that you suggest but we *are* married.' She gestured to her belly. 'The important thing is the baby and he and I agree on that.'

353

Nella walked over to the trench and balanced on its edge, a manoeuvre which sent waterfalls cascading down its sides. 'I don't think you understand how Gus thinks. But I understand. He wants a normal life. That's what he always told me. And it won't be normal with you.'

Then you don't know him, flashed through Krista. 'That is not how Gus is any longer,' she said.

Nella pointed into the trench, which was a deep one. 'If I was being truthful, I would say I wish I could throw you into one of these and you would disappear.'

'Is that an English joke?'

Nella laughed nervously. 'Of course.'

'And I could push you in too, and no one would ever believe a pregnant woman could do such a thing.'

'I almost wish you would.' Nella cried.

The sun was slanting across the path and a couple of the muscovy ducks on the pond in the distance were having a spat.

Krista focused on the ducks. 'Have you and Tilly been talking?'

'No. Why?'

She shook her head. 'Nothing. Only she . . . No, nothing.'

Nella was intrigued. 'You shouldn't listen to Tilly. She's often a bit wild.'

'She thought I might want to go back to Germany.'

'Tilly said that?' A secretive, cunning look streaked across Nella's features. 'It's a good option,' she murmured. 'As we discussed once before?'

354

'You will take that back, Nella.'

Nella looked everywhere except at Krista. 'Yes,' she said. 'I should.'

A cloud sailed over the sun.

Krista went into battle. 'You could not know what it took to get me here and you will not know what it took to keep on going. There were times when I wanted to die. Can you understand that? Perhaps you can? But that desire is powerful and becomes a habit. I had to will myself not to give in to it. I had to stamp on its temptations. But, to live, I had to ignore the rules of good behaviour and what I had been taught was right.'

'I see.'

The uneasy combination of terror and fear, and the fragmentation of her thoughts, which had fuelled Krista for so long and from which she was desperate to free herself, had become second nature. 'So you will now know that I have become a formidable enemy. I know what it takes to survive. And once that is learned, it is never unlearned. I am prepared to do most things. Perhaps you will never face such a thing. Perhaps you will. But it makes me very difficult to get rid of.'

'Stop, stop, Krista.'

'There.' Krista eased her aching back against the bench. 'It is said.'

The sun had re-emerged, a little weaker, a little less golden, and it was noticeable that, on some of the trees, the leaves were on the turn.

Nella sighed and sat for a long time in silence. Finally, she spoke in a more moderate and conciliatory way. 'That was quite a speech.'

'Do you understand what I am saying, Nella?'

Nella looked this way and that. 'You're right. We are all in danger of going a little mad, especially me. I don't know about Teddy.' Her lips tightened. 'His feelings are so fierce and I can't see him being rational about it for a long time. It's sweet the way he defends me.' She turned her head and gazed over the Common. 'It's so nice to have that. Being defended, I mean. It makes up for . . . a lot of things.'

Krista took a deep breath. 'We should have peace, Nella.'

Nella held out a hand.

Krista took in the panorama of normal life rolling out across the Common. The trees, the patchy grass, the church spire and the traffic. For a moment, she experienced a sensation of rising above all the noise and past conflict into a sphere where hope was not a ghost and shadows did not threaten.

She looked down at the proffered hand. Any civilized being would accept it and ignore the risk.

Yet one thing was for sure in Krista's mind. Until her dying breath, she would use the powers she possessed to ensure that her baby — *the invader she must protect* — knew that he or she was loved.

She took the hand. 'Peace, then, Nella. Yes, and gladly. But if any of you suggest again that I should leave my baby, I will not account for my actions.'

★ ★ ★

Krista left the encounter shaken, but did not say anything about it to Gus.

Not through choice, and not from any fault of hers, Nella had suffered and publicly and Krista felt that the other woman was entitled to some privacy.

In a rare invitation, the Cliftons were invited to the Swithins' house in an adjacent road for what their hostess warned them would be a 'scratch' supper. 'But isn't it more important,' Judy Swithin added, 'for us all to begin to socialize again?'

Nobody wished to dispute that.

The evening had been enjoyable, and feeling that all was well with the world, Julia, Gus and Krista (no Tilly) said their goodnights to the Swithins and walked back home through a warm night.

Getting ready for bed, Krista removed her precious stockings and rolled them up, then, as she stowed them in the drawer, her fingers brushed against the package containing the gun.

She pulled it out.

'I was hoping . . . ' Gus had come up behind her.

'Yes?' She held out the gun like a votive offering.

'That you're happier. Would I be correct?'

'I am,' she replied. 'Can't you tell?'

She took aim at the window. 'Are you going to teach me to use this?'

Gus took it away. 'Not at the moment. Possibly I might have to, if we end up in Berlin.'

'Gus, since there's no need for it here, you must take it away.'

'You feel you can yield it up?'

She held his gaze. 'I do.'

A smile leaped into his eyes. He took the package from her, unwrapped it, and checked out the gun before rewrapping it and putting it away. 'I will take it back to Berlin when I go.'

Later on, in bed, Gus was lying close to her, breathing quietly and comfortably.

'Gus, what was Teddy to you?'

'Questions, questions,' he murmured. 'You know he was my friend. My best friend.'

Krista looked across the dark mass of his shape under the blankets. 'I talked to Nella the other day. It was all right. We managed. But Teddy is still swearing vengeance, she said.'

Gus had become instantly wakeful, as she knew he would.

She wanted to explain to Gus what she was thinking. Teddy was undoubtedly angry for his sister and almost — that old-fashioned thing — angry for his family's honour. Yet there were other elements, too, not least a profound sense of betrayal and not just for Nella.

Jilted.

The implications of the word hit Krista with a percussive shock.

At a stroke, it fell into place. Teddy loved Gus and, by encouraging the marriage that had never taken place, he would have ensured keeping him close.

She felt her way carefully. 'Gus, Nella said something which made me wonder about what Teddy is up to. He is very angry with you. I think . . . ' She very nearly blurted: *Teddy loves*

you. Instead, she said, 'Nella also hinted . . . '
Krista slid into German. 'She hinted that he was
so angry it might direct his decisions at the
council.'

There, it had been said.

'I'm not going to answer that one because I
can't.' Gus sounded annoyed. He sat up and
tucked the sheets and blankets around Krista's
shoulders. 'Will you ever let a man go to sleep?'

★ ★ ★

Just after dawn, the back wall of Number 26
collapsed with a shocking sound resembling an
explosion.

Gus leaped up and padded down the corridor
to the window overlooking the gardens.

Not yet properly awake, Krista found herself
cowering against the pillow; all the old demons
springing into life.

Returning, Gus took in the situation and was
at her side in an instant. 'It wasn't a bomb,
Krista. It's Number 26. Remember, I pointed it
out.' He shifted her awkward, pregnant shape
against him and cradled her.

Krista fought for control. 'I don't want to be a
trouble to you. But a bang.'

He stroked her head. 'Bugger the bangs.'

After a moment, she managed a feeble laugh.
'Bugger the bangs.'

'The baby won't like you being anxious.'

She took his hand in hers. Her slender fingers
slid around his masculine palm. 'Understood.'

'Good,' he said softly.

359

A few minutes later, fire engines clanged up outside and screeched to a halt. 'There are quite a few of them,' Gus reported from the bedroom window. Krista joined him there.

A couple of firemen swung down from the vehicle and padded up to the front garden. There was no fire, and after checking on the rest of the building they were on their way again.

First thing in the morning, before breakfast, the ruin recorder knocked on the door.

Gus let him in. 'I admire your rapid response, Mr — ?'

'Forrest.' He nodded to Krista. 'The fire services are always quick off the mark and phone us. It's important to get the 'Danger' notices up.'

'The damage looks bad,' said Gus. 'Is it?'

'It is.'

'No one hurt?'

'Not as far as I could see. You must have known the owners?'

'Not really. We knew the neighbours at Number 24, of course. Do you know what will happen to Number 26?'

'Demolished, I imagine.' Mr Forrest spoke with real regret.

'And Numbers 24 and 28?'

'We shall have to wait and see.'

'And us?'

Mr Forrest made some notes. 'The council is looking to build blocks of flats.' It was obvious he was taking care to sound neutral. 'It's a way of rehousing several families in one go.' He stuck his pencil into his pocket. 'But I will be reporting this to the relevant parties. If Mrs Orville is at home, do please send her my regards.'

After breakfast, Gus asked: 'Do you want an adventure?'

'Why not?'

Gus and Krista let themselves out of the house by the scullery door. In the back gardens, except for a cluster of birds in the sycamore tree sounding off, quiet reigned. There was a glow to the morning, a lushness, she thought, a ripeness and an autumn smell of damp leaves. Gus guided Krista carefully through the hole in the damaged wall and into the Johnsons' abandoned garden. Keeping a tight grip on her hand, he helped her to pick her way through the freshly scattered rubble and plaster.

Peering over the wall into Number 26, she gave an audible intake of breath. It was so familiar and, yet, so unfamiliar.

The back wall of the top storey had been peeled away like an onion, exposing a bathroom and a bedroom. As a result, the side wall had buckled under the strain and, its moorings ripped apart, the house had sagged and been brought to its knees.

Gus anchored his hand firmly under Krista's elbow. 'The ground floor still looks intact. Perhaps it will be possible to rebuild.'

Krista peered at the stricken house. 'I hope no one was in there. Julia said she had seen a man disappear into a house about here.'

Gus frowned and said, 'The firemen would have found them if anyone had been in there.'

'What's that?'

He followed the line of her pointing finger.

Snaggled on to a beam extruding from the heaped scree of brick and plaster was a furry object. 'A teddy bear, I think.'

'Can we get it?'

Gus levered himself up over the wall and retrieved it. Filthy and minus an eye, it was still recognizably a teddy.

Krista held it to her chest and dust sifted over her dress. 'It deserves a chance. Like us.'

They picked their way back over the abandoned garden, leaving dark footprints in the overgrown, dew-slicked grass. The birds stepped up their clatter and chatter and Krista stopped to look up at a cluster of them in the sycamore. 'It must have been nice here once. Very peaceful.'

Back at Number 22, Tilly had arrived home and was brewing up a small amount of real coffee in the kitchen.

With her hair scraped back into a turban made from a head-scarf and wearing Moroccan leather slippers with trodden-down backs, she seemed cheerful enough if a little withdrawn. 'I thought you could all do with a treat in our post-war, rationed Britain.' She added wryly, 'Not even a Labour government, it seems, can beat the rationing.'

'Patience. It will happen,' said Gus, who was delighted to see her. 'I've missed you, Tilly.'

Krista and Tilly exchanged greetings: polite and tactful, each tacitly acknowledging that it was necessary to take care with the other. Krista admired the Moroccan slippers and Tilly commented on how well Krista was looking. That was all. The ease between them had vanished.

'Did Krista tell you about our jaunt to see the paintings?' Tilly asked Gus.

'She did.' Gus slipped an arm around Tilly's shoulders. 'It was good of you.'

Julia arrived in the kitchen. '*That* smell.' She was dressed in her good cotton frock with a cardigan draped over her shoulders. Tilly handed a cup over to Julia, who took it and said, 'You look a bit pale, Tilly. Have you been overdoing it?'

Tilly said angrily, 'No.'

Gus was delighted to be with his sisters and their bond was evident in the banter, the glancing references to old events, old jokes, family matters that did not require full explanations. Having laid out the rescued bear on newspaper on the sideboard, Krista sat down and watched them with her chin in her hand.

She concentrated on the coffee. How wonderfully — joyously — rich it tasted, triggering memories of the foods and taste sensations for which she yearned.

Eighteen, seventeen...

'*How* did you get the coffee?' Gus accepted a cup and inhaled deeply.

'You look as though you're about to purr.' Tilly bent over and kissed Gus on the cheek.

'I am.'

'What's that?' Tilly had noticed the bear.

'A teddy bear. I'm rescuing it.'

With an awkward jerk, Tilly turned her back and there was a jittery crash on to the hob as she banged down a saucepan. 'You don't want *that*,' she said, her voice darkening. 'It looks like a tiny corpse.'

'Yes, I do.' Krista touched its battered face with a fingertip. 'He will recover.'

She placed a hand over her coffee cup to shield it in case any drop of the precious coffee should spill. Gus looked fondly at them both.

22

Julia was holed up with Teddy in a dive in Rupert Street in Piccadilly. The gin was trickling nicely down to her stomach and sending out the glow which she had grown to welcome, even to rely on.

'How are things with Michael?' Teddy asked.

The base of her neck tingled with an increasingly familiar mixture of shame, confusion and excitement. 'Fine. He's nice enough.' She pushed back her hair. 'And useful to you?'

He gave Julia a quick half-smile as if to say: *You're learning fast.* 'I've been meaning to ask. Your Mr Forrest was in contact the other day about the house that collapsed.'

'He's not *my* Mr Forrest.' Julia assessed the level of gin in her glass. It was astonishing how it went down so quickly. 'He drops in quite frequently. Something of a pest, actually. It's sad about the house. The back wall collapsed.'

'Has he inspected Number 22?'

'I believe so. Gus has the report.'

Teddy signalled to the waiter for refills. There was a tiny, but pregnant, silence. 'You couldn't get hold of it for me, could you, darling? It would be useful.'

'What on earth for?'

'Could you?'

'It's possible.'

The waiter placed a second gin-and-something in front of Julia and she anticipated with pleasure the evening ahead. It would be spent in this noisy, smoky club, becoming pleasantly drunk.

'Only, I would ask that you don't let Gus know,' Teddy was saying. 'Do you think you could do that? I'll come and get it.'

'Teddy, I'm not sure. I don't know what Gus would do if he found out.'

'He won't find out. I'll give it back to you within the day. Once I've copied it.'

The voice of prudence muttered in her ear, but only in a feeble way. Julia drew a pattern in the frosting on her glass. 'Stupid question, but are you wanting to get at Gus in some way?' She glanced up from under her eyelids. 'I would understand why.'

'Now, how could I possibly do that?' Teddy nodded at an acquaintance standing by the bar. 'You've been reading thrillers again, Jules. That's not to say I wouldn't mind giving Gus a punch. But reading a report on the house isn't exactly training a gun on him, is it? As I told you, the council has employed me to work with the surveyors in the area and every bit of information is helpful. They are a bit slow on releasing the documentation to people like me. It all has to go through endless procedures. You know the sort of infuriating thing? I'd like to get ahead.' He sent Julia one of his affectionate, but increasingly rare, smiles. 'That's all.'

Julia saw the logic. 'I suppose.'

One of Teddy's friends, a small man with suspiciously black hair, came and stood by their table. Ignoring Julia, he said, 'Teddy, will I be seeing you later?'

'You will,' said Teddy.

Julia watched them talking. Not for the first time, she realized that the kind of man Martin had been was out of fashion and it was the sharp-suited operators in clubs like this who were calling the shots.

The man moved off and Teddy turned his attention back to her. 'Sweetheart . . . We deal together very well, don't we?'

'Do we?' She was aware she must sound bleak and unhelpful and it was not how she wished Teddy to view her. It would be far, far better to suggest that she was positive and in control. She eyed her cocktail. 'Yes, we do deal well together, Teddy. I trust you and it's lovely that we are still talking to each other. Let's make a pact never to fall out.'

Into the inscrutable features crept something which Julia analysed as relief, but she couldn't be sure.

'You might find this hard to believe, but I miss Gus. He and I . . . ' He killed the rest of the sentence. 'Perhaps in the future, when everything has died down?' His tone became brisk. 'You haven't told Gus about our meetings, have you? Or about your other meetings?'

He inflected the word 'other' very delicately, in a way that made it seem practically obscene.

'No. No,' she got in quickly. 'And I don't want Gus, or anyone, to know. Will you promise me, Teddy?'

Teddy breathed in sharply — a triumphant little hiss. 'That depends.'

'*Teddy!* Don't tease me.'

Immediately, he backed off. 'No, of course not. It was a joke, sweetheart.'

Julia decided that discretion was the better part of valour. Even if Teddy was up to no good with the council — and she had no proof — she was not going to be the one to jeopardize the new understanding between them. Its proceeds were far too enjoyable.

'So,' he was saying, 'the report?'

She pushed her glass over to him. 'Could I have another, darling Teddy, and I'll see if it is in his desk?'

They agreed it would be unwise for Teddy to come to the house again. He suggested that, since Julia was the one going to all the trouble to help him, he would take her to a matinee on the following Tuesday. 'So we can have some fun, sweetie. You deserve it.' He clinked his glass against hers. 'Chocolates and all.'

On the Tuesday morning, having checked that Krista was out, Julia went into Gus's study.

At the best of times, the study was too small and it had been made smaller by the arrival of a cumbersome filing cabinet. This had been delivered in a van the previous week by two preternaturally silent men in brown overalls who lugged it into the house and nailed it to the floor. Gus said it had been necessary for his papers.

Unsurprisingly, after all the trouble to install it, it was locked but it was easy enough to go through Gus's desk drawers. The first one revealed a stack of neatly assembled household bills and not much else. As she worked through them, her cheeks burned and she was almost deafened by a pulse thumping in her ears. God knew what Martin would have thought of this behaviour — searching in Krista's things, now this. And the other things, too.

The bottom drawer yielded a buff folder on which was written 'Number 22' in Gus's handwriting. She grabbed it, rifled through and found the report signed by Mr Forrest.

She handed it over to Teddy in the foyer of London's New Theatre, where J. B. Priestley's *An Inspector Calls* was playing. Having arrived early — how stupid to appear so keen, she thought — she had been forced to circulate around the foyer, pretending to study the carved panelling and gilding and to look perfectly at ease.

Her agitation was partly owing to Teddy being late, which she felt was rather insulting, and partly down to her conscience. Feeling guilty made her slightly queasy and prone to resentment, which she knew was not attractive. The upshot was that, when he eventually arrived, her greeting was a cold one.

'Hey, what's this?' He held her by the shoulders. 'Smile for me, sweetie.'

Julia obeyed reluctantly. Teddy frowned and removed his hands. 'Let's not make a drama out of this. I'm sorry I'm late. Have you brought the report?'

The hint of ice in his voice made her panic. Extracting it from her handbag, she thrust it into Teddy's hand and he skimmed through it. 'Aha. Perfect.' All coldness had vanished and he turned the charm on Julia. 'I'll return it as promised, so no need to worry.'

'I know you will. But are you sure — ' She didn't get the chance to ask her question.

'As sure as eggs are eggs.' Teddy resurrected the old saying from their childhood. 'Look, if it will make you feel better, I'll confess to Gus when I return the papers.'

Julia suspected Teddy had no intention of doing anything of the sort but she did not want any more difficulty between them.

By now, a crowd had gathered in the foyer. There was noise, laughter, a sense of anticipation. This is our reward for living under the cosh of war, Julia thought, and she felt it thrill down her body into her toes. Perhaps this was the moment when life would begin again; when pleasure and colour and sensuous experience would all return.

'Look, sweetie, I'm so sorry but I can't come to the play after all. Something's come up.' Taking up one of Julia's gloved hands, he pressed into it a small box of chocolates. 'Will these make it up to you? I practically had to bribe the Minister for Food to get them.'

With that, Teddy steered Julia towards the usher, handed over her ticket and, without a backward glance, limped away.

★　★　★

Later that evening, in a hotel bedroom, Julia undressed in front of Michael.

The two of them had eaten a dinner composed

370

of tastes of which she dreamed. The richness of the wine sauce, the very fishy-ness of the sole, suggested another life which Julia had only seen in films. Over dessert, Michael had made it plain that he was looking forward very much to another kind of dessert. The humour was heavy-handed but Julia was not going to take offence. Why should she?

Of course there was a niggle. Actually, more like a problem. Since the first occasion, she realized that going to bed with Michael presented its dangers. Pregnancy and, God forbid, disease were terrors that dogged women and they were so little discussed that she found it difficult to know what to do. Should she ask him to provide precautions? But she couldn't quite bring herself to raise the subject of contraception with him and sensed that Michael considered it something for Julia to deal with. The situation struck her as amusing. Here she was, taking off her clothes and doing all sorts with Michael in bed, but she could not have told anyone the first thing about him.

'Women,' Tilly had once said with her lecture look that Julia found infuriating, 'have been forced into a condition of perpetual fear over this sort of thing because men know they would not be able to control them otherwise.'

The hook on the fastening on her suspender belt had been pulled out of shape and Julia had to tug at it hard. Would she dare to ask Tilly for contraceptive advice? One of her stockings, which she had draped over the chair, fell to the floor but, in her half-naked state, she hesitated to bend over to retrieve it. She solved the problem by dipping down and scooping it up.

It helped that Michael had no pretensions to be dashing; he was manoeuvring out of his trousers in anything but a graceful manner. In bed, however, he was pretty bold and had more than a good idea of what Julia wanted. Towards the end, swollen with desire and greed, she uttered a cry which seemed to please him.

Julia went home in a taxi. Looking out into the dark, autumnal streets, she told herself for the umpteenth time since she had begun this business that maybe she would be able to manage a double life.

The following Saturday, the postman delivered the morning post at the usual time before breakfast. Julia bore it down to the kitchen and stacked it on the table. Thanks to Krista, the dingy kitchen was turning out to be a nice place in which to spend time and she felt a rush of affection for all the familiar things in it. The blue-and-white china, the green-lidded storage tins and the bread board with the outline of a loaf carved into it.

Humming, she measured out oats for the porridge, put them on a low gas on the stove and made a pot of tea. Drinking it, she made her plans which, hopefully, meant she would not be spending too much time at Number 22.

So thinking, Julia gave herself up to the contemplation of her new, and secret, life of nice dinners, taxis and meeting people. Also, she wanted to get to know better what went on in the world. Despite her marriage, it was now clear that she had been innocent about many things — money, politics, business — and it was time to rectify her ignorance.

Gus walked into the kitchen. 'You're up early.' He placed an affectionate hand on her shoulder. 'Trust you had a good evening.' He sat down, saying, 'Give us some tea, dear sister,' and took up the first letter from the pile of post and slit it open.

There was silence, followed by the exclamation: 'What the hell?'

'Bad news?'

Gus put down the letter. 'It's from the solicitors working for the council. Apparently, they have read Forrest's report and have concluded that the foundations of the houses in our part of the terrace are unstable. They want to requisition it and demolish it.'

A fearsome jolt went through Julia. 'That's ridiculous, Gus. The council can't just take it.'

Gus got to his feet. 'Not if I have anything to do with it.'

Krista interrupted them. 'Is there something wrong?'

Despite her advanced pregnancy, her dress, which had been run up by Ada's mother from some blue material which Krista had discovered in the attic, was too loose and fitted badly over the shoulder. Gus helped her into a chair. Easing herself down, Krista placed a hand on her belly. I used to do that, thought Julia.

'The council deems the house unsafe. It wants to demolish it and to build a block of flats in its place,' said Gus.

'Tell them no.' Krista accepted the bowl of porridge which Julia placed in front of her.

Gus was rereading the letter. Reaching behind him, he pulled open a kitchen drawer. 'Where's the bloody pencil we keep in here?' Unearthing a stub, he set about annotating the letter.

Krista made valiant attempts to eat the porridge but gave up.

'I thought it would do you good,' Julia said mechanically. 'The baby.'

'You're right,' said Krista, picking up the spoon. 'Thank you.' She swallowed a couple of mouthfuls. 'May I see the letter?' Gus handed it over and she read it carefully, taking her time to decipher the council jargon. 'In Germany we would probably have to bribe someone to get this overlooked. Can you do this here?'

Gus actually laughed. 'No. It doesn't work that way here.'

'*Ach so.*' Krista returned to the letter. 'It says you must contact the solicitor immediately.' She placed a finger on the signature on the letter and there was a small, cold silence. 'Gus, you have seen that the name of the solicitor in charge is Teddy Myers?'

★ ★ ★

Julia felt she had no option but to visit Teddy in his office and demand to see him.

Teddy wasn't there when she arrived at nine-thirty on the dot on Monday morning. His secretary, a grey, bustling woman in a twinset that was puckered and bobbled from too much washing, suggested that Julia wait on one of the uncomfortable chairs set aside for clients.

Julia sat impatiently, longing for a cup of tea, but the secretary was not going to offer one. She both understood, and didn't understand, what Teddy was up to. 'You're sure he is due in this morning?' she ventured after half an hour, to be informed sharply that he was.

The windows in the office required cleaning and dust had accumulated in the corners of the room and on the furniture. Of all the friends, Teddy had always been the tidy one and the state of the office struck Julia as odd.

Eventually, she found herself facing him across the forbiddingly large desk in his office. There was no point in mincing words. 'You wanted me to give you that report in order to get at Gus.'

Equally, Teddy did not bother to pretend. 'Fair game, Julia.'

'You can't destroy our home because Gus chose to marry a woman other than your sister.'

He shifted his bad leg. The dark circles under his eyes seemed to have deepened. 'Don't flatter yourself, Julia. I don't care enough about the Cliftons to put myself to the effort. Losing a house is not the end of the world. There are hundreds of thousands in the same boat. Have you read the newspapers? Refugees are swarming all over Europe like a biblical plague.'

She said desperately, 'The house is all we've got.'

'Get another one. You will have the funds. No one is proposing not to compensate you.'

Julia searched for her cigarettes in her bag and

tried to think clearly. What she said now would probably set them all on a course from which it would be impossible to row back. 'Being jilted is awful and what Gus did is pretty shocking, but it's not the first time it's happened and won't be the last.' She shoved the cigarette case over to Teddy but kept her hand on it, which forced him to look at her. 'Nella will find someone else.' His fingers brushed against hers as he picked up the case. 'What good will it do, Teddy?'

Teddy took his time to light up. 'I have very little say over council decisions. All I do is supply them with legal advice. If I'm pushed, I would have to admit that I approve the idea of new homes. It's what the country needs and it will help to get businesses up and running.'

'Oh, my God.' A shock wave rippled through Julia. Not only was she an innocent but she had been positively stupid. 'You and Michael. Michael and the concrete. You're making money off the backs of each other. Michael talked about providing his concrete for affordable homes.'

Teddy was amused by her indignation. 'If you can see past your own interests, sweetheart, you will see that we all have a duty to make this country work again after what has happened.'

'With corruption?'

A telephone rang in the next room.

'Could I remind you that you have slept with Michael for the price of a dinner?' He sounded very understanding and not at all accusatory, which brought a lump into her throat. 'I hope you got good champagne and food out of it. We missed all that for so long.'

376

Julia shook herself mentally. What she had done, she had done, and she was damned if she would allow herself to cry over it.

Teddy opened a drawer and took out a file. 'Being sorry or outraged won't change anything. If I'm disgusting, so are you. But I don't think that going after something I want, or need, is disgusting. And, in your case, it's all very discreet and no one is going to get hurt. As for the house? That was damaged anyway and nothing to do with me.' He extracted the report from the file and pushed it over to her. 'Here it is. For what it's worth, I would have read it sooner or later. You just helped me speed things up, that's all, sweetie.'

Her fingers felt cold and disobedient. Nevertheless, she managed to stuff it into her handbag. 'To think,' she began and checked herself.

Teddy moved over to the bookshelf between streaked, grimy windows and finished the sentence for her. 'Weren't you going to say: 'To think that I — ' Teddy, that is — 'was the man in whom you were interested'?' Julia felt the blood storm into her cheeks. 'To talk frankly is a good thing, wouldn't you say? In fact, it's probably the only thing left that keeps us sane. So, I will be frank. I can only say that, if I was going to be interested in anyone, it would be you.'

All of them together. Walking. Teddy with his arm draped loosely around Gus's shoulders. The girls bringing up the rear.

A golden circle.

She stared at the back turned on her. Teddy was being far from frank — even she got that.

There was an evasion lying beneath his words, a swerving from the truth, however well meant.

'Don't lie to me. *Please.*' Teddy did not respond but she sensed a struggle and groped her way towards the explanation. 'Please.' She was conscious of the breath on her lips and a surge of the wilder feelings which were becoming familiar.

She watched his now-rigid figure and something prodded her on — no matter that she was again risking humiliation. But, these days, that's how she appeared to function. 'If you married me, then you wouldn't have to worry.'

'Stop it.'

'Think about it. I would do very well for you, Teddy. We understand each other and know each other. I wouldn't expect . . . ' She lost a little of her flow. 'I wouldn't expect what I had before. That's not possible. I make you comfortable. You give me security.'

Finally, Teddy turned round to face her. 'You're a nice person, Julia.'

'No, I'm not,' she said. 'Not any more.'

It was true.

Teddy sent her an odd, vulnerable smile which made Julia catch her breath with pity. 'The war did for me in more ways than one. In a certain way. This is difficult to say, but do you understand? The crude mechanics.'

'I see.'

'I expect you do and you don't.' Teddy slapped the palm of his hand against his bad leg and winced. 'That's not an accusation but just how it is. You can't possibly see the kind of mixed-up stuff in my body. But I'll let you into another secret, Julia, because you've tried to be open with me. It goes deeper than that. I have lost interest in loving man, woman or beast. Or in conducting a relationship, a marriage or whatever. Up on that mountainside, waiting to die, I lost the ability. I bet if you ask that German bride of Gus's, she would say something similar. I recognize the look. She and I — we've experienced the worst, seen the worst, and now we will always expect the worst. I don't know whether to be sorry for Gus or think it bloody serves him right.'

Beaten, she turned her head away and stared at the window and it was impossible now to stem the embarrassing tears rolling down her cheeks.

'Don't cry, Julia.'

She tried to wipe her face with her sleeve.

'Does it make it any better that I regret how I feel? I wish it were otherwise. You're right. We would probably have done very well together.'

Julia pulled on her gloves and rallied whatever shreds of pride and energy she had left. 'At least things are clear between us.' She rose from the chair. 'Teddy, you should get these offices cleaned. They won't impress clients.'

Teddy laughed. 'Indeed.'

'But, since we have been honest with each other, I must tell you that we will fight you over the house. I don't understand what you are doing or why, but it seems you're involved and I'm implicated.'

'You don't understand what I'm doing?' He shut the desk drawer with a snap. 'Despite what I

379

said, I do love one person very much, and that's Nella. If I am not to have a family, I will do what I can for her. It's a matter of honour.' He took a look at her face. 'It's not Greek revenge tragedy, Julia, but near enough.'

'So what are you going to do?'

Teddy stared steadily at her. 'You tell me.'

'Oh God,' said Julia.

★   ★   ★

Extraordinarily, a poetry festival being held in south London ('*That* will be a winner,' said Gus unkindly). But Julia thought it was a brave venture when so many people had other things to worry about.

Tilly, who had been asked to read her latest work, came home to prepare. She was very short-tempered, thin and uncooperative, especially with Krista.

Julia took her to task. 'You're behaving badly,' she told her one afternoon as they sat in the drawing room, where they had lit the first fire of the season. 'You were the one who said we had to be kind to her.' Picking up a log from the basket, she wedged it carefully into the grate. 'You were right. Krista isn't bad.'

Tilly was surrounded by poetry volumes on the sofa but seemed to be having difficulty keeping still. She held up one: ' "Stars, sun, moon . . . I can't reach you. I can't get at you." '

A finger of unease poked Julia. 'You don't seem yourself.' She peered at her sister's white, shuttered features. 'Are you ill?'

380

' "We do not know our own souls, let alone the souls of others," ' Tilly read out in a hoarse voice. 'So true.'

Julia tried again. 'We shall have to think about finding a nanny.'

Tilly threw down the book. 'I hate this baby.' She began to cry with an anguish and hopelessness which frightened Julia.

'What is it, Tilly? *What?*'

Tilly dried her eyes. 'Sorry. It's nothing. Forget it.'

'Tell me what's the matter,' Julia begged.

Tilly looked at her with swollen eyes. 'I said forget it.'

On the day of the poetry festival Julia got herself down to the venue, which was a room opening off the council chamber of the town hall. There she sat on a hard chair among a — very — small audience and listened to a number of poets, some of whom were terrible. But a handsome, dissolute-looking man was good.

Tilly began: ' "The swirl of dreams in the jungle of the id . . . " '

She was good, too, but it struck Julia that her poems were overfull of images of death and grief. Watching her sister's tense, absorbed face as she read aloud in her new hoarse voice, she concluded that something was very definitely wrong.

At the end, Julia convinced Tilly to return to the house, rather than join her fellow poets in the pub. It was evening rush hour and people were on their way home. A grey mass surged towards

381

station entrances and bus stops. Julia slipped her arm under Tilly's elbow and, thus linked, they made their way towards the Common, Tilly's bright-yellow scarf and black cape as always drawing glances. Julia's brown lace-up shoes had recently been mended and they emitted a small squeak at intervals.

Tilly suddenly stopped. 'I feel like a circus pony.'

Julia pushed her forward. 'Your poems are interesting, Tilly.'

'Are they? Do you mean that?' She sucked the compliment down greedily.

The street lights glowed orange and the buses lumbered up and down the pitted streets.

Tilly squeezed Julia's hand. 'I feel all eaten up.'

Julia's shoe squeaked for the umpteenth time. 'If I said I'd managed to get hold of some eggs and have made a sponge cake, would that make you feel better?'

'Cake?' Tilly brightened. 'Well, that solves life's problems.'

Returning to the house, they hung up their outdoor things and went down to the kitchen. The saucepans gleamed, Krista's herbs scented the air and Ada had been in and left a loaf of bread wrapped in a cloth on the table.

The rescued teddy bear had been propped up against the dresser. Tilly inspected it. It had been washed until fluffy and a pirate's patch now hid its missing eye, giving it a rather appealing, cut-throat look. Tilly poked it. 'Hello. What's your name?'

'Hans,' said Julia sarcastically.

She gave Tilly a slice of cake but Tilly managed to eat only a tiny portion.

'You're overdoing it, Tilly.'

'The trouble with being outrageous is that the satisfactions last for increasingly little time,' she confessed. 'So you have to try it out again.'

'No, you don't. Just say no.'

'Which just goes to show you don't know anything about it.'

Julia nearly said: *But I do.*

'For goodness' sake,' she said instead. 'Find something to do. Get a job. Work for a charity like I've been doing. It helps, Tilly.'

Tilly didn't reply. Julia finished her tea and got up to peel the potatoes.

'Aren't the potatoes Krista's neck of the woods?' Tilly said.

'She needs to rest. I offered to do them today.' The peelings looped down into the sink and she felt a familiar cramp in her guts. Thank God. For a day or two she had been agonizing that the unthinkable had happened and she might be pregnant, and she had been frightened at how deeply fearful she had felt.

The knife scraped against the potato flesh. 'Tilly, when you . . . ' She ground to a halt. 'I mean . . . taking precautions when you . . . '

'When you sleep with someone, you mean? Are you sleeping with someone?'

'No,' said Julia, far too quickly.

'Suit yourself.' Tilly turned her face away and stared out of the window.

Silence fell, broken only by the scrape of the

383

knife and Tilly's cup clinking against the saucer. The pile of potatoes grew and Julia stacked them into a bowl and poured cold water over them.

'Sex is interesting,' Tilly offered up out of nowhere. 'Sometimes, it works with the most surprising people. Sometimes, with ones you don't think you fancy. Don't take it too seriously, Julia. It's only an appetite.'

Julia closed her eyes. Everything about that statement went against the grain. *Oh, Martin, so much else died when you did.*

Where was she going? What was she doing?

She took a deep breath. 'If I wanted to have a little adventure, where would I go for contraception?'

23

When the first soldier threw her to the floor, Krista lost possession of her body and imagined that she had learned everything about helplessness. Not so: she discovered that in pregnancy, where she had no control of her body whatsoever, the helplessness was of a different order.

The first weeks had dragged. Then the pace picked up to a gallop and she was breathless from the speed of it. Her feet swelled, she suffered from indigestion and her back was painful. Having done some research in the medical section of Herr Laube's bookshop, she deduced that she had had so little to eat towards the end of the war that it had affected her muscles and bones. The last time she had seen him, Dr Lawson prescribed iron pills and dark beer, both of which made her feel worse.

Never mind. She was glad that the baby would be born into this glorious autumn.

The last days of pregnancy were in sight. 'Herr Laube, I need something to divert me,' she said, as she sorted out the ledgers, which she now did regularly. 'Something to make me laugh.'

Herr Laube suggested *One Pair of Hands* by Monica Dickens. 'It's an account of the author's cooking and maiding experiences for the upper classes, which are both awful and ridiculous enough to take your mind off your discomforts.'

The last was uttered in German, with politeness and the slanting humour on which she had grown to rely. 'But you will laugh too, Mrs Clifton. I guarantee it.'

And she did but she also appreciated the ironies. As funny and clever as were Monica Dickens's sly observations of the upper classes for whom she worked, she only got away with them because she, too, belonged to the selfsame upper classes.

'Ah,' said Herr Laube, 'but she is an exile from her class.' He patted Krista's hand. 'Just like you and I are exiles. It is uncomfortable and a sad place to be but we can see things more clearly. Some of the best writers are exiles.'

Still unsure of what to expect from her sisters-in-law as the pregnancy advanced, Krista kept her discomforts to herself. Julia was friendly enough, but preoccupied, and increasingly away from the house. Tilly? Well, Tilly had noticeably absented herself in spirit.

Whenever she was around — which wasn't that much — Tilly swung between indifference and being over-helpful. When it was the latter, she was uncannily prescient at anticipating what Krista might be feeling or experiencing. 'Your ankles will probably swell,' she would toss unexpectedly into a conversation, 'but don't worry. It's normal.' Or: 'Isn't it funny how one's hair gets thicker when pregnant?' She had even presented Krista with a book entitled *Pregnancy and Early Childcare*.

'Will Krista be able to understand it?' asked

386

Julia in her practical way. 'The jacket's a bit stained.'

'It *is* second-hand, if that's what you are getting at, Julia. I picked it up in one of those shops that sells things people don't want any more. They are, by the way, doing a roaring trade.'

'Tilly, I am grateful.' Krista rifled through the pages and felt a little sick. Some of the diagrams were terrifying.

'I've read up about it all,' said Tilly. 'So if you need help when the action begins.'

Both Julia and Krista found themselves staring at Tilly.

'I don't believe I heard that,' said Julia.

Think of the harvest, Krista told herself. Think of ripened wheat, fragrant apples, beans, beets, blackberries, cabbage, cantaloupe, corn, cucumbers, eggplant, grapes, herbs, onions, peaches, pears, peppers, potatoes, raspberries, squash, tomatoes, watermelons and zucchini.

Pacing around the garden which, after her efforts during the summer, had begun to assume a shape, and a promise, she recited the list to herself. *Blackberries and beets. Cantaloupe and cucumbers.*

During the final stages of the pregnancy the midwives turned up with a maternity pack containing waterproof paper, draw sheets and maternity pads. Sisters Jackson and Baldwin were both brisk, matter-of-fact young women who did not look as though much would flap them. They examined Krista, asking her lots of questions as they joked and exchanged flippant remarks. For the first time, Krista felt that she was not being judged for who she was. In their eyes, her nationality did not matter, only her cervix and uterus did.

Gus surprised her by saying, 'We must go to church.'

'Really?' Gus had never shown any urge to do so before.

'Insurance policy.'

She laughed. 'We Germans approve of such sensible precautions.'

'Krista, was that a joke?'

She said proudly, 'Yes.'

Gus put on his Sunday suit and red silk tie, while Krista was in the yellow cotton dress with a cardigan over it and a pretty straw hat (Gus had insisted that she pay a visit to the milliner's which had arrived on the High Street). Gus made her stand in the hallway while he adjusted its brim. 'We have to look the part,' he said. Out they went to Matins, held in the church at the centre of the Common; afterwards they picked their way along the paths and debated whether or not they were hypocrites. Gus said they were and Krista pointed out that they were in a club of many.

Krista asked Gus if he had been a churchgoer before the war.

'No,' he replied. 'It did not attract me.' He looked grim. 'It would be good to believe.'

There was such a gap, Krista reflected, between what one wanted to do and what one was capable of doing. Who would not wish to be settled, loved and content?

This conversation was a milestone for she and Gus were tackling a topic which didn't carry any obvious war baggage.

Her arm was linked into his. They were exactly like all the other couples criss-crossing the Common. There was a leisureliness in the collective pace — *Look, we can take our time* — which suggested peace was settling in. Many of the men were in demob suits and the women wearing hats which had obviously been refurbished more than once. Now two of the people walking home to a Sunday meal, she and Gus were becoming as ordinary as they were and she was thankful.

She said as much to Gus. In English.

'I love the way you say things.' Gus took her by surprise. 'It's quite formal, which is sweet.' With his free hand he touched Krista's hand resting on his arm.

They took an indirect route back to the house and detoured down one of the streets leading off the Common. This was a street which had escaped the bombs and it had a settled, tranquil, prosperous look quite different from the turmoil that still reigned in their own terrace. A number of the houses had porches decorated with glazed tiles. The windows had been cleaned in quite a few of the houses and, in some of the front gardens, shrubs and plants flowered in reds and oranges and an occasional purple.

The colours reminded her of home, when every second of summer and early autumn was to be relished. Clinging on to Gus's arm, she told him about it. After the endurance test of the bone-aching winters, the warmth arrived in grand-opera style — swaggering and unmissable — and the scent of blossom drifted through the boulevards. Cafes sprouted on to the pavements and the aroma of proper coffee sifted out from their interiors. There was noise, street life, parties and music until the first chill barged in.

'I loved all that, too,' he said. 'I wonder if any of it will survive?'

Krista stopped to admire a dark-red dahlia which had toppled against a fence. A ray of sun hit the spot between her shoulder blades, and the peppery smell of the dahlia filtered up as she bent to take a closer look. The flower scents and the warmth on her back were delicious and the tart pang of her homesickness vanished. How nice life could be when the past was forgotten, washed clean of death and suffering. When they could live with optimism and pleasure in the small things and worry about dahlias and clothes pegs.

The baby kicked — testing the hard muscle of her uterus. She straightened up.

'Do you remember that night when our baby was conceived?' he asked.

'I do.'

'Good.' Gus removed his hand from her elbow and slid his arm around Krista's waist. His fingers rested gently, possessively, on her swollen belly and she did not flinch.

She looked up at him. 'I find it all extraordinary.'

Gus looked down at her. 'So do I, Krista. Shall we go home?' Again, he adjusted the brim of her pretty hat. 'You look very respectable, Mrs Clifton. Do you think people are taken in by us?'

'Are we taken in by us?'

They continued to the top of the street, where Number 22 came into sight. Krista tightened her grip on Gus's arm. 'This business with the council. Do you think you can outwit Teddy?'

'We have our differences but we are old friends.'

'Old friends can be the worst if things go wrong. Teddy wishes you harm because of Nella and that is bad enough. But there is something else which he might never say. Perhaps he doesn't even know himself.'

'Krista.' Gus sounded a warning note.

Did she dare? Could she trust herself to handle this cleverly? She slid into rapid German. 'I have to say this, Gus. Because if you don't already know, you must be told. The knowledge might protect you, might make what Teddy does more understandable. Teddy loves you, Gus. As a lover, I mean. That is why he will do what he can to ruin you. Because you have left him.'

Gus looked straight ahead. 'I'm afraid you don't know what you're talking about.'

'Not so, Gus.' She chose her words carefully. 'Yes, it is none of my business, but I learned to read faces to stay alive. I became very good at it. I do not know Teddy but, from what I have seen of him, I know that you have hurt him badly.'

'Be careful what you say and where. Homosexual men can end up in prison.'

It was an implicit admission that Gus knew.

* * *

On their final visit before the baby's due date, the two midwives made their usual thorough examination and, for the first time, Krista found it intrusive and uncomfortable.

'Baby hasn't turned,' said Sister Jackson, a frown on her freckled forehead. 'We could be in for a breech.' She leaned down to Krista, who was trapped on the bed. 'But not to worry about Baby, do you hear? We'll arrange for you to get into hospital.'

After they left, Krista sat gingerly on the edge of the bed and struggled to keep calm. You have survived so far, she reminded herself. Do not give in.

Easy to say.

There was no God who looked out for you and no guarantee of survival, precepts which applied to childbirth in particular. The drained, weeping ghost of Lotte rose up into the room. *I wanted children.*

Towards the end, she made Krista eat her portion of food. *I'm going to die anyway and you must live. Have courage, my Krista.*

There was no God — however many times she put on a hat and went to church.

On hearing of the midwife's reservations, Gus said that of course Krista must go into hospital and he would pay whatever was needed. It was agreed that Krista would be admitted into St Thomas' Hospital two days before her due date.

After the arrangements were made, Krista sought out Gus in his study, where he was writing up a report. 'I don't want to be an expense,' she said.

He got up from the chair and put his arm around her. 'What else would I spend money on?'

A week before the baby was due, Krista woke late, her abdomen rigid. She stared at the ceiling. *God. Lotte. Baby.* Turning her head, she checked the clock. It was eight-thirty and Gus would have left for the bank.

Sliding her legs over the edge of the bed, she levered herself upright and made for Gus's dressing room. His suit and tie were gone and his hairbrush had been thrown down on the chair. Krista restored it to the dressing table.

It was only a small movement but a pain speared between her legs, and flowed up and over her belly.

Crawl under the bed. Hide. Instead, she made for the window and made herself look out on the flat swathe of the Common. *Breathe. Look at the green. See how soothing it is.*

The milkman clopped by. Minutes later, the postman came into sight. He was whistling. So ordinary, she thought. Concentrate on the ordinary. Gradually, she mustered sufficient control to deal with the pains, which arrived regularly.

It was not long before she realized that she must get help and she stumbled out of the bedroom. Crouched over the banister on the landing, she called out but there was an answer neither from Julia, nor from Tilly, who she knew was in the house.

She hauled herself up the two flights of stairs to Tilly's bedroom. Its door was ajar, revealing a fully clothed Tilly scrunched up on the bed and breathing heavily. Krista knocked. Tilly didn't stir.

'Tilly, I need help.'

The room was bomb-blast untidy, with an unfamiliar length of blue-and-gold-patterned material doing duty at the window as a curtain. Where had that come from? Clothes were strewn over the floor and the room, which smelled of a concoction of lily of the valley scent, face powder and alcohol, needed airing.

'Tilly, can you help me?' A contraction hit Krista, forcing her to slump down on to the end of Tilly's bed.

Tilly opened her eyes. 'What?' It took her a second or two to understand what was going on. Then she did. 'Bad?'

'I don't think I can get to hospital. I don't think I can walk.'

Instantly, Tilly was on her feet, blazing with the necessity to cope with this emergency. Firing questions at Krista, she coaxed her back down to her bedroom and made her sit in the chair while she remade the bed with the waterproof paper. 'Lie on this. I'll phone the midwife and see if we can get an ambulance.'

'Thank you.' Krista focused on a crack in the ceiling. With each contraction, its dimensions and pathway across the ceiling appeared to change.

Her laboured breathing sounded very loud in the silence.

The convent. Grey, solid, an unhappy place. The soldiers. Grey SS, khaki and dun Soviets. Her desk at the ministry. A pot of sharpened pencils and neat stacks of paper.

A tidal river of images from her past splashed through her mind.

This house. Hostility. Her foreignness.

Was she safe?

She could smell blood — a well-known smell. Her sinews were stretching, cracking, yelling their displeasure.

Tilly returned and slipped into the chair beside the bed. 'There's a bit of a problem. A big building has collapsed near Waterloo and all the ambulances are out there. And both the midwives are out on call. I can't get hold of Gus. The person at the number I have for him seemed a bit vague. They said he was out on an assignment.' Her enlarged face hung over Krista's. 'You'll have to put up with me.'

Tilly maintained watch beside her, referring repeatedly to the clock on the bedside table so that she could measure the time between contractions.

'Seven minutes, Krista, that's good.'

'Four minutes, Krista. Excellent.'

'I can't wait, Krista, to see the baby.'

At one point, she took Krista's hand and held it uncomfortably tight. 'I'm afraid you have to brace here. This bit is the worst.'

Because her brain had turned to mush, the question formed slowly. How did Tilly know?

Her body was in the grip of ever-more-extraordinary sensations. Turning her head,

Krista looked towards the window. The words slipped from her in German — the language of her people and her past. '*Hilf mir.*'

Tilly ferried in hot water from the kitchen in the kettle, poured it into the bowl and bathed Krista's forehead. Krista listened to the splash of water on china, the trickles of it being wrung from the cloth. Later, Tilly rubbed her back with soft, circular pats. 'Nice,' she murmured, sliding for a few seconds into longed-for semi-consciousness. Waking, Krista cried out until the pain overpowered her and carried her down to a subterranean place.

Tilly checked the clock. 'I'll try to phone the midwives.'

She disappeared.

Where was Tilly?

She was alone. *She had always been alone. Would always be alone.*

Sister Jackson did not arrive until late afternoon, by which time Krista was exhausted.

What was happening? The midwife's hands moved here . . . there . . . over her tortured body.

The frown was back on Sister Jackson's forehead. 'Listen to me, Mrs Clifton. You should be in hospital but it is too late. Baby's cord has prolapsed, which sometimes happens with a breech. So I am going to ask you to be very obedient and very brave. Can you do that for me?'

Speak in German. Please.

'You are not to push. Do you understand?'

Tilly was there by the bed. 'I can see a bit of your baby.'

She slipped in and out of a strange blackness.
'*Is she in trouble, Sister?*'
'*We must get the doctor. This is serious.*'

Tilly's voice rising wildly. Tilly sobbing, almost hysterically, and Sister Jackson sharply admonishing her to pull herself together.

Then, later, Tilly sounding urgent and determined. '*If there's a choice, Sister, save the baby, not the mother. That's been agreed.*'

Was she delirious?

Where was Gus?

Why didn't she have a mother to help her? Stupid question: she had always been alone.

Gus.

She must not have heard Tilly correctly.

'Mrs Clifton, are you listening?' Sister Jackson bent over, put her face close to Krista's and spoke with a whispering urgency. 'The doctor is on his way but it is going to take a little time. Please listen. The left buttock is going to be born first but it has to be born slowly. You must make a huge effort to help me manage it.'

Make a huge effort.

Sister Jackson's voice hissed and bubbled in her ear. 'As soon as the body is born we must wrap towels around it, otherwise Baby will get cold and the shock will make it gasp for air while the head is still not born. That is not good because it might inhale fluid which . . . well, let's leave it at that. Also, a towel will help me to steady the body, which can be slippery.'

More effort, more . . . more...

'It's a boy,' cried Tilly.

Krista tried to respond but failed.

'We must get the head out.' Sister Jackson was talking across her. 'Now.' In a move that made Krista cry out, she released the body and allowed it to hang down. 'Push, Mrs Clifton.'

It was painful. My God, it was painful. Then it wasn't. A baby gasped and sneezed in the room which, only a few seconds before, had resounded with Krista's cries.

'All done, Mrs Clifton.' Sister Jackson placed a warm, moving object on Krista's abdomen.

Tilly cried out, 'A boy!' She raised her hands in a dramatic gesture of welcome. With her fair hair streaming down her shoulders, and her billowing kimono, she resembled a primitive goddess.

My son. I have a son.

So small. So compact. Breathing? Gingerly, she touched his damp head with a fingertip. Her fingers were scarlet from birth blood — the colour of war and death but also the colour of life. There would be no more death.

Sister Jackson moved around the bedroom tidying up the mess.

'*Danke*,' Krista managed to say. 'You are skilled.'

Sister Jackson's sensible features softened. 'We got there.' She glanced at the watch pinned on her apron. 'You did well, Mrs Clifton. Some mothers panic and make it worse, but you got through. I'm going to wash your son and put him down in the cradle and then I must go,' she said. 'Sister Baldwin will call in on you very soon.'

Tilly hovered over the bed. 'Do you feel like a mother, Krista?'

Krista looked up at Tilly. 'I don't know. More battered by a hammer.'

After Sister Jackson had washed and changed Krista and taken her leave, Tilly placed a tray with tea and toast in front of Krista. 'I've got hold of Gus, who's coming as fast as he can. You must eat.' Dropping dramatically to her knees beside the cradle, she touched the baby's head. 'Your mother has been battered by a hammer. Yes, I suppose that's how it is.'

Not so long later, a breathless Gus clattered up the stairs and perched awkwardly on the side of the bed. 'Krista, are you all right?'

At the sight of him, an immense gladness and relief filled her. 'I am.' She pointed feebly towards the cradle. 'Your son.'

'I'm sorry, I'm sorry I wasn't here to greet him.' He hauled himself to his feet. 'Can I pick him up?'

But Tilly interposed herself between Gus and the cradle. 'Let me.' She lifted up the baby and held him out to Gus. 'Say hello to him. But you can hold him for only a second.'

Save the baby, not the mother.

Krista said, 'Tilly, Gus can hold him for as long as he likes.'

Tilly turned on her heel and left the room.

Cradling him inexpertly, Gus went over to the window and gazed down into the countenance of his new son. Krista watched. This was a moment of peace and acceptance, of sweetness and anticipation.

Gus looked up. 'I know you're supposed to say things like, 'He's just like my father,' or some such. But he looks . . . Krista, he looks just like he is.'

Although she felt that to move even her mouth would be painful, Krista smiled. 'That is good, Gus. He shouldn't be anything but himself.'

The baby stirred, mewed and then sneezed. Gus brought him back to Krista. 'I suspect you need your mother.'

With an effort, Krista eased herself upright. 'Should I feed him?'

Gus grinned. 'That's generally what happens.' He laid the baby beside Krista and helped her to plump up the pillows. 'Do you want me to leave?'

'Stay.'

Krista unbuttoned her nightdress and Gus gave her the baby. Nervous, very weak, unsure, she glanced up at Gus. 'Go on,' he murmured.

Almost drunk with sensation, Krista did her best and was rewarded by the baby latching on to her breast. Almost at once he understood what was required and began to suck. She gazed down at her flesh, his flesh, her nightdress. So many shades of white. Her vision blurred into this world of white. *The nun's starched scapulars. The borrowed dress for the dance she went to with Lotte. The white cross painted on the convent's chapel roof.*

Her son rooted at her nipple. The tug on her flesh was not unpleasant. In fact, it was a lovely, peaceful feeling of the kind she had experienced on sun-filled Sundays strolling in the Charlottenburg, past the art galleries and crowded cafes.

Then she thought: no. It is a much bigger, better feeling than that.

'He will be a citizen of the world.' With no warning, tears of thankfulness sprang into her eyes. 'Will he?'

Sister Baldwin arrived. One look at the scene inside the bedroom, and she took control. 'Mrs Clifton must rest,' she said.

Krista wiped away the tears. 'My husband has only just arrived. He wants to see his son.'

'Plenty of time for that,' said Sister Baldwin. 'Believe you me. We have rules and rules are to be obeyed.' Her face shone with youth and earnestness. 'Mothers and Babies need rest.'

'*Aber*, this is a special moment,' said Krista.

Sister Baldwin pursed her lips and, for a second, Krista read the word *foreigner*. But it vanished as quickly as it had come.

'Sister, I promise I'll leave in a couple of minutes.'

Gus sat down on the bed and Krista imagined she smelled rain, autumn leaves and bonfires. Sated, the baby released her breast and she closed her eyes.

'I'll hold him,' said Tilly, arriving from nowhere. 'Give him to me.'

'Steady on,' said Gus.

Krista's eyes snapped open. 'Gus?'

'I've already told Sister Baldwin that I can look after him,' Tilly continued, in a curiously insistent tone of voice. 'While Mrs Clifton sleeps, Mr Clifton and I can amuse ourselves with choosing names.'

'I want him here, Tilly.'

Nevertheless, Tilly scooped up the baby from Krista. 'No need for concern,' she said. 'You just rest and everything will be dealt with. I'll bring him back.'

Sister Baldwin thrust her face at Krista's. So good-natured. So bossy. So unseeing. 'Miss Clifton is right. Baby will be perfectly fine.'

Gus held the door open for Tilly to pass through with the baby. The door handle had a habit of sticking. It did so now and, trapped and exhausted, Krista watched it rattle away before it did its duty and the door shut.

★   ★   ★

In the early hours, Krista woke suddenly. From the dressing room next door came the sound of Gus sleeping the sleep of the exhausted.

Her son needed her. Of that, Krista was absolutely convinced.

With an effort, she stood upright and went over to the cradle. It was empty. Unsteady from the birth and fogged with sleep, her mind worked sluggishly. Where would the baby be? Why wasn't he here?

Run. Hide. Danger.

The terrors and horrors of old hovered, waiting to claim her back. She pressed a hand over her eyes.

Go.

Making her way in fits and starts, and hampered by the nightdress which slapped against her legs, Krista again made a painful ascent to Tilly's bedroom. She was shivering

402

— from shock, she imagined, and loss of fluid.

The light was on in Tilly's bedroom and she was propped up in her bed, hair tousled, with the swaddled, sleeping baby on her lap. One hand rested on the baby's torso.

'Tilly, I'll take him now.' Krista edged into the room.

Tilly's gaze locked on to Krista's. 'No, he's fine here. Go and sleep. Leave him to me.'

She sounded reasonable. Very.

Krista supported herself on the back of the chair. 'Tilly, give him to me.'

'Sister Baldwin would be angry if she knew you were up.'

Krista shuffled over to the bed. Tilly snatched up the baby and said, in the ultra-reasonable voice, 'You're in no state to deal with him. Why don't you feed him and then leave him to me?'

'If I have to call Gus, I will.'

'Krista, aren't you overreacting?' Tilly dropped her voice. 'I understand, I really do. Your experiences must have left you jumpy and suspicious, I suppose.' Easing the baby off her lap, Tilly tucked a pillow under his back and made sure that the shawl was not covering his face. 'Look at you, Krista.' She swung her legs over the side of the bed and stood up. She pointed to the blood seeping on to Krista's nightdress. 'You're not very well, you know, and won't be thinking straight. Believe me. You should be sleeping and giving yourself a fighting chance.' Her voice was almost a caress. 'Come on, sister-in-law, you've just had a difficult birth. You shouldn't be wandering around.'

403

Placing a hand on Krista's shoulder, Tilly made to push her down on to the bed.

Krista resisted. 'No.'

Tilly sighed. 'I'm only trying to help. You must trust me.'

Krista could smell her own milky and bloodied body. Her insides had turned to water. The tangle of nightdress around her legs was like a manacle. Trembling, she picked up her son. 'Thank you. I will take him downstairs.'

Tilly hovered, almost blocking Krista's passage. Krista pressed the small body to her breasts. The baby snuffled and rooted. How good was that? It meant he knew who she was and what she would give him. Milk, flesh, life. The baby emitted small, increasingly urgent cries.

'Feed him.'

It was a huge effort. Holding him. Helping him. Sweat sprang on to her upper lip. *Don't flinch.*

'Here, let me.' Tilly helped Krista to adjust the angle at which she held him to make the process more comfortable, then she sat quietly beside mother and son and watched.

Save the baby, not the mother.

'What time is it?'

Tilly glanced at the clock on her dressing table. 'Just after four.'

'Tilly, did you tell the midwife to save the baby but not me if there was a choice?'

Tilly looked startled. 'Were you hallucinating?' She smiled. 'How could I possibly say something like that?'

404

The baby had finished feeding. Tilly hauled Krista to her feet. 'Now, will you do what you're told? Go back to bed and I'll bring the baby down behind you. Just in case you stumble.'

Back in the bedroom, Krista crawled into bed and fell asleep as soon as her head hit the pillow. When she awoke, it was morning: a peaceful, joyous morning and a son had been born.

She turned her head. There was no baby in the cradle.

24

'Mrs Orville, if you want me to help you,' said Dr Rowan, 'you must let your knees fall apart. But you are not helping me.'

Julia, whose every instinct shrieked at her to run and hide, tried to relax and to do what Dr Rowan asked. 'Sorry,' she said as Dr Rowan probed away. 'I can't help thinking this is one of God's jokes on women.'

''Fraid so. But you could look at it this way — that at least we are beginning to get a little control over our bodies.'

Julia had got herself to Harley Street and was being examined by the doctor whom Tilly had recommended. Sitting in the waiting room and surrounded by potted plants and second-rate oil landscapes hanging on the plush wallpaper, she had almost fled. God knew how Tilly knew about all this.

A tall, handsome woman, Dr Rowan turned out to be sympathetic and, when Julia asked falteringly for help with contraception, she said briskly, 'It's a very good thing you have come to me.'

'You don't disapprove?'

'Mine is not a moral role.' Dr Rowan indicated that Julia should undress and get herself up on the examination couch. 'All I shall say is that women have a right to a sexual life, whether they are married or not, if they wish it.'

Julia was intrigued. 'Are you a feminist?'

'Aren't all women? Every woman must surely believe that she has the freedom and the right to do with her life and her body as she wishes.'

This was a novel idea for Julia and she would have liked to have signalled her approval. However, this proved to be difficult given the position of naked vulnerability in which she now found herself. Instead, she concentrated on the elaborate plaster rose in the centre of the ceiling.

Dr Rowan was nothing if not thorough. 'All fine. Everything looks healthy. How many sexual partners? Periods? Pregnancy? I see that — '

Julia cut her off. 'I lost it. After my husband was killed.'

Dr Rowan inserted a finger and frowned in concentration. Julia wondered if the flush that burned on her cheeks had reached her cervix.

'Good, good . . . ' Dr Rowan explained exactly what she was checking and what she was going to do. Taking up a dome-shaped rubber object from the table, she smeared it with jelly and, after a small tussle, placed it inside Julia. 'There. I think that is the correct size.'

Julia felt it snap into place. With the sensation came the notion that her old identity had been snapped away with it and she had been changed — into what, and into whom, she did not know.

'Are you all right, Mrs Orville?'

The humour of it suddenly struck Julia. How could she be thinking these thoughts in *this* position?

Dr Rowan made Julia practise inserting and removing the Dutch cap behind a chintz screen

407

and her new-found vigour faltered as she struggled to master the intricacies. The thing itself was almost malicious in its intractability and the jelly, which got everywhere, smelled horrible. Shuddering at the idea, she envisaged it springing out mid-coitus or, if she was in haste, being impossible to insert.

'It's better than nothing, Mrs Orville.' Dr Rowan had, evidently, witnessed contraceptive struggles many times.

Finally, she triumphed. Having promised Dr Rowan she would return to report her progress, she paid there and then (she did not want to risk a bill arriving at the house). She left the surgery with the packages stuffed into her handbag, their subversiveness weighting it down.

Walking down Harley Street towards Oxford Street, Julia reflected that the ushering-in of her new personal era happened to coincide with changes in the world at large. Atom bombs, Soviet hostility, a Labour government which had booted out the old-school Conservatives. All these were big events to which she had not paid much attention. Yet, prompted by the changes happening to her, she was beginning to take better notice of them.

Julia spent the following night with Michael Hebden in the hotel. Neither of them intended this to happen but it had been very late when they reached the room and, what with one thing and another, it was easier.

Breakfasting with him in the room was rather enjoyable. Michael was such an easy companion, merely passing over the minuscule pat of butter and tea in silence and not demanding conversation — for which she was grateful.

Going home in her evening clothes was a bit more of a problem but Michael organized a taxi for six a.m. and she was able to scuttle into it. Sitting well back in the seat, she felt a glow of sexual satisfaction that considerably outweighed the slight worry of having to explain away her absence for the night.

Stepping into Number 22, she sensed at once that some event had taken place. There was a hushed, almost strange, atmosphere, as if every inhabitant was locked in Sleeping Beauty's drugged sleep, plus a new loamy smell of disinfectant and slops.

The baby?

If Julia was truthful, she had not wished to be at the birth or to participate in its drama or to hear the cries of pain turning to cries of welcome. It was too raw . . . too close to the bone for her.

Hoping that her absence had not really been taken on board, she slipped off her shoes and tiptoed up the stairs. Halfway up, she encountered Tilly standing like a drowsy nymph on the landing. She was holding a wrapped bundle which she held out to Julia. 'Don't know where you've been but you'd better say hello to your nephew.'

Looking down at the baby enshrouded in a shawl, Julia's heart convulsed. 'He's tiny.'

'But so perfect. Made from alabaster, Jules. He reminds us of what life should be. Productive and fertile, and filled with sweetness.'

This was a slightly unsettling Tilly in full flight. 'Isn't it a bit early for that sort of thing? How's Krista?'

Tilly fussed over the baby's shawl. 'What do you think? She's just had a baby. Exhausted, I imagine.'

'Why are you looking after him?'

'He slept in my room. The midwife was very stern — they are very stern, these girls — and said Krista needed rest. So . . . ' Tilly smiled. 'I did my bit.'

'I've never known you do your bit.'

'Have it your way, Julia.'

Julia took a closer look at the rumpled, puffy-eyed Tilly. 'Have you been up all night?'

'Keeping vigil, actually,' said Tilly.

'Why don't I take him and you go and get some sleep?' Tilly had been known to behave oddly when she hadn't slept properly, and, judging by her appearance during the last few months, that was happening frequently. 'I'll go and see Krista. Won't the baby need feeding or something? Give him to me.'

Tilly shrugged but handed over the bundle. 'If you must.'

The baby was not heavy, but he was awkward to hold. Julia tested his weight on one arm and shifted him carefully to the other. Knocking on Gus and Krista's bedroom door, she edged in and was stopped in her tracks.

It was as far from being the decorous, pin-neat sanctum of her parents as it was possible to be. The room had an untidy, heated air, with the sweet, rusty smell of blood permeating it. Dark,

410

elemental events had taken place in it and it was still to return to normal.

Krista was lying in bed on her side, a hand pressed to her stomach. Seeing Julia with the baby, she struggled upright. 'Please, please give him to me.' She sounded a little unhinged. 'He's safe.'

'Of course he is.' Julia handed over the baby and went to open the window and air the room. 'Why would you think he wasn't?'

Krista calmed down. 'No reason.' She shook her head. 'I think I must have had a nightmare.'

'Do you need to feed him?'

Krista looked puzzled. 'I suppose I should. The midwife said he should be fed every four hours exactly. How funny that babies should be so regular. Who would have thought it? But Sister Baldwin was very clear and she said that, even if he was crying, I mustn't feed him until four hours were up.' She looked up at Julia. 'What do you think? I fed him at about four in Tilly's bedroom.'

It occurred to Julia that life in the house was going to change irrevocably and she wasn't sure that she was either in tune with it, or equipped with the patience to deal with the almost certain disruptions. 'Perhaps his nappy needs changing?' she offered with what authority she could muster, which was not that much. 'I remember hearing somewhere that if you don't change them frequently they can get bad nappy rash.'

Julia retrieved the baby and bore him over to the table under the window, where several terry-cloth nappies were stacked. He was tiny, oh

411

so tiny. Unwrapping him like a piece of rare porcelain, she peeled away the wet nappy. The baby opened his eyes and looked up at her, catching and anchoring her own gaze. She felt a disconcerting tenderness. Was it possible? Was it *possible* to feel love?

Gus emerged in his dressing gown from his dressing room as Julia wrestled with a nappy pin. 'Congratulations on your son, Gus.' The baby was making mewing sounds. 'He's superb.' Julia managed to truss up the baby in a clean, fresh nappy, God knew how as she had had no practice at all, except for the couple of times she had been called to help out with a baby at the RAF station.

For a few seconds, Julia held him against her breast and inhaled the scent of a baby — and was transported back to her Gethsemane when, bloodied and anguished, she had cradled her dead daughter and begged for it not to be true.

The baby's head brushed against her chin: *I am here.* With a sigh of surrender, Julia cupped his head in her hand and kissed his small cheek. 'Hello,' she said.

Krista unbuttoned her nightdress. Disturbed by the sight of a swollen breast on the thin torso, Julia averted her gaze. 'Gus, I think we need to hire a maternity nurse. I don't know why we didn't plan for it before. I won't be able to cope with the extra work and nor will Krista. There'll be extra laundry, shopping and cooking.'

'I will manage,' said Krista, gazing down at her son.

'You're right,' said Gus. 'I will see to it.'

'I don't want anyone taking him over.' Krista's voice trembled.

'It's for the best,' said Julia.

'He's mine,' Krista cried. '*He's mine*. No one will take him. Do you understand?' Her face contorted, the colour rushed into her cheeks. 'Never. *Never*.'

With a swift movement, Gus knelt down beside the bed, a gesture which took Julia by complete surprise. 'Don't, Krista. There's no need.' His voice was tender, caressing almost, and new to Julia. 'No one will hurt anyone else. You are safe, sweetheart. You are. So is he.'

Julia's hand slid across her stomach in the old, defensive gesture. The intimacies in this fetid, untidy room were theirs — and she was excluded from the hesitant, but ongoing, consolidation of the marriage between her brother and this strange woman. Yes, she knew enough from her own happy marriage to understand what she was witnessing.

'Sorry, sorry,' said Krista.

'It's all right,' said Gus. 'Yes?'

The isolations of Julia's widowhood had never appeared so savage or so marked.

'You must get your strength back,' said Gus. 'A nurse will help.'

Krista had pulled herself together. 'We don't need a nurse,' she said in a far more reasonable way. 'We need more help in the house. That would be better. I am sure Ada would like some more work.'

'Then you shall have it,' said the new, tender Gus.

413

Krista raised her eyes and, for a second, a tiny second, flashed a look at Julia.

'Thank you, Gus.' A silence fell, and then Krista said, 'I would like to call him Carsten.'

'Carsten!' exclaimed Julia before she had had time to think. 'But that's a foreign name.'

'Julia!' said Gus.

Julia bit her lip in frustration at her own tactlessness. 'But it's a nice one,' she added lamely.

'It could be Carsten,' said Gus with only the smallest of hesitations.

'You don't like it, Gus. I can tell,' said Krista. 'It's just . . . it is a reminder for me . . . of where I came from.'

Gus got to his feet. 'Krista, believe me, with a name like that here he'll get teased at school. Children are not kind. Why don't we make it his second name and give him an English one.' He put his finger under her chin and made her look up at him. 'He's going to be brought up here, Krista. Isn't he? We must think of him. What about Richard? Or Theo?'

Julia found herself holding her breath.

'Theo Carsten Clifton.' Krista's lips were so pale and dry that Julia thought they might crack open. 'I agree.'

★   ★   ★

Theo, as he now was, did not settle easily into life and cried a lot, very often in the evenings. As Julia predicted, he also developed a bad nappy rash, making him even more wretched, and

414

Krista was guilt-stricken about that, which impeded her recovery.

She looked awful. Her hair lost its pregnancy lustre and her skin its bloom. There were circles under her eyes and when she was particularly tired she lost her grasp on English.

The thought crossed Julia's mind that Krista almost resembled a figure from the terrible photographs of the death camps that had been published in the press. They had made her think and, along with everyone else, she questioned if the British powers that be *had* known about them all the time and had kept the information from the public. And, if so, were the British as morally culpable as the Nazis because they didn't do anything about them?

'How could you British have done anything?' Krista roused herself from her maternal torpor when Julia raised the subject with her. 'How could you, if we in Germany could do nothing?'

Her admirably fair response went a long way in raising Krista further in Julia's good books.

She did her best to help, bullying Krista to eat and drink and taking over the baby whenever necessary.

In the afternoons, she often sat with him in the drawing room while Krista slept. That was the time she grew to know the exact curve of Theo's skull. The set of his ear. His cries, which were different according to what he needed.

One day, he grizzled without stopping in his basket beside her and, desperate to quieten him, she scooped him up. The crying ceased and, with a baby's snuffly sigh, he lay against her breast and was at peace.

She held him tightly. Her capacity for love was variable and rusty from disuse, but recognizable, and this baby had infiltrated himself into her inner psyche — a wailing, milky, nuzzling trigger for the feelings that she had buried with her daughter.

That said, Julia always handed him back to his mother with some relief.

Naturally — and why would she imagine otherwise? — Tilly was not being much help. But it was always best not to rely on Tilly. On being approached, Ada had agreed to take on more work for the Cliftons and had been surprisingly firm on insisting that she was paid more money. 'That's the law of demand and supply,' said Michael Hebden when Julia mentioned it.

'If we are going to be thrown out into the street, should we bother to order coal and wood for the winter?' Julia asked Gus. 'Or try to get the basin in the bathroom mended?'

'God knows,' said Gus. 'I'm doing my best to find out what the position is.'

From bitter experience, Julia knew that when there was a wind, it whistled through any gap in the house it could find. Fuel was expensive and Julia ordered Ada to stuff newspaper into any of the windows that could remain closed once winter had arrived. She and Krista discussed the matter and the decision was also taken to camp in the drawing room during the coldest weeks, where the fire would be kept permanently burning.

'You look like a caged rabbit.' Tilly caught

416

Julia one morning, list in hand, checking over the kitchen store cupboard. 'You need to get out more.'

'I see you are taking your own advice.' Julia was at her wryest.

Tilly was dressed to go out in a black cape, with a necklace of very large wooden beads around her neck.

'Any other hints?' asked Julia.

'Live,' said Tilly. 'What else?' She reached over and untied the unflattering scarf which Julia had wound into a turban around her head, releasing Julia's hair to tumble down over her shoulders. 'A word in your ear, Jules. *Never* hide your hair.'

Live.

Tilly did up the top button of the cape. 'I'm thinking of taking off for Italy.'

'Really?' Julia had heard this too often to take it seriously. 'Isn't it impossible to travel? You have to have papers and things. And you can't rely on the trains.' She recollected a snippet she had overheard in the Blue Feather about robberies on trains. 'Europe isn't safe yet.'

'Where there's a will . . . ' said Tilly, her eyes gleaming strangely. 'You know how I love Italy. And here is dull, dull, dull . . . ' To Julia's astonishment, she began to cry.

Julia's initial irritation turned into concern. 'Have you been drinking too much again? Tilly, you must look after yourself.'

Tilly shrugged. 'Drink, pills, I'll take whatever does the trick.'

Julia gave a nervous laugh. 'Don't say that, Tilly.'

417

If it was peace for which Julia yearned, it was in short supply. Theo's evening crying drove her to shut herself up in her bedroom. But it wasn't peace that Julia craved. She wanted to get dressed up and to drink, talk and smoke at the Blue Feather, in the Ritz, in a dive off Piccadilly.

Would Martin be turning in his unmarked grave?

No use thinking about *that*.

But she did think about it and her thoughts distilled more promisingly than she had anticipated. The one sure thing in this mess was that Martin had loved her and she was pretty sure he would not begrudge Julia her bid to carve out some fun from her bereaved life.

'You know,' she said to Michael, as they lay in bed in the hotel room which was becoming as familiar as her bedroom at Number 22, 'this has helped me to make sense of the losses and struggles.' Michael reached over and patted Julia's thigh. After a minute, she added, 'Funny how Teddy understood that.'

'That's his business.' Michael sounded very dry. 'Don't read too much into the milk-of-human-kindness *schtick*.'

A shocked Julia processed the implications. 'Are you suggesting that he . . . arranges these things as his business? He told me he was just being nice.'

Michael backtracked. 'A slip of the tongue.'

She recalled her previous conversation with Teddy, when he had denied this. This time, although shocked, Julia was more ready to accept that there was a side to Teddy about which it was best not to enquire. Furthermore, if she had been stupid and allowed herself to be not exactly pimped, but to be compliant with Teddy's schemes, she had to accept the consequences. At times, she felt thoroughly bewildered by the situation and upset by her own behaviour. Yet, if she was truly honest, she no longer minded enough about morality to stop what she was doing.

'Don't fret about it, Julia,' Michael reiterated. 'There're more important things.'

On balance, she supposed, with the new realism that continually took her by surprise, there were.

Did she please Michael? Did she dare ask him?

Julia quickly corrected this unconscious bias as feeble. If posed at all, the question should surely be: did they please each other? Without a doubt, she was better at sex since meeting him. This puzzled her a little for she and Martin had enjoyed a sex life that had been both tender and filled with emotions — if a little awkward and embarrassed at first. Her encounters with Michael were not in the same league of tenderness and respect but they were character- ized by a deftness and invention which she and Martin had not shared.

★ ★ ★

As October advanced, Number 22 got colder and draughtier.

Wrapping her cardigan tightly around her, Julia was heading downstairs and almost collided

419

with Gus as he emerged from his bedroom. He asked her: 'You didn't know anything about the letter from the council, did you?' Horrified, Julia's gaze flew to his. 'You see, I suspect that you did.'

She was seven years old again, and had been caught stealing a humbug from the tin which the cook kept on the top shelf of the cupboard. The chewy sweetness and the fascination of its black and white stripes had done for her.

'Julia?' Gus did not sound angry, more affectionate than anything else. Yet there was also a faint suggestion of menace. She knew from old that Gus normally defended his sisters come what may, but there was a line.

She hoped to God that her guilt was not reflected in her face. 'I'm not sure what you mean.' She followed Gus down to the hall.

'The reason I ask is because you act oddly whenever it's mentioned.' He reached for his coat and put on his hat. 'Could I be right?'

In the bedroom upstairs, Theo wailed. Immediately, Gus looked up, every bit of him concentrating on what was happening to his wife and son.

She breathed in hard.

Satisfied that Theo's wails were just normal and run-of-the-mill, he turned back to her. 'It's odd how Teddy appears to be involved and how he's got hold of certain information. Isn't it? Were you anything to do with it, Jules?'

Of course Gus would think along those lines. His work in cagey areas made him predisposed to do so. She and Tilly had never fathomed what

420

he did exactly but, whatever it was, she was pretty sure Gus would know how to ferret out information.

It would be a good thing to confess. A lovely release.

'Don't be silly, Gus. If Teddy is involved, it's because he's furious with you.'

Gus searched for a scarf on the peg. His son was still crying. 'If you have done anything, Julia, I don't know what I would do.'

Up shot one of her eyebrows. 'Murder me?'

'I would find it very hard to forgive you.' Gus turned round and apprehension trickled down Julia's spine. This was a Gus who was a stranger to her: the Gus who had done things in the war about which she knew little. 'Nothing is more important than Theo, and Krista's comfort. I mean to keep the house.'

'But Teddy says . . . '

'Bugger what Teddy says,' he said. 'Have you any idea what Teddy gets up to these days?'

Apprehension turned to dread. 'How would you know?'

Gus draped the scarf around his neck. 'Don't ask. But he's not the man we used to know. And he's consorting with some odd types.'

With that, Gus was gone, the front door banging shut behind him, leaving Julia with an open mouth. It was so unlike Gus to swear.

★ ★ ★

Julia licked a finger, rubbed at the surface of the mirror and peered into it. It was far too small a mirror but her mother had forbidden big mirrors because she believed they encouraged vanity.

Her cut-off torso was reflected back from the smeary surface and it both reassured and alarmed her. The black wool dress with the boat neckline and cinched-in waist, which had been paid for with money and coupons donated by Michael, was very becoming. (If there was one thing to be said for the war, it had kept women thin.)

She had done her hair differently and her skin looked good, too. So clever had she been with Michael's money that some had been left over and she had taken herself off to Elizabeth Arden's salon to have a facial. Lying there, being creamed and pampered, Julia felt as if she had died and gone to heaven. She left the salon smelling of roses.

The woman reflected in the mirror — or what she could see of her — was unrecognizable. Before the war, that woman would never have visited a beauty parlour, and certainly not planned to return to one on a regular basis. Somehow, she had changed from the polite, well-bred and not concerned with facials, cold cream and French knickers middle-class wife, into a woman with an indeterminate label and only her name to remind her of what she had once been.

The dress was a success. When she took off her coat in the restaurant, she noted the flicker of lust in Michael's eye.

'Clever Julia,' he said. 'Good choice.'

There hadn't been that much to choose from

422

in the depleted department stores but Julia didn't let on.

Michael's reaction had boded well but the good mood did not last and, over dinner, he became more withdrawn and preoccupied. When she enquired if something had happened, he cut her off.

He might think her a fool but she knew there was something wrong and, after sex, during which he had been very attentive and sweet, Michael revealed what it was. Rolling over, he lay on his back with an arm covering his eyes. 'That's it, lass. I won't be seeing you again.'

Julia felt a small electric shock speed through her body. To say this was a surprise was an understatement. Once absorbed, it was followed by an instinctive reaction: Michael did not find her attractive enough.

'Is there someone else?' The thought of another woman made her very angry. 'If so, why bother with this evening?'

Michael laughed but he was not amused. 'If only it was that simple.' He removed his arm from his face. 'Someone has found out about you and they are threatening to go to the local press.' He let a beat elapse. 'And my wife.'

She didn't need the implications to be spelled out. Pulling herself upright in the bed, she said, 'You're being blackmailed.'

'Pretty, isn't it?' His jaw tightened, giving him a much more rugged look. 'It happens and it happens more than you think. If you figure in the local church and charity arena you're fair game.' He swung his legs over the side of the bed and sat up. 'I don't want my wife to know but it will probably come out.'

'Not necessarily.'

He glanced over to Julia. 'I hope you don't feel this was a waste.'

It was not much in the way of a compliment but it was probably all she would get from a man such as Michael. She thought of the affection that had been growing, and the sexual satisfaction she'd enjoyed. All in all — and despite her initial shrinking — plenty had been gained from these encounters, not least the excitement of having a disgraceful secret.

'No, it wasn't wasted,' she told him.

'Good. You are a good lass.'

The sheet tangled around her feet as she made haste to get out of the bed. It seemed ridiculous to be tearful while struggling to tug on her tight girdle. But there it was. Michael made haste to get dressed, too, which saddened Julia as it suggested he was impatient to shake her off.

Their goodbyes were perfunctory.

'Don't worry about Michael,' said Teddy when he and Julia next met. They were back at the Blue Feather and Julia had told Teddy what had happened and how worried she was for Michael. 'He'll survive. Believe me. By and large, the men who hold the purse strings do. He will take steps to shut the gossip down.'

'Oh,' said Julia, who was feeling flat and uncertain. 'We needn't have said goodbye?'

'Who knows?'

Perhaps Michael *had* wished to get rid of her,

thought Julia, her affection for him shifting suddenly.

She and Teddy were sitting close together at the bar, and the G&Ts were not slow in arriving. 'I must introduce you to someone else. Plenty more fish in the sea.'

'Good Lord.' She hadn't considered 'someone else' — other than Teddy, of course. 'There's no need.'

Teddy's expression was as deadpan as ever. 'You'll get over Michael. Oh, yes, you liked him well enough but I think you liked what he gave you more. Dinners, et cetera. Am I right?'

Julia swirled the ice around her glass. She had come to recognize his cynicism.

'Sweetheart, you are so much more attractive these days. Do you mind me telling you that? Good hair, nice clothes. And you're a lot more experienced. Men enjoy women like you.'

Julia flushed at the 'women like you' for it had been said with just a hint of condemnation. She pulled herself up short: why should she feel condemned or ashamed? Michael had taught her that men certainly didn't.

'Better still, men will appreciate you. They'll want you on their arm.'

What Teddy was saying could have been disgusting but, somehow, it wasn't. Yet there were remnants of the teachings from her upbringing that still swam at the back of Julia's mind. 'But not as their wife?'

'Ah, that's another matter.' He pushed his glass gently to and fro on the bar. 'But do you want to go down that route when there are others to choose from?'

Swish went the ice in the glass. 'You know you've put me in a very awkward position with Gus?'

'Yes.'

At the other end of the bar, a woman in a tight satin dress threw back her head and laughed. 'Oh, you,' Julia heard her say to the man sitting beside her.

Everyone was sick of the war. People wanted to drink, eat, dress in colours and fornicate. They wanted to make money. Somehow, Teddy had got himself in on it all and, by association, so had she.

'You used me, Teddy.' For a moment, he resembled the Teddy of old: young and handsome, crackling with energy and humour. 'Apart from anything else, it was cruel of you. Particularly . . . ' She stopped.

Teddy reached for Julia's hand. The touch was light and uncommitted — and she knew then that any hope she might have nurtured was truly lost. 'Sweetheart, I've told you that if I ever wanted what you are suggesting, it would be with you. But it's not going to happen for a very good reason.' He raised a wry eyebrow. 'You did understand what I told you last time?'

'Yes.' The blush burned brightly on her cheeks. 'I hadn't been thinking of sex,' she said, greatly daring. 'I was thinking of companionship. Loyalty to one another. Perhaps, love.'

She knew she was approaching the heart of the matter. 'Who do you love, Teddy? Surely someone?'

There was a flash of violent emotion on his features — a grief and yearning which Julia had not seen before. 'I'm not the sort of person who loves,' he said. 'Apart from my sister.'

The noise level reached a crescendo and she had to raise her voice. 'You're lying, Teddy.'

He shrugged.

There was a long, long silence. Teddy contemplated his glass with a bent head. Eventually, he lifted it. 'As I was saying, sweetheart, now Michael's off the scene, I want to introduce you to someone else.'

'No, thank you, Teddy.' Julia made to get to her feet but he reached over and pushed her back on to the seat.

'I think you will,' he said, and there was no mistaking the menace. 'You are in this now, Julia. Remember that.'

She sat utterly still, shocked.

Teddy fiddled with his cigarette case. Julia stared at her drink. 'I see.'

Two gins later, she tallied up the pros and cons of her position. Whichever way she looked at it, she was trapped. Either by Teddy and his designs or in glum widowhood.

The best thing would be — the thoughts tumbled squiffily around her head — the best thing would be . . . the *prudent* thing would be. What? If, say, Krista had died in childbirth, it would have left her, Julia, to look after the baby for Gus and to run the house. Then she would be a respectable woman with a purpose.

When she mentioned this to Teddy, he said, 'Sweetie, I don't think so. Do you?'

25

Minet said, 'Time to leave the documents, Clifton. You're Berlin-bound again.'

He and Gus were holed up in the house in Lord North Street. Gus had just handed over his report on the German steel industry and Minet had done a quick rifle through. During the Reich's glory years, the state of German steel had been carefully monitored by the henchmen and there was plenty for him to digest and — if the service was so minded — to pass on to a British steel industry eager to pinch a rival's methods.

Gus's feelings were mixed and Minet saw this. 'I gave you fair warning,' he said. 'I know it's not the best timing with the birth of your son. But it never is.' He sent Gus a smile which was surprisingly genuine. 'For the future, I have you tagged as Head of Station somewhere. If all goes well. Possibly Beirut. Istanbul? Bear it in mind, Clifton. Meanwhile, you work your arse off in Berlin, with or without your wife, and we'll train you in the techniques. It is an extremely tricky and fluid situation out there and we need all the linguists we can lay our hands on. For this trip you're still working for the bank. Investment opportunities — although that's a bit of a joke at the moment. Understood? But for future trips the FO will give you a title and a role. Be prepared to come and go while we monitor what

428

is going on with the Soviets. Have you got your wife under control?'

'I'll ask her.' Gus was his most sarcastic.

'Still determined to continue with her?'

'Yes.'

Minet's eyebrows got busy again. 'Then she will earn her keep, too.'

Gus made no comment.

'We will be keeping an eye on her, Gus. I'm afraid we must.'

It crossed Gus's mind that this was a threat more than a reality. Both men were aware that keeping an eye on Krista would undoubtedly waste hard-pressed resources.

'You'll need three things in the job,' Minet continued. 'Personality is key, so don't turn into a colourless spook. The capacity to make and to keep friends who will help out at the right moments.' He pushed the steel report to one side. 'A sense of humour about the skulduggery business is also vital. Some of us get carried away with the mumbo-jumbo of secrecy, which is ridiculous. You are there to keep the country safe not to take top bill in a pantomime.'

Minet got down to detail. 'A unit is being set up, Number 5 CCU. They want any intelligence they can get their hands on. Political, military, economic.' And so the briefing continued.

'I'll finish, as I sometimes do, by warning you that you can never discuss this with anyone other than us. That includes the wife until such time as we bring her in. Otherwise we have to kill you.'

Minet enjoyed his jokes. If it was a joke.

Still faintly surprised at the turn his life had

429

taken, Gus listened carefully.

A young man's love affair with Germany had resulted in his becoming an interrogator. An anonymous observer had taken note of his work and talked to someone else. Astonishingly, the men in the shadows had not kicked up over his protest about Bad Nenndorf. Or his marriage. *So-and-so knew your father and that will do.* The hand which had tapped him on the shoulder had ushered him into a parallel world very quietly. *You can join our club.*

When he and Teddy were still talking to each other, they had wrangled over various subjects: appeasement and socialism, the causes of poverty and unemployment. They had taken their opinions seriously. So they should have done, but neither would have called himself political.

In the aftermath of the war, it was increasingly obvious to Gus that subtlety and non-confrontation were needed, not the simplicities offered by politicians. Listening to Minet, it was ever clearer that the Soviet bear had turned hostile and was intent on finding out the exact extent of western progress with atomic weapons. Influenced by de Gaulle, France was anti-British, Britain was on its knees psychologically and financially, and everything, and everyone, was vulnerable. People. Nations. Democracy. The stinking, displaced, violent, desperate hordes unleashed on this broken Europe must be fed, sheltered, persuaded back into civilization.

★   ★   ★

430

Krista was feeding Theo in bed and Gus was getting dressed.

It had been a fractured night, with the baby failing to settle until the early hours, and they were both tired.

Watching Gus button up his shirt, she said, 'I think you will not be talking to me any more of your work?'

'What gives you that idea?'

Krista placed Theo carefully in the hollow between two pillows and slid out of bed. She smelled of tousled warmth and ever so slightly of milk and it made his senses stir in a way that Nella's scent never had. 'You forget that I lived in a country where everyone had secret work. I can read the signs.'

He allowed her to do up the last button. 'I wish I could answer your questions.' He dropped his hand over hers. 'There's no one I would rather tell.'

Krista laughed. 'The one thing you learned was to never ask questions unless you were sure.'

'Krista . . .'

She smiled and gave him a get-out. 'Maybe I am wrong.' Reaching up, she turned down the collar of his shirt. 'You know something? I wanted to thank you.'

'For what?'

'For our son.'

The way she pronounced the word 'son' delighted Gus.

'And for bringing me to a country where I can be straightforward. I know people hate me for being German but that is a perfectly normal

431

reaction, not a terrorized one or one full of paranoia. I am grateful you have given me a chance to have a proper life.'

'Not quite.' Gus wanted to be clear. 'Remember? You will be asked to work for our side and you might not like that.'

The atmosphere between them was full of unsaid things.

Krista checked the now-sleeping Theo. 'When I think what could have happened to me, the price is a small one.' Picking up the hairbrush, she proffered it to Gus. 'Did you see where it was? On the top. I am better. I do not know what you are doing now. Probably, something against my country, but I understand that is how things have to be for the present. It might not always be so.'

At that moment, Gus wished fervently that his life — their life — was uncomplicated and transparent.

'Krista?'

She eyed him shrewdly — and, also, with a tenderness that was new to him. 'Gus, we know the worst of each other. Yes? We must promise never to have secrets from one another.' She added, 'I know you will have work secrets.'

'What about your beauty secrets?' He tried to make light of the request.

'Not those, of course.'

Gus traced the blue vein snaking down from the base of her neck to her chest, towards the full breast. She did not flinch, which made him feel absurdly pleased. 'I'll do my best.'

Gritty-eyed and slightly light-headed, he took

himself down into the kitchen and found a dishevelled Tilly making tea. 'You look terrible, brother.'

'I could say the same about you.'

Tilly poured boiling water into the teapot. 'I heard the baby in the night.' She sounded hoarse and there were dark circles engraved under her eyes. 'I keep thinking he has no idea where he is and he's frightened.'

'He's only a few weeks old, Tilly. Of course he doesn't have any idea.'

'I reckon he's not settled or happy. It worries me, Gus.'

Gus was used to Tilly speaking her mind and he needed his breakfast. Praying that it was the case, he said, 'Theo is beautifully looked after by his mother who, I agree, is tired, but she is perfectly in control.'

'Here. Have some tea.' She settled on to a chair. 'It takes a bit of getting used to, Gus.' She tapped a spoon on the table. 'Once upon a time, Julia and I were your main concern. Now, we're not. But that's fine. It was always going to happen.'

'What's brought on the melodrama?'

'The truth.'

'I'll never lose interest. But be merciful. The baby kept us awake.' He pulled the cup of tea over to him. 'I'm going to be away for a couple of weeks, perhaps more.'

Tilly jerked her head round and the fair hair swung wildly with her. 'I'll help out.'

She had got to her feet and was staring down at him in a meaningful way.

'Gus, I'm thinking of going away myself. Soon. I'm losing my energy here and the will to write. I've worked out that my allowance would cover my costs.'

Gus had heard these sorts of plans before from Tilly. 'Wouldn't you miss the partying too much? Where would you go?'

'Where do you think? Italy. Herbs on a hillside and blue skies. Blazing poppies.' She held up a hand and he noticed that her nails were bitten to the quick.

'No poppies at this time of year.'

'Don't be so literal.'

Something nagged at Gus but he could not work out what. 'More tea?' He refilled the kettle and struck a match. It flared into the gloom. Swivelling round, he took a good look at Tilly while the flame burned up towards his fingers.

'Pasta, olive oil . . . '

Tilly was rolling out a list made up of the usual suspects, which she did whenever she talked about Italy. But the hoarseness was harsh and rasping and her blue eyes were bruised and weary.

'Good luck with getting the right papers.'

Tilly wasn't done. 'You're settled now, Gus. Julia and I are ever-squarer pegs rattling in this round hole. We have to do something. I don't know what Jules is plotting but I am determined to establish myself elsewhere.'

Theo's reedy wail percolated down to the kitchen, triggering in Gus both irritation and an up-welling of love so intense it was almost painful. A response, he imagined, typical to the new parent.

434

Abandoning Tilly to her castles in the air, Gus went upstairs to help.

Krista was endeavouring to soothe Theo, holding him against her shoulder as she administered little feathery pats to his back. At Gus's entrance he quietened.

'He knows you,' said Krista. Theo's downy head was resting neatly in the concave between her collarbone and shoulder.

'Anything the matter?'

She had gone pale, a sure sign she was agitated. 'No, he just wants to go to sleep but will not allow himself to.' She transferred Theo over to the other shoulder. 'Gus, is there any news about the house?'

This wasn't the first time she had asked and Gus suppressed a sigh, reminding himself that a history lay behind her question. *Bombs. Ruins. Rape.*

'This is England and people aren't herded from their homes, if that's what you're worried about.'

'It would be nice to know.' Real worry and tension underlay her words and Gus reminded himself that losing a place of safety was the thing most dreaded by anyone who had been displaced.

He sat down on the bed. 'If the worst comes to the worst, we move. And you never know where the job will take us.'

'This is your home and it should be your son's home. Anyway, where would we go? There are no houses to move to, I think. No, we have to stay here.' She kissed the top of Theo's head and shot

435

Gus a look. 'Are you sure we cannot bribe someone?'

Gus barked with laughter. 'Krista, I love your ruthless side. Promise me that you'll stop fretting. It will affect Theo.'

She squinted down at her son. 'You think so? Well, then, I must stop.' She got to her feet and laid the quietened baby down on the bed. 'I must make sure that Theo is safe and comfortable.' She was getting her colour back but Gus noticed that she clamped down on her lip in the old way. '*Safe.*'

'*We* must make sure that Theo is safe and comfortable,' he reminded her. 'We.' He ran through the options. 'I'll contact Teddy and see if we can talk it through.'

Krista sent him a look of profound gratitude.

Later that morning, Gus rang Teddy's secretary and asked for an appointment. A paid-up member of the dragon class, the secretary was uncooperative. 'Mr Myers would not be able to see you for a week.'

'Tell him to make time.' Gus was curt to the point of rudeness. 'Understand?'

After that, he took a bus to the council headquarters and asked to see Mr Forrest, who happened to be in his office. Returning reassured by their conversation and even more determined to fix things with Teddy, he retreated into his study and spent the rest of the morning combing through all the available papers and Mr Forrest's report. Krista found him there, with the papers from the house file spread over the desk.

'Ask Teddy,' she said, 'if he is doing this

because he loves you.'

'*Loves* me? We've been through that.'

'You know what I mean,' she said, with great pity, even tenderness. Gus stared at his wife, astonished by their deepening collusion. 'Keep asking him, Gus. In whichever way you can.'

The first rule of interrogation is to know the answers to the questions you are about to ask.

Late in the afternoon, Gus made for Johnson Alley, known to the locals as 'pickpocket central', where the offices for Myers, Ruby and Wilson were situated. The bombing had blocked off the north entrance to the alley and, until the rubble was cleared, it was possible to access the office only from Fleet Street. At the best of times nothing but a meagre light filtered between the overhanging buildings and, at night, a sharp eye out was needed.

At the offices, Gus was conducted by a uniformed messenger boy along a corridor which had once been painted in white, but this had mutated into the dun colour now universal to the country. In the rooms opening off the corridor, young women hunched over typewriters. None of them looked up.

Gus was ushered into Teddy's office, which he knew of old. A large, unappealing room with a couple of small windows overlooking the alley, it was furnished with bookshelves and a substantial desk stacked with box files.

All very familiar — as indeed was the sight of Teddy ensconced at the desk, a tray laid with a coffee pot and cups beside him. He did not look up from the document he was annotating.

After a moment, he said, 'You have a nerve coming here.'

Gus sat down in the chair facing Teddy, positioning his hat on the large expanse of desk between them, and waited. The hard chair and the cheerless office reminded him of the mean rooms in which he had worked in Germany.

Gus waited. It was a tactic he had often used and he knew how to ride it out.

As might be expected, the bookshelves were stuffed with law and reference books, plus, Gus noted, a selection of dictionaries. 'I see you still have the dictionaries,' he remarked into the heavy silence. 'They are as rare as the Koh-i-Noor.'

In the early days as an interrogator, Gus had formally requested a German dictionary and had been told by the unit head that there weren't any. Furthermore, he was briefed that it was unwise, in the interests of national security, to consult one at a library. After giving the problem some thought, and on the premise that this definitely would be in the interests of national security, Gus stole one from a friend who he knew wouldn't miss it (he planned to give it back sometime soon).

Teddy carried on writing.

In interrogations, the we-know-everything-already illusion is highly effective. To bring it off, the more you know about a prisoner's background — his culture, his customs, his family, his work colleagues — the more successful the results.

Teddy pushed several of the papers to one side

438

— having forgotten, perhaps, that Gus had a knack for reading upside down.

It was easy work to decipher: 'Hebden Associates. Building Materials', 'Thomas Spart. Architect'. There was also a letter with a foreign letterhead, which carried a Zurich address.

Teddy levelled a cold gaze on Gus. 'So?'

In interrogations, choosing a technique and holding it steady is crucial.

'Teddy, it's good to see you.' There was no response. 'I think you know why I'm here. I've come to talk about plans for the terrace and the houses.'

'Nothing to do with me, Gus.'

Gus smiled in a reasonable manner. 'Are you sure? According to council minutes, you have been present for several meetings.' He recited a couple of dates. 'You were heard joking with Councillor Cleave about the situation. Councillor Cleave later said he didn't think it was a very good joke.' He paused. 'You might as well tell me, Teddy.'

Teddy did not reply.

'Can we put aside the bad blood between us for this conversation? Let me take an educated guess about what has happened. I have hurt you and Nella, just as surely as you were hurt on that Italian mountainside, and you wish to punish me. I understand.'

Gus kept up the reasonable tone and friendly manner.

The dragon of a secretary barged into the office and hovered adoringly over Teddy. 'Do you need anything, Mr Myers?'

'No, thank you, Miss Philby.'

Gus watched her departing back. 'She's in love with you, Teddy.'

'Shut up, Gus.'

'I know how much Nella means to you. And you want to avenge her, perhaps? Particularly if you can make some money out of it.'

'Shut up, Gus,' Teddy repeated.

Bait your hook to suit your fish.

'How friendly are you with the director of Hebden Associates?'

Teddy shifted in his chair. 'Don't know who you're talking about.'

'He met you at the council. There is a record of the meeting.'

Teddy was nonplussed but fought back. 'You've been talking to Julia.'

Gus was thrown. 'What's Julia got to do with it?'

'You'd better ask her.'

Teddy was using a classic tactic of deflecting from the central question.

Find the vulnerable points. Then probe to find a tiny shift in emphasis, or behaviour.

'The council threaten to requisition my house on the grounds that it is irreversibly damaged. This is not correct. You know that. I know that. And a surveyor's report will back me up. Please will you help me to get it removed from the list?'

'The chap who inspects the houses thinks differently.'

'I've talked to Mr Forrest. He doesn't. He thinks it's possible to demolish Number 26 and to repair the others.'

Again, Teddy shrugged. 'Well, it's in black and white in the council files.'

'Did you bribe Mr Forrest to alter the report?'

Anger sparked in Teddy's dead eyes. 'Yes, actually.' The words dripped with sarcasm. 'That's what I do.' He moved awkwardly and caught his leg on the side of his desk. 'Do you think for a minute I would get away with anything like that? As you correctly say, I'm working for the council, which means I don't deal with individuals. In case you hadn't appreciated this, the council has been directed by the Labour government to provide housing. This means difficult, and at times distressing, decisions have to be made. It's for the greater good.'

The atmosphere in the room grew poisonous.

'And where would demolishing still-viable houses fit into the greater good, Teddy?'

Teddy looked down at his hands clasped on the desk. 'Ah, Gus. Do we have to?'

'You were like my brother, Teddy, and I loved you. I know you loved me, too.'

'I'm doing my job, Gus.'

The only thing that matters, Gus, is the lucre. Was it? Had it been the motivator?

An interrogator was trained to unearth the exact point when the man or woman being questioned had made the choice to step over the line. Sometimes, they had done it for the best of reasons — *I needed to feed my family* — only to find they could not stop there, that they could no longer control their involvement. Gus stood up and went over to the window, which was

441

streaked and smeared with dust and ash. The phone on Teddy's desk rang. From his standpoint at the window, Gus stared down into the gloomy alley.

The call terminated, Teddy addressed Gus's back. 'That was the Housing Officer. The all-clear has been given on the housing projects. Even if I wished it, there's nothing I can do.'

'You mean you don't *want* to do anything.' Gus turned around.

'The contractors are lined up. Builders. Suppliers. Architects. Just think of how many jobs that means, Gus. I've done good work. A lot of businessmen will be thanking me. England should be thanking me.'

'What are the margins on projects such as these?' Teddy named a figure and Gus asked, 'Are you reluctant to do anything because you will be getting a couple of per cent extra on the rake-off?' He was conscious of a slight hesitation. Would he have been immune in the circumstances? Gus checked himself: to speculate in such a way would be to lose the advantages of the exchange, a classic error. 'I'm sure you went into it all with the best of intentions, but then opportunities became too tempting.'

'Take that back.' Teddy struggled painfully to his feet. 'Otherwise, I'll sue you.'

The moment of intersection?

'I think not.' Gus was pretty sure by now that he had found that vulnerable point. 'Prove me wrong.' It was astonishing to think that he and Teddy had once been only a cigarette paper apart. 'We don't understand each other any more. But that's fine. I'll find another way to keep the house.'

'For the record, attempting to obstruct the council is against the law.'

Interrogate anyone and it is the small details that often prove the most revelatory. A primary task is to disinter potentially useful strategic information.

'Are the contracts for this brave new world handled entirely by you, Teddy?'

'As it happens.'

Their gazes collided and Gus held his steady. 'I see.'

'Fuck off, Gus.'

'Is the bank account in Switzerland?'

'I don't know what you're talking about.'

Gus reeled off the Zurich address he had memorized earlier.

'Get out.'

Strolling over to the desk, Gus glanced over the papers. ''Hebden', 'Spart'. Quite a community.'

Teddy steadied himself on the bookshelf. For a moment, Gus thought he was about to hurl a book at him.

'I agree with you, Teddy, that we need new houses. Lots of them. But what you will be doing to us is for very different reasons.' He hoped to God that Krista had got it right. 'You want to avenge what you see as a personal betrayal of you by me.'

'Is that what being married to a German does to you? Turns you into a third-rate pseudo-psychologist. You disgust me, Gus. You treat my sister like dirt and then you expect me to embrace you like the brother you say I was.' He pointed to the door. 'Leave. Now.'

He limped over to Gus and hooked his arm under Gus's. His grip was surprisingly ferocious and he was more powerful than he seemed. Having grabbed his hat, Gus found himself propelled down the corridor. If any of the busy typists in those rooms had looked up, the sight might well have struck them as farcical.

At the entrance to the offices, Teddy pushed Gus through the door and into the alley. 'Get lost.'

Gus stumbled, righted himself and turned back. 'You will get found out, Teddy.'

Teddy was gripping the door frame with an expression as hard and hostile as Gus had ever seen when interrogating the enemy.

Gus walked away down the alley. This end of it was lit by only an inadequate street light. It was growing dark and a gritty, sooty menace was palpable in the bombed and maimed city, with its hissing gas leaks, exposed cables and craters.

He stopped to put on his hat and to button up his coat.

Without warning, an arm whipped around his neck and tightened. 'So what did happen, Gus, to make you marry a Kraut?'

It was impossible to speak. Teddy was forcing Gus's head back against his chest and the pressure was becoming intolerable. The pain in his windpipe swallowed up conscious thought. Just as blackness threatened, his army training kicked in.

Dodging sideways, he twisted round and the movement sent Teddy off balance and crashing against the wall. Gasping, his eyes watering, Gus stepped out of reach. After a few seconds, he managed to get out: 'You bloody fool. You could have killed me.'

In the November dusk, it was difficult to make each other out clearly.

'God knows why I didn't.'

Gus coughed and retched up bitter-tasting fluid. 'You're a fool, Teddy. And, as it turns out, no better than anyone else.'

'You know, do you?' Teddy propped himself up against a doorway. 'Yup, I suppose you do.'

Gus shivered with shock and the chill.

'But I know you, Gus, through and through. Boy, adolescent, man. I was the unpredictable one and you were the honourable, decent one. It irritated me that you had a natural justice built into you, but I admired it, too. You wanted to right the wrongs. But I knew — I know — your soft side and your weaknesses. It didn't make any difference to me. You knew mine. Something happened to make you betray me and Nella. What was it?'

His chest was still heaving painfully.

'*What was it, Gus?*'

Gus heard his breath rattle, felt the lurch of his empty stomach, the burn of alcohol in it. There was the never-to-be-forgotten taste of ashes and cheap brandy and triumphalism in his mouth.

Gus was drunk. So were the men he had blagged a lift with. Their truck had sprung a puncture and he and the men debouched inside what remained of the nearest building while it was being repaired.

It turned out to be a chapel in the ruins of a convent. It was a nightmare place; the air was rank with dust and the floor scattered with masonry. The three women . . . girls . . . were slumped down in a corner. At the sight of the men heading towards them, one of them got up, raised her skirt, leaned back against the wall and turned her head away.

They were waiting. They knew what was coming and it was useless to resist. Even British soldiers.

Gus was vomiting when the first one raped Krista, and semi-oblivious when the second one took over. When the third, a runty chap with a moustache, stood up and unbuttoned his flies, some sense filtered through his brain.

With a cry, Gus lurched forward. 'Stop.'

'Sir, she's mine.'

'That's an order. Get off them.'

'Spoils of war, sir. You know that. Anyway, they're German.'

With his flies open, the runty one seized hold of Krista and dragged her in front of Gus. 'Go on, sir,' he said. 'Have her after me. You know you want to.'

She had raised her face to his and those great eyes had hooked him on to a rope of sickening desire, pity, rage and horror at what he, Gus, had become.

'I will feel the guilt for the rest of my life,' he told Krista later. 'I will never forgive myself for allowing this to happen.'

'It's normal. For war. It's what soldiers do. It happened all over Europe.'

'No, no. It isn't. It mustn't be normal.'

It was the secret they shared. It was the secret that took Krista to a new life in the house on Clapham Common.

Teddy moved over to Gus and grabbed his arm. A passionate, grieving touch.

'Tell me.'

'We're done, Teddy.' With that, Gus raised his hand and, using its edge, smashed it down hard on to Teddy's wrist.

'*Gus . . .* '

Teddy's cry of love and hate reverberated down the alley as Gus picked his way over the rubble and headed for the lights of Fleet Street at the end of it.

26

'I won't be gone too long,' said Gus, easing the bulky pram, with a sleeping Theo inside it, out of the scullery into the back garden. It was a bit of a tussle. 'Why do we have to put him out anyway?'

'The book Tilly gave me says babies need fresh air every day,' Krista replied. 'It's safe here. I couldn't put him out in the front.'

The soil having been softened from recent rain, it was difficult to wheel the pram over the grass and Gus positioned it by the back door. They stood looking down at their son.

'So,' Krista said. 'It begins and you will be coming and going for a while.'

Gus's explanations were vague. Of course. He simply told Krista that he was needed to help set up planning and evaluation units in the British Zone in Germany to deal with the backlog of enemy prisoners and would be seconded there for several months. With trips home, of course.

'I understand,' she said, feeling her mouth twist with apprehension. 'Can you tell me where?'

'No,' he said gently. 'I can't.'

He told her instead about the 'town majors', the officers who had been sent out to establish local government in the *Stadtkreis* or *Landkreis*, the small administrative districts in the British Zone.

'My people will hate it,' she said.

'I know. But these men will try to get life going again. Help business and commerce and industry.' He cleared his throat and asked a trifle gruffly, 'Will you miss me?'

She was so much better. The baby's routine was stabilizing. The hundred little tasks that were required to keep him fed and clean, his tiny bottom free of rash, kept her busy and occupied her mind. She loved to hold him and could spend hours watching the milky little mouth and the sudden changes in his colour as he cried or slept or fed.

She loved him. *She loved him.*

Gus was waiting for her answer. Krista glanced at Theo and smiled at Gus. 'I will miss you, Gus.'

'Sure?'

'Would I lie to you?'

'I count on you not lying.' He reached out and drew her close. Kissing her on the mouth, he said, 'I never thought I would be happy.'

She looked up at him. 'Nor me.'

'Do you feel settled? Do you think this can become your life?' He added, 'I care about you. Very much. I can't imagine you not being here.'

It was a moment filled with unexpected sweetness.

'So Nella?'

'Nella has gone,' Gus cut in. 'I'm so sorry for hurting her. I can't deny I loved her, but you know all about that.' Gus took hold of both her hands. 'I pray she will find a life of her own.'

The clang of bottles out on the south side of the Common indicated that the milkman was doing his rounds. In the distance a factory hooter sounded. A tiny breeze rustled the leaves on the trees in the back gardens. The sun had come out and it was beautifully warm.

'I'll be back,' said Gus.

He had said that before, in Berlin.

'I'll be back,' said Gus after all that happened had happened, and he and the men prepared to leave. He was still a little drunk. To be honest, she didn't consider that night to be better or worse than any of the others. They all merged. One man, two men . . . no point in counting.

But back he had come to the convent, time and time again, bearing tins of spam and chocolate. Too late for Lotte. But not too late for her.

Frequently, he could not stay, but on occasion he drew Krista into a corner to talk to her. At first they had nothing to say to each other and their exchanges were like digging into saturated clay. 'Your German is excellent,' she told him. 'And your English likewise,' was the reply. They kept their distance whenever they talked. He did not want to touch her. She could not bear him to get too close to her. But he knew that she knew he was useful and that she would use him. Soon afterwards, he secured her the job on his team, which needed all the help it could get, and they worked together. A lot. The rhythms between them were established. Questions. The pause for answers. More questions fielded between them. 'I know they are your countrymen and it must be hard for you,' he said. 'They are my countrymen and I

450

have to find out if they are guilty,' she replied.

Gus and Krista sat side by side in the autumnal garden, with their son sleeping in the pram beside them. Gus put his arm around her. 'I shall really miss you.'

With a little cry, she turned to him. 'And I you.'

★ ★ ★

Julia had taken to dressing more carefully and Krista noticed that she wore lipstick every day, which most women could not because they had to hoard their supplies. The tweed costume was now rarely seen, discarded in favour of a glossy mink cape which Julia maintained, with an air of suppressed excitement, had belonged to her mother, plus a selection of dresses with enviable full skirts.

Once or twice the telephone went and a man would ask for Julia. One of the male voices was familiar, but it was not until later that Krista realized it had probably been Teddy Myers. He would have known it was Krista answering the phone and the exchange was cut short.

Tilly was not around much either, which meant Krista was alone in the house for a lot of the time. One of her happier outings was wheeling Theo in the pram up the High Street to introduce him to Herr Laube. He had been serving another young mother at the time and Krista found herself discussing routines with her, which was very pleasant, particularly as it did not seem to make a blind bit of difference that Krista

451

was German. Herr Laube said what a fine baby Theo was, presented him with a picture book about Noah's ark and asked if she would please bring him back often.

Most of the time, she was on an even keel. None of the buzzing in her head, no black moments, no nightmare images — just the negotiation of mundane everyday tasks — but she would have given a lot to have known where in Germany Gus was. It seemed he had been gone longer than three weeks and she would have liked to picture him travelling through the clanking, dirty Ruhr, or taking delight in a sparkling Moselle river, or scratching his head as the teams faced the task of getting Hamburg up on its feet.

Home. Her country. Homesickness lashed her from time to time but she dealt with it. No doubt the Allies would try to wipe out the immediate past. Even before she left Berlin, they had begun burning Nazi literature, flags and yards and yards of bunting, and anyone caught with Nazi memorabilia was punished. That was the easy bit. It would be harder to rid the imprint of the Reich from the national mind.

In London much lay in ruins, too, and the elation of being victorious did not appear to have lasted very long. What had she found over here: a dull, depleted country, with shrill and unkind people? Yes. Yet she had also found kindness and tolerance.

One morning, Krista was suddenly, completely awake. Within two seconds, she was bolt upright in the bed, a prickle crawling up her spine.

452

She was familiar with that sensation. It meant danger.

Julia was away and Tilly had told her that she would not be coming home until later in the week. Except for herself and the baby, the house was empty.

Someone was coming up the stairs.

Adrenalin pumped through her. From the bed, she could just see Theo's cot in the room across the landing, which was doing duty as his nursery.

Something was not right.

Burglars? Or a homeless person sleeping in one of the damaged houses?

How different the sound of a furtive footstep was to a normal one. First the toes and then the little smack of the heel on the floor.

A figure, which she could not make out clearly, slid into view and into the room containing the cot.

Toes followed by heel. Almost noiseless.

Her instincts screamed: *Danger*. Whipping out of bed, she picked up the poker from the fireplace and ran across the landing into the baby's bedroom. 'What are you doing?'

Someone was bending over and lifting up a sleepy Theo.

'Stop!'

With Theo in her arms, the figure turned round.

'Tilly! What are you doing?' Krista fumbled behind her for the light switch and flipped it on.

'Nothing.' She looked peculiarly white and very thin, with staring eyes. 'Don't look at me like that.'

Krista tightened her grip on the poker. 'Tilly, give Theo to me. He needs a feed.'

Tilly grasped Theo even tighter and the baby sneezed. 'Actually, I've just come to say goodbye to him before I go. I'm sorry to have startled you. I should have let you know. He was crying, you know. I thought you might be neglecting him.'

She sounded so sensible and concerned. Yet Krista caught a grief and desperation under the reasonable tone. She couldn't identify why exactly, only that it was there. 'Tilly, give me Theo, please.'

'He's perfectly happy with me.'

Krista fought to keep control. Tilly was going mad. She *was* mad. Was Krista herself going mad? Lowering her voice, she said softly, 'Tilly, Theo isn't your baby. He's mine and Gus's.'

Holding him close to her heart in the way that mothers did, Tilly cradled Theo in the crook of her arm, her form flowing into his. 'He could have been,' she said.

Krista groped for an explanation. Why would someone like Tilly possibly want Theo? 'You will have to be more direct, Tilly.'

Tilly tucked the shawl around Theo. 'There are things.'

'What things? Tell me.'

Tilly smoothed the corners of the shawl into a cocoon. 'I'm a mother, too, Krista.'

'Then where is your baby?'

'That's the point,' said Tilly, sidling towards the door.

Krista moved closer but, executing a neat

feint, Tilly jabbed her foot so hard on Krista's ankle that it gave way and she dropped down. She cried out and struggled to get upright. Backing out of the bedroom, Tilly used her free arm to bang the door shut.

Krista heard her running down the stairs. Wrenching open the door, she leaned over the banister. 'Stop and tell me what happened.' Tears of pain were blurring her vision. 'Tell me where your baby is and we can work something out. What about the father?'

Tilly was halfway down the stairs and she called back, 'The father? I'm afraid there are a few contenders for that exalted position.'

Krista focused on the sight of her son's small head. *Think.*

She had fought a daily battle to detach herself from the past but, hard to accept as it was, it was impossible — and she had only a few seconds to capture Tilly's attention.

Divert. Disarm. Shock.

'Would you like to know how many Soviets raped me in one afternoon?'

'What?' That made Tilly whip round. 'Bloody hell, Krista.' She glanced down at Theo. 'You won't believe me, but I'm sorry to hear that.'

Krista edged down the stairs. 'I am telling you so you will know that I am not shocked. All sorts of things go on in a war. Being raped is one. Sleeping with a lot of people is another. It is not important. My only advantage over you was that, because I did not have much food for a long time, I did not get pregnant.'

Theo was waking up. There was much

455

snuffling and flinging out of his arms, then the cry of alarm, tinged with imperious impatience, and Krista's breasts responded with a rush of milk. Tilly shifted him on to her shoulder. 'So you win in the moral-high-ground stakes. Does that please you? I gave my son away. I thought I didn't want him. I thought I couldn't have him. Except . . . ' Her eyes were huge, and it was only then Krista took on board that Tilly's pupils were dilated. 'I *did* want him. I do want him. More than I can possibly say. More than I can write.' Theo was crying in earnest. Tilly moved him into the crook of her elbow and rocked him. Back and forth. 'He would be almost two by now.'

Back and forth.

Krista's feet slid over the wood, gathering hair-like splinters. Ignoring them, she continued down the stairs. 'I understand. I do. Really. I am the one person who would understand you, Tilly.'

Everything in the house — clocks, water in the pipes, air — seemed to be frozen.

She tried again. 'The women were raped. Not once. Not twice. But many, many times. All day they were raped. Every day.'

'This was you?'

'All women.'

'Not the British, I hope.'

'Mostly the Soviets, Tilly, but not always. Conquering armies all behave in the same way. The Soviets raped us and then they wanted us to dance or eat with them. Or darn their uniforms.'

Another step down.

456

'I remember one of them, a major. He had a harmonica, it was a German one. He played it like an angel and we were so starved of music that we could not move. We were yearning, aching, to hear something beautiful. But it was almost worse than being raped because to listen made you feel again.'

Tilly seemed hypnotized by the words and Krista was getting closer.

Theo cried. The sound crackled through her body and the front of her nightdress was wet. 'At least let me feed him, Tilly. He will suffer if I don't.'

'You don't understand, Krista, precisely because you have Theo.'

Theo's wails were reaching an impossible pitch. She knew the arc of them. Hunger. Anger. Desperation. Fear.

Tilly ignored them. 'At the time, it seemed the perfect solution. The moment it happened, I felt relief. Joyous that whole damn thing was over and dealt with. All solved with a simple signature: a childless family was made happy and I was free to carry on as if nothing had happened.'

'Yes,' said Krista. 'I can understand.'

'Then doubt creeps in. Then more than doubt. An agony starts up, a longing, which burns like acid.'

Tilly was sounding very sane and very mad, in one and the same breath. It was perfectly possible to be both. Krista knew that.

Her feet were growing cold and unresponsive. The light of the deepening dawn clothed the two figures in the bare hallway in a chilling, eerie light.

'But why are you doing this, Tilly?' Theo wailed.

'Nobody wants you here, Krista.' Tilly spoke calmly and matter-of-factly. 'You should go back home and rebuild Germany. Isn't that what's happening? Because there are no men, it's the women who are pitching in, I'm told. You're needed.'

'You have a point, but Gus and Theo also need me.'

'Everyone's replaceable.' Tilly's eyebrows twitched upwards. 'There. That's the truth.'

Krista flexed a foot; it was in danger of going completely numb. 'You think I should go back to Berlin and become a *Trümmerfrau*?' She kept her eyes fixed on Tilly's face, trying to read it, trying to anticipate.

'Is that what they call the women? You know your country. It will rise again. Of course it will, but it needs every able-bodied woman. You should go. It's your duty.'

'I will not leave my baby.'

Wrong, wrong, she thought. She was reminding Tilly that she had abandoned her son.

For a few seconds, Theo was quiet.

Tilly walked over to the front door. A brown attaché case had been placed beside it. 'When you first came, Julia and I often wondered if you were really married. We never saw a photograph.'

'Tilly, you will not be able to take Theo anywhere in this state.'

Using her free hand, Tilly opened the front

door, then she bent down and picked up the case. Theo was now rigid and scarlet. 'Shush,' she said tenderly.

Traffic sounds filtered in from the road outside: a grating of car gears and the rattle of a badly fitted exhaust. The cold seeped in, grimly harsh and unforgiving.

'How will you feed him, Tilly? He doesn't know about a bottle.'

Theo gave such a piercing wail that both women jumped.

'For the love of God, Tilly, let me feed him. *Please.*'

With a sigh, Tilly kicked the front door shut and surrendered the baby.

'Tilly, why don't we go and make a cup of tea in the kitchen?'

The kitchen was freezing but Krista didn't dare risk fetching her dressing gown. She unbuttoned the front of her nightdress and, curled like an ammonite against her, Theo began to feed. *Thank God. Thank God.*

Tilly shut the kitchen door and blocked it with a chair.

Krista shifted Theo to ensure that he got a better hold on her breast. His bite was becoming powerful and her flesh shrank.

How did madness arrive? Seeping in like the tide? Smashing through you like a bullet? For Tilly, surely, was mad.

'When are you going to Italy?'

Tilly removed her cape to reveal the flowing black skirt and an emerald-green jumper. 'Afternoon boat train.'

459

'Is anyone coming with you? You shouldn't go on your own.'

Tilly filled the kettle and lit the stove, taking two attempts to light a match. 'None of your business.' She looked away. 'I am going on my own. No one . . . ' she inflected the words, 'wants to come with me.'

The gas hissed and bubbled under the kettle.

'Tilly, you don't look very well.'

If she made it to the scullery, Krista calculated, and out through the door, she could make an escape over the garden walls.

'I'm fine, Krista.'

To Krista's astonishment, Tilly was making a pot of tea as if nothing was happening — carefully warming the pot, spooning in the leaves, pouring in the water.

'Krista, listen. I've worked it all out. I'm going to take Theo with me. You can disappear back to Germany.' She poured out a cup of tea and pushed it across to Krista. 'I'm only thinking about you, Krista. You'll be happier in your own country.'

It sounded plausible. Easy to picture as a newspaper headline:

HOMESICK AND BRITISH-HATING GERMAN BRIDE RETURNS TO HER HOMELAND

Easy, too, to think of the platitudes that would be handed around, like pass the parcel, by anyone who discussed the scandal.

Krista helped herself to a precious spoonful of

sugar and forced down a mouthful of the tea. 'Tilly, how do you think you will get away with kidnapping Theo? The police would be looking for you.'

'No, they would be searching for *you*. They would think *you* had taken Theo. Except looking for you in Europe would be like trying to find . . . ' She gave a shrug. 'A needle in a haystack. That old cliché.'

'And if I don't go? If I stay here?'

Tilly stared at Krista. 'You will go.'

Careful. 'But if I agree to go, why take Theo to Italy?'

'Because I can look after him better.'

What was going on in Tilly's drugged brain?

'If you have had a baby then you must know that I'm not leaving Theo.'

Tilly's gaze shifted around the kitchen and came to rest on a heavy copper saucepan on the shelf.

'If you go, Gus will probably be happier with Nella.' She ticked off the points on her fingers. 'She suits him, Krista. She's duller than you, but there we are. She knows how to live our life here.'

'I thought you didn't care about convention.'

Again, Tilly shrugged.

'But if I disappeared, Tilly, and Nella married Gus, they would look after Theo, not you.' Tilly shivered. 'After you bring him back from Italy, that is.'

A hectic flush mounted into Tilly's cheeks.

'Tilly, you will have other children.'

Tilly's dilated pupils reflected her tragedy. 'I

gave my son away and I thought it would be fine. It was fine. Afterwards, I went to a party. And that was all right. I went back to work. And that was all right. Then it wasn't, and now my days and nights are filled with him.' Her voice was pure, undiluted yearning. 'I long for him. I don't know where he is, nor can I ever know.'

Krista's arms crept ever tighter around Theo. 'Could you not have kept him? Somehow?'

Babies born in Berlin were given away, too. They were tossed away.

Think. Clearly and practically.

'That's the terrible thing,' Tilly answered. 'I probably could have done. It would not have been easy, but possible. Others did it. I tried to get rid of him while I was pregnant but couldn't go through with it. I got myself posted to Scotland, and I suppose I could have come home with him, pretending I had adopted an orphan. Instead, I left him there. Maybe I would have got away with a story of a whirlwind marriage that ended in tragedy. Julia would have fallen for it.' Her fingers laced into each other. 'But I didn't do any of that because I was quite clear that I didn't wish to be encumbered. I had another life to lead and I ran away from the neat, boring house and regular meals.' She looked down at Theo. 'I wanted poetry.'

Crouched in the convent chapel, Krista and Lotte had talked about neat, boring lives and how they longed for them.

'There was too much going on in my neck of the woods. Too much coming and going. Blind eyes were turned left, right and centre. Perhaps it

462

would have been different if I had been in the regular services.'

Theo's breath fell softly on Krista's exposed breast; his head lay on her bare forearm, his stomach pressed against hers. They were one. Joined in flesh and need. She would never let him go.

Tilly was forgetting that, for Krista, danger was an old friend. With a jolt she realized that she had never felt as at home in England as she did now, at this moment, facing a threat.

'Longing for him is like a hunger I can never satisfy,' Tilly continued. 'Or a thirst. I was so wrong.' She paused. 'But how can you know?'

Think.

'Have you written about it, Tilly?'

'Oh, God.' Tilly pressed her hand to her mouth.

'Perhaps you can show me the poems?' Krista buttoned up her nightdress. 'Why don't you get them while I change Theo?'

Tilly shot to her feet with such force that her chair fell over. 'You're staying here. I'll do the nappy.' Her blonde hair fell over her shoulder. A Valkyrie, thought Krista. A Valkyrie — and just as mad. 'Get into the pantry.'

Where she was standing, Tilly was blocking the escape route through to the scullery. Krista did not wait another second. Clutching Theo, she pushed the chair aside and was out of the kitchen, up the stairs, through the front door and down the front steps.

Tilly was behind her. 'Stop her,' she shouted. 'Stop her.'

With bruised toes, her breath hammering painfully out of her lungs, sweat trickling down her spine, Krista made it out of the gate. Mr O'Connor from Number 18 was also turning into the street. At the sound of the shouting, he looked round.

Krista ran up to him. 'Please, please . . . ' The words tumbled out: thickly accented, foreign. 'You remember me? When I first arrived? Help me.'

'There you are, Krista.' Tilly ran up. 'Oh, hello, Mr O'Connor. So sorry about this. Please forgive us. My sister-in-law hasn't been well since the baby was born. She is getting better but sometimes . . . ' The rest of the sentence trailed away into insinuation.

His timetable interrupted, and clearly anxious to be on his way, Mr O'Connor looked frozen with embarrassment. 'If you think you have it under control, Miss Clifton.'

'Yes. It's nothing to worry about, Mr O'Connor.'

Tilly sounded like the perfect sister-in-law. What would he think of this woman in the street clad only in her nightdress? 'Please could you let me sit in your house?' Desperation fractured Krista's grasp on English — and she knew he would see her as out of control.

'My dear Mrs Clifton,' said Mr O'Connor, pulling his hat further down over his eyes, speaking in tones of dislike — as he had done on that first meeting a year ago. 'I think you need to go inside with Miss Clifton.' He looked at Tilly, then salvaged some good manners. 'Should I call the doctor for you?'

Tilly slid her arm around Krista's shoulders in a brutal grip. 'My sister-in-law is German, as you probably know. It's had an effect on her. The defeat, you understand, and coming here. She's not been at all well.'

'German . . . ' The repeated word crackled between them. '*German.*' He glanced at his watch. 'If you're sure you can deal with this, Miss Clifton. Otherwise — '

'No, thank you.' Tilly cut him off. 'It's not . . . er, unusual.' She tightened her grip. 'Come on, old girl. Let's go in and make a cup of tea.' She sent Mr O'Connor a conspiratorial smile. 'I find that when Mrs Clifton is upset a cup of tea always helps.'

27

The front door closed behind them, sealing Theo, Krista and Tilly into the house.

The hallway was not as chilly as the kitchen but it was no place of refuge either.

What next? Where next? She knew now that Tilly was perfectly capable of snatching Theo and spiriting him away before she could get any clothes on. Anyway, Tilly was faster and stronger.

Tilly knelt down by the case and snapped it open, revealing a pair of blue knitted bootees on top of the pile of clothes she had packed.

Nothing else in Krista's experience . . . rape, bombardment, ruins . . . had ever been so chilling as the sight of those bootees.

'Tilly,' she said very gently, 'you must get help for your hurt and your loss. That is the way to deal with it, not in taking my baby. He can't possibly replace your own.'

'I'm not ill, Krista.' Tilly stuffed her scarf into the case and shut the top.

'You cannot kidnap a baby because you want yours back.'

Tilly stood upright. She had never looked more beautiful or more terrible. 'But I can. It's your word against mine, Krista. What would the average Brit think? Here's an English girl who did her bit during the war and here's the German one who fought against us. The war changed us. I don't know about the Germans but the British are much ruder than they used to be. Restless, too. And hating the enemy is a rewarding sensation.'

Krista needed to keep Tilly talking. 'I agree. In Germany,' she said, 'people called the aftermath the *Stunde Null*, Zero Hour. It implies that the slate had been wiped clean and we can start again.' She kept her eyes fixed on Tilly. 'Everyone is greedy for food, colour, warmth and the good things, don't you think? For sex, parenthood, and a comfortable doze after a meal rich in fat and sugar.'

Tilly raised an eyebrow. 'That's absolutely right.'

The satiated baby was snuggled into the warmth of Krista's arms but he needed changing. What were her options? Nappy change or not, she was not going to go upstairs, thus allowing Tilly to block off escape routes.

'Theo needs settling,' she said. 'He needs a bit more of a feed.' Reaching out to the coat stand, she unhooked the nearest coat on it and thrust her bruised and bloodied feet into a pair of outdoor shoes which were underneath it. 'I will go into the drawing room.'

In the drawing room, she steadied herself against a chair.

What time was it?

She heard Tilly go upstairs.

What time was it?

Oh, God, she had forgotten to wind the clock in the drawing room. Laying Theo down on the sofa, she put on the coat, and used its belt to hitch up her nightdress so it was out of sight. Glancing out of the window, she calculated it

467

was about eight forty-five and people were on their way to work. Traffic was now moving steadily around the Common and a stream of workers, strung out like spiders' legs, moved in the direction of the Underground.

As Krista tried frantically to think, a car drew up outside the house. The passenger door opened and out slid Julia.

Walking down the path, Julia appeared a little unsteady and she was having trouble with her high heels. Krista snatched up Theo and went to meet her.

Julia crept into the hall.

'Julia! Thank goodness!'

Julia started visibly. She exuded a blurred, tumbled, early morning quality — which spoke of sex and little sleep. It wasn't unattractive. 'What on earth? Is everything all right?'

'It's Tilly, Julia. I think something has happened to her. She says she wants to take Theo with her to Italy.'

'What?' Julia shrugged off her coat, revealing a low-cut, aquamarine evening dress and shoulders which had obviously been powdered the previous evening but now only sported odd patches of it. 'Are you making this up?'

Krista clutched the now-sopping Theo to her chest. 'I don't think Tilly is very well.'

'Are *you* ill?' Julia was stripping off her long gloves.

'Julia,' said Krista, 'Tilly is suggesting that I return to Berlin and leave Theo with her. This is not rational and I think it is Tilly who is ill. I beg you to talk to her.'

468

'Krista, have you been drinking?'

On cue, Tilly clattered down the staircase carrying a bag from the top of which protruded a rubber cot sheet. 'Julia! Oh, bugger. I thought you were out for the duration, being a dangerous woman and all that. How's the night life? I trust you're being careful. It's not much fun if you make a mistake.'

Julia flushed a painful red. Her gaze travelled from Tilly's drained features to the bag by her side and focused on the rubber sheet. 'Why are you going off with that?'

'Because I'll need it for the baby.'

Julia stiffened. 'Tilly.' She was very sharp. 'What do mean, 'the baby'?'

'Hasn't Krista told you?'

Julia moved towards Tilly. 'Don't be ridiculous.'

Krista shivered. The old weariness and sickness of heart was almost too much to bear. 'Tilly wishes to take Theo with her because she thinks it would be better if I left Gus and returned to Germany.' She spoke as calmly as she could manage. 'Tilly, please explain to Julia what you want to do.'

Julia threw her coat on to the hall chair. Close up, Krista could see that her lipstick had bled into the fine lines around her mouth, giving it an oddly bleached look. 'Tilly, what *is* all this? Are you really not feeling well?'

'Never better.' Tilly was upbeat. 'You agree with me that the Germans deserve all that is coming to them?'

Julia shook her head. 'No. And nor do you. All

that's past. We have to do what our dear vicar says and love one another.'

'I thought you couldn't bear them because they killed Martin.'

'Yes . . . ' Julia was obviously deeply shocked by what she was hearing. 'But what you're suggesting is mad and wrong, Tilly.' She peered at her sister. 'Have you taken something? Tell me you haven't. Are you listening? It's unthinkable. You can't steal other people's babies.' She was struggling for control. 'Unthinkable and criminal, Tilly. Theo belongs to Gus and Krista. He's our family's future.'

Tilly put down the bag. 'Someone took mine.'

'Your what?'

'I had a son. Two years ago.' Tilly gave a little cry. 'Two years, five days and four hours ago. Actually.'

Julia rocked on her high heels. 'With whom?'

'I don't know, Julia. There were several candidates.'

'Oh, God,' Julia choked. 'Where?'

'I had him in Scotland. I gave him away and none of you were ever the wiser. It wasn't easy. It took nerve but you can always find a way. The nice doctor knew of a family who were desperate for children. It seemed the best solution.'

Krista weighed up whether she dared go upstairs to dress and change Theo's nappy.

'How could you have done that?' Julia looked as though she had been punched in the stomach.

Tilly's face reflected the hell that she was experiencing. 'You know, I could have pretended to be a widow or something. But I didn't want to

470

keep my son at that time. I wanted him gone.'

Julia collapsed on to the hall chair. 'You gave away your son.' She looked up at her sister. 'Tilly, I would have had him.' She looked utterly agonized. 'I could have adopted him. Given him a home here.'

'Stop it.'

'A home and a family, Tilly.'

'Shut up, Julia.'

Tilly's gaze shifted to Krista. She nudged the case in the direction of the door and Krista tensed, ready to run. Tilly made a move towards Krista. 'No, Tilly.' Julia sprang to her feet, awkward on her high heels, and interposed herself between them.

'*Don't* interfere.'

As Tilly tried to dodge around Julia, her foot tripped Julia up and she went crashing to the floor, throwing out an arm to break her fall.

She cried out.

'Oh my God, Julia,' cried Krista.

Streaming tears, Julia struggled into a sitting position and dropped her head into her hands.

Krista was trembling. 'Tilly, help Julia. Quick!'

'It's the worst thing,' said Tilly, as if nothing had happened, 'aching for a child you can never have. The doctor wouldn't tell me where he went. Of course. But it makes me angry with myself and everyone else. It was as if I had taken an axe and chopped off my own limbs. Nothing helps, you know.' She stared at Krista. 'Not even the pills.'

Julia groaned but Krista didn't dare go to her aid. 'Tilly, please.'

471

'Shut up.'

When the questioning has reached a stalemate, use the diversion.

Krista turned to Tilly and hissed, 'Your baby will search for the rest of his life for his parents. Did you realize what you were doing to him when you gave him away? I am an orphan, so I know. You have condemned him.'

Tilly went very still.

'Below the belt, Krista. I'd like to see you try having an illegitimate baby in this country. You wouldn't appreciate that.'

'But you did not try. You said you did not want him.' Krista turned what facts she had to hand back on Tilly — a classic tactic. 'Believe me, Tilly, I know about being abandoned. It is not good.' Holding Theo ever more tightly, she said: 'From now on, neither Gus nor I will let Theo out of our sight.' An ammonia stink rose from the baby — her baby. 'Go to Italy, Tilly. When you have gone, I will talk to Gus and we will decide if you can come back here.'

' "Neither Gus nor I",' Tilly repeated. 'Ah.'

Julia eased off her high heels and managed to haul herself to her feet. She was dead pale and shaky with shock. 'Tilly, you have to leave now. I order you to do so.'

'And what if I don't?'

'You will. And you won't come back for some time.' Julia was only just holding herself together. 'If you go and stay away for a bit, I promise I will say nothing to Gus . . . or to the police.'

'Police?'

'Yes, police.' There was a pause. 'You would be

472

in trouble. And there would be a scandal.' Julia sobbed. 'Oh, Tilly, what have you done? What have you become?'

'As if I shouldn't ask the same question of you, Julia.'

All the same, Tilly removed the rubber cot sheet from the bag and laid it ceremoniously on the bottom stair. 'You win. I'll be in Italy. I don't know when I'll be back.' Picking up the bag and the case, she let herself out of the house.

Relief surged through Krista. As sharp as she had ever experienced. Sharper than the worst times in Berlin.

'Julia, are you all right?'

Julia was swallowing hard and still looked dazed. 'I feel very odd.'

There was a silence.

'I can't believe it . . . ' Julia was almost inaudible. 'Who is Tilly? She's not my sister any more. How could she think she could get away with it?' She pressed a finger against white lips. 'I'm sorry about this. Tilly is ill. Hopefully, only temporarily.'

'Should we not get Tilly to the doctor?'

'I think it would be better if she went away. I think it would sort her out.' Julia inhaled a shuddering breath. 'Will you keep quiet about this? Please? Even to Gus? Especially to Gus. I think we have dealt with the situation. There's been enough upset in the family.' The blue eyes were sad beyond measure. 'We have to stick together, don't we? And there's no harm done.'

Theo stirred and whimpered. 'Julia, why don't you go and lie down? After I've changed Theo,

473

I'll bring you a cup of tea.'

The women exchanged a glance. Halting at the turn of the stairs, unsteady and stooped with weariness, Julia looked down at Krista. 'A cup of tea would be lovely.'

★ ★ ★

Before she put Theo in his pram, Krista went upstairs with him to check on Julia, who had been sick and had now taken a sleeping pill. She was sunk in sleep, her head turned away from the door, fair hair spilling over the pillow. In sleep, she was softened, rounded, beautiful, which was how her husband must have seen her, and others seldom did.

A little later, Krista manhandled the pram outside the scullery door and positioned it so that the late autumn sun fell over the raised hood. Theo was washed, changed and fed.

Keeping a tight eye on it from the kitchen, she made herself a cup of tea, splashed brandy into it and sat down in the sun beside the pram.

Sixteen, fifteen . . .

No.

Concentrate on her son. How lucky she had been in the end. How lucky she was to have Gus. Thank God, Theo had not been born into the ruins and the fire, like so many had been. She thought about the coming winter and of how she would wrap her son up against it and hold him fast to her.

Don't think about Tilly.

She would teach him to appreciate the sparkle

of frost on stone, the delicate traceries of bare branches and, when winter was over, the excitement of spring as it crept in with colour and warmth. She would teach him to be grateful to be alive, fed, warm, loved.

The tea was hot, so hot, but she almost gulped it down as if it might be her last cup on earth. The shock of the morning was obviously threatening to bring on the old habits. *No*, she told herself. *No*.

What would happen to Tilly? Would Julia consult Dr Lawson about her? She checked the time. In an hour or so, Tilly would be catching the afternoon boat train, and perhaps she would find peace in Italy. When Julia woke up, they would talk about Tilly carefully and honestly.

Inside the house, the telephone rang. She hesitated. Theo was asleep and she did not want to leave him even for a minute. But the phone continued to ring and she ran upstairs to Gus's study.

'Krista,' said a female voice. 'Could I speak to Julia?'

'I'm afraid she can't come to the phone.' The voice had a familiar ring. 'Is that Nella?'

'How clever of you to recognize my voice.' Krista explained that Julia had not been very well and was sleeping late. 'Oh. That's a pity.'

Krista said, 'I am sorry but I cannot talk at the moment. I cannot leave Theo.'

'Is something wrong with the baby? Didn't you say when I saw you last that he cries in the evenings? I was wondering . . . Have you consulted a doctor? I asked my mother and she's recommended one. I told Julia about him. She was going to give you a name.'

Krista cut her off. 'Theo is fine. But I must go. I am sorry.'

Nella was not listening. 'Should you not get a nurse or a nanny? To give yourself a bit of time off?' Nella's concern was genuine and she sounded anxious to be friendly. '*I* would love to look after him for an afternoon. Or whatever would be helpful. Would you consider it?'

'Thank you,' said Krista, 'but no.'

Nella was not to be dissuaded. 'Why don't you take our telephone number, just in case you do?'

Colour intruded on her vision. A flash of blue. No, it was green.

Emerald green.

'No!' Krista heard herself shout. 'Help!'

'What? What?'

'It is Theo . . . Tilly is taking him.'

Leaving Nella gabbling into the telephone, she pelted down the stairs into the kitchen and out into the garden.

'Tilly, *stop!*'

Tilly was climbing over the dividing wall into Number 24, with Theo held tightly to her chest.

'*Stop!*'

She ran towards them and was felled by a hunk of stone hidden by smaller pieces of rubble. Smashing down on to it, her knee immediately wept blood.

Tilly made a dash for the short flight of stairs flanked with iron railings which led up to the house. Masonry had been scattered over it, making any false step perilous. Tilly took them at speed and disappeared through the damaged door into the house.

Krista screamed after them. 'It's dangerous in there. If you come back, we can talk, Tilly.'

She threw herself up the steps. One, two, five, seven, ten.

Inside the abandoned house, it was quiet. Poised in the entrance, Krista breathed in the clues. She knew about ruined places, she knew how and where people hid when at bay.

There was a slight noise — nothing much, possibly a piece of wood shifting. But it was enough.

The layout of Number 24 would be that of Number 22, only in reverse and she ran over it in her head. The noise had come from the hall area and Tilly was likely to be there, waiting for a moment to get out of the front door, which might be difficult to open.

Blood seeped out of her knee. She looked down. A mistake. *She was back moving through the Berlin ruins, stealing, fighting. Staying alive.* She flexed it and suppressed a groan as a thousand knives drove into her leg.

Then she heard Theo's startled wail and lurched forward into the hallway. Floorboards cracked. Plaster trickled here and there. On reaching the hall, she noted the front door was blocked by a fall of plaster.

There was a flutter of material, a crunch of shoes on rubble — and Tilly shot past her, back out on to the stone steps.

'Someone help me!' screamed Krista.

A figure in a blue coat swung over the wall,

ran over to the steps and blocked Tilly's passage. 'Tilly, what on earth are you playing at? What are you doing with the baby?'

Tilly was panting. Sweating. Chalk-white. 'What does it look like? Theo is coming with me.'

Nella spoke sharply. 'You can't take Gus's baby. Tilly, are you listening to me?'

'Not 'Gus's baby',' Tilly mimicked. 'Can we be sure of that? Can we ever be sure? But you would like him to be your son, wouldn't you?'

Krista was edging towards Tilly who, hampered by Theo's weight and by her full black skirt, was precariously balanced on the top step. What to do? What next? If Tilly got back down into the garden, she could make a getaway through the passage around the side of the house. Grabbing a handful of the skirt, Krista managed to stop Tilly in her tracks.

Nella was standing on the bottom step. 'Tilly, I don't know what's going on but you've got to be reasonable.' She moved up to the second step. 'You'll get yourself into trouble.'

Third step.

Tilly struggled to release her skirt. 'I'm not giving him up.'

The sight of her son's body clamped to Tilly's gave Krista a steel edge. 'Nor am I. Make no mistake.'

Who would move first?

Nella was negotiating a pile of rubble on the penultimate step.

'Any further and I'll kill you,' Tilly flung over her shoulder to Nella.

'I could say the same to you,' said Nella

fiercely. 'It's just words. I could say, 'I'll kill you',
too. It doesn't mean anything.'

No? Krista knew better.

It was the eyes that always gave the game away.
A flick to left or right and Krista would know
which way Tilly was going to go.

Correct. Tilly's eyelids dropped, lifted and she
threw a split-second glance into the house's
interior. Krista let go of Tilly's skirt and hobbled
forward. 'Don't.' With her free hand, Tilly shoved
Krista against the iron railings, knocking her on
to her injured knee. Then she turned to go back
into the house.

'No,' cried Krista.

Nella threw herself after Tilly, grabbed her and
hauled her back on to the steps. Krista, seizing
that half-second of opportunity granted by
Nella's surprise attack, wrested Theo away from
Tilly and — somehow, somehow — got herself
back down into the garden.

'Give him to me.' Bending down, Tilly picked
up the nearest piece of masonry, a large one.

'Have you gone mad? You might hit the baby.'
Nella made a grab for Tilly's arm. Tilly swung
round and brought the lump of masonry hard
down on Nella's shoulder. With a scream, Nella
subsided.

Cradling her son, Krista looked up at Tilly,
and the terror that she had experienced once
again burned through her soul. In that
moment, she understood that war's imprint was
with her for ever. If Tilly threatened Theo, she
would kill her. It was as simple as that and she
would do it without a second thought and with

no guilt. That's how it was.

Crouching down, and without taking her eyes off Tilly, she felt with her free hand for something — anything — that would make a weapon. Earth sprouted under her nails as, determined, murderous, she searched for a stone . . . a piece of wood . . . a brick. Yes, she had a brick. Gratefully, she grasped it and rose to her feet.

Tilly was having difficulty manipulating the masonry. As she held it aloft, it threatened to slip out of her grasp. But she was taking aim. Krista tensed and twisted her body to shield her son. Tilly's face was a parody of itself: huge pupils, staring eyes and bright-red lips. Tears rolled down her cheeks.

Krista raised the brick. 'Tilly . . . think . . . *Don't* . . . '

Nella launched herself at Tilly. 'You can't take Gus's baby.'

'Shut up, Nella.' Tilly lurched towards Nella, who stuck out her hands and pushed Tilly away. Hard and vicious.

Taken by surprise, Tilly was driven backwards. Her feet fought for purchase on the treacherous scree, failed to get any in the dust and rubble, and down the steps she went.

There was a noise reminiscent of a wet sheet splitting . . . like a tree falling . . . as Tilly's head smashed and bounced on the lumps of masonry lying at the bottom. A groan issued from her stretched mouth as she rolled over and ended up face down in the rubble, where she lay twitching. Then, after a few horrified, frozen seconds had elapsed, she was quiet.

In the sycamore tree a dove set up a call which was echoed by its mate.

Nella's hands fell to her sides. 'What have I done?' she asked Krista in an ominously calm voice.

Krista dropped her brick back on to the grass. Then she laid Theo on the ground. Easing herself down beside Tilly, she searched for a pulse at the wrist and just below the ear. *Bitte, bitte. Please, please not.*

Nothing.

She looked up at Nella.

No prayer would work miracles here. She had seen death too often. Tilly was dead and, if she had any doubts, the lack of fresh blood flowing from the dent at the back of her head confirmed it.

A dark, glistening liquid stained the rubble on which was smeared a cat's cradle of fair hairs. Shaking violently, Nella sank down on to the step.

'Nella, help me turn her over.'

'I can't touch her.' Nella shrank back. '*I can't.*'

'Then take Theo and put him in the pram.' Nella did not move. 'Do you hear me, Nella?'

'Have I killed her?' Nella's whisper was hoarse and agonized. 'I have killed her.'

'Yes.'

The sound which escaped Nella was a mixture of muffled scream and a sob. Krista got to her feet. 'Nella, you must be quiet. Go and put Theo in the pram.'

'Yes . . . yes . . . '

'Put Theo in his pram and wheel it over to the wall where I can see him.'

Krista watched Nella climb through the damaged wall and settle the baby.

She turned her attention to Tilly. Gently, she rolled her over, and, as gently, she smoothed back the bloodied hair. The fall had battered Tilly's nose and cheeks, and she wiped away the earth from the grazes and pulled down the black skirt.

Nella had returned. 'I'll go to prison.' Her tone was disconcertingly deadpan. 'I can't. I can't, Krista.' She gazed down at Tilly's body. 'I will kill myself first.'

'You'll do nothing of the sort. It was a mistake, Nella. The court will understand that.'

'I'll still go to prison. Manslaughter. You know that. I know that. The lawyers will get me.'

Nella was right. Krista knew about clever questioning and what it could achieve. 'I will tell them the truth.'

Nella bit her knuckle. 'For God's sake, a jury's not going to take your word.'

Nella *had* pushed Tilly. A clever lawyer could well convince a jury that the blow was meant to be fatal.

Tilly's lifeless face looked up at them. In death, the mouth had clenched, her hand flung stiffly out, her forefinger stained with ink. How many had Krista seen like that — stretched out in their last attitudes, jaws clenched, useless weapons still to hand? Too many, far too many. This was to return to the worst: the deaths, the violence, the scavenging, the willingness to step

482

over any boundary to survive.
   She and Lotte had done so.
   She and Gus had done so.
   She and Nella?
   'Help me, Krista.'

28

To survive, one had to be focused and clear. And ruthless.

Tilly was dead and there was nothing to be done. It had been a terrible mistake.

Her blue, staring eyes bulged under their heavy lids. Stooping down, Krista closed them, shutting down for ever the poetry, the fire and the grief which had been Tilly.

Think. Be logical.

'Listen carefully, Nella. We must bury Tilly. It would be impossible to carry her elsewhere so it will have to be here. Nobody lives at this house at the moment. It is a risk but by the time someone does live here, all traces . . . ' She pointed to the darkened patch of earth into which Tilly's blood had puddled. 'The traces will have gone. But we will have to dig deep.'

Nella laughed hysterically and pressed a shaking hand to her mouth.

'Try to take this in, Nella. Tilly said she was on her way to Italy. If she is not here, most will assume she caught the train.'

'But they'll expect her to come back.'

'Yes, but they also know that it was a foolish thing to do. If it is anything like Germany, it is very dangerous travelling in Europe, plus it would be almost impossible for anyone to find out if she got to Italy.' Krista struggled for a moment. 'Nobody knows what is happening.

Communication is non-existent. Then, if she does not come back, it will be as though something dreadful happened to her. It has been the fate of many.' She looked up into Nella's lost face. 'Very many.'

'How could this have happened?'

'It did happen and you must be strong and brave and cunning over it for the rest of your life because, if we do this, you must never, ever talk about it. And, if I am to help you, you must help me.' What was right? What was best? What should she do? 'Are you sure you don't want to go to the police?'

'No. *No.*' A chalk-white Nella glanced over her shoulder. 'Won't we be seen?'

'Julia is asleep. She has taken a sleeping pill. There is no one in this house or next door. But we have to bury her. Now.'

Nella threw her a look as if to ask: *How are you capable of this?*

'Do what I tell you. See the tree at the bottom of the garden? Help me get her over there. We can't bury her in the middle of the garden. It would be too obvious.'

'Oh, God.' Nella averted her face from Tilly's body.

'Pick her up.'

The body was awkward to manoeuvre and appallingly heavy. Krista's knee was on fire and Nella was sobbing so much she was almost useless. But, with Tilly slung between them, they managed to stagger over to the sycamore, where they released her. Tilly thumped on to the earth and came to rest on her side. After a moment, the body appeared to move and settle as if she was still alive. Observing this, Nella shrieked.

'Nella, be quiet.'

A few blades of grass, now dyed scarlet, stuck to the deep gouges on Tilly's temple. Twigs and dust streaked down the back of her skirt and the ends of her blonde hair were grey with dust.

A starburst of bloodstains splattered Nella's blue coat and, increasingly frantic, she dabbed at it.

'Don't waste your energy, Nella,' Krista was icy calm. 'We must dig. As deep as we can. It will take time. So be prepared. Stay here and don't move.'

'Don't leave me. Don't leave me.' Nella hunched over and retched into the grass. 'Sorry, sorry.' She straightened up, her hair dampened by sweat and vomit.

'I'm getting tools from the shed. I'm not leaving you.'

It was no use thinking about her knee: she had to get over the wall into the garden of Number 22. As she did so, Krista glanced up at Julia's bedroom. The curtains were still drawn tight.

She returned to Nella with a spade and a fork. 'Start there.' She pointed to a patch of earth. 'If you loosen the soil with the fork, I will dig. We will change places every fifteen minutes.'

Nella stared at her. 'You seem to know what you're doing.' Taking off her coat, she let it drop to the ground.

I do, she nearly said. *I buried the Sisters.*

They dug.

Despite the recent rain, the earth under the

topsoil was sawdust-dry from the summer and sifted into fine dust. At a lower level, a claggy London clay impeded their work. The roots of the sycamore seemed to rise to meet and to clash with the spade. Again and again, Krista drove it down into their fibrous flesh.

Sweating. Aching. Ripping the tendons.

'What is the time, Nella?'

Half an hour had elapsed.

Were they being watched? Krista continued to scan the silent terrace with its bomb wounds. Her instinct, sharpened into watchfulness, warned her not to take anything for granted.

An hour had gone by.

Sweat slicked Krista's body. Over by the wall, Theo slept on in the pram — worn out, perhaps, by events.

It was Nella's turn to dig and she did so with frantic, unproductive stabs of the spade. Every so often, she gave a sob. Somehow, the pile of dug earth mounted.

The earth walls of what was to be Tilly's grave yielded lumps of white chalk, worms, a fragment or two of blue-and-white china, a penny.

An hour and a half.

The work was fearsomely hard, Krista was already exhausted, and Nella's pitiful sobbing did not help.

The hole they had dug was now approximately four feet deep — from experience she knew that it should have been six or so but there was no more time. She let the spade fall to the earth.

Crouching down by Tilly's felled form, Krista's pity almost choked her. Tilly seemed to be gently curled, as if in sleep. She looked both surprised and, somehow, at peace.

Gus had loved Tilly. Very, very much.

Cupping her hand gently around one of Tilly's cheeks, Krista knew that she had loved her, too. That kind, unhappy, beautiful girl.

Strange and terrible as this was, Krista was also doing it for Gus. In this way she would be shielding him. He would never be faced with the pain of knowing his sister had tried to steal his son. Instead, he would grieve for the restless adventurer, who would live on in his mind in that form. He would grieve mightily, and that grief would be full of regrets and questions that could never be answered. He and she would agree that Tilly had taken one risk too many. Later, perhaps many years later, as the subject came up once more, Krista would suggest that Tilly would have died (or vanished) doing what she wished — journeying towards the sunlit, wooded slopes of Italy. *Take comfort from that*, she would say.

This way was better, far better.

Gus, I am doing this because I love you.

A frantic Nella inspected their work. 'Surely this will do?'

Krista dashed a hand across her sweaty face. Was Nella going to last? 'We must get Tilly in,' she said and got to her feet. 'One, two, three . . . Nella.'

Nella grabbed Tilly's shoulders and heaved. Krista grasped her legs. Tilly's head fell on to her chest and a noise between a sigh and a gasp came from the dead lips. With a huge effort, the

488

two women lifted her to the side of the trench and rolled her over the lip of what was now her grave.

For a second, Tilly's body was held in the balance: between life and death, between the here and the vanished. Then she lolloped over and slid into the grave, bringing down with her a shower of earth. Krista picked up Nella's coat, pulled Tilly's black skirt down over her legs and covered her face tenderly with the blue coat, to form her shroud.

'Goodbye, Tilly.'

Tilly was joining the hundreds and thousands of unknown dead. All the victims of war.

Nella hid her face with her filthy hands.

Pushing the earth back was hellish and they were both exhausted. Still it was easier work this way round, and done sooner, and left a mound of earth over the grave. Nella stamped on it and kicked the earth residue around the garden. Fetching masonry, planks, bricks, whatever they could lay their hands on, they scattered them over Tilly's grave.

It was growing cold.

Nella seized Krista's arm. 'Why have you done this?'

'Because it was an accident and you were trying to help me. It is the rule we learned. We help each other. Always. Ever. Now go.' Krista pointed to the side passage of Number 24. 'Go that way and, remember, we haven't seen each other today at all. Meet me at the bandstand at eleven o'clock in two days' time.'

Nella obeyed and vanished out of sight.

In his pram, Theo opened his eyes and looked up at his mother. Bending over, she smiled at him. '*Liebling*.'

Nevertheless, her tears fell for the burden she must now carry.

Law and justice glued peace together. In war, they didn't.

★ ★ ★

During the next two days, Krista made careful, unobtrusive checks on the hidden grave and was satisfied that nothing marked it as being out of the ordinary.

Woken by Theo in the early hours, she thought of Tilly lying there, and as she fed him in the grey-white light of dawn, her knee throbbing, she wished she could pray.

Meticulously, she went over every detail to make the story watertight. Her story. Nella's story.

Nella looked bad when they met. She was as pale as death and a patch of eczema ran down her neck, which she tried to hide with a headscarf.

Berlin maquillage.

'I keep reliving it,' she muttered. 'I keep . . . feeling what it was like when I pushed her and hearing her head . . . Oh, God.' She clapped a hand to her mouth and her wild, agonized gaze sought out Krista's.

Krista scrutinized Nella's face. Was this going to go wrong because Nella's nerves would not hold?

'Nella, you must stop it.' She led her over to a bench and snapped on the brake of the pram. 'Otherwise it won't work.'

'How can you be so calm, with Tilly rotting in the next-door garden?' Nella looked wildly around. 'I'm not sure I'm strong enough. To battle with the guilt.' She seemed wary of Krista. 'And the horror of . . . it. For the rest of my life.'

'Our lives,' Krista reminded her. She tucked Theo's blanket more securely around him. 'Do you want to go to the police?'

Nella was crying hard. 'I can't.'

Theo had settled into a doze. Krista folded her hands in her lap. 'The correct thing is to go to the police, but whether it is the right thing, I do not know.'

They exchanged glances. 'Because we tried to cover it up, you would be in the dock beside me,' Nella pointed out.

Krista reflected for a moment. 'I could not risk leaving Theo without his mother so I would lie if I had to.'

'No one would believe you because . . . '

Krista sighed. 'You have told me already. Because I am German?'

Silence fell between them, broken by the sound of two boys calling to each other as they played football on the grass.

'Something like that.'

'It is your coat in the grave. Not mine. I could deny all knowledge.'

Nella eyed Krista, hostility and disgust written all over her face. 'Is that why you put it in the grave? Your insurance policy?' She pressed one knuckle against the other.

Krista reached over and took Nella's hand with the whitened knuckle into hers. 'No, Nella. Not that. I said that we help each other. That is what we do.'

'*Why* have you helped me?' The rash flamed on Nella's neck. 'I would tell you that I'm grateful. But . . . ' She paused. 'That is the wrong word.'

'Tell me, if you loved a sister like you love Teddy, would you prefer to think that she had died trying to do something she wanted to do, or that she was drugged and slightly mad and stealing a baby?'

Nella closed her eyes.

'You must go away for a while,' said Krista. 'Sooner or later, you will be questioned, as I will be. You need to know what you are going to answer. You will be asked about your friendship and when you last saw Tilly and what you discussed. You could say that you warned Tilly not to travel to Italy because it would be dangerous, but you must think of a date when you might have had this conversation. Never say too much. Remember they will try to pretend that they know everything. It is a technique. They do not.'

Nella was staring at Krista with astonishment. 'How do you know all this stuff?' Understanding crept in. 'You're in the same business as Gus.'

'I know about asking and answering the questions, if that is what you mean.' Krista leaned over and touched her son's warm, soft cheek.

She was aware that Nella would be fighting a battle, the biggest of her life, and one which Krista knew intimately: the battle with conscience and fear.

Krista stood up and snapped off the pram brake. 'You know, the war was awful. Terrible. But it taught me some important things, Nella. A person does not have more than one or two chances. If you do not take them, they never come back.'

'And what about the rule of law? I was too panicked to think when it happened, terrified of being locked up.'

Krista stared down at the pretty, but now ravaged, features. 'You can change your mind. You can go to the police. You can pay your dues.' She, too, found she was shaking from the enormity of what might lie ahead. 'I cannot. But I must not stop you.'

Nella was silent.

'Your choice, Nella.'

Her silence was complicity.

Turning the pram homewards, Krista said, 'Neither of us will be free of this. Ever. We will carry Tilly night and day until our own deaths. It will pull us down many times, very many, and the only people we can speak to about it is each other. So we must keep each other strong.'

'Yes,' said Nella. She glanced down to Theo in the pram, and there was grief and longing expressed in every line of her body. 'It's all set in stone now, isn't it?' She gave a long, sobbing sigh. 'I will get Teddy to change the demolition order on the terrace. That's all I can do.'

They were silent.

Nella tied her headscarf back on. 'An eye for an eye,' she said. 'Or something like that. Perhaps that isn't the right phrase?'

You can't have Gus's baby.

'When you come back, Nella, come and see us. Come and help me look after Theo, if you like.'

The two women exchanged bleak, wintry smiles. Then Nella walked away, her pretty hair blowing out under her scarf, and Krista watched her until she turned into a small dot.

★   ★   ★

Gus arrived home in December, when temperatures were dipping alarmingly.

Julia and Krista had taken care to provide for the coming cold. Wood and coal had been ordered. Ada had stuffed newspapers around the windows and Krista had potted up her fragile plants, wrapped them in sacking and put them into the shed.

Julia, shocked and saddened by Tilly's behaviour, discussed Tilly obsessively with Krista. They both agreed that going to Italy was the best thing for her; it was where she would have the chance to live more healthily. The conversations were reassuring to both of them. In this new spirit, Krista was the first person to whom Julia confided her plans.

It so happened that Gus arrived back on the day Julia was putting them into action.

Throwing his hat on to the table, he kissed

494

Krista's cheek. 'What's going on?' He pointed to the suitcases by the front door.

Krista was about to tell Gus when Julia ran down the stairs. She was wearing a soft green dress and had done her hair differently. She looked beautiful. 'Hello, Gus. I'm glad I caught you before I went.'

Gus looked astonished. 'Where are you going?'

'I've been offered a flat to live in near Sloane Square. It's owned by one of Teddy's friends and he needs a tenant to keep it lived in and clean. You know, I'll be doing him a favour.'

Krista and Julia avoided each other's eye.

'This friend of Teddy's, who is he?'

'His name is Ian.' She snapped open her handbag and stuffed a headscarf into it. 'It's going to be fun.'

'Will Ian stay in this flat?'

'Don't be stuffy, Gus.' Julia sounded a warning note.

He caught Julia by the arm. 'Be careful, Jules. You must know that you always have a home here.'

'Sweet of you, Gus.' Julia turned away and busied herself finding her coat on the coat stand. 'I've thought a lot about the future.' She slotted an arm into the sleeve. 'Ask yourself, Gus. Do I really have a future here? You have a wife and a son. You don't need me. I don't want to become the equivalent of a maiden aunt.' She smiled wryly. 'And don't give me the nonsense about marrying again.'

'You will marry again. I'm sure.'

'Eligible men are like hens' teeth and, anyway,

half of them have gone mad. It's not like before. Even I can see that. Martin is dead . . . He's gone, and there's nothing I can do about it. I want to have a life, not an existence. But I will be back very often to see my adorable nephew.'

A taxi drew up outside the house.

Julia buttoned up her coat, stood on her toes and kissed Gus. After a tiny hesitation, she kissed Krista also, not once but twice on the cheeks. 'Continental fashion, yes?'

Krista smiled. 'Yes.'

'Goodbye, you two.' Julia picked up the suitcases and was gone.

Gus always took a bit of time to settle after returning from a mission. Knowing this, Krista proposed a walk. They put Theo into the pram and pushed him up to Herr Laube's bookshop, where Krista introduced Gus. Within a few minutes, both men were talking in German and Herr Laube had fetched down from the shelves his prized illustrated volume of Ludwig of Bavaria's castles.

Later that evening, after eating the supper Krista had prepared, they went up to the drawing room. Under Krista's tuition, Ada had learned to lay a fire expertly. Gus lit it and poured out their evening nip of whisky. The newspaper was ready to hand by Gus's chair.

'This is nice.' Gus sank into it. 'Julia has probably got a lover, hasn't she?'

'Probably.' Krista went over to pull the curtains. Big, fat snowflakes were drifting down but in the spring the colour would return and London would no longer be grey. 'It is snowing, Gus.'

She thought of the flakes that would mask Tilly's grave.

After a moment, she said, 'Julia is a grown woman and a widow. Why shouldn't she have a lover?'

Gus reached for the paper. 'I'm not sure about the people she is mixing with.'

'Teddy's friends? Are they so bad?'

Gus took his time to reply. 'I don't know any more.'

The fire spluttered and she picked up the poker to deal with it. 'If Julia wants a man in her bed and to enjoy her life, then she should.'

She stepped back and carefully brushed down her skirt where ash had smeared on it.

Gus watched. 'You take such care with your clothes. I know you think you'll never have any more and that makes me sad.'

'No need, Gus.'

He looked up. 'Come here, Krista. Please.'

Tilly's shadow hung over Krista, heavy, sullen and potentially destructive. But she would live with it. She must live with it.

She knelt down beside him and he took her face in his hands. 'Do you know, you smell of flowers?'

She thought briefly of the flowers which had bloomed around the convent — whites and yellows and the powder-blues. A bitter grief streaked through her, to be doused when Gus kissed her.

I am alive.

She reached over and touched his mouth with a fingertip. 'Gus, I am so glad you are home.'

Even later, she lay in their bed beside Gus as he slept, and listened out for the first stirrings of her son.

I am alive.

After all, and after everything, the desire to live never died, until you were half-dead. *That* she had discovered.

That desire had never been so strong, or so undeniable, as at that moment — before she met Gus — when the air was filled with German lamentation and the roads were choked with Germans . . . fleeing . . . stumbling . . . dying . . . and she and Lotte and the others had hidden in the convent.

And on that night, too, when Gus had lurched into the convent and done what he did.

With his flies already open, the small soldier with mean eyes seized hold of Krista and reached under her skirt. The thought of him inside her, the filthy horrible memories of all the men who had raped her, was too much. She would die — she would die — if it happened again with a man like this one. Disgusting, vicious, ruthless with victory.

There wasn't any way she was going to get out of this.

But she was going to live. She would make sure of that.

The drunk officer with dark hair was looking straight at her, deep into her eyes. Something sparked. Something moved and they exchanged a message. What it was, and how it was possible, she did not know. She knew only that it was important.

With a little cry, she shook off the other one and pulled him down on top of her. 'There,' she said, her hand reaching for the place between his legs. Her fingers sought and found what she was looking for and what he wanted.

There.

Take it.

In that way, they slept for some hours, she partially bearing his weight on the cold, stone floor. By the time he shook himself into consciousness, the men, knowing that they were in trouble, had fled. Gus raised himself on to an elbow. His dark eyes were shadowed and anguished. 'Did I . . . did I do anything to you? I was so drunk I can't remember.'

Lotte was slumped by the wall, barely breathing.

'Did I?' he repeated. 'If I did, I deserve to be hanged.'

Did I?

He reached over and stroked her cheek. 'Tell me the truth.'

'You did,' she said.

Gus bowed his head. 'Then I will repay.'

Acknowledgements

As always, I owe many thanks to many people.

First of all to Jessica Leeke and Clare Ledingham, the crème de la crème of editors, who have lavished their expertise and patience on the book, plus the crack team at Michael Joseph and Penguin and my agent, Judith Murray. My gratitude is immense. I would also like to thank Isabelle Grey, who sent me her copy of *Getting to Know England 1950–1952*. My grateful thanks also to Antony Mair who gave me permission to use two stanzas from 'Cloudless' and 'Agnes' taken from *Brighton Stanza Poets: Anthology 2014*. Also a huge thank you to Charlotte Gere who gave me invaluable details about life in post-war Chelsea and lent me her copy of *Recording Ruin* by A. S. G. Butler.

I have consulted many books in the writing, all of which have been invaluable. These include: *Alone in Berlin* by Anonymous; *Languages at War: Policies and Practices of Language Contacts in Conflict* edited by Hilary Footitt and Michael Kelly; *Hanns and Rudolf: the German Jew and the Hunt for the Kommandant of Auschwitz* by Thomas Harding; *Otherwise Occupied: Letters Home from the Ruins of Nazi Germany* by Michael Howard; *A Strange Enemy People: Germans Under the British 1945–50*, by Patrick Meehan; *Call the Midwife* by Jennifer

Worth; last, but not least, the brilliant *Savage Continent: Europe in the Aftermath of World War II* by Keith Lowe who has kindly given me permission to quote from it; I have taken details and scenarios from all of these and hereby acknowledge my debt to them.

My beloved friends have put up with me (and I mean put up with me) as I wrote this. I could not do without them. To Benjamin, Adam, Lucinda and Alexia, and Eleanor, my most tender thanks.

We do hope that you have enjoyed reading this large print book.

Did you know that all of our titles are available for purchase?

We publish a wide range of high quality large print books including:
Romances, Mysteries, Classics General Fiction Non Fiction and Westerns

Special interest titles available in large print are:
The Little Oxford Dictionary Music Book Song Book Hymn Book Service Book

Also available from us courtesy of Oxford University Press:
Young Readers' Dictionary (large print edition) Young Readers' Thesaurus (large print edition)

For further information or a free brochure, please contact us at:
Ulverscroft Large Print Books Ltd., The Green, Bradgate Road, Anstey, Leicester, LE7 7FU, England. Tel: (00 44) 0116 236 4325 Fax: (00 44) 0116 234 0205